MIC

RELL

LETTERED BY
STEF PURENINS

SERAFINA

and the

BLACK CLOAK

The Graphic Novel

BASED ON THE BEST-SELLING NOVEL BY

ROBERT BEATTY

DISNEP • HYPERION

LOS ANGELES   NEW YORK

First Hardcover Edition, April 2023
First Paperback Edition, April 2023
10 9 8 7 6 5 4 3 2 1
FAC-034274-23048
Printed in the United States of America

This book is set in Comic Spans/Chequered Ink Ltd; ImaginaryFriend BB/Blambot
Designed by Braeden Sherrell and Phil Buchanan

Library of Congress Cataloging-in-Publication Data is available.
Hardcover ISBN 978-1-368-07222-9
Paperback ISBN 978-1-368-07690-6

Visit www.DisneyBooks.com

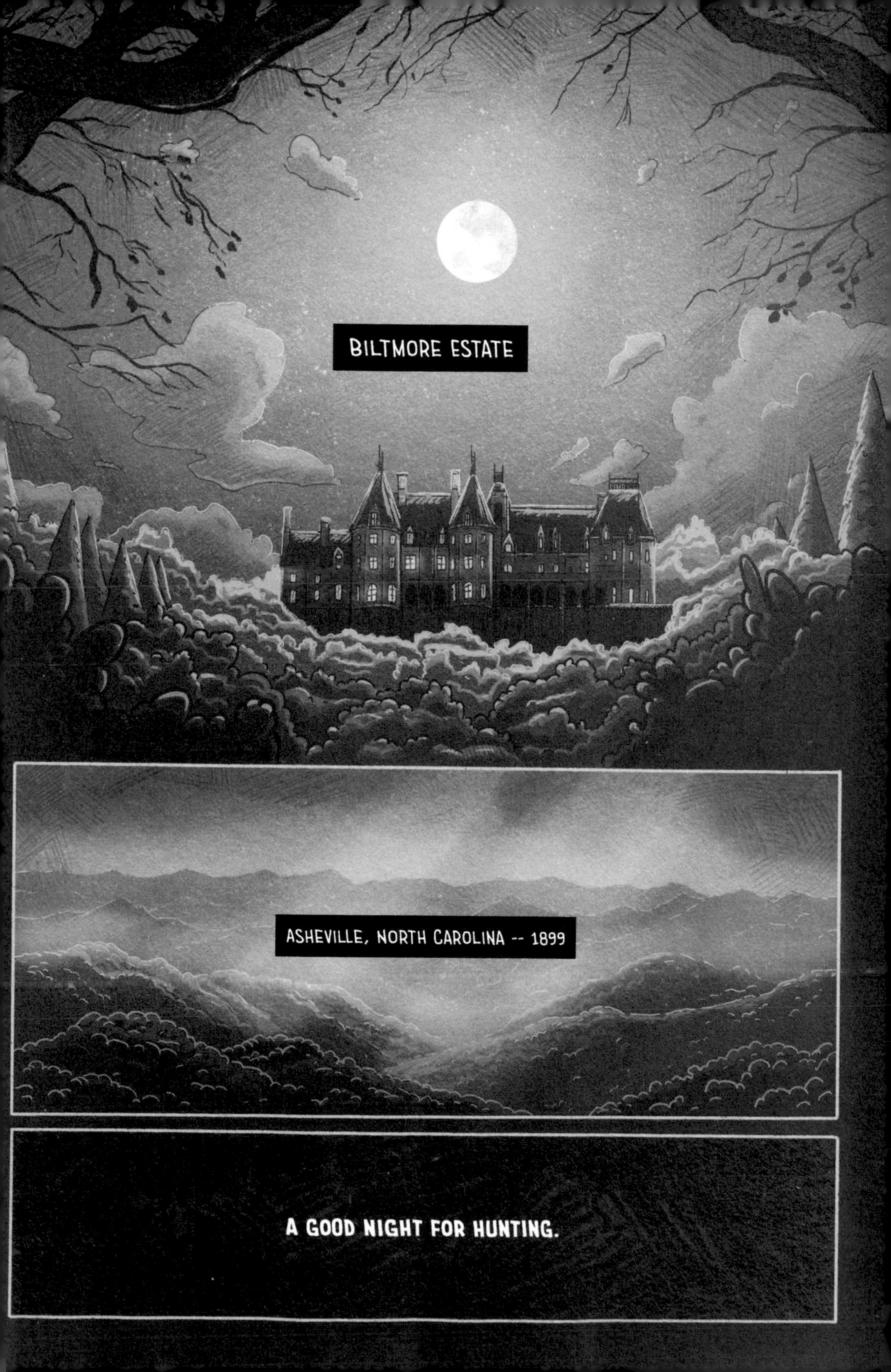
BILTMORE ESTATE
ASHEVILLE, NORTH CAROLINA -- 1899
A GOOD NIGHT FOR HUNTING.

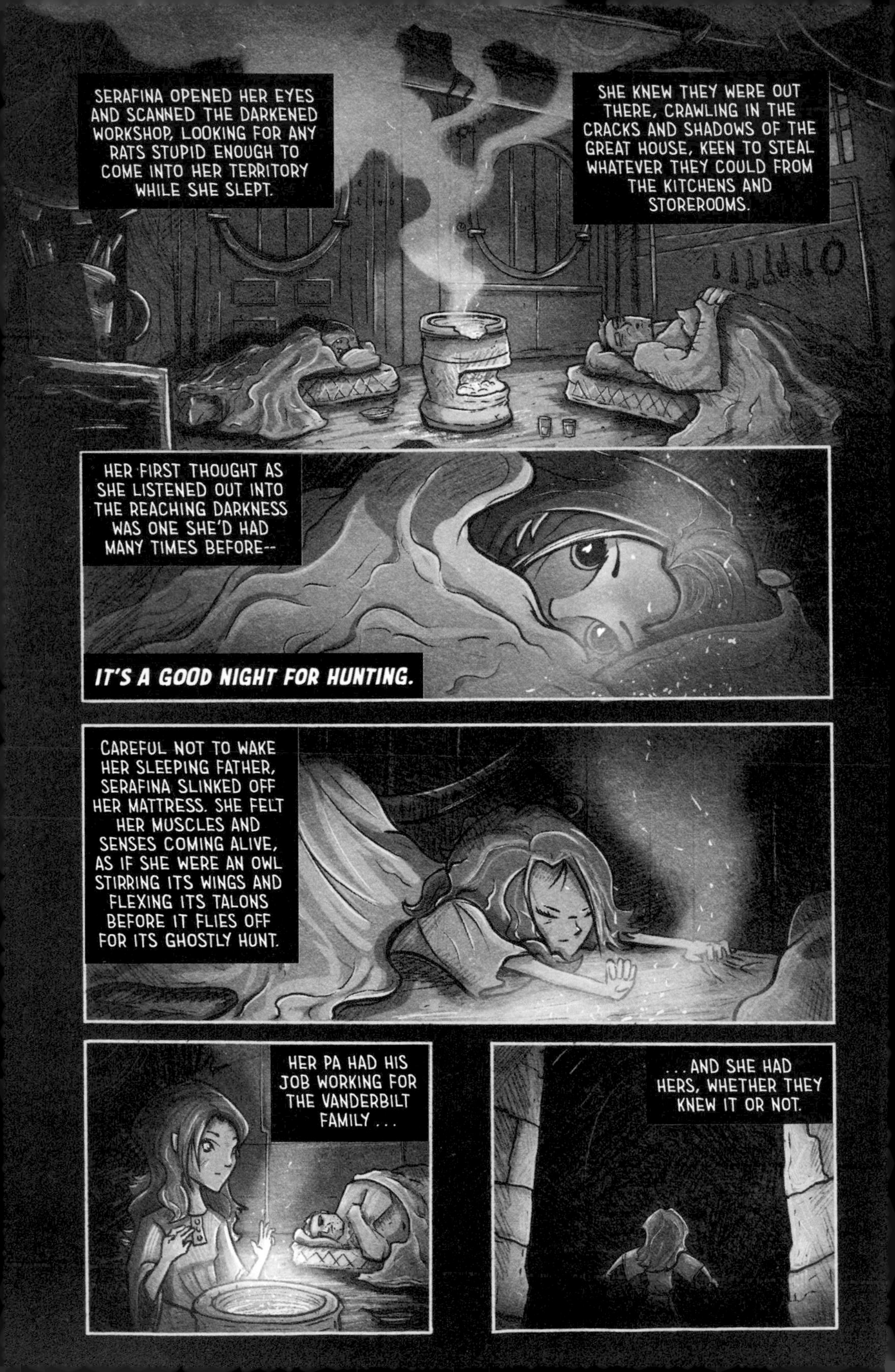
SERAFINA OPENED HER EYES AND SCANNED THE DARKENED WORKSHOP, LOOKING FOR ANY RATS STUPID ENOUGH TO COME INTO HER TERRITORY WHILE SHE SLEPT.
SHE KNEW THEY WERE OUT THERE, CRAWLING IN THE CRACKS AND SHADOWS OF THE GREAT HOUSE, KEEN TO STEAL WHATEVER THEY COULD FROM THE KITCHENS AND STOREROOMS.
HER FIRST THOUGHT AS SHE LISTENED OUT INTO THE REACHING DARKNESS WAS ONE SHE'D HAD MANY TIMES BEFORE--
IT'S A GOOD NIGHT FOR HUNTING.
CAREFUL NOT TO WAKE HER SLEEPING FATHER, SERAFINA SLINKED OFF HER MATTRESS. SHE FELT HER MUSCLES AND SENSES COMING ALIVE, AS IF SHE WERE AN OWL STIRRING ITS WINGS AND FLEXING ITS TALONS BEFORE IT FLIES OFF FOR ITS GHOSTLY HUNT.
HER PA HAD HIS JOB WORKING FOR THE VANDERBILT FAMILY . . .
. . . AND SHE HAD HERS, WHETHER THEY KNEW IT OR NOT.

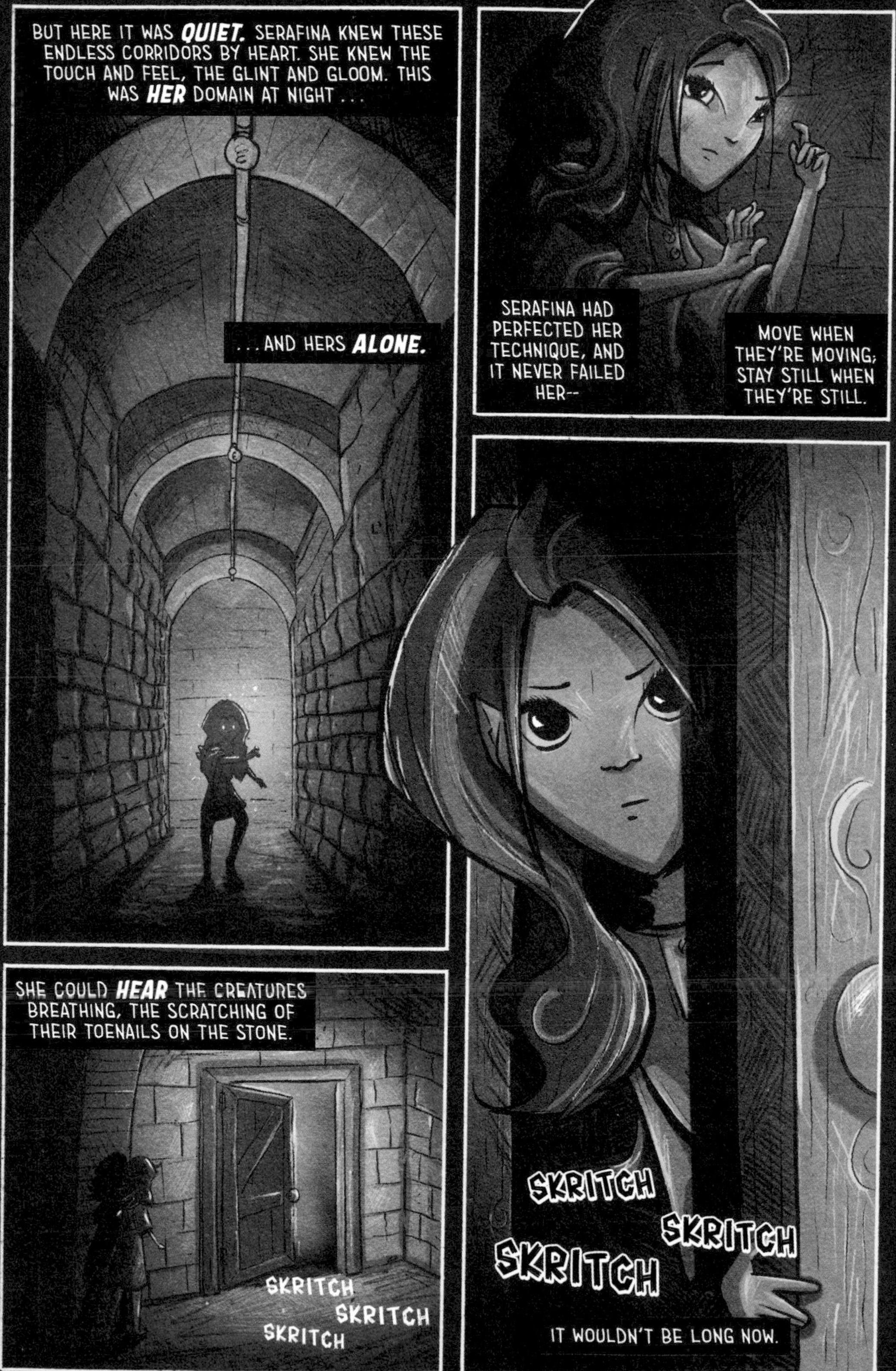

BUT HERE IT WAS QUIET. SERAFINA KNEW THESE ENDLESS CORRIDORS BY HEART. SHE KNEW THE TOUCH AND FEEL, THE GLINT AND GLOOM. THIS WAS HER DOMAIN AT NIGHT . . .
. . . AND HERS ALONE.
SERAFINA HAD PERFECTED HER TECHNIQUE, AND IT NEVER FAILED HER--
MOVE WHEN THEY'RE MOVING; STAY STILL WHEN THEY'RE STILL.
SHE COULD HEAR THE CREATURES BREATHING, THE SCRATCHING OF THEIR TOENAILS ON THE STONE.
SKRITCH
SKRITCH
SKRITCH
SKRITCH
SKRITCH
SKRITCH
IT WOULDN'T BE LONG NOW.

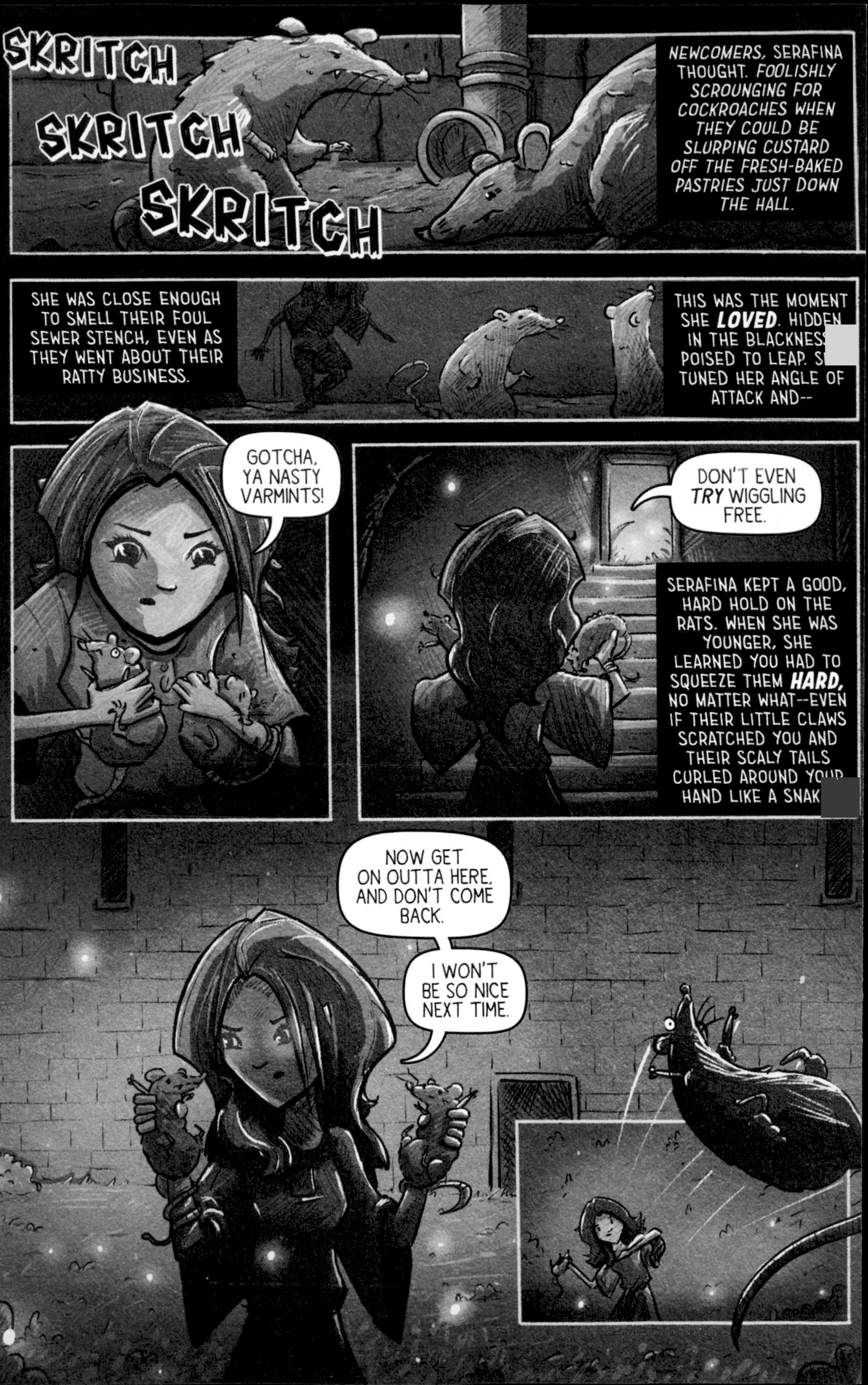

SKRITCH
SKRITCH
SKRITCH
NEWCOMERS, SERAFINA THOUGHT. FOOLISHLY SCROUNGING FOR COCKROACHES WHEN THEY COULD BE SLURPING CUSTARD OFF THE FRESH-BAKED PASTRIES JUST DOWN THE HALL.
SHE WAS CLOSE ENOUGH TO SMELL THEIR FOUL SEWER STENCH, EVEN AS THEY WENT ABOUT THEIR RATTY BUSINESS.
THIS WAS THE MOMENT SHE LOVED. HIDDEN IN THE BLACKNES POISED TO LEAP. S TUNED HER ANGLE OF ATTACK AND--
GOTCHA, YA NASTY VARMINTS!
DON'T EVEN TRY WIGGLING FREE.
SERAFINA KEPT A GOOD, HARD HOLD ON THE RATS. WHEN SHE WAS YOUNGER, SHE LEARNED YOU HAD TO SQUEEZE THEM HARD, NO MATTER WHAT--EVEN IF THEIR LITTLE CLAWS SCRATCHED YOU AND THEIR SCALY TAILS CURLED AROUND YOU HAND LIKE A SNAK
NOW GET ON OUTTA HERE, AND DON'T COME BACK.
I WON'T BE SO NICE NEXT TIME.

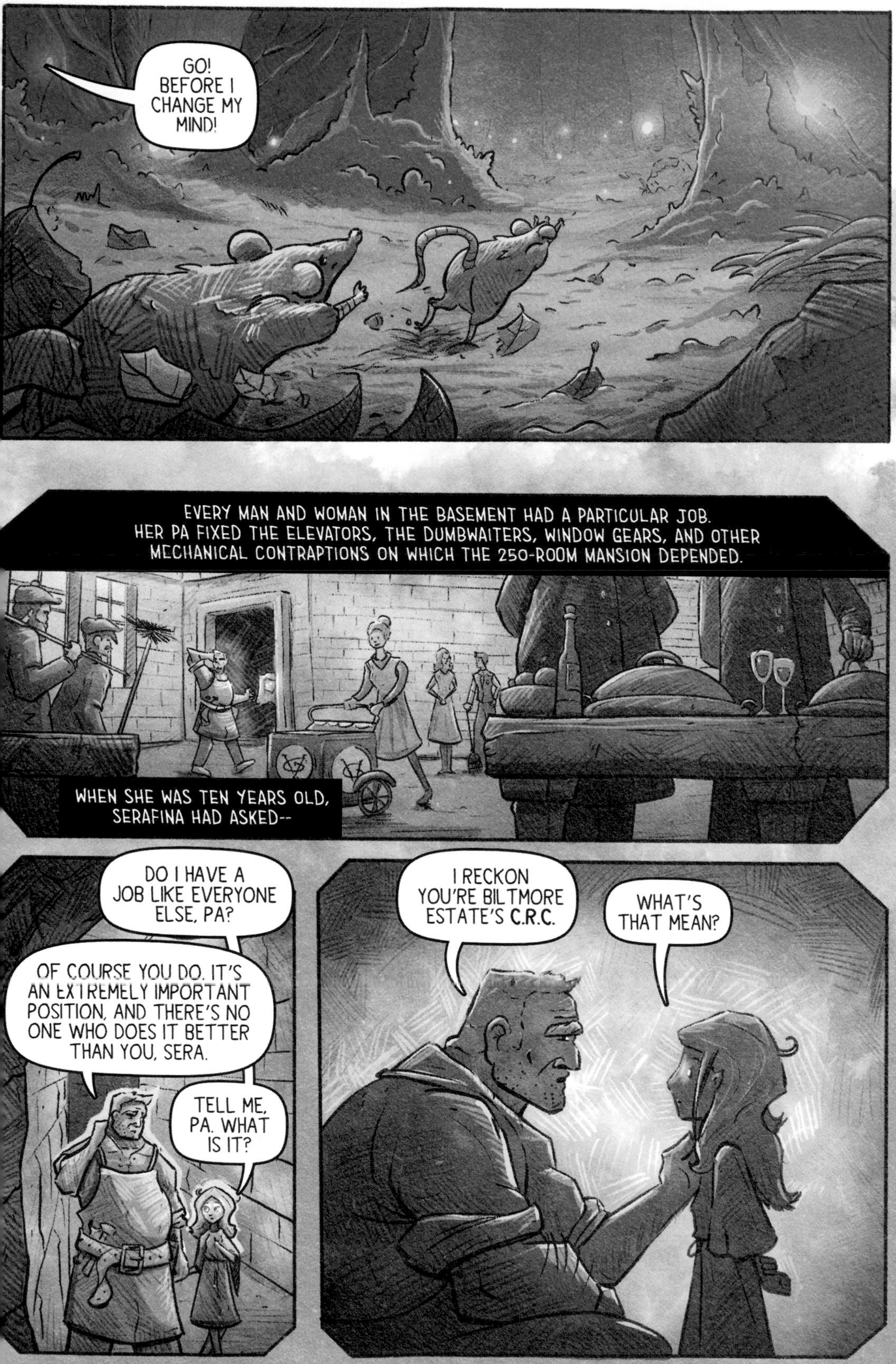
GO! BEFORE I CHANGE MY MIND!
EVERY MAN AND WOMAN IN THE BASEMENT HAD A PARTICULAR JOB. HER PA FIXED THE ELEVATORS, THE DUMBWAITERS, WINDOW GEARS, AND OTHER MECHANICAL CONTRAPTIONS ON WHICH THE 250-ROOM MANSION DEPENDED.
WHEN SHE WAS TEN YEARS OLD, SERAFINA HAD ASKED--
DO I HAVE A JOB LIKE EVERYONE ELSE, PA?
OF COURSE YOU DO. IT'S AN EXTREMELY IMPORTANT POSITION, AND THERE'S NO ONE WHO DOES IT BETTER THAN YOU, SERA.
TELL ME, PA. WHAT IS IT?
I RECKON YOU'RE BILTMORE ESTATE'S C.R.C.
WHAT'S THAT MEAN?

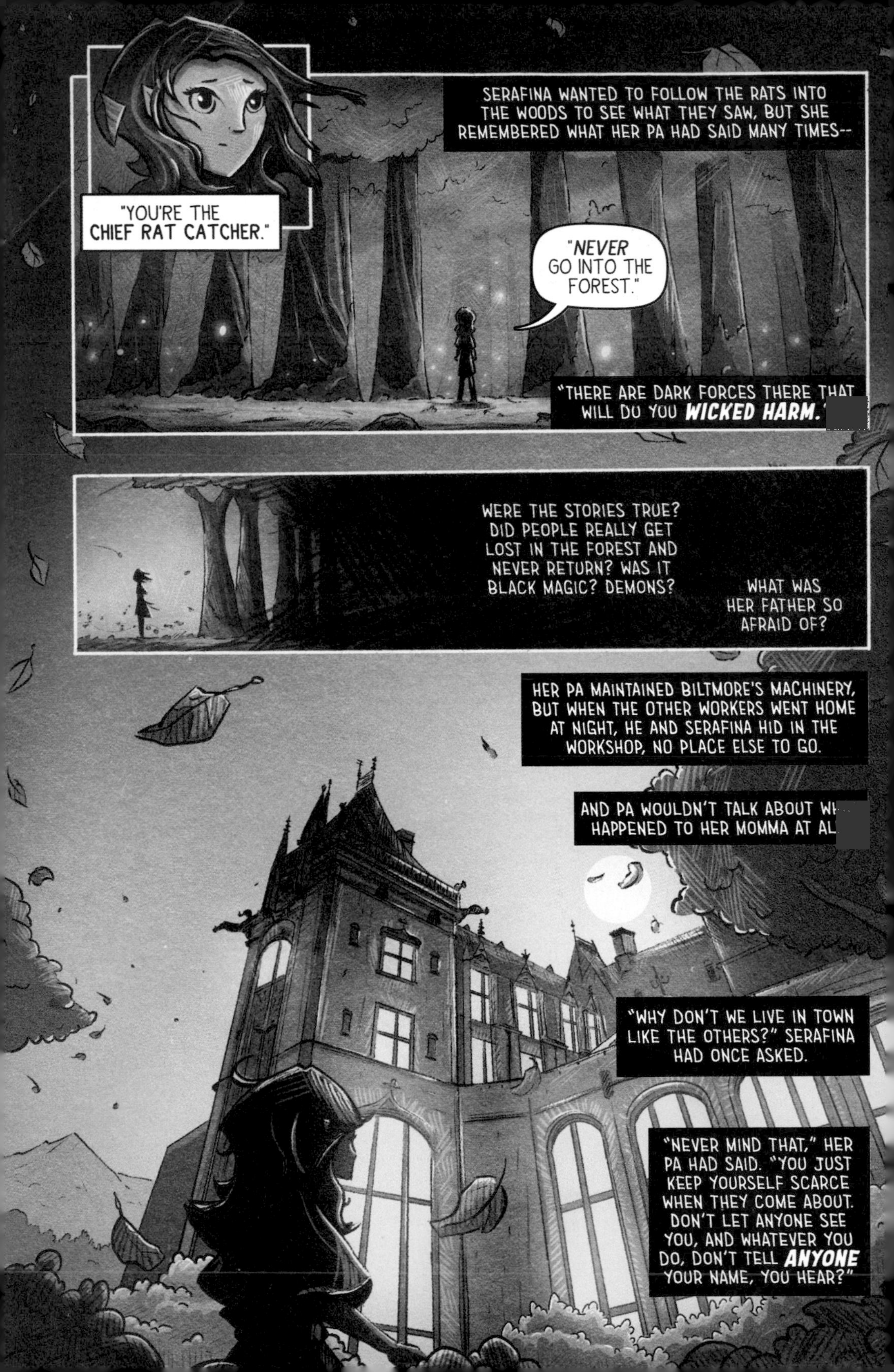
SERAFINA WANTED TO FOLLOW THE RATS INTO THE WOODS TO SEE WHAT THEY SAW, BUT SHE REMEMBERED WHAT HER PA HAD SAID MANY TIMES--
"YOU'RE THE CHIEF RAT CATCHER."
"NEVER GO INTO THE FOREST."
"THERE ARE DARK FORCES THERE THAT WILL DO YOU WICKED HARM.[redacted]
WERE THE STORIES TRUE? DID PEOPLE REALLY GET LOST IN THE FOREST AND NEVER RETURN? WAS IT BLACK MAGIC? DEMONS?
WHAT WAS HER FATHER SO AFRAID OF?
HER PA MAINTAINED BILTMORE'S MACHINERY, BUT WHEN THE OTHER WORKERS WENT HOME AT NIGHT, HE AND SERAFINA HID IN THE WORKSHOP, NO PLACE ELSE TO GO.
AND PA WOULDN'T TALK ABOUT WH[redacted] HAPPENED TO HER MOMMA AT AL[redacted]
"WHY DON'T WE LIVE IN TOWN LIKE THE OTHERS?" SERAFINA HAD ONCE ASKED.
"NEVER MIND THAT," HER PA HAD SAID. "YOU JUST KEEP YOURSELF SCARCE WHEN THEY COME ABOUT. DON'T LET ANYONE SEE YOU, AND WHATEVER YOU DO, DON'T TELL ANYONE YOUR NAME, YOU HEAR?"

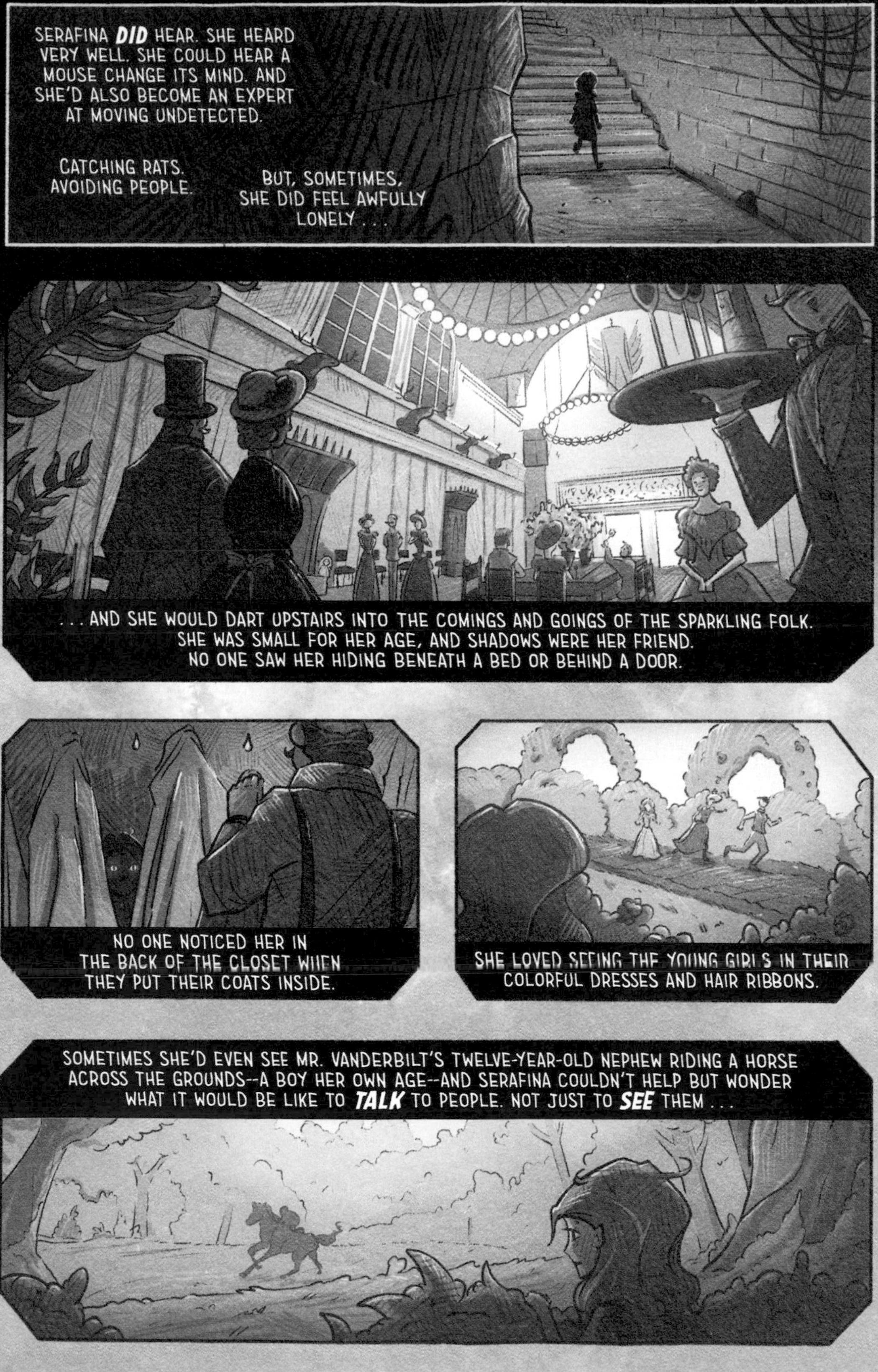
SERAFINA ***DID*** HEAR. SHE HEARD VERY WELL. SHE COULD HEAR A MOUSE CHANGE ITS MIND. AND SHE'D ALSO BECOME AN EXPERT AT MOVING UNDETECTED.
CATCHING RATS. AVOIDING PEOPLE.
BUT, SOMETIMES, SHE DID FEEL AWFULLY LONELY . . .
. . . AND SHE WOULD DART UPSTAIRS INTO THE COMINGS AND GOINGS OF THE SPARKLING FOLK. SHE WAS SMALL FOR HER AGE, AND SHADOWS WERE HER FRIEND. NO ONE SAW HER HIDING BENEATH A BED OR BEHIND A DOOR.
NO ONE NOTICED HER IN THE BACK OF THE CLOSET WHEN THEY PUT THEIR COATS INSIDE.
SHE LOVED SEEING THE YOUNG GIRLS IN THEIR COLORFUL DRESSES AND HAIR RIBBONS.
SOMETIMES SHE'D EVEN SEE MR. VANDERBILT'S TWELVE-YEAR-OLD NEPHEW RIDING A HORSE ACROSS THE GROUNDS--A BOY HER OWN AGE--AND SERAFINA COULDN'T HELP BUT WONDER WHAT IT WOULD BE LIKE TO ***TALK*** TO PEOPLE. NOT JUST TO ***SEE*** THEM . . .

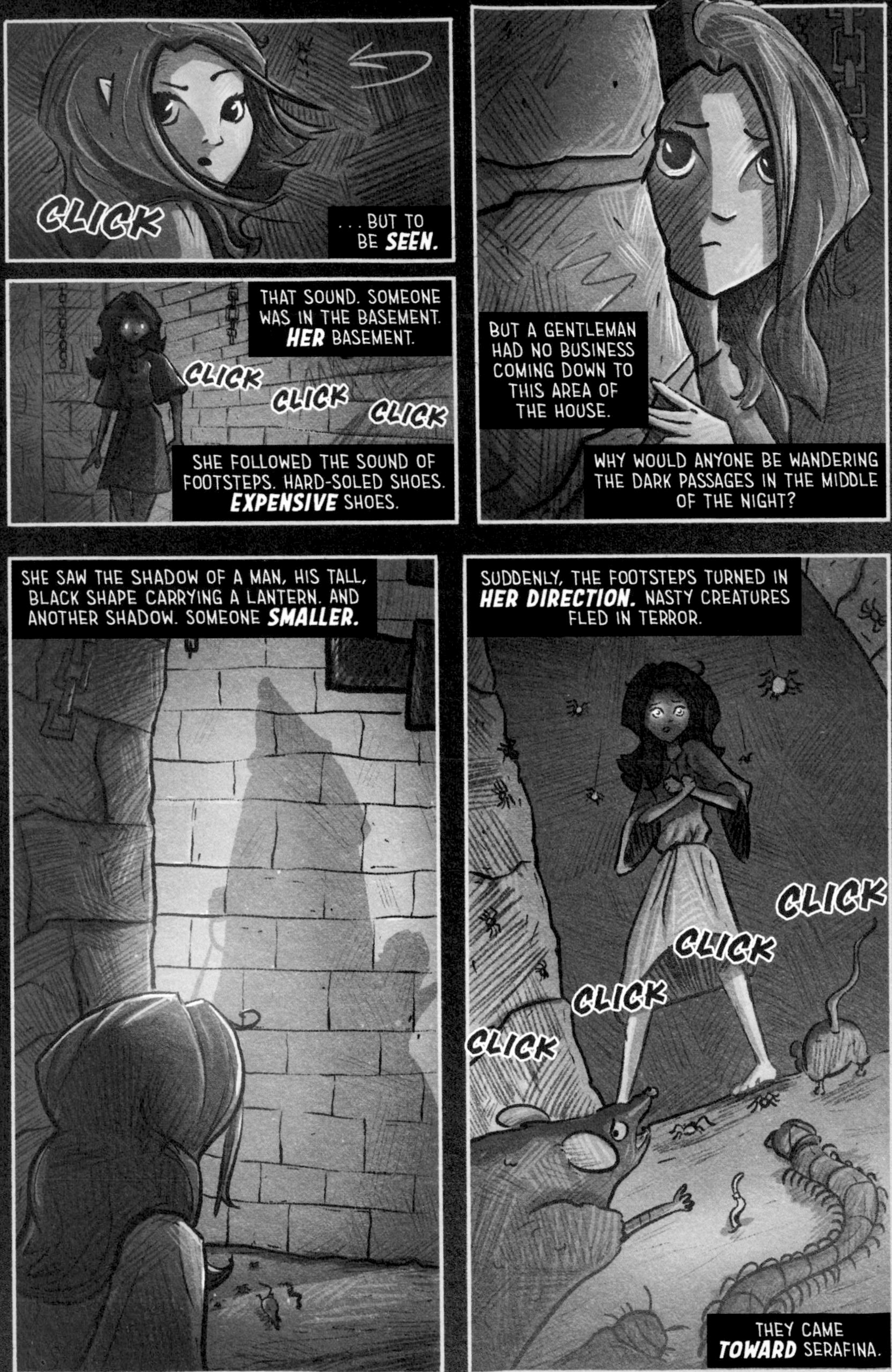
CLICK
. . . BUT TO BE SEEN.
THAT SOUND. SOMEONE WAS IN THE BASEMENT. HER BASEMENT.
CLICK
CLICK
CLICK
SHE FOLLOWED THE SOUND OF FOOTSTEPS. HARD-SOLED SHOES. EXPENSIVE SHOES.
BUT A GENTLEMAN HAD NO BUSINESS COMING DOWN TO THIS AREA OF THE HOUSE.
WHY WOULD ANYONE BE WANDERING THE DARK PASSAGES IN THE MIDDLE OF THE NIGHT?
SHE SAW THE SHADOW OF A MAN, HIS TALL, BLACK SHAPE CARRYING A LANTERN. AND ANOTHER SHADOW. SOMEONE SMALLER.
SUDDENLY, THE FOOTSTEPS TURNED IN HER DIRECTION. NASTY CREATURES FLED IN TERROR.
CLICK
CLICK
CLICK
CLICK
THEY CAME TOWARD SERAFINA.

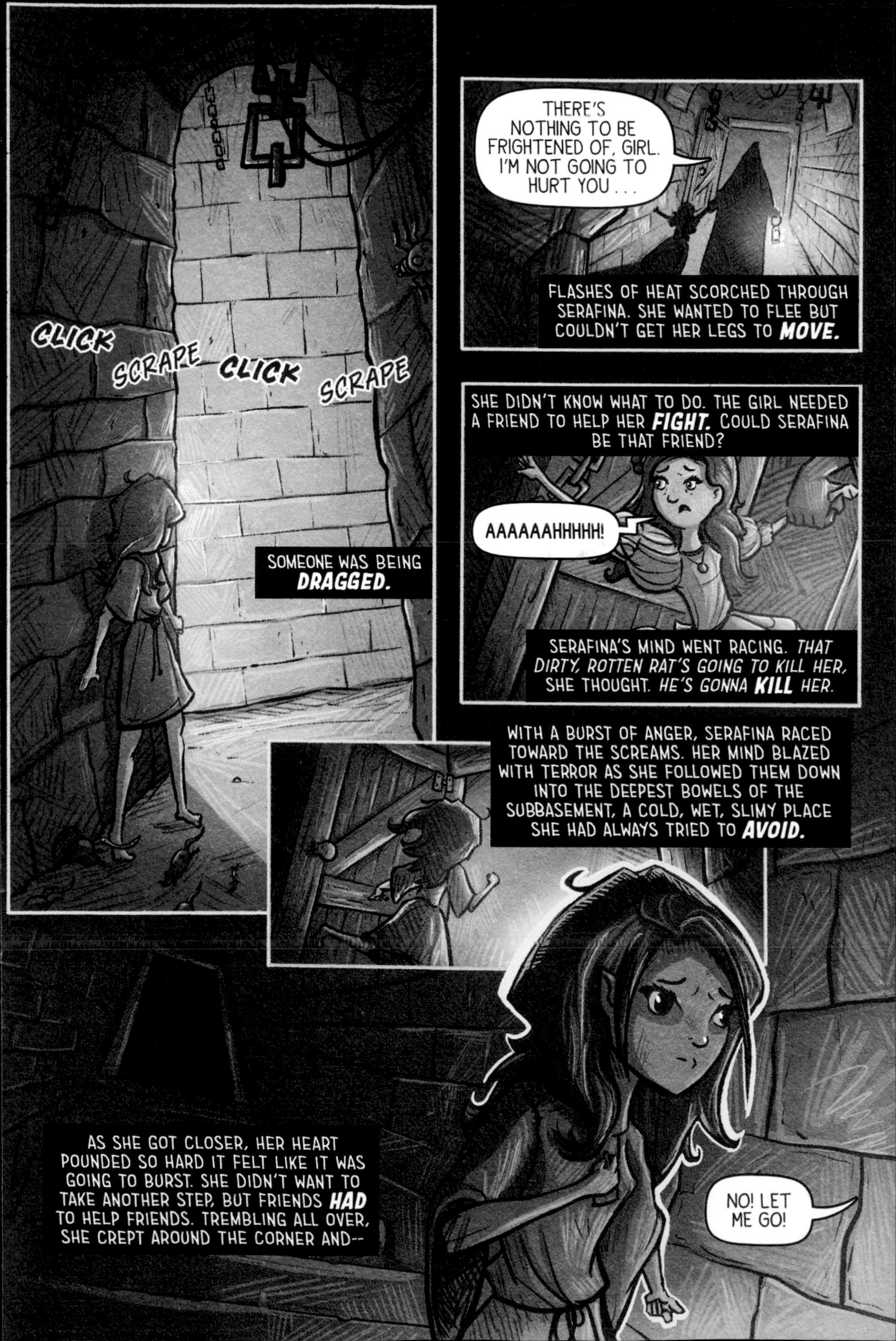
CLICK
SCRAPE
CLICK
SCRAPE
SOMEONE WAS BEING DRAGGED.
THERE'S NOTHING TO BE FRIGHTENED OF, GIRL. I'M NOT GOING TO HURT YOU . . .
FLASHES OF HEAT SCORCHED THROUGH SERAFINA. SHE WANTED TO FLEE BUT COULDN'T GET HER LEGS TO MOVE.
SHE DIDN'T KNOW WHAT TO DO. THE GIRL NEEDED A FRIEND TO HELP HER FIGHT. COULD SERAFINA BE THAT FRIEND?
AAAAAAHHHHH!
SERAFINA'S MIND WENT RACING. THAT DIRTY, ROTTEN RAT'S GOING TO KILL HER, SHE THOUGHT. HE'S GONNA KILL HER.
WITH A BURST OF ANGER, SERAFINA RACED TOWARD THE SCREAMS. HER MIND BLAZED WITH TERROR AS SHE FOLLOWED THEM DOWN INTO THE DEEPEST BOWELS OF THE SUBBASEMENT, A COLD, WET, SLIMY PLACE SHE HAD ALWAYS TRIED TO AVOID.
AS SHE GOT CLOSER, HER HEART POUNDED SO HARD IT FELT LIKE IT WAS GOING TO BURST. SHE DIDN'T WANT TO TAKE ANOTHER STEP, BUT FRIENDS HAD TO HELP FRIENDS. TREMBLING ALL OVER, SHE CREPT AROUND THE CORNER AND--
NO! LET ME GO!

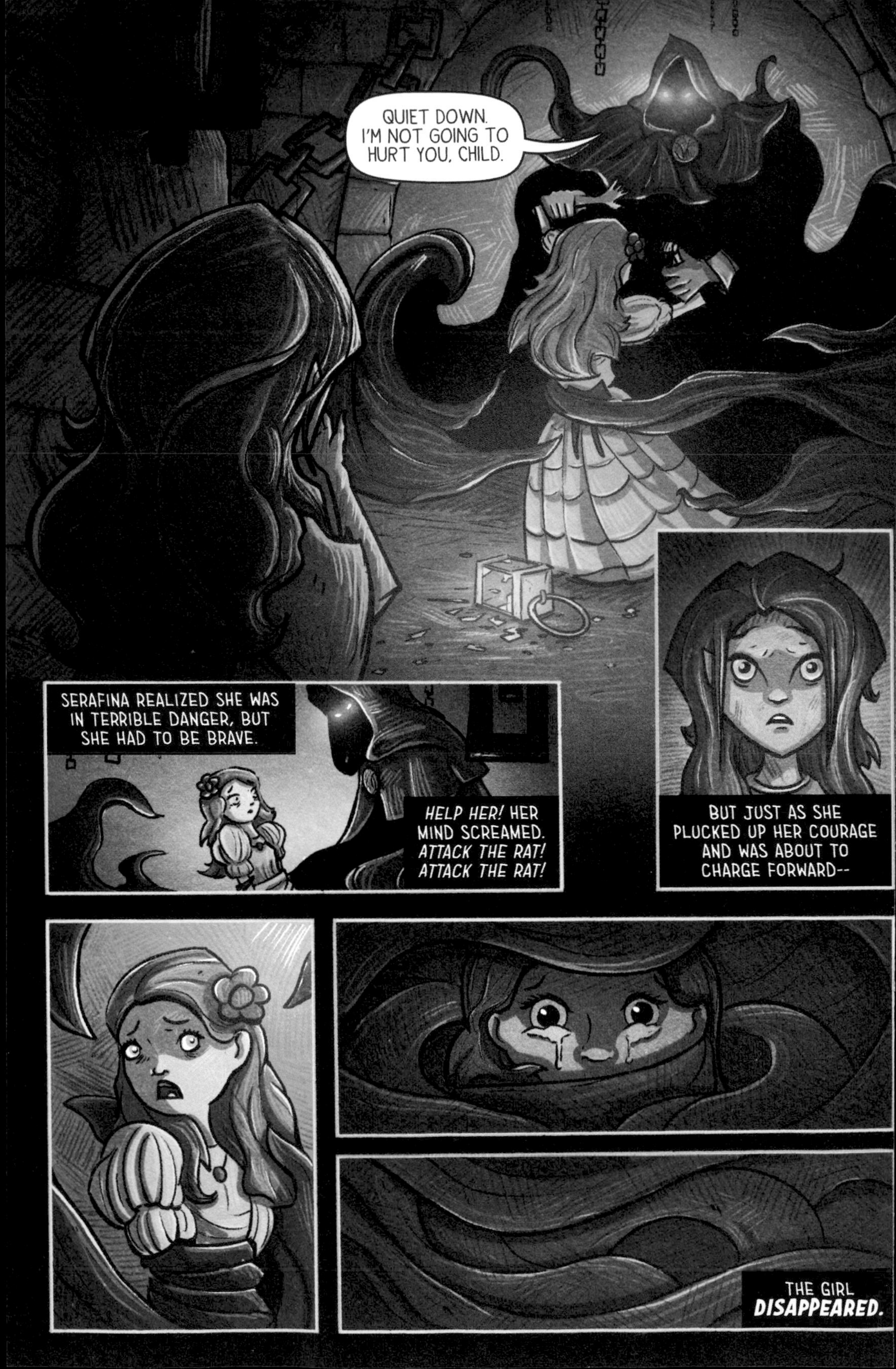
QUIET DOWN. I'M NOT GOING TO HURT YOU, CHILD.
SERAFINA REALIZED SHE WAS IN TERRIBLE DANGER, BUT SHE HAD TO BE BRAVE.
HELP HER! HER MIND SCREAMED. *ATTACK THE RAT! ATTACK THE RAT!*
BUT JUST AS SHE PLUCKED UP HER COURAGE AND WAS ABOUT TO CHARGE FORWARD--
THE GIRL **DISAPPEARED.**

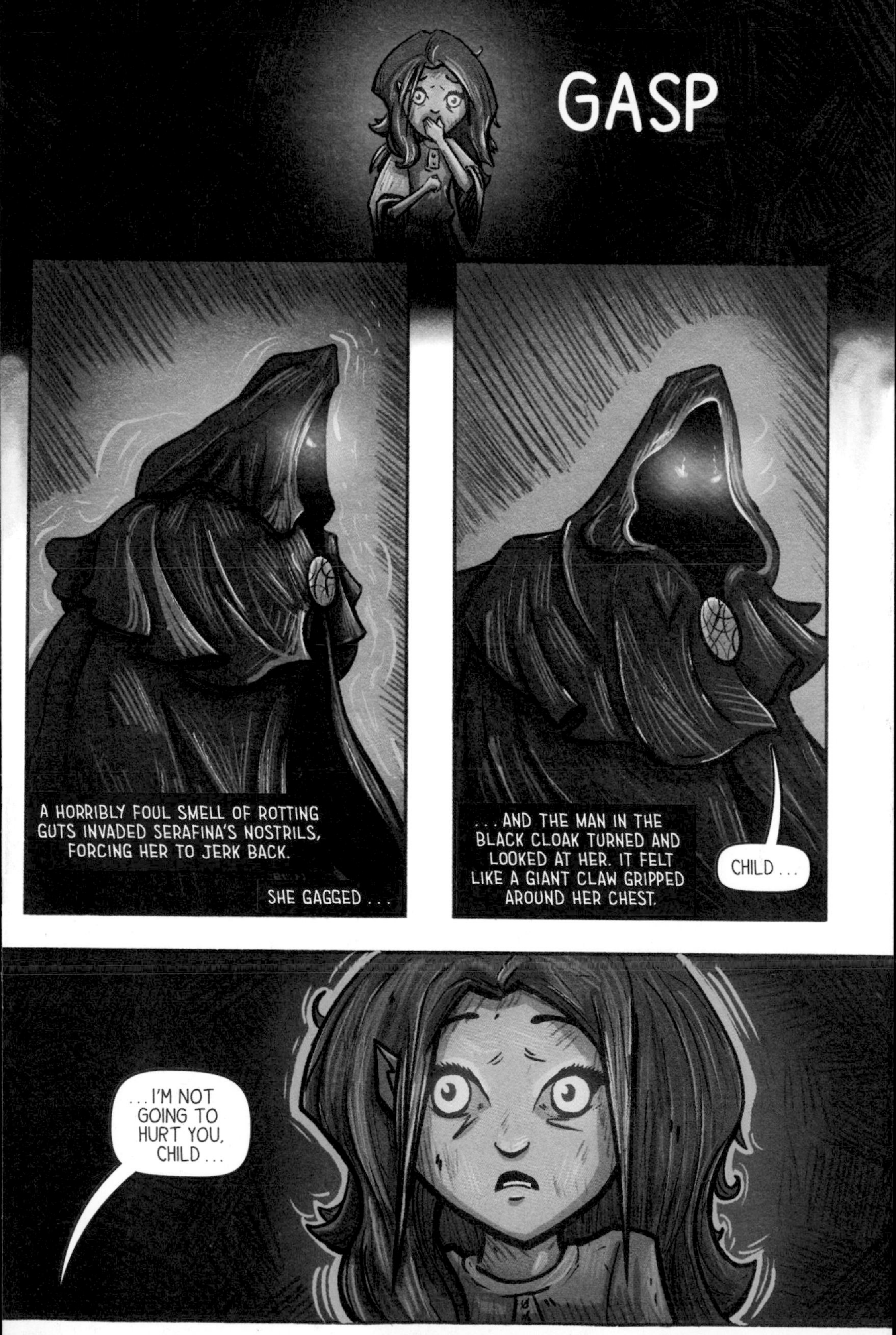
GASP
A HORRIBLY FOUL SMELL OF ROTTING GUTS INVADED SERAFINA'S NOSTRILS, FORCING HER TO JERK BACK.
SHE GAGGED . . .
. . . AND THE MAN IN THE BLACK CLOAK TURNED AND LOOKED AT HER. IT FELT LIKE A GIANT CLAW GRIPPED AROUND HER CHEST.
CHILD . . .
. . . I'M NOT GOING TO HURT YOU, CHILD . . .

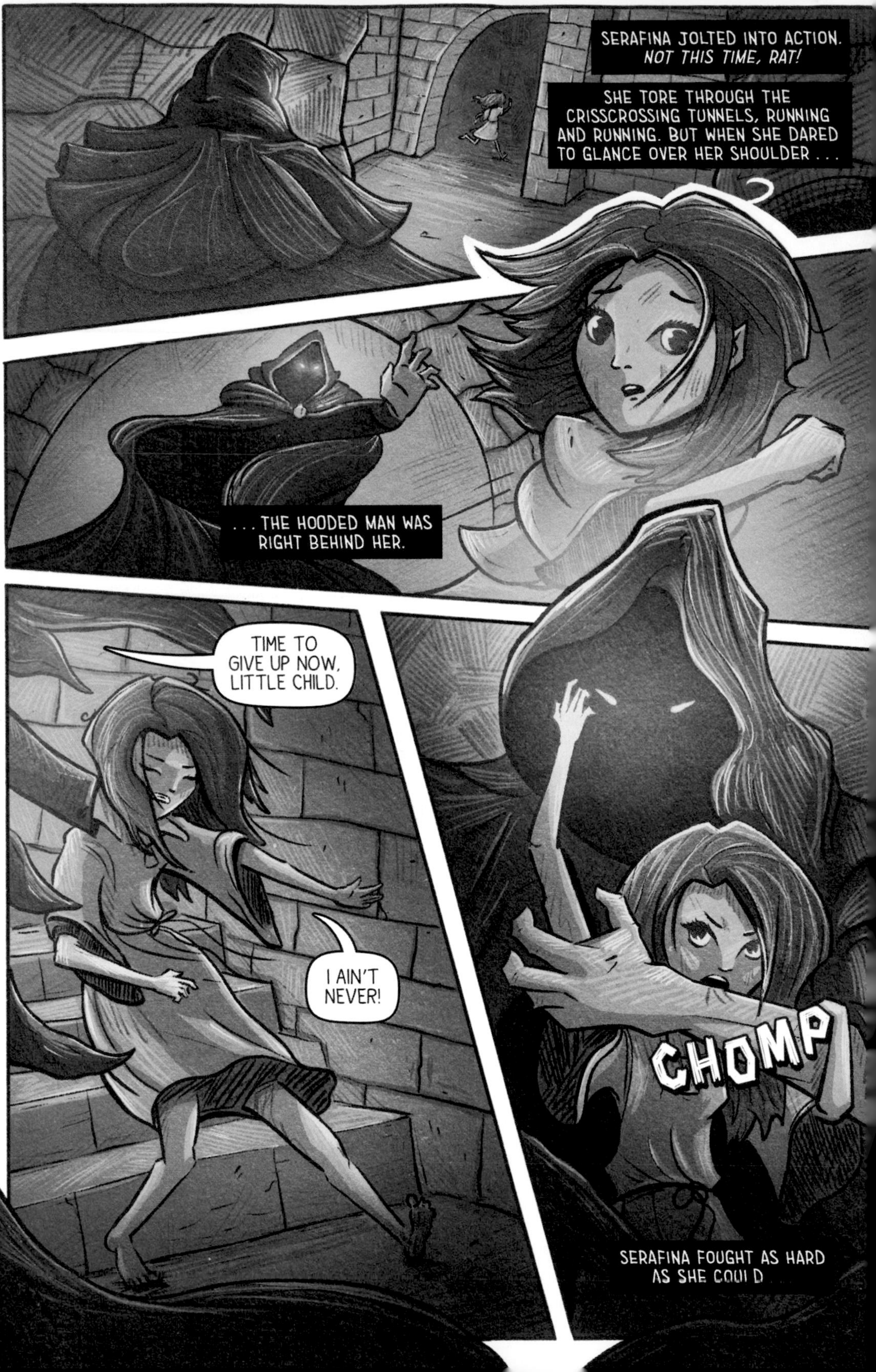
SERAFINA JOLTED INTO ACTION. *NOT THIS TIME, RAT!*
SHE TORE THROUGH THE CRISSCROSSING TUNNELS, RUNNING AND RUNNING. BUT WHEN SHE DARED TO GLANCE OVER HER SHOULDER . . .
. . . THE HOODED MAN WAS RIGHT BEHIND HER.
TIME TO GIVE UP NOW, LITTLE CHILD.
I AIN'T NEVER!
CHOMP
SERAFINA FOUGHT AS HARD AS SHE COULD

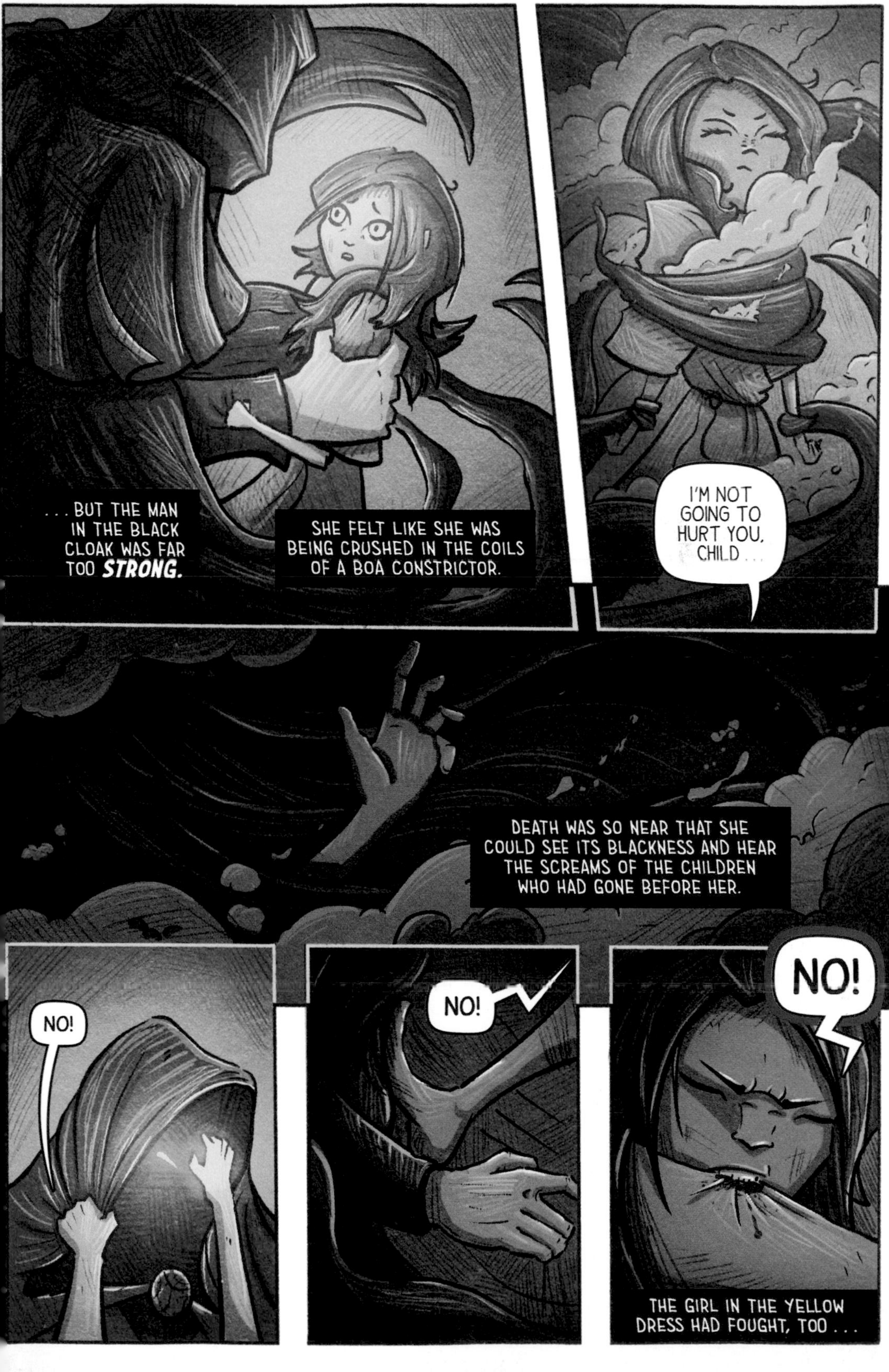
. . . BUT THE MAN IN THE BLACK CLOAK WAS FAR TOO STRONG.
SHE FELT LIKE SHE WAS BEING CRUSHED IN THE COILS OF A BOA CONSTRICTOR.
I'M NOT GOING TO HURT YOU, CHILD . . .
DEATH WAS SO NEAR THAT SHE COULD SEE ITS BLACKNESS AND HEAR THE SCREAMS OF THE CHILDREN WHO HAD GONE BEFORE HER.
NO!
NO!
NO!
THE GIRL IN THE YELLOW DRESS HAD FOUGHT, TOO . . .

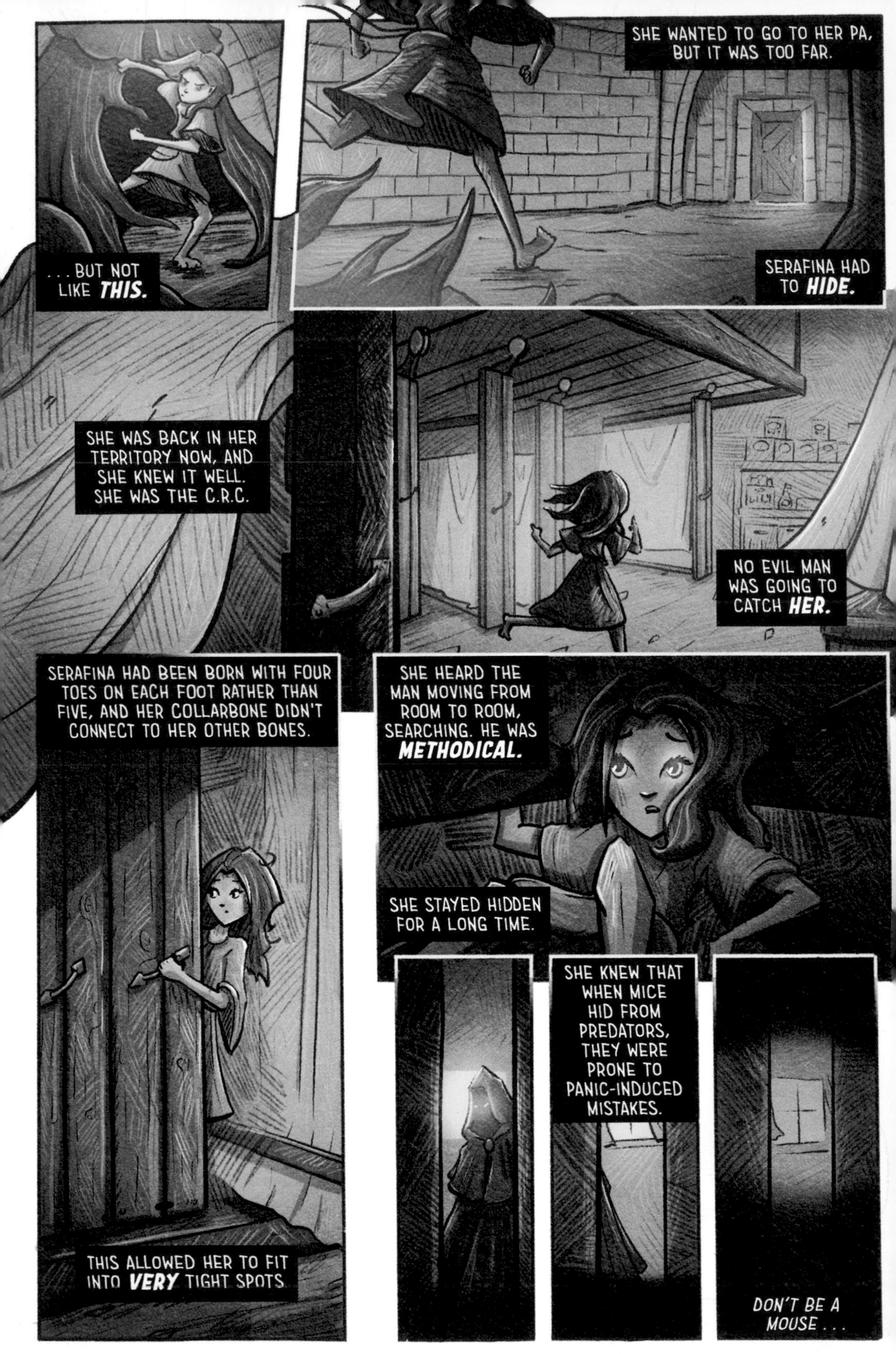
. . . BUT NOT LIKE THIS.
SHE WANTED TO GO TO HER PA, BUT IT WAS TOO FAR.
SERAFINA HAD TO HIDE.
SHE WAS BACK IN HER TERRITORY NOW, AND SHE KNEW IT WELL. SHE WAS THE C.R.C.
NO EVIL MAN WAS GOING TO CATCH HER.
SERAFINA HAD BEEN BORN WITH FOUR TOES ON EACH FOOT RATHER THAN FIVE, AND HER COLLARBONE DIDN'T CONNECT TO HER OTHER BONES.
THIS ALLOWED HER TO FIT INTO VERY TIGHT SPOTS.
SHE HEARD THE MAN MOVING FROM ROOM TO ROOM, SEARCHING. HE WAS METHODICAL.
SHE STAYED HIDDEN FOR A LONG TIME.
SHE KNEW THAT WHEN MICE HID FROM PREDATORS, THEY WERE PRONE TO PANIC-INDUCED MISTAKES.
DON'T BE A MOUSE . . .

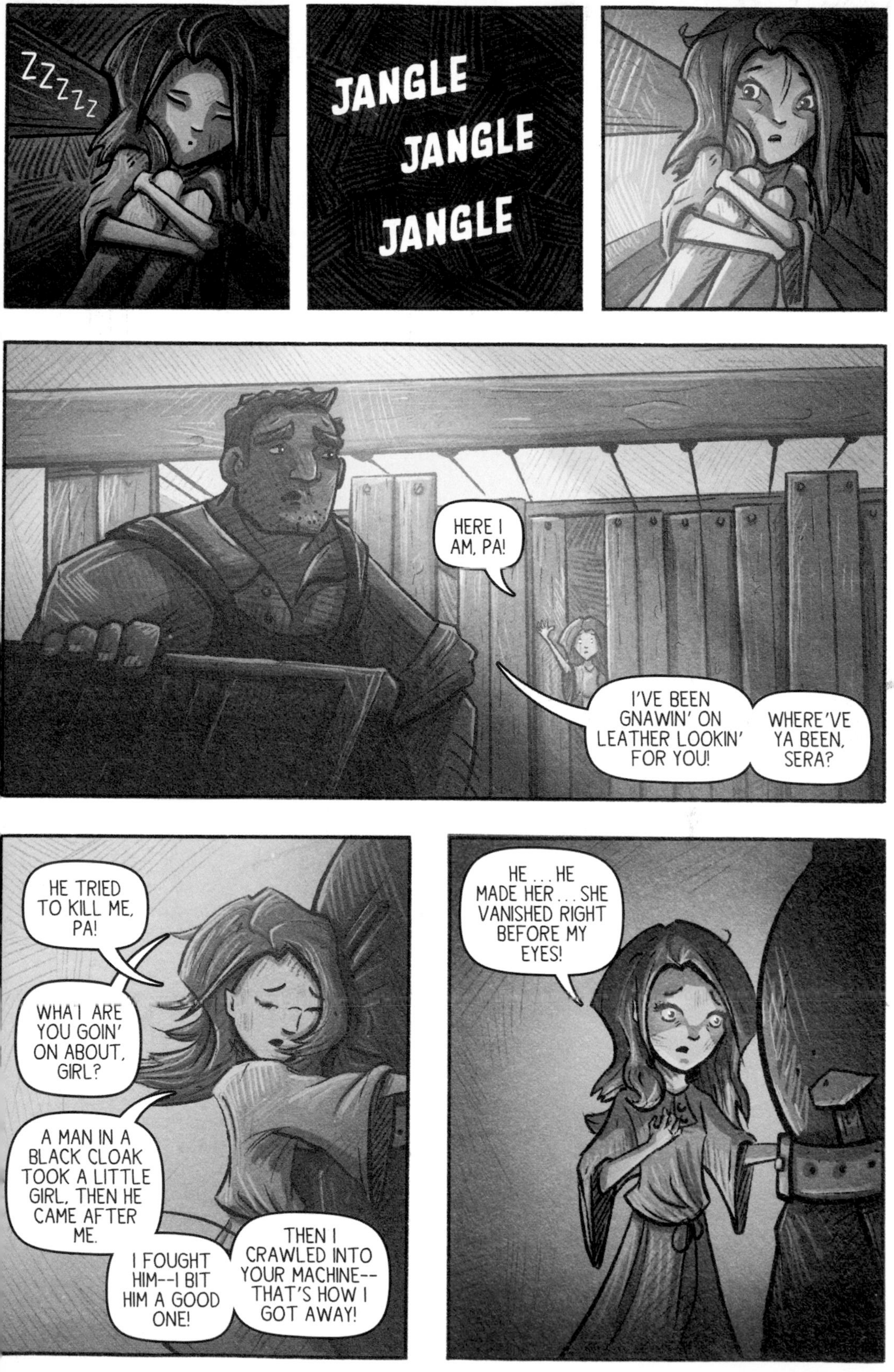
ZZZZZ
JANGLE
JANGLE
JANGLE
HERE I AM, PA!
WHERE'VE YA BEEN, SERA?
I'VE BEEN GNAWIN' ON LEATHER LOOKIN' FOR YOU!
HE TRIED TO KILL ME, PA!
WHAT ARE YOU GOIN' ON ABOUT, GIRL?
A MAN IN A BLACK CLOAK TOOK A LITTLE GIRL, THEN HE CAME AFTER ME.
I FOUGHT HIM--I BIT HIM A GOOD ONE!
THEN I CRAWLED INTO YOUR MACHINE--THAT'S HOW I GOT AWAY!
HE . . . HE MADE HER . . . SHE VANISHED RIGHT BEFORE MY EYES!

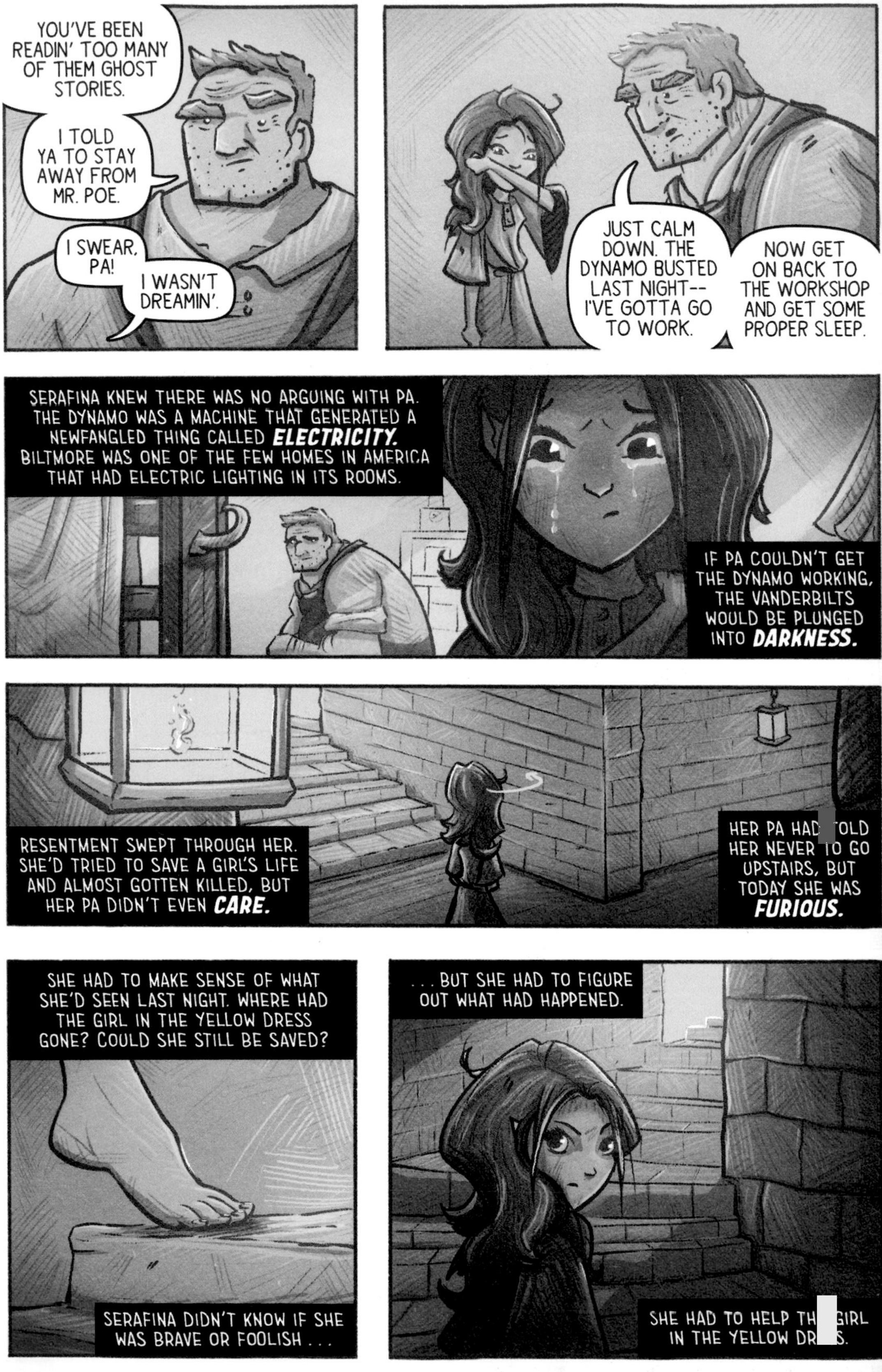
YOU'VE BEEN READIN' TOO MANY OF THEM GHOST STORIES.
I TOLD YA TO STAY AWAY FROM MR. POE.
I SWEAR, PA!
I WASN'T DREAMIN'.
JUST CALM DOWN. THE DYNAMO BUSTED LAST NIGHT-- I'VE GOTTA GO TO WORK.
NOW GET ON BACK TO THE WORKSHOP AND GET SOME PROPER SLEEP.
SERAFINA KNEW THERE WAS NO ARGUING WITH PA. THE DYNAMO WAS A MACHINE THAT GENERATED A NEWFANGLED THING CALLED ELECTRICITY. BILTMORE WAS ONE OF THE FEW HOMES IN AMERICA THAT HAD ELECTRIC LIGHTING IN ITS ROOMS.
IF PA COULDN'T GET THE DYNAMO WORKING, THE VANDERBILTS WOULD BE PLUNGED INTO DARKNESS.
RESENTMENT SWEPT THROUGH HER. SHE'D TRIED TO SAVE A GIRL'S LIFE AND ALMOST GOTTEN KILLED, BUT HER PA DIDN'T EVEN CARE.
HER PA HAD TOLD HER NEVER TO GO UPSTAIRS, BUT TODAY SHE WAS FURIOUS.
SHE HAD TO MAKE SENSE OF WHAT SHE'D SEEN LAST NIGHT. WHERE HAD THE GIRL IN THE YELLOW DRESS GONE? COULD SHE STILL BE SAVED?
SERAFINA DIDN'T KNOW IF SHE WAS BRAVE OR FOOLISH . . .
. . . BUT SHE HAD TO FIGURE OUT WHAT HAD HAPPENED.
SHE HAD TO HELP TH GIRL IN THE YELLOW DR S.

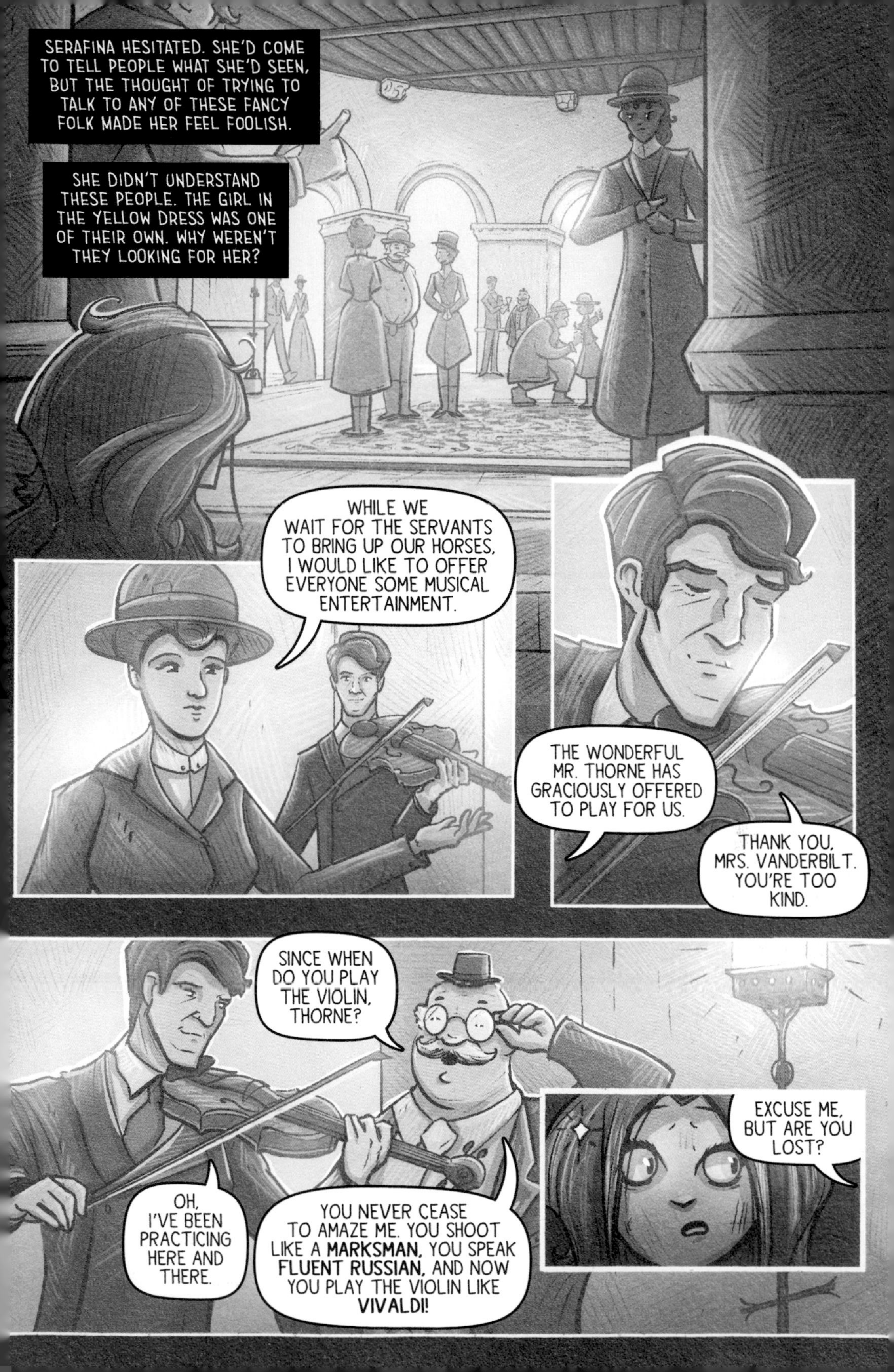
SERAFINA HESITATED. SHE'D COME TO TELL PEOPLE WHAT SHE'D SEEN, BUT THE THOUGHT OF TRYING TO TALK TO ANY OF THESE FANCY FOLK MADE HER FEEL FOOLISH.
SHE DIDN'T UNDERSTAND THESE PEOPLE. THE GIRL IN THE YELLOW DRESS WAS ONE OF THEIR OWN. WHY WEREN'T THEY LOOKING FOR HER?
WHILE WE WAIT FOR THE SERVANTS TO BRING UP OUR HORSES, I WOULD LIKE TO OFFER EVERYONE SOME MUSICAL ENTERTAINMENT.
THE WONDERFUL MR. THORNE HAS GRACIOUSLY OFFERED TO PLAY FOR US.
THANK YOU, MRS. VANDERBILT. YOU'RE TOO KIND.
SINCE WHEN DO YOU PLAY THE VIOLIN, THORNE?
OH, I'VE BEEN PRACTICING HERE AND THERE.
YOU NEVER CEASE TO AMAZE ME. YOU SHOOT LIKE A **MARKSMAN,** YOU SPEAK **FLUENT RUSSIAN,** AND NOW YOU PLAY THE VIOLIN LIKE **VIVALDI!**
EXCUSE ME, BUT ARE YOU LOST?

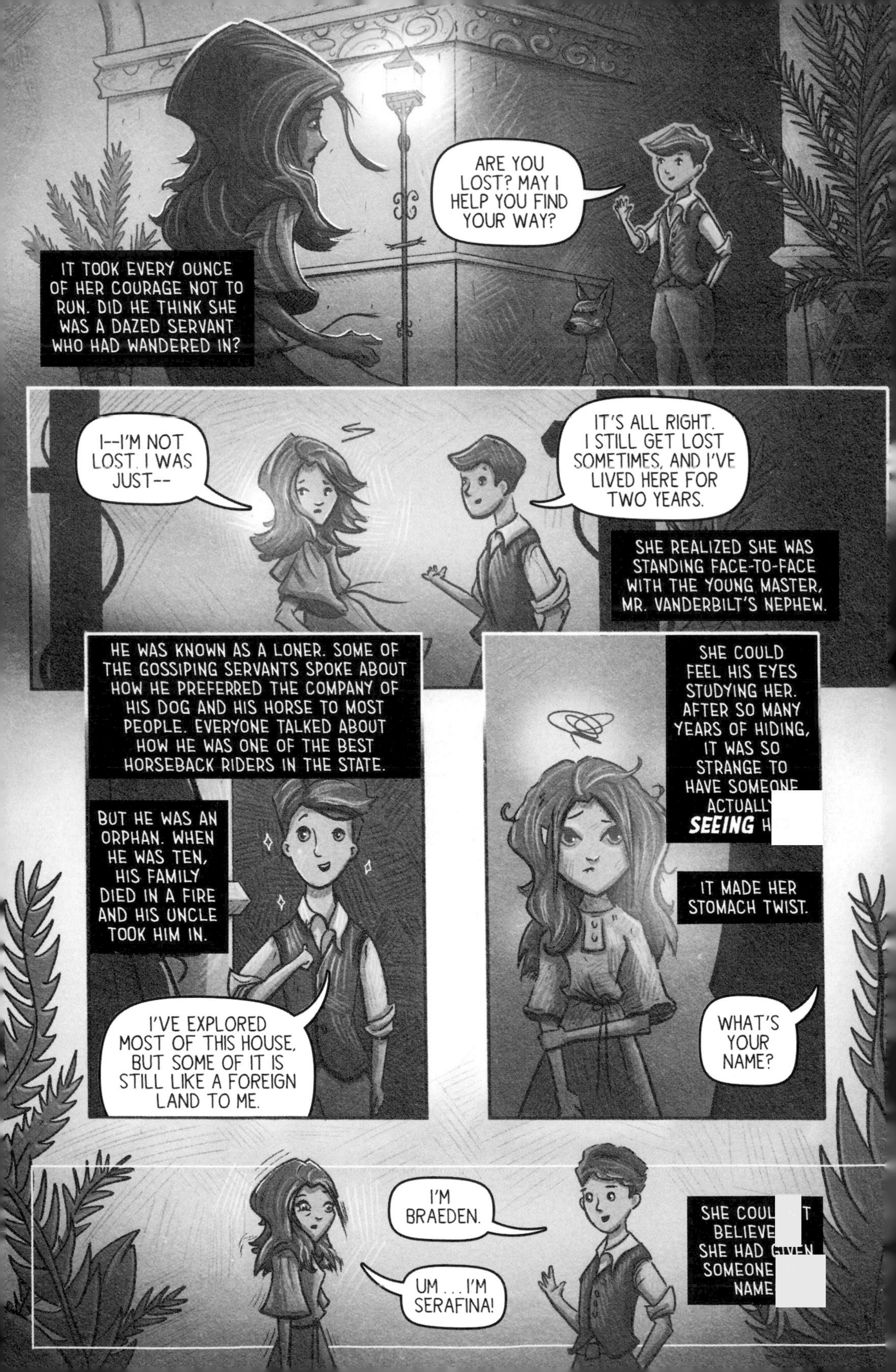
ARE YOU LOST? MAY I HELP YOU FIND YOUR WAY?
IT TOOK EVERY OUNCE OF HER COURAGE NOT TO RUN. DID HE THINK SHE WAS A DAZED SERVANT WHO HAD WANDERED IN?
I--I'M NOT LOST. I WAS JUST--
IT'S ALL RIGHT. I STILL GET LOST SOMETIMES, AND I'VE LIVED HERE FOR TWO YEARS.
SHE REALIZED SHE WAS STANDING FACE-TO-FACE WITH THE YOUNG MASTER, MR. VANDERBILT'S NEPHEW.
HE WAS KNOWN AS A LONER. SOME OF THE GOSSIPING SERVANTS SPOKE ABOUT HOW HE PREFERRED THE COMPANY OF HIS DOG AND HIS HORSE TO MOST PEOPLE. EVERYONE TALKED ABOUT HOW HE WAS ONE OF THE BEST HORSEBACK RIDERS IN THE STATE.
BUT HE WAS AN ORPHAN. WHEN HE WAS TEN, HIS FAMILY DIED IN A FIRE AND HIS UNCLE TOOK HIM IN.
I'VE EXPLORED MOST OF THIS HOUSE, BUT SOME OF IT IS STILL LIKE A FOREIGN LAND TO ME.
SHE COULD FEEL HIS EYES STUDYING HER. AFTER SO MANY YEARS OF HIDING, IT WAS SO STRANGE TO HAVE SOMEONE ACTUALLY *SEEING*
IT MADE HER STOMACH TWIST.
WHAT'S YOUR NAME?
I'M BRAEDEN.
UM . . . I'M SERAFINA!
SHE COUL T BELIEVE SHE HAD GIVEN SOMEONE NAME

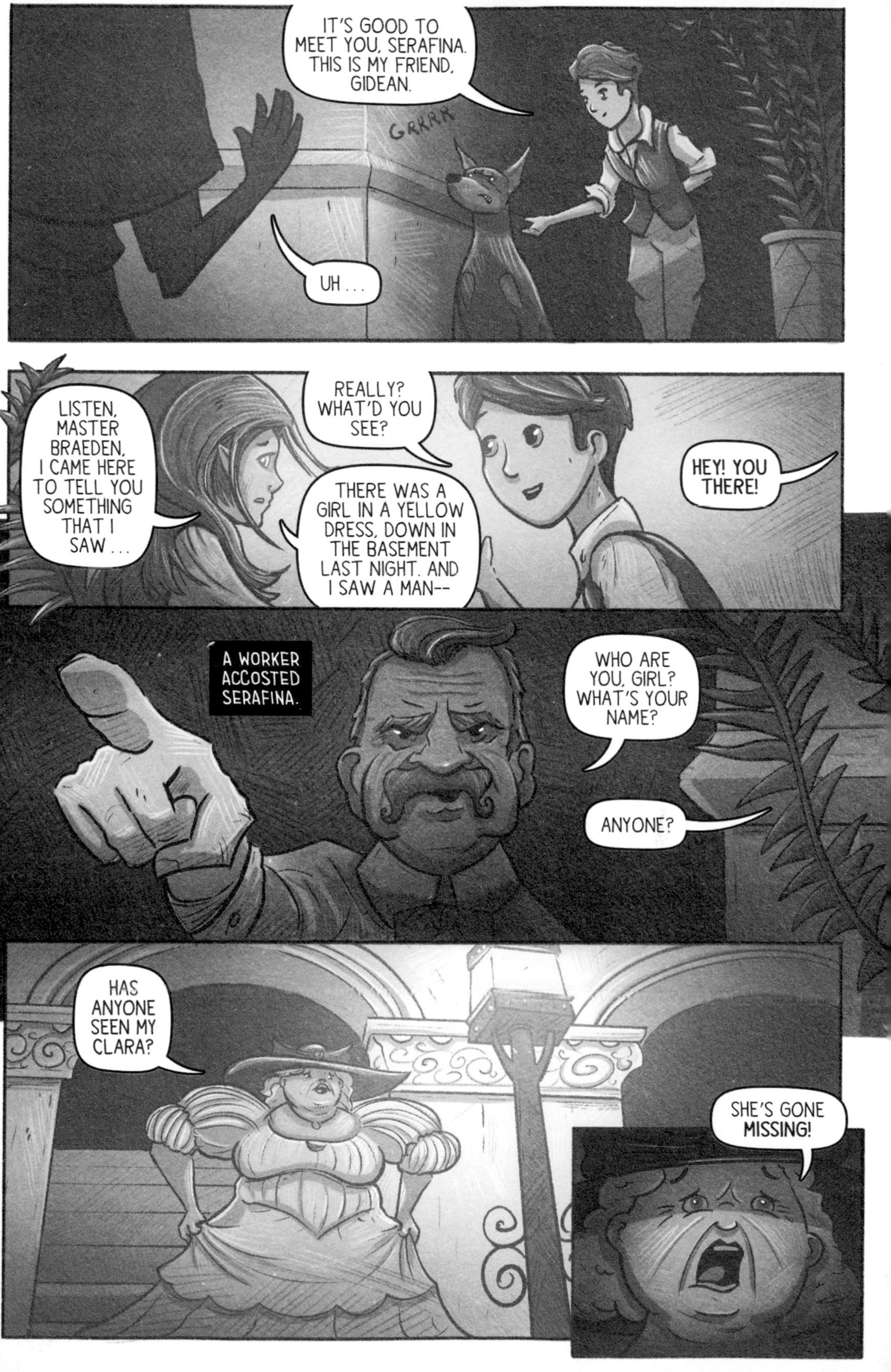
IT'S GOOD TO MEET YOU, SERAFINA. THIS IS MY FRIEND, GIDEAN.
GRRRR
UH . . .
LISTEN, MASTER BRAEDEN, I CAME HERE TO TELL YOU SOMETHING THAT I SAW . . .
REALLY? WHAT'D YOU SEE?
THERE WAS A GIRL IN A YELLOW DRESS, DOWN IN THE BASEMENT LAST NIGHT. AND I SAW A MAN--
HEY! YOU THERE!
A WORKER ACCOSTED SERAFINA.
WHO ARE YOU, GIRL? WHAT'S YOUR NAME?
ANYONE?
HAS ANYONE SEEN MY CLARA?
SHE'S GONE MISSING!

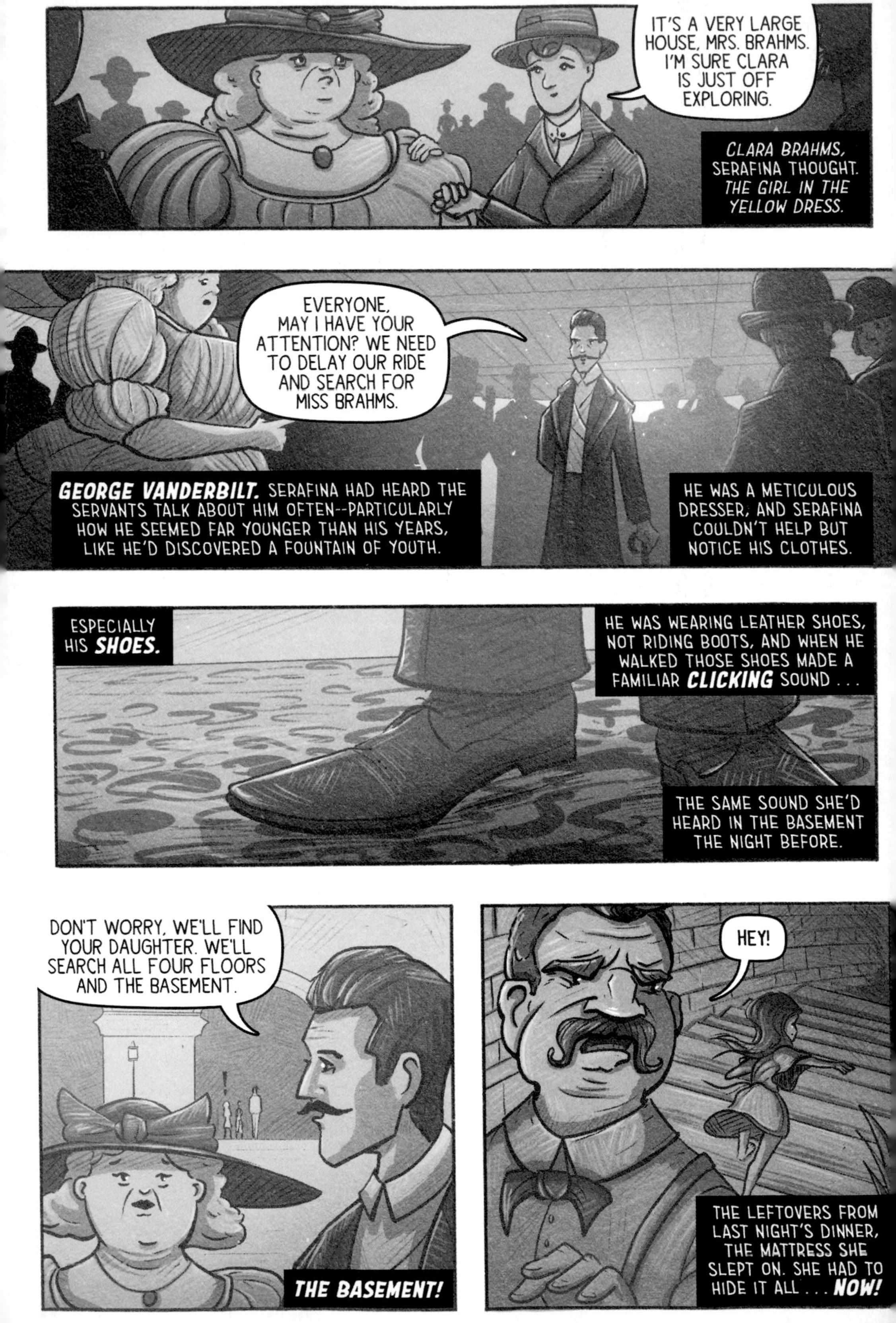
IT'S A VERY LARGE HOUSE, MRS. BRAHMS. I'M SURE CLARA IS JUST OFF EXPLORING.
CLARA BRAHMS, SERAFINA THOUGHT. THE GIRL IN THE YELLOW DRESS.
EVERYONE, MAY I HAVE YOUR ATTENTION? WE NEED TO DELAY OUR RIDE AND SEARCH FOR MISS BRAHMS.
GEORGE VANDERBILT. SERAFINA HAD HEARD THE SERVANTS TALK ABOUT HIM OFTEN--PARTICULARLY HOW HE SEEMED FAR YOUNGER THAN HIS YEARS, LIKE HE'D DISCOVERED A FOUNTAIN OF YOUTH.
HE WAS A METICULOUS DRESSER, AND SERAFINA COULDN'T HELP BUT NOTICE HIS CLOTHES.
ESPECIALLY HIS SHOES.
HE WAS WEARING LEATHER SHOES, NOT RIDING BOOTS, AND WHEN HE WALKED THOSE SHOES MADE A FAMILIAR CLICKING SOUND . . .
THE SAME SOUND SHE'D HEARD IN THE BASEMENT THE NIGHT BEFORE.
DON'T WORRY, WE'LL FIND YOUR DAUGHTER. WE'LL SEARCH ALL FOUR FLOORS AND THE BASEMENT.
THE BASEMENT!
HEY!
THE LEFTOVERS FROM LAST NIGHT'S DINNER, THE MATTRESS SHE SLEPT ON. SHE HAD TO HIDE IT ALL . . . NOW!

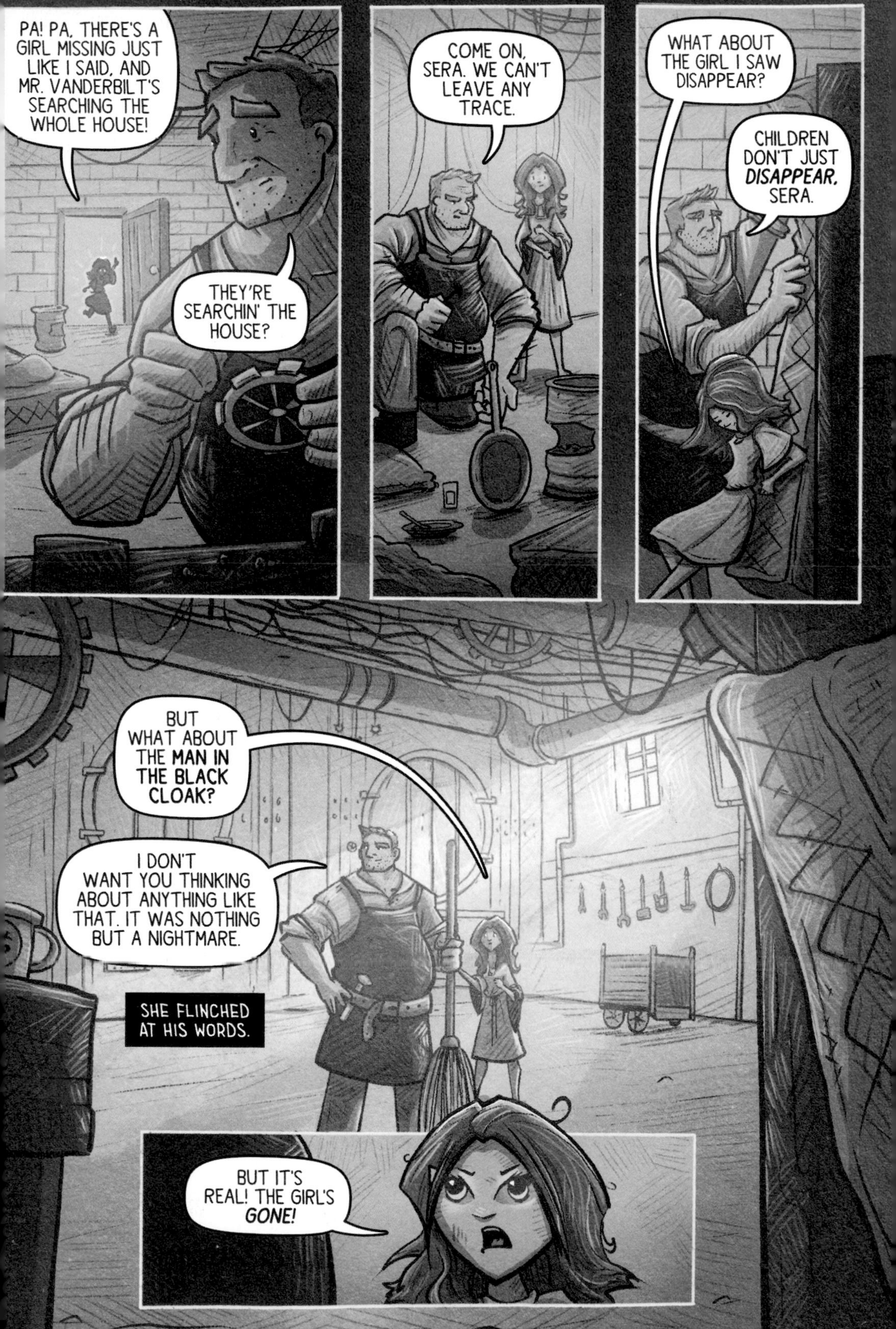
PA! PA, THERE'S A GIRL MISSING JUST LIKE I SAID, AND MR. VANDERBILT'S SEARCHING THE WHOLE HOUSE!
THEY'RE SEARCHIN' THE HOUSE?
COME ON, SERA. WE CAN'T LEAVE ANY TRACE.
WHAT ABOUT THE GIRL I SAW DISAPPEAR?
CHILDREN DON'T JUST ***DISAPPEAR,*** SERA.
BUT WHAT ABOUT THE **MAN IN THE BLACK CLOAK?**
I DON'T WANT YOU THINKING ABOUT ANYTHING LIKE THAT. IT WAS NOTHING BUT A NIGHTMARE.
SHE FLINCHED AT HIS WORDS.
BUT IT'S REAL! THE GIRL'S ***GONE!***

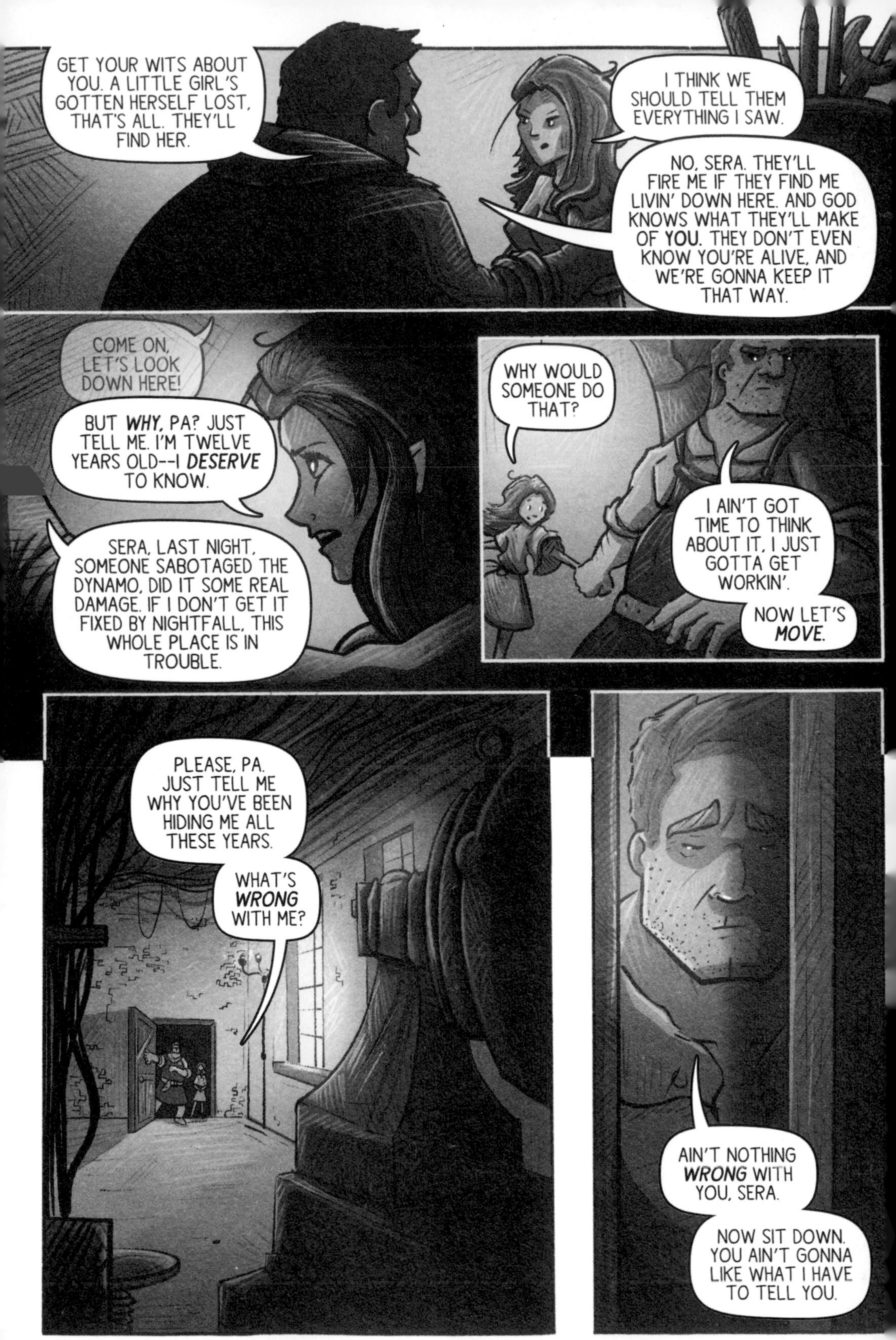
GET YOUR WITS ABOUT YOU. A LITTLE GIRL'S GOTTEN HERSELF LOST, THAT'S ALL. THEY'LL FIND HER.
I THINK WE SHOULD TELL THEM EVERYTHING I SAW.
NO, SERA. THEY'LL FIRE ME IF THEY FIND ME LIVIN' DOWN HERE. AND GOD KNOWS WHAT THEY'LL MAKE OF **YOU.** THEY DON'T EVEN KNOW YOU'RE ALIVE, AND WE'RE GONNA KEEP IT THAT WAY.
COME ON, LET'S LOOK DOWN HERE!
BUT ***WHY,*** PA? JUST TELL ME. I'M TWELVE YEARS OLD--I ***DESERVE*** TO KNOW.
SERA, LAST NIGHT, SOMEONE SABOTAGED THE DYNAMO, DID IT SOME REAL DAMAGE. IF I DON'T GET IT FIXED BY NIGHTFALL, THIS WHOLE PLACE IS IN TROUBLE.
WHY WOULD SOMEONE DO THAT?
I AIN'T GOT TIME TO THINK ABOUT IT, I JUST GOTTA GET WORKIN'.
NOW LET'S ***MOVE.***
PLEASE, PA. JUST TELL ME WHY YOU'VE BEEN HIDING ME ALL THESE YEARS.
WHAT'S ***WRONG*** WITH ME?
AIN'T NOTHING ***WRONG*** WITH YOU, SERA.
NOW SIT DOWN. YOU AIN'T GONNA LIKE WHAT I HAVE TO TELL YOU.

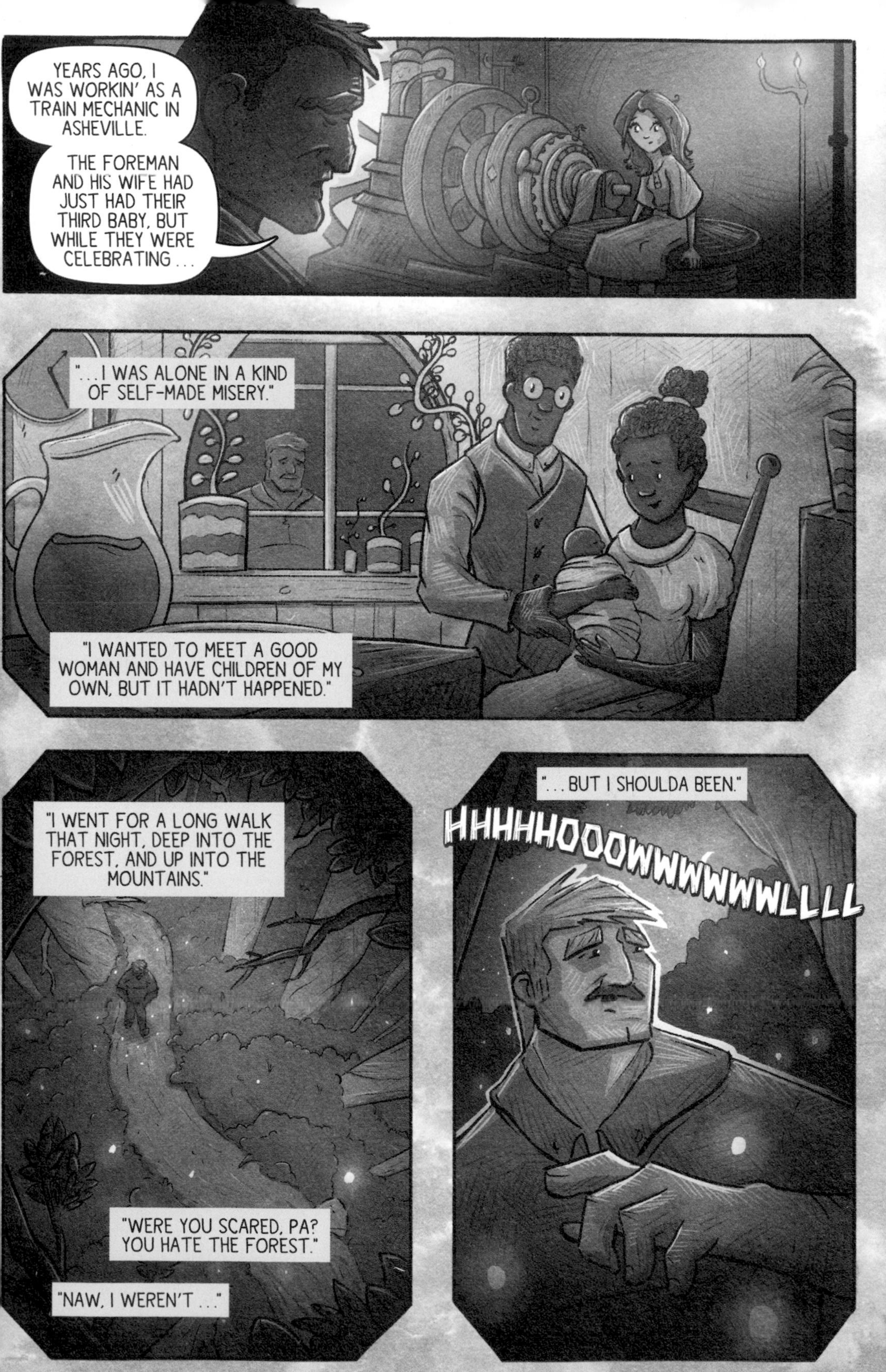

YEARS AGO, I WAS WORKIN' AS A TRAIN MECHANIC IN ASHEVILLE.
THE FOREMAN AND HIS WIFE HAD JUST HAD THEIR THIRD BABY, BUT WHILE THEY WERE CELEBRATING . . .
". . . I WAS ALONE IN A KIND OF SELF-MADE MISERY."
"I WANTED TO MEET A GOOD WOMAN AND HAVE CHILDREN OF MY OWN, BUT IT HADN'T HAPPENED."
"I WENT FOR A LONG WALK THAT NIGHT, DEEP INTO THE FOREST, AND UP INTO THE MOUNTAINS."
"WERE YOU SCARED, PA? YOU HATE THE FOREST."
"NAW, I WEREN'T . . ."
". . . BUT I SHOULDA BEEN."
HHHHHOOOWWWWWWLLLL

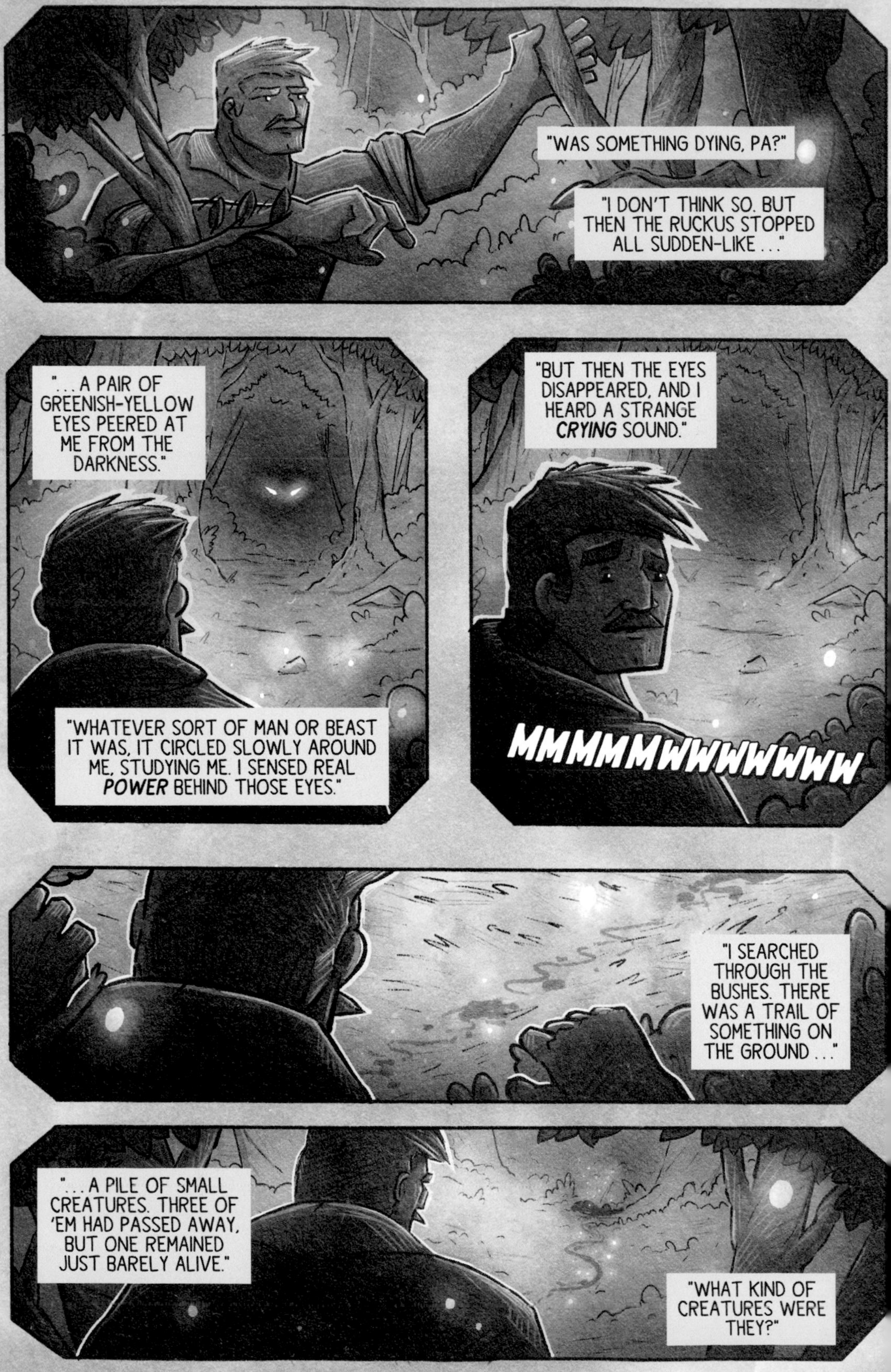
"WAS SOMETHING DYING, PA?"
"I DON'T THINK SO. BUT THEN THE RUCKUS STOPPED ALL SUDDEN-LIKE . . ."
". . . A PAIR OF GREENISH-YELLOW EYES PEERED AT ME FROM THE DARKNESS."
"WHATEVER SORT OF MAN OR BEAST IT WAS, IT CIRCLED SLOWLY AROUND ME, STUDYING ME. I SENSED REAL *POWER* BEHIND THOSE EYES."
"BUT THEN THE EYES DISAPPEARED, AND I HEARD A STRANGE *CRYING* SOUND."
MMMMMWWWWWWWW
"I SEARCHED THROUGH THE BUSHES. THERE WAS A TRAIL OF SOMETHING ON THE GROUND . . ."
". . . A PILE OF SMALL CREATURES. THREE OF 'EM HAD PASSED AWAY, BUT ONE REMAINED JUST BARELY ALIVE."
"WHAT KIND OF CREATURES WERE THEY?"

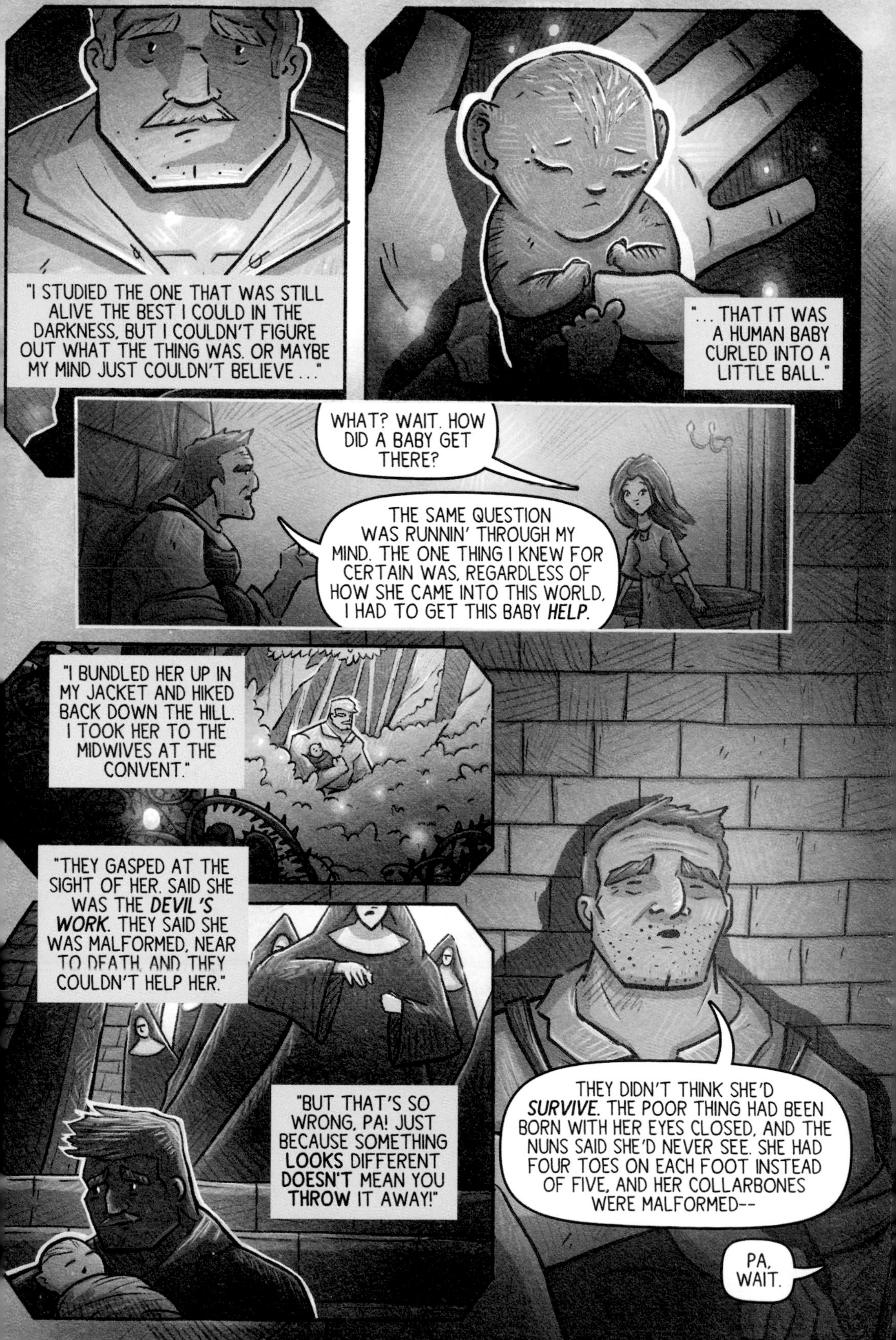
"I STUDIED THE ONE THAT WAS STILL ALIVE THE BEST I COULD IN THE DARKNESS, BUT I COULDN'T FIGURE OUT WHAT THE THING WAS. OR MAYBE MY MIND JUST COULDN'T BELIEVE . . ."
". . . THAT IT WAS A HUMAN BABY CURLED INTO A LITTLE BALL."
WHAT? WAIT. HOW DID A BABY GET THERE?
THE SAME QUESTION WAS RUNNIN' THROUGH MY MIND. THE ONE THING I KNEW FOR CERTAIN WAS, REGARDLESS OF HOW SHE CAME INTO THIS WORLD, I HAD TO GET THIS BABY ***HELP***.
"I BUNDLED HER UP IN MY JACKET AND HIKED BACK DOWN THE HILL. I TOOK HER TO THE MIDWIVES AT THE CONVENT."
"THEY GASPED AT THE SIGHT OF HER. SAID SHE WAS THE ***DEVIL'S WORK***. THEY SAID SHE WAS MALFORMED, NEAR TO DEATH, AND THEY COULDN'T HELP HER."
"BUT THAT'S SO WRONG, PA! JUST BECAUSE SOMETHING **LOOKS** DIFFERENT **DOESN'T** MEAN YOU **THROW** IT AWAY!"
THEY DIDN'T THINK SHE'D ***SURVIVE***. THE POOR THING HAD BEEN BORN WITH HER EYES CLOSED, AND THE NUNS SAID SHE'D NEVER SEE. SHE HAD FOUR TOES ON EACH FOOT INSTEAD OF FIVE, AND HER COLLARBONES WERE MALFORMED--
PA, WAIT.

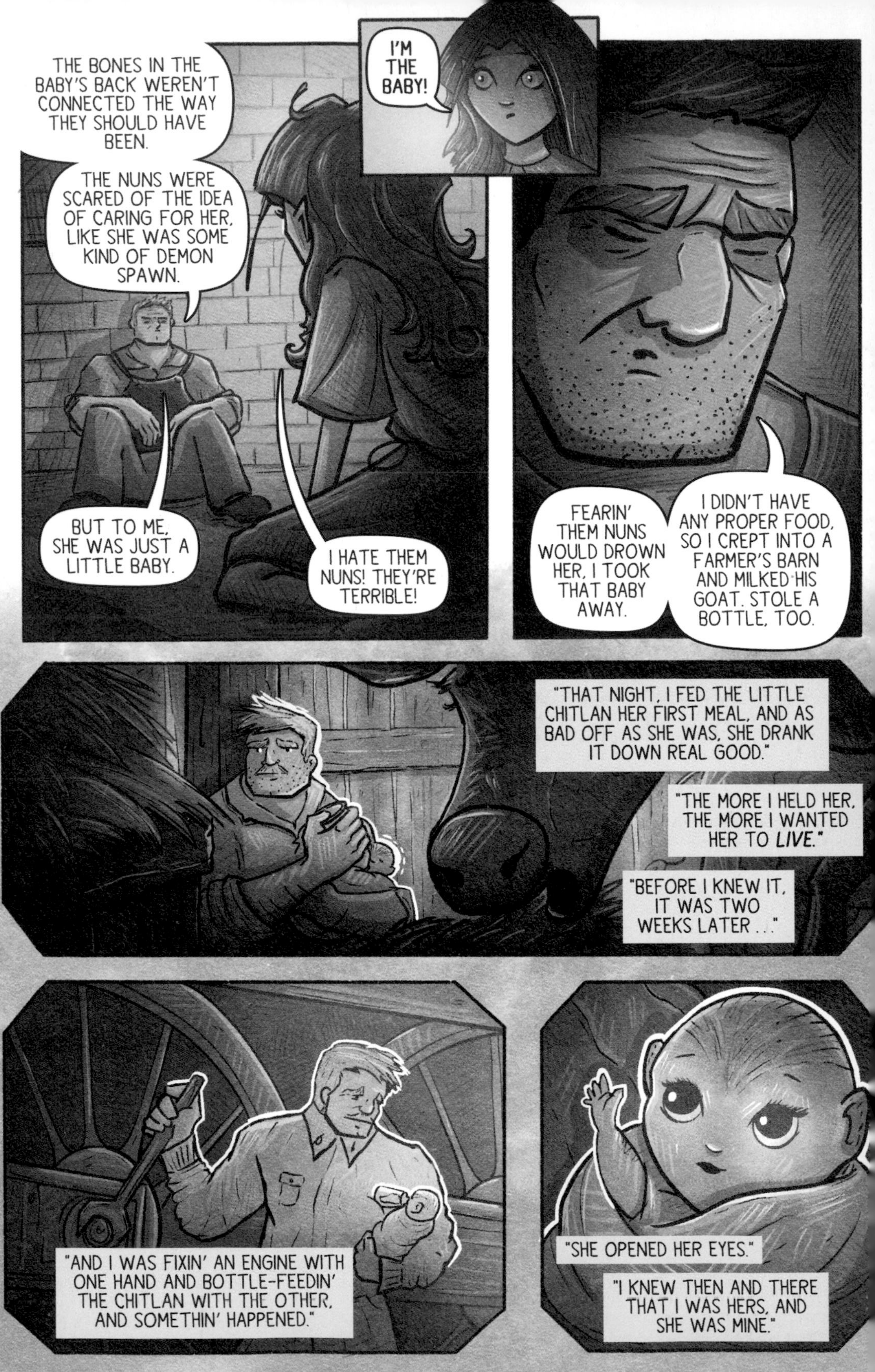
THE BONES IN THE BABY'S BACK WEREN'T CONNECTED THE WAY THEY SHOULD HAVE BEEN.
THE NUNS WERE SCARED OF THE IDEA OF CARING FOR HER, LIKE SHE WAS SOME KIND OF DEMON SPAWN.
BUT TO ME, SHE WAS JUST A LITTLE BABY.
I HATE THEM NUNS! THEY'RE TERRIBLE!
I'M THE BABY!
FEARIN' THEM NUNS WOULD DROWN HER, I TOOK THAT BABY AWAY.
I DIDN'T HAVE ANY PROPER FOOD, SO I CREPT INTO A FARMER'S BARN AND MILKED HIS GOAT. STOLE A BOTTLE, TOO.
"THAT NIGHT, I FED THE LITTLE CHITLAN HER FIRST MEAL, AND AS BAD OFF AS SHE WAS, SHE DRANK IT DOWN REAL GOOD."
"THE MORE I HELD HER, THE MORE I WANTED HER TO *LIVE*."
"BEFORE I KNEW IT, IT WAS TWO WEEKS LATER . . ."
"AND I WAS FIXIN' AN ENGINE WITH ONE HAND AND BOTTLE-FEEDIN' THE CHITLAN WITH THE OTHER, AND SOMETHIN' HAPPENED."
"SHE OPENED HER EYES."
"I KNEW THEN AND THERE THAT I WAS HERS, AND SHE WAS MINE."

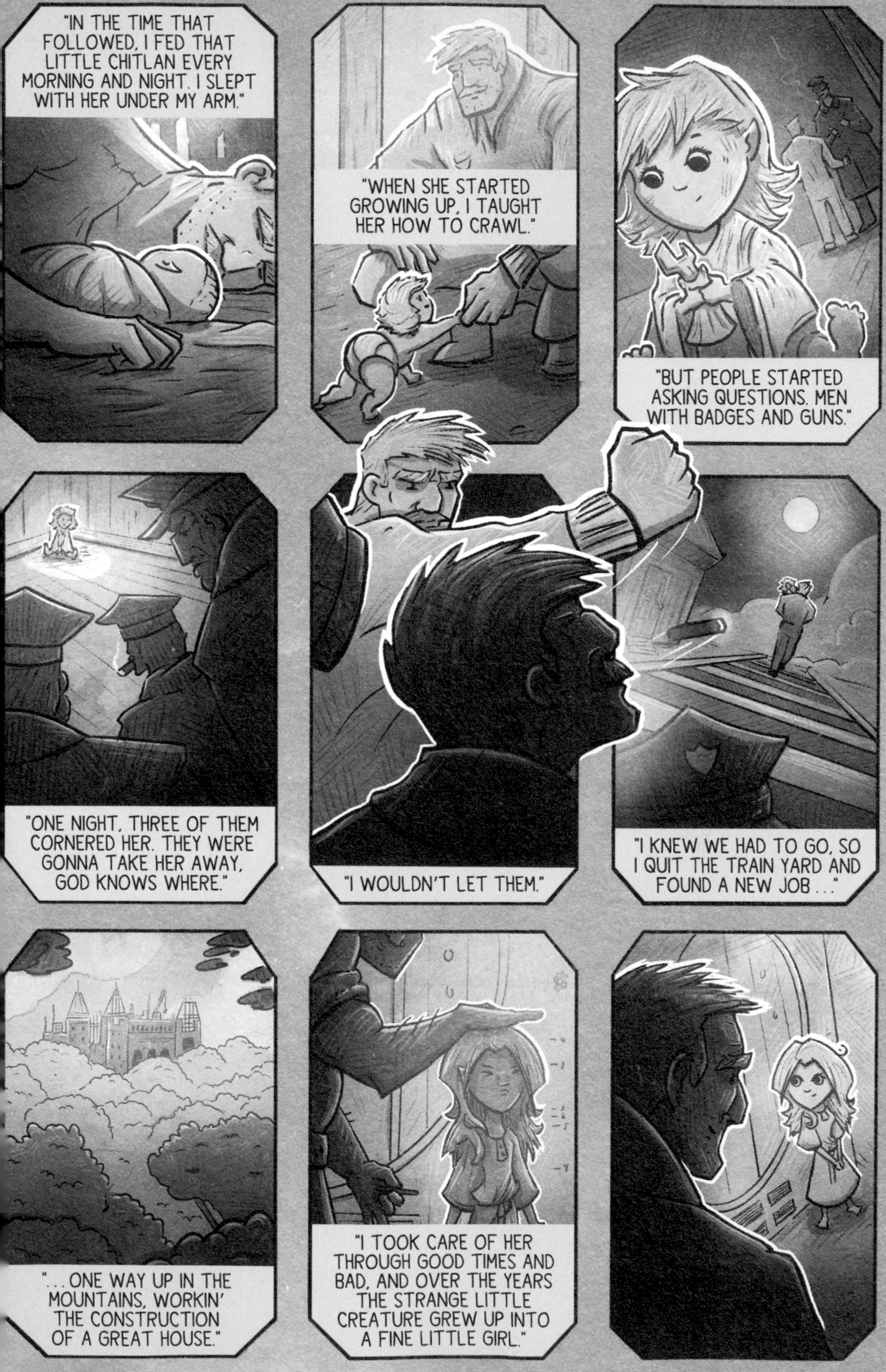
"IN THE TIME THAT FOLLOWED, I FED THAT LITTLE CHITLAN EVERY MORNING AND NIGHT. I SLEPT WITH HER UNDER MY ARM."
"WHEN SHE STARTED GROWING UP, I TAUGHT HER HOW TO CRAWL."
"BUT PEOPLE STARTED ASKING QUESTIONS. MEN WITH BADGES AND GUNS."
"ONE NIGHT, THREE OF THEM CORNERED HER. THEY WERE GONNA TAKE HER AWAY, GOD KNOWS WHERE."
"I WOULDN'T LET THEM."
"I KNEW WE HAD TO GO, SO I QUIT THE TRAIN YARD AND FOUND A NEW JOB . . ."
". . . ONE WAY UP IN THE MOUNTAINS, WORKIN' THE CONSTRUCTION OF A GREAT HOUSE."
"I TOOK CARE OF HER THROUGH GOOD TIMES AND BAD, AND OVER THE YEARS THE STRANGE LITTLE CREATURE GREW UP INTO A FINE LITTLE GIRL."

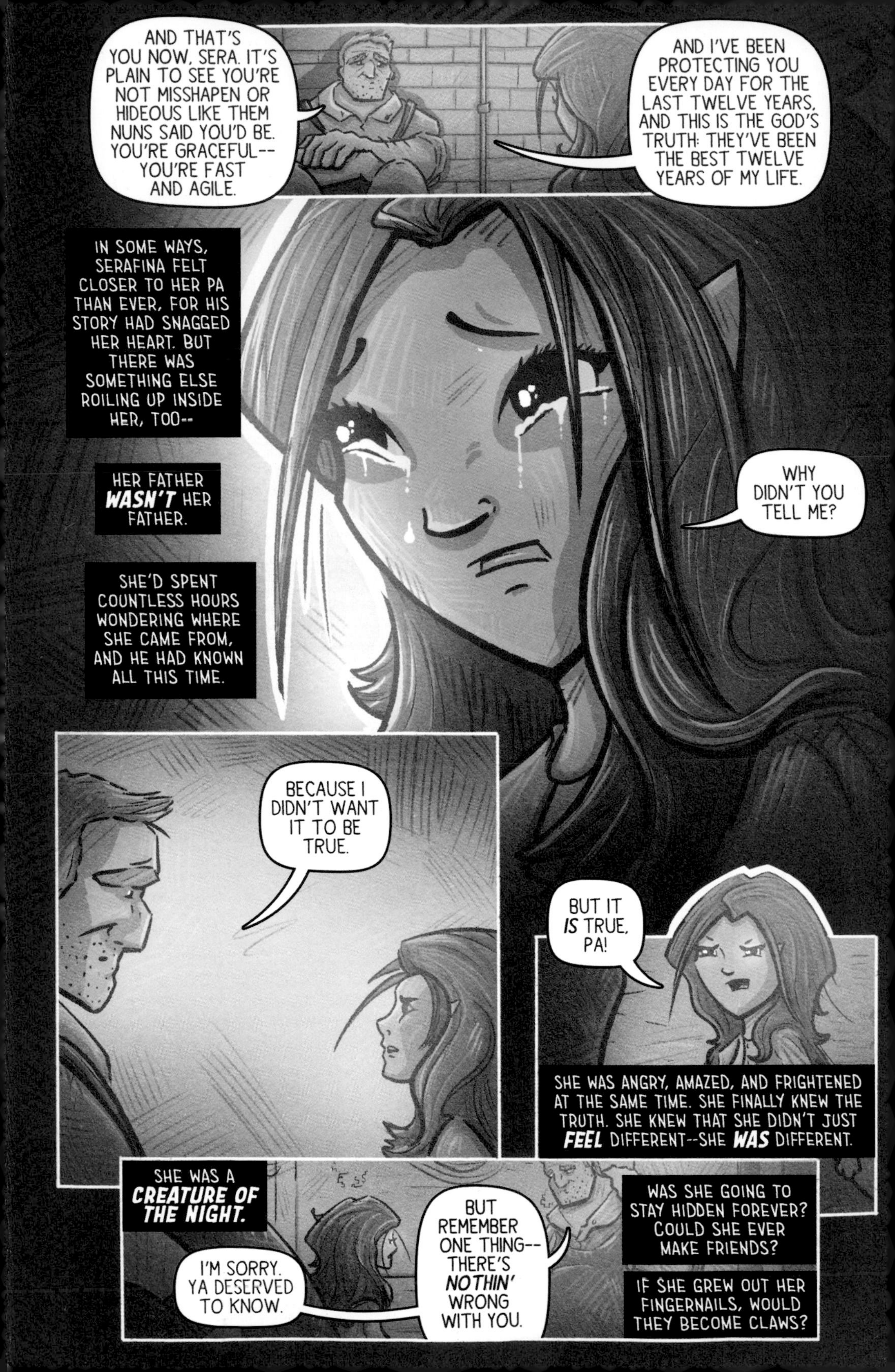
AND THAT'S YOU NOW, SERA. IT'S PLAIN TO SEE YOU'RE NOT MISSHAPEN OR HIDEOUS LIKE THEM NUNS SAID YOU'D BE. YOU'RE GRACEFUL-- YOU'RE FAST AND AGILE.
AND I'VE BEEN PROTECTING YOU EVERY DAY FOR THE LAST TWELVE YEARS, AND THIS IS THE GOD'S TRUTH: THEY'VE BEEN THE BEST TWELVE YEARS OF MY LIFE.
IN SOME WAYS, SERAFINA FELT CLOSER TO HER PA THAN EVER, FOR HIS STORY HAD SNAGGED HER HEART. BUT THERE WAS SOMETHING ELSE ROILING UP INSIDE HER, TOO--
HER FATHER ***WASN'T*** HER FATHER.
SHE'D SPENT COUNTLESS HOURS WONDERING WHERE SHE CAME FROM, AND HE HAD KNOWN ALL THIS TIME.
WHY DIDN'T YOU TELL ME?
BECAUSE I DIDN'T WANT IT TO BE TRUE.
BUT IT ***IS*** TRUE, PA!
SHE WAS ANGRY, AMAZED, AND FRIGHTENED AT THE SAME TIME. SHE FINALLY KNEW THE TRUTH. SHE KNEW THAT SHE DIDN'T JUST ***FEEL*** DIFFERENT--SHE ***WAS*** DIFFERENT.
SHE WAS A ***CREATURE OF THE NIGHT.***
I'M SORRY. YA DESERVED TO KNOW.
BUT REMEMBER ONE THING-- THERE'S ***NOTHIN'*** WRONG WITH YOU.
WAS SHE GOING TO STAY HIDDEN FOREVER? COULD SHE EVER MAKE FRIENDS?
IF SHE GREW OUT HER FINGERNAILS, WOULD THEY BECOME CLAWS?

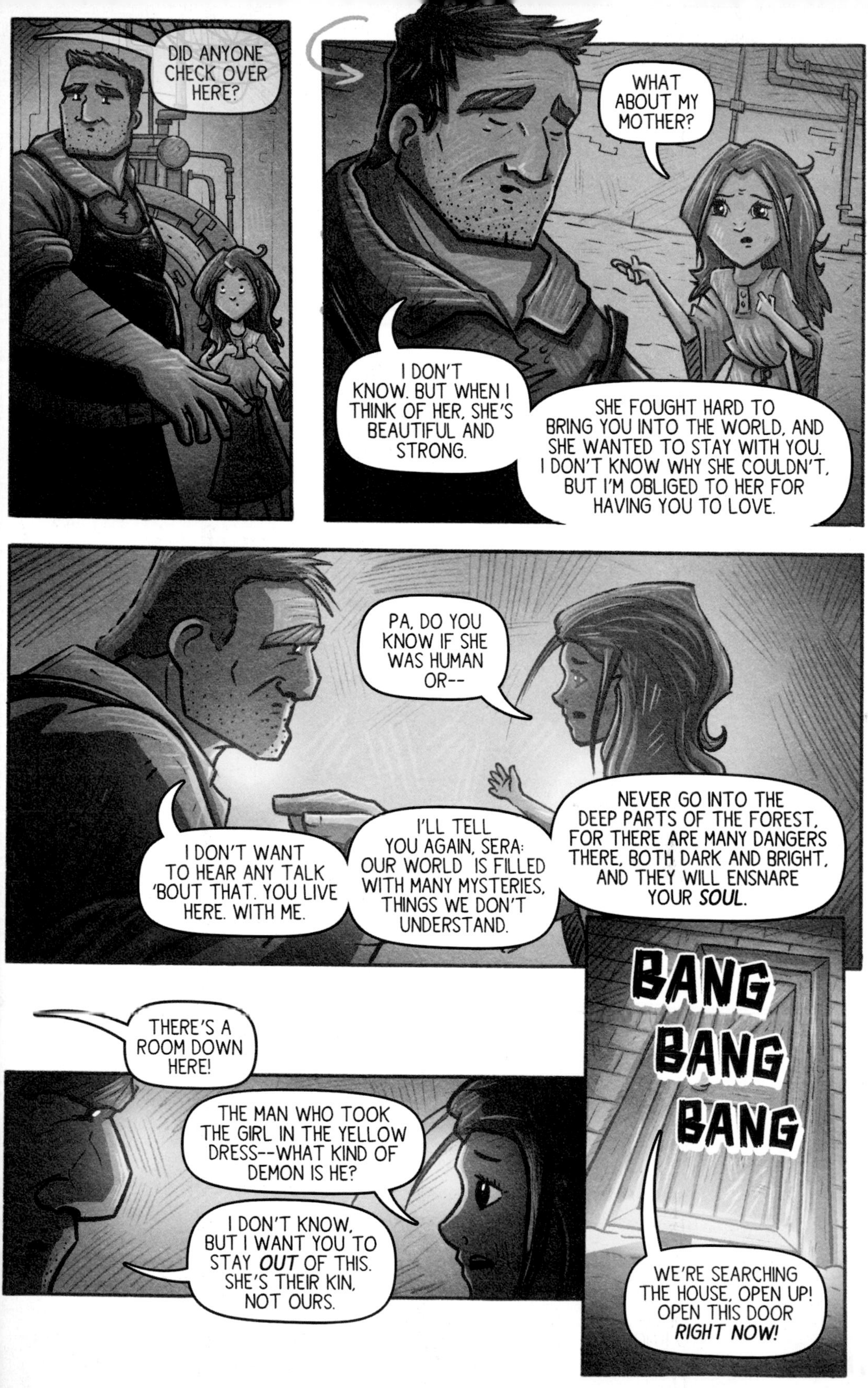
DID ANYONE CHECK OVER HERE?
WHAT ABOUT MY MOTHER?
I DON'T KNOW. BUT WHEN I THINK OF HER, SHE'S BEAUTIFUL AND STRONG.
SHE FOUGHT HARD TO BRING YOU INTO THE WORLD, AND SHE WANTED TO STAY WITH YOU. I DON'T KNOW WHY SHE COULDN'T, BUT I'M OBLIGED TO HER FOR HAVING YOU TO LOVE.
PA, DO YOU KNOW IF SHE WAS HUMAN OR--
I DON'T WANT TO HEAR ANY TALK 'BOUT THAT. YOU LIVE HERE. WITH ME.
I'LL TELL YOU AGAIN, SERA: OUR WORLD IS FILLED WITH MANY MYSTERIES, THINGS WE DON'T UNDERSTAND.
NEVER GO INTO THE DEEP PARTS OF THE FOREST, FOR THERE ARE MANY DANGERS THERE, BOTH DARK AND BRIGHT, AND THEY WILL ENSNARE YOUR *SOUL*.
THERE'S A ROOM DOWN HERE!
THE MAN WHO TOOK THE GIRL IN THE YELLOW DRESS--WHAT KIND OF DEMON IS HE?
I DON'T KNOW, BUT I WANT YOU TO STAY *OUT* OF THIS. SHE'S THEIR KIN, NOT OURS.
BANG
BANG
BANG
WE'RE SEARCHING THE HOUSE, OPEN UP! OPEN THIS DOOR *RIGHT NOW!*

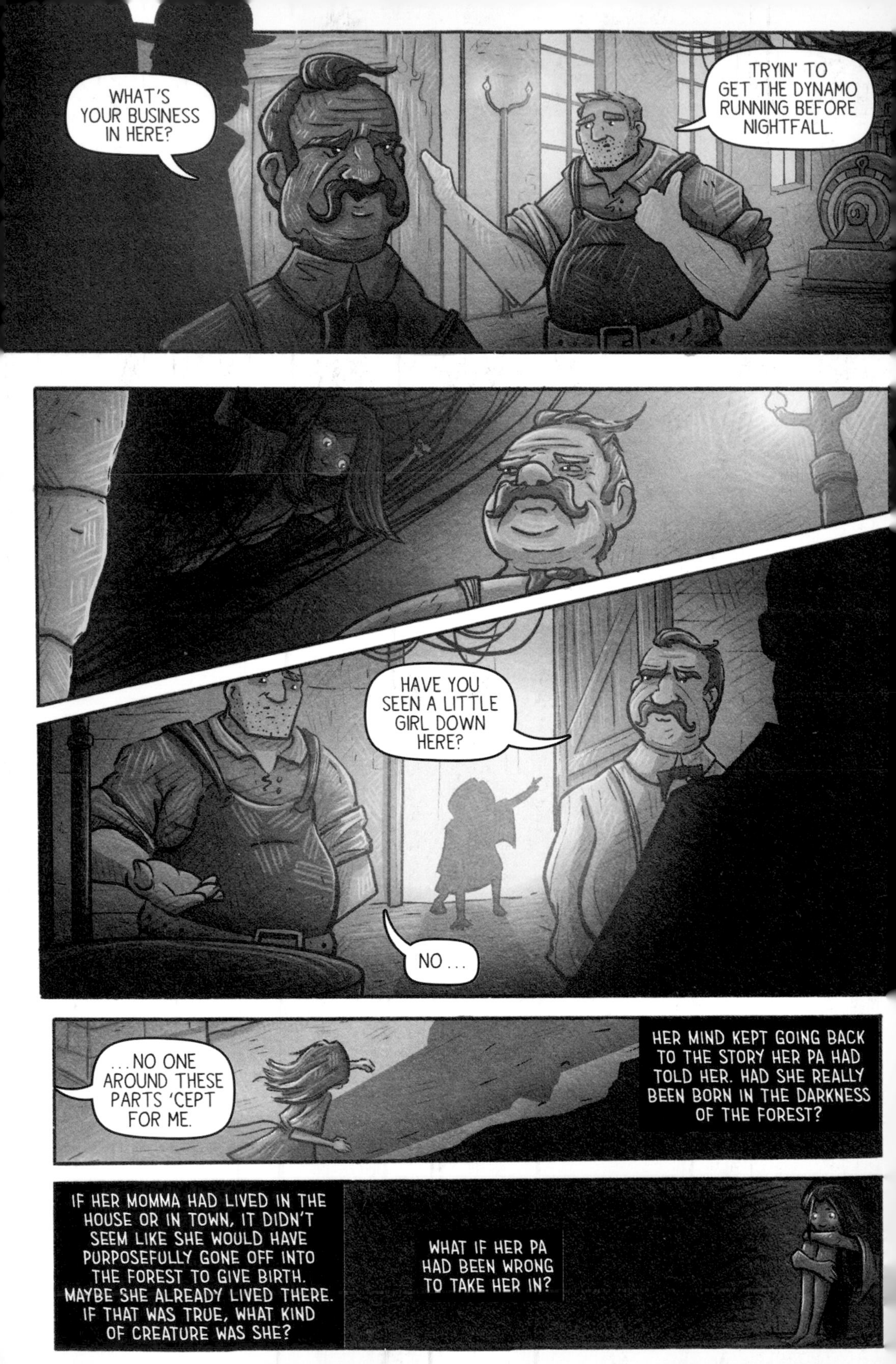
WHAT'S YOUR BUSINESS IN HERE?
TRYIN' TO GET THE DYNAMO RUNNING BEFORE NIGHTFALL.
HAVE YOU SEEN A LITTLE GIRL DOWN HERE?
NO . . .
. . . NO ONE AROUND THESE PARTS 'CEPT FOR ME.
HER MIND KEPT GOING BACK TO THE STORY HER PA HAD TOLD HER. HAD SHE REALLY BEEN BORN IN THE DARKNESS OF THE FOREST?
IF HER MOMMA HAD LIVED IN THE HOUSE OR IN TOWN, IT DIDN'T SEEM LIKE SHE WOULD HAVE PURPOSEFULLY GONE OFF INTO THE FOREST TO GIVE BIRTH. MAYBE SHE ALREADY LIVED THERE. IF THAT WAS TRUE, WHAT KIND OF CREATURE WAS SHE?
WHAT IF HER PA HAD BEEN WRONG TO TAKE HER IN?

BRING THE LIGHT OVER HERE!

YOU'RE TOO LOUD, SERAFINA THOUGHT AS THE SEARCH PARTY PASSED HER BY. *YOU'RE NEVER GOING TO FIND ANYONE THAT WAY. YOU'VE GOT TO CATCH THE RAT.*

AS THE CORRIDOR CLEARED, SERAFINA CONCOCTED A PLAN: IF SHE WANTED THE YOUNG MASTER, BRAEDEN, TO BELIEVE HER STORY, SHE NEEDED EVIDENCE.

THERE WAS NO SIGN OF CLARA BRAHMS OR THE MAN IN THE BLACK CLOAK. BUT THERE WERE RED DRIPS ON THE WALL AND SHARDS OF GLASS FROM A LANTERN.

LAST NIGHT HAD **NOT** BEEN A DREAM.

ON HER WAY BACK, SHE SPOTTED SOMETHING THAT GAVE OFF A PUTRID SMELL, BUT IT WASN'T A RAT.

IT WAS A **GLOVE.**

IT WAS MADE OF FINE BLACK SATIN, BUT INSIDE, IT WAS FAR MORE DISGUSTING THAN ANY RAT CARCASS SHE'D EVER FOUND.

THERE WERE PATCHES OF **SKIN** THAT HAD BLACK SPOTS AND GRAY HAIRS. IT WAS AS IF THE OWNER OF THE GLOVE HADN'T JUST BEEN OLD BUT AGING **RAPIDLY.**

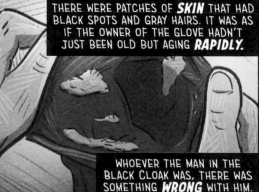

WHOEVER THE MAN IN THE BLACK CLOAK WAS, THERE WAS SOMETHING **WRONG** WITH HIM.

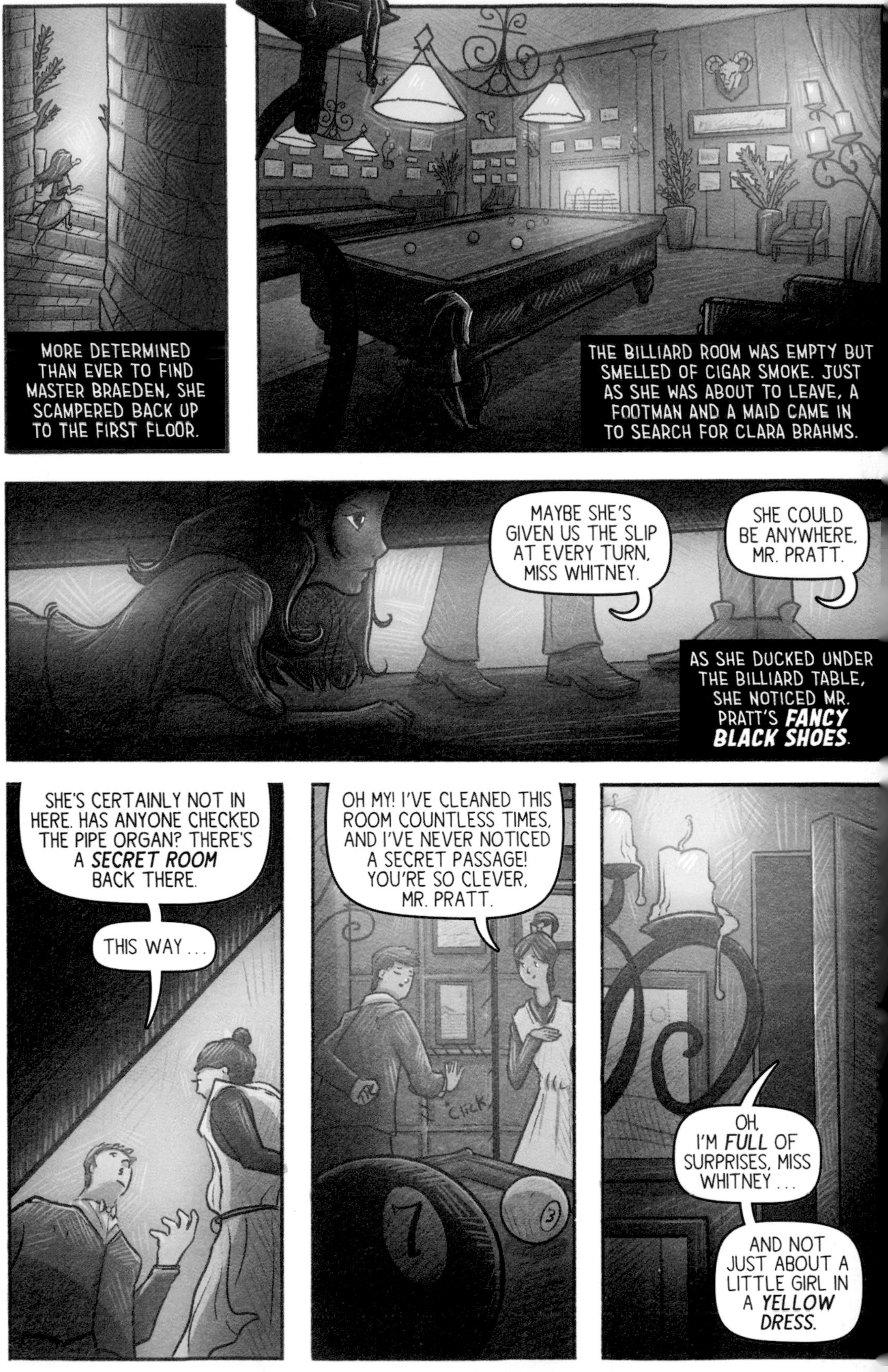
MORE DETERMINED THAN EVER TO FIND MASTER BRAEDEN, SHE SCAMPERED BACK UP TO THE FIRST FLOOR.
THE BILLIARD ROOM WAS EMPTY BUT SMELLED OF CIGAR SMOKE. JUST AS SHE WAS ABOUT TO LEAVE, A FOOTMAN AND A MAID CAME IN TO SEARCH FOR CLARA BRAHMS.
MAYBE SHE'S GIVEN US THE SLIP AT EVERY TURN, MISS WHITNEY.
SHE COULD BE ANYWHERE, MR. PRATT.
AS SHE DUCKED UNDER THE BILLIARD TABLE, SHE NOTICED MR. PRATT'S ***FANCY BLACK SHOES***.
SHE'S CERTAINLY NOT IN HERE. HAS ANYONE CHECKED THE PIPE ORGAN? THERE'S A ***SECRET ROOM*** BACK THERE.
THIS WAY . . .
OH MY! I'VE CLEANED THIS ROOM COUNTLESS TIMES, AND I'VE NEVER NOTICED A SECRET PASSAGE! YOU'RE SO CLEVER, MR. PRATT.
CLICK
OH, I'M ***FULL*** OF SURPRISES, MISS WHITNEY . . .
AND NOT JUST ABOUT A LITTLE GIRL IN A ***YELLOW DRESS***.

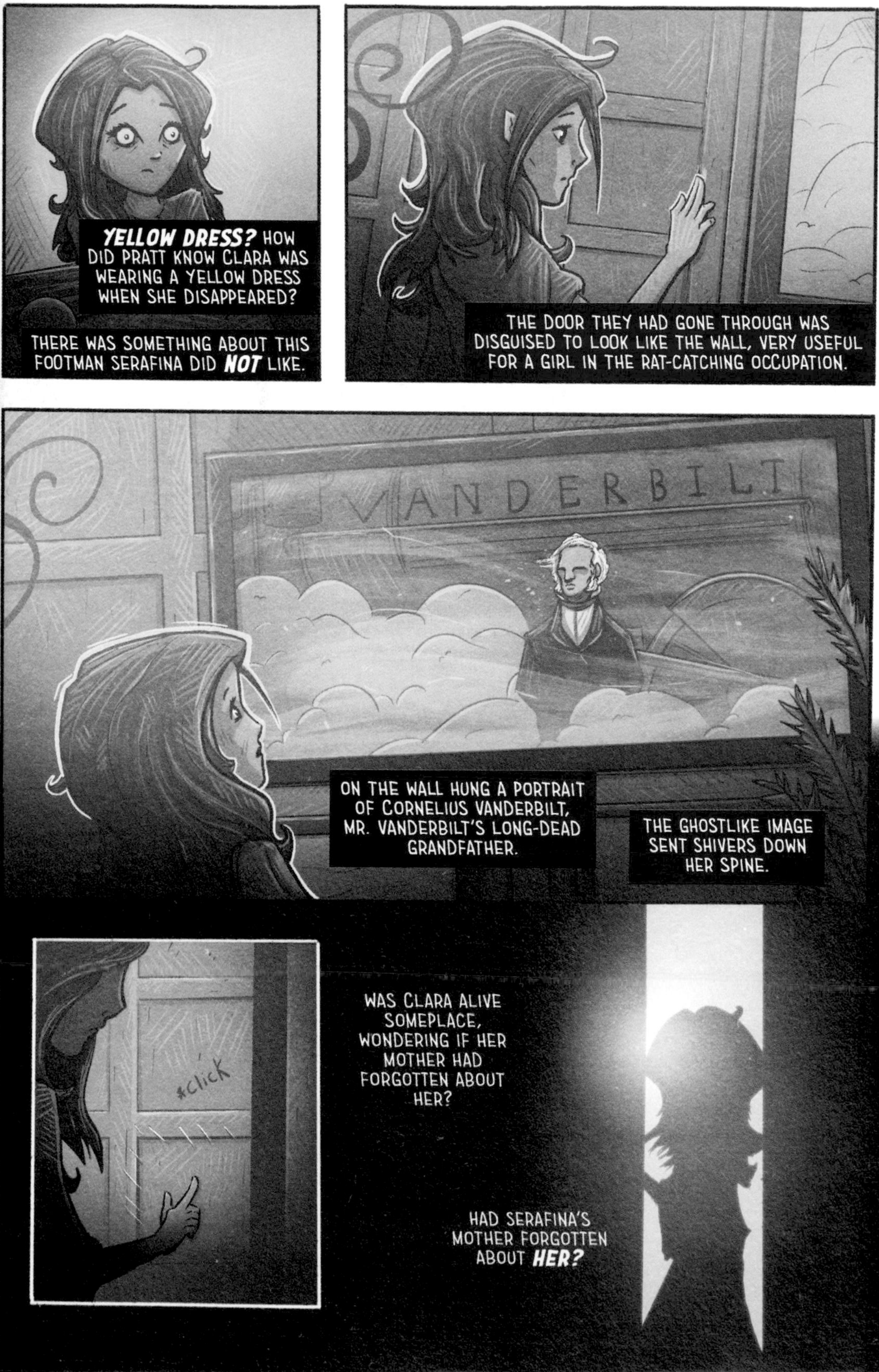
YELLOW DRESS? HOW DID PRATT KNOW CLARA WAS WEARING A YELLOW DRESS WHEN SHE DISAPPEARED?
THERE WAS SOMETHING ABOUT THIS FOOTMAN SERAFINA DID NOT LIKE.
THE DOOR THEY HAD GONE THROUGH WAS DISGUISED TO LOOK LIKE THE WALL, VERY USEFUL FOR A GIRL IN THE RAT-CATCHING OCCUPATION.
VANDERBILT
ON THE WALL HUNG A PORTRAIT OF CORNELIUS VANDERBILT, MR. VANDERBILT'S LONG-DEAD GRANDFATHER.
THE GHOSTLIKE IMAGE SENT SHIVERS DOWN HER SPINE.
*click
WAS CLARA ALIVE SOMEPLACE, WONDERING IF HER MOTHER HAD FORGOTTEN ABOUT HER?
HAD SERAFINA'S MOTHER FORGOTTEN ABOUT HER?

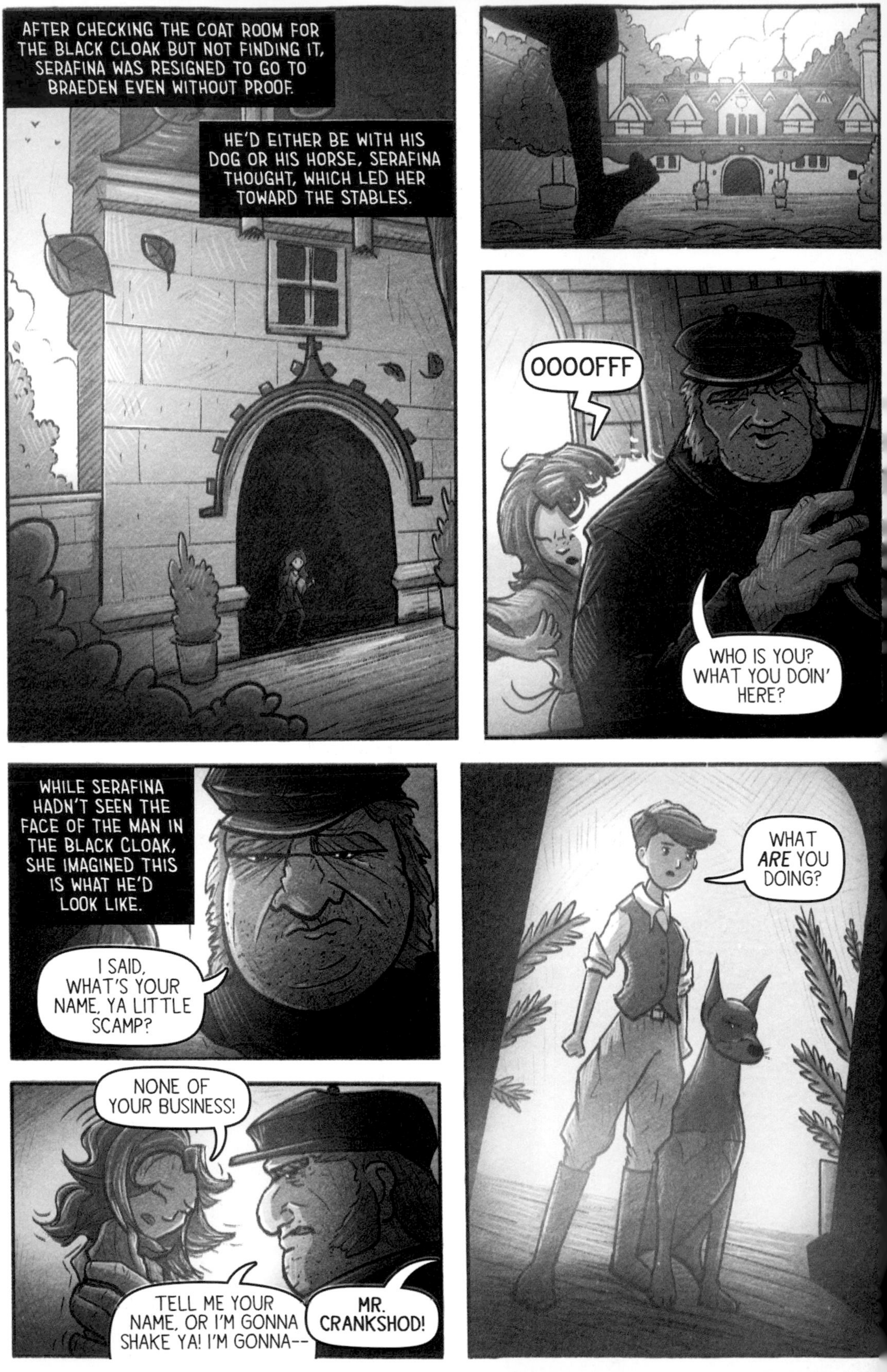
AFTER CHECKING THE COAT ROOM FOR THE BLACK CLOAK BUT NOT FINDING IT, SERAFINA WAS RESIGNED TO GO TO BRAEDEN EVEN WITHOUT PROOF.
HE'D EITHER BE WITH HIS DOG OR HIS HORSE, SERAFINA THOUGHT, WHICH LED HER TOWARD THE STABLES.
OOOOFFF
WHO IS YOU? WHAT YOU DOIN' HERE?
WHILE SERAFINA HADN'T SEEN THE FACE OF THE MAN IN THE BLACK CLOAK, SHE IMAGINED THIS IS WHAT HE'D LOOK LIKE.
I SAID, WHAT'S YOUR NAME, YA LITTLE SCAMP?
NONE OF YOUR BUSINESS!
TELL ME YOUR NAME, OR I'M GONNA SHAKE YA! I'M GONNA--
MR. CRANKSHOD!
WHAT *ARE* YOU DOING?

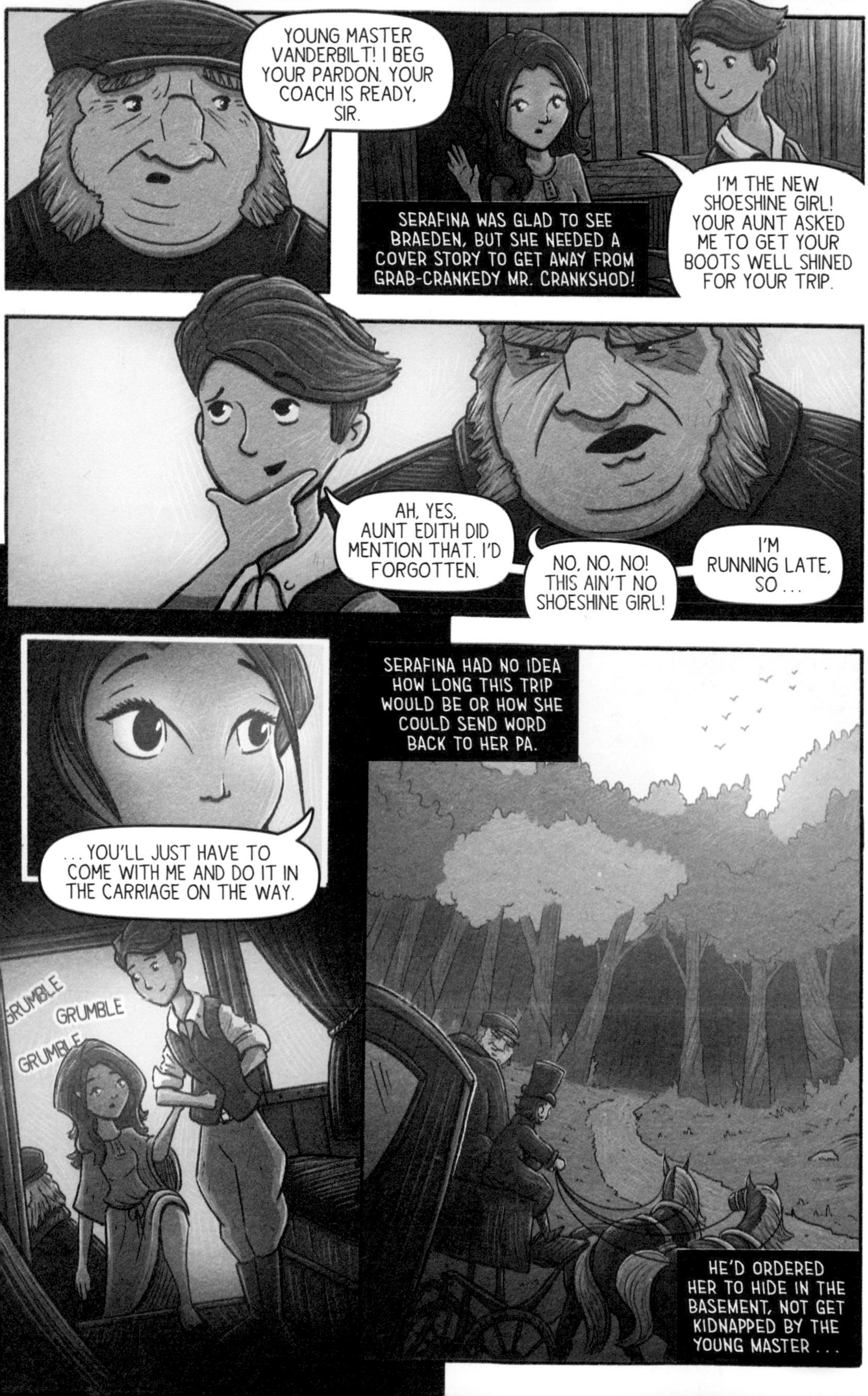
YOUNG MASTER VANDERBILT! I BEG YOUR PARDON. YOUR COACH IS READY, SIR.
SERAFINA WAS GLAD TO SEE BRAEDEN, BUT SHE NEEDED A COVER STORY TO GET AWAY FROM GRAB-CRANKEDY MR. CRANKSHOD!
I'M THE NEW SHOESHINE GIRL! YOUR AUNT ASKED ME TO GET YOUR BOOTS WELL SHINED FOR YOUR TRIP.
AH, YES, AUNT EDITH DID MENTION THAT. I'D FORGOTTEN.
NO, NO, NO! THIS AIN'T NO SHOESHINE GIRL!
I'M RUNNING LATE, SO . . .
. . . YOU'LL JUST HAVE TO COME WITH ME AND DO IT IN THE CARRIAGE ON THE WAY.
GRUMBLE
GRUMBLE
GRUMBLE
SERAFINA HAD NO IDEA HOW LONG THIS TRIP WOULD BE OR HOW SHE COULD SEND WORD BACK TO HER PA.
HE'D ORDERED HER TO HIDE IN THE BASEMENT, NOT GET KIDNAPPED BY THE YOUNG MASTER . . .

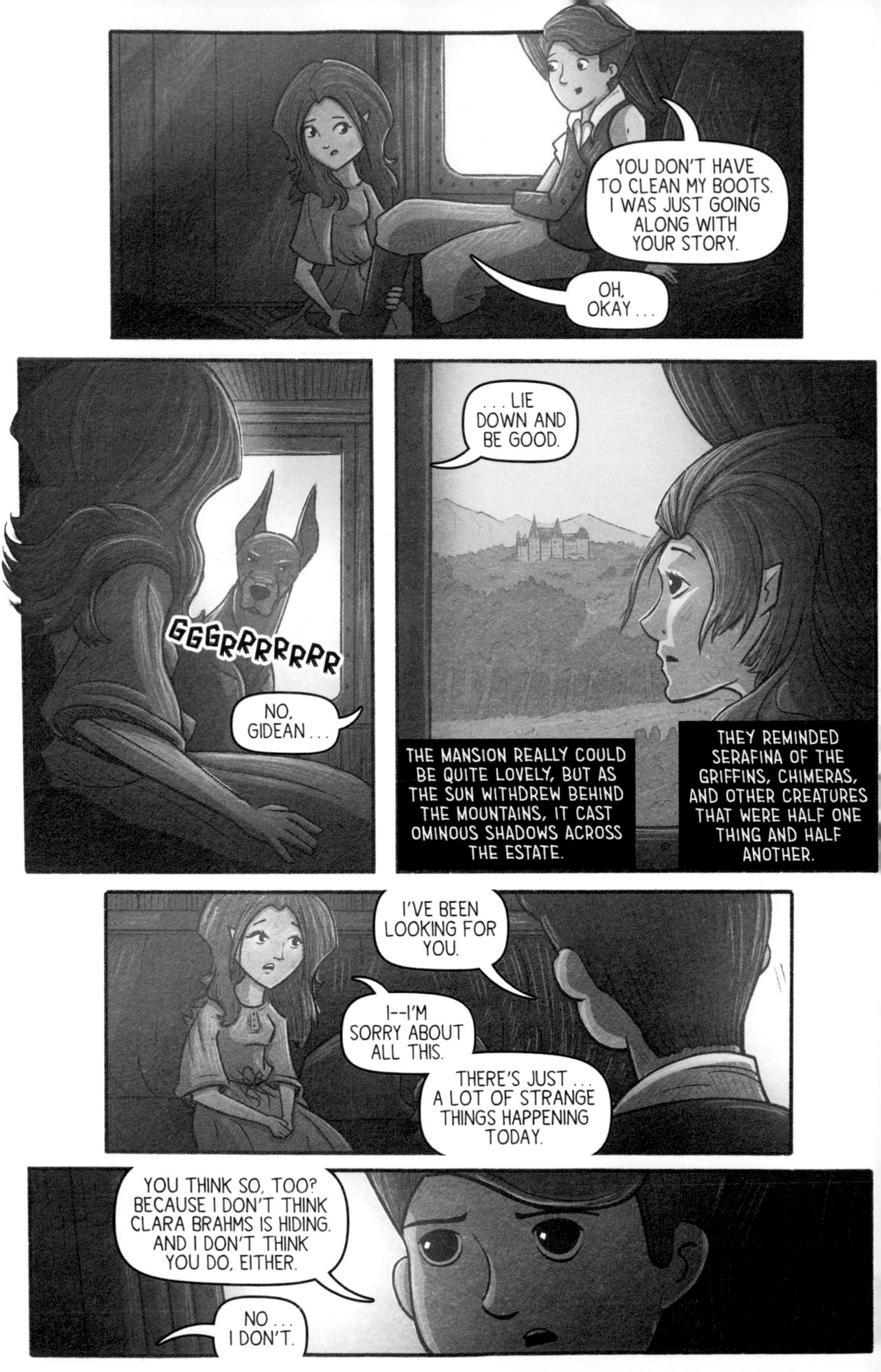
YOU DON'T HAVE TO CLEAN MY BOOTS. I WAS JUST GOING ALONG WITH YOUR STORY.
OH, OKAY . . .
GGGRRRRRRR
NO, GIDEAN . . .
. . . LIE DOWN AND BE GOOD.
THE MANSION REALLY COULD BE QUITE LOVELY, BUT AS THE SUN WITHDREW BEHIND THE MOUNTAINS, IT CAST OMINOUS SHADOWS ACROSS THE ESTATE.
THEY REMINDED SERAFINA OF THE GRIFFINS, CHIMERAS, AND OTHER CREATURES THAT WERE HALF ONE THING AND HALF ANOTHER.
I'VE BEEN LOOKING FOR YOU.
I--I'M SORRY ABOUT ALL THIS.
THERE'S JUST . . . A LOT OF STRANGE THINGS HAPPENING TODAY.
YOU THINK SO, TOO? BECAUSE I DON'T THINK CLARA BRAHMS IS HIDING. AND I DON'T THINK YOU DO, EITHER.
NO . . . I DON'T.

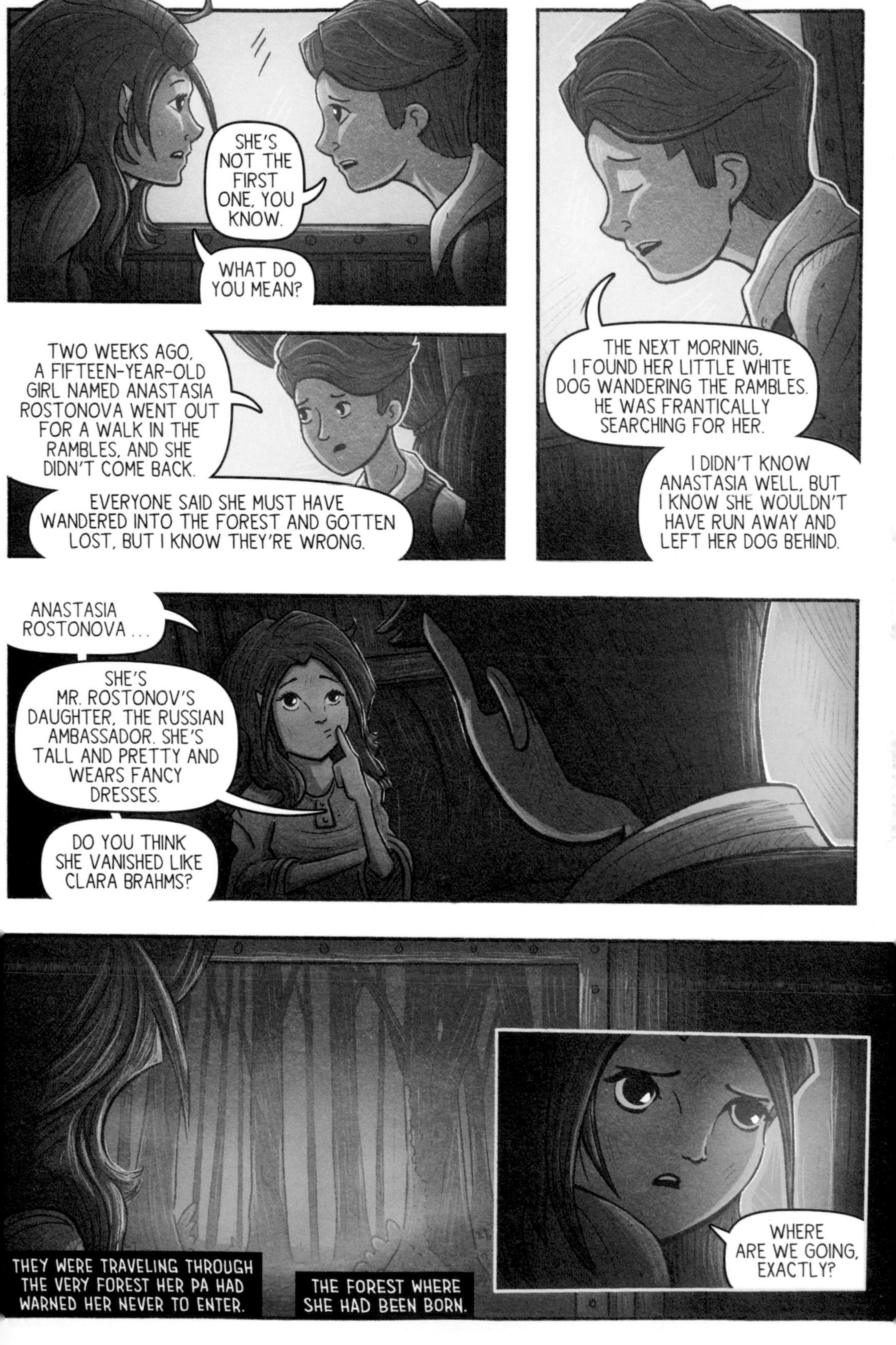
SHE'S NOT THE FIRST ONE, YOU KNOW.
WHAT DO YOU MEAN?
TWO WEEKS AGO, A FIFTEEN-YEAR-OLD GIRL NAMED ANASTASIA ROSTONOVA WENT OUT FOR A WALK IN THE RAMBLES, AND SHE DIDN'T COME BACK.
EVERYONE SAID SHE MUST HAVE WANDERED INTO THE FOREST AND GOTTEN LOST, BUT I KNOW THEY'RE WRONG.
THE NEXT MORNING, I FOUND HER LITTLE WHITE DOG WANDERING THE RAMBLES. HE WAS FRANTICALLY SEARCHING FOR HER.
I DIDN'T KNOW ANASTASIA WELL, BUT I KNOW SHE WOULDN'T HAVE RUN AWAY AND LEFT HER DOG BEHIND.
ANASTASIA ROSTONOVA . . .
SHE'S MR. ROSTONOV'S DAUGHTER, THE RUSSIAN AMBASSADOR. SHE'S TALL AND PRETTY AND WEARS FANCY DRESSES.
DO YOU THINK SHE VANISHED LIKE CLARA BRAHMS?
THEY WERE TRAVELING THROUGH THE VERY FOREST HER PA HAD WARNED HER NEVER TO ENTER.
THE FOREST WHERE SHE HAD BEEN BORN.
WHERE ARE WE GOING, EXACTLY?

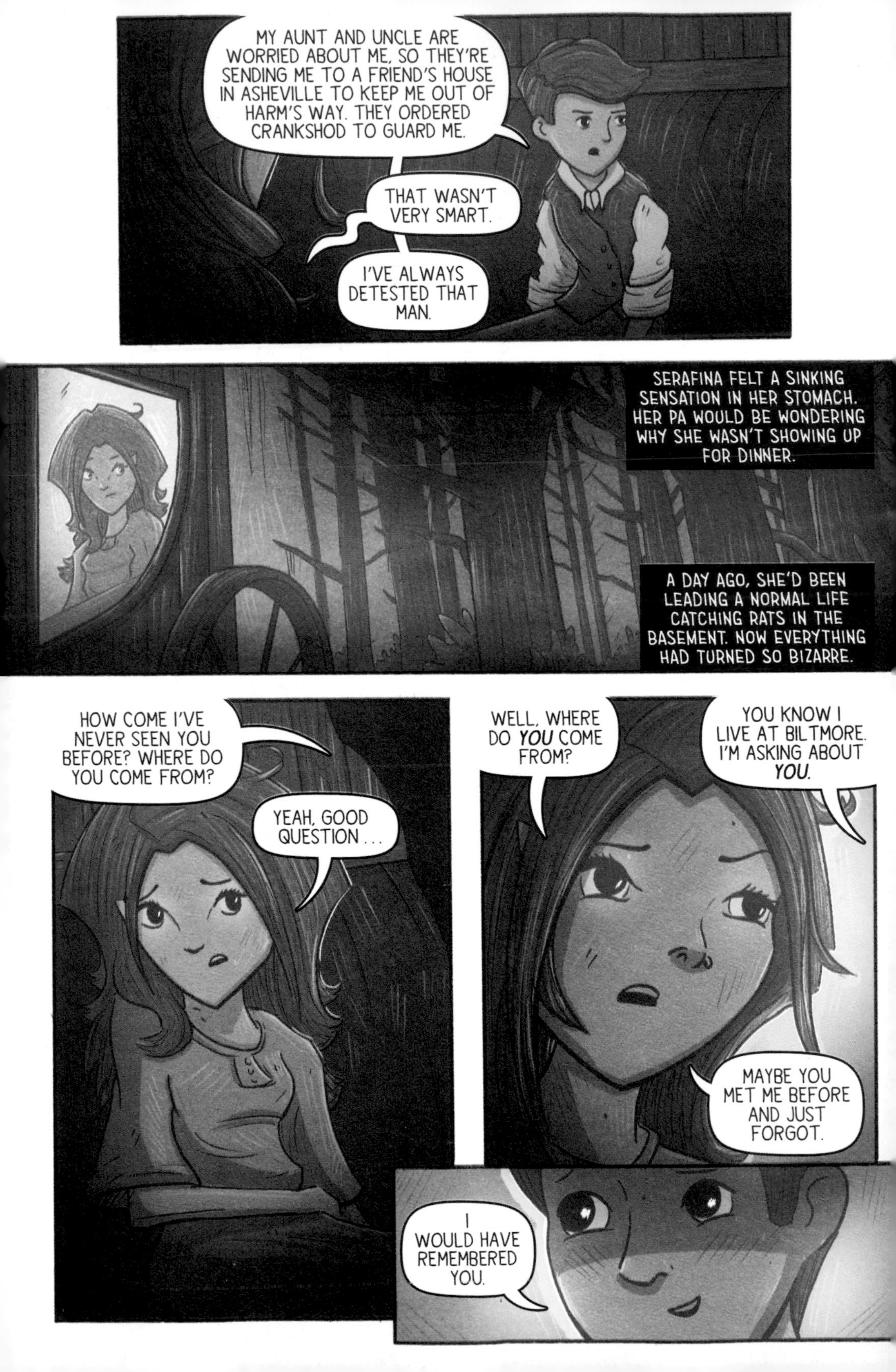
MY AUNT AND UNCLE ARE WORRIED ABOUT ME, SO THEY'RE SENDING ME TO A FRIEND'S HOUSE IN ASHEVILLE TO KEEP ME OUT OF HARM'S WAY. THEY ORDERED CRANKSHOD TO GUARD ME.
THAT WASN'T VERY SMART.
I'VE ALWAYS DETESTED THAT MAN.
SERAFINA FELT A SINKING SENSATION IN HER STOMACH. HER PA WOULD BE WONDERING WHY SHE WASN'T SHOWING UP FOR DINNER.
A DAY AGO, SHE'D BEEN LEADING A NORMAL LIFE CATCHING RATS IN THE BASEMENT. NOW EVERYTHING HAD TURNED SO BIZARRE.
HOW COME I'VE NEVER SEEN YOU BEFORE? WHERE DO YOU COME FROM?
YEAH, GOOD QUESTION . . .
WELL, WHERE DO *YOU* COME FROM?
YOU KNOW I LIVE AT BILTMORE. I'M ASKING ABOUT *YOU.*
MAYBE YOU MET ME BEFORE AND JUST FORGOT.
I WOULD HAVE REMEMBERED YOU.

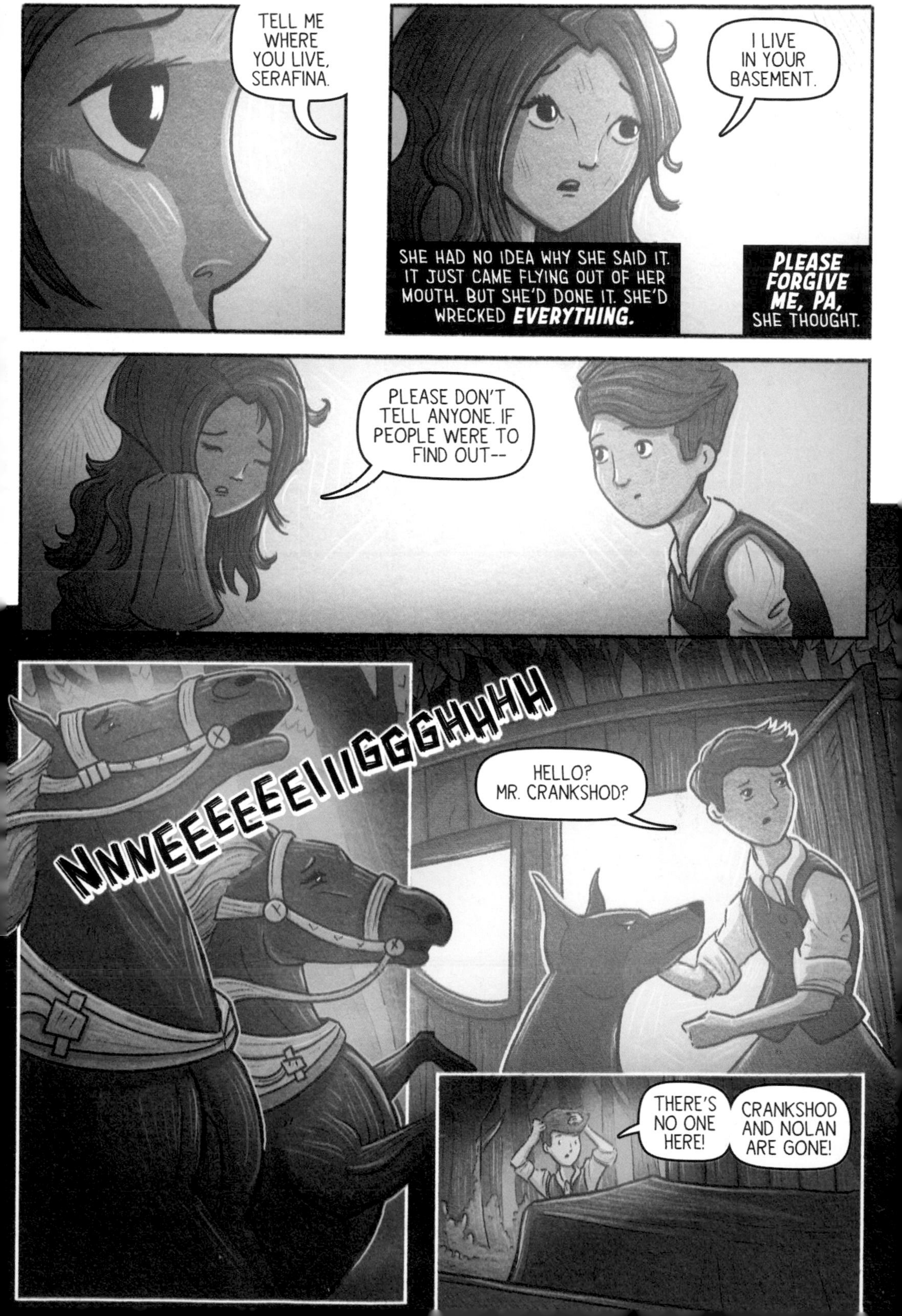
TELL ME WHERE YOU LIVE, SERAFINA.
I LIVE IN YOUR BASEMENT.
SHE HAD NO IDEA WHY SHE SAID IT. IT JUST CAME FLYING OUT OF HER MOUTH. BUT SHE'D DONE IT. SHE'D WRECKED EVERYTHING.
PLEASE FORGIVE ME, PA, SHE THOUGHT.
PLEASE DON'T TELL ANYONE. IF PEOPLE WERE TO FIND OUT--
NNNEEEEEEEIIIGGGGHHHH
HELLO? MR. CRANKSHOD?
THERE'S NO ONE HERE!
CRANKSHOD AND NOLAN ARE GONE!

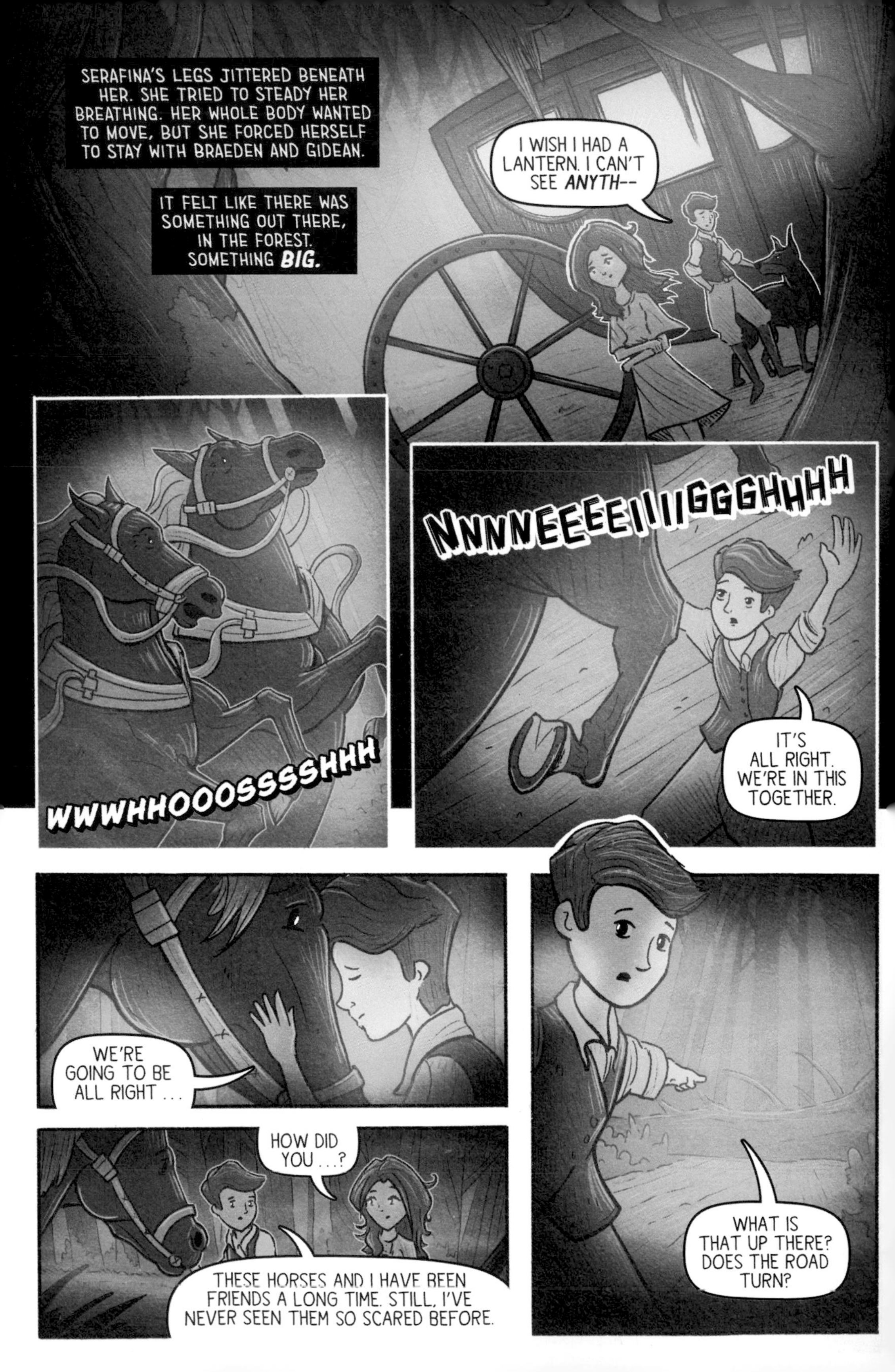
SERAFINA'S LEGS JITTERED BENEATH HER. SHE TRIED TO STEADY HER BREATHING. HER WHOLE BODY WANTED TO MOVE, BUT SHE FORCED HERSELF TO STAY WITH BRAEDEN AND GIDEAN.
IT FELT LIKE THERE WAS SOMETHING OUT THERE, IN THE FOREST. SOMETHING **BIG.**
I WISH I HAD A LANTERN. I CAN'T SEE **ANYTH--**
WWWHHOOOSSSSHHH
NNNNEEEEIIIIGGGHHHH
IT'S ALL RIGHT. WE'RE IN THIS TOGETHER.
WE'RE GOING TO BE ALL RIGHT . . .
HOW DID YOU . . .?
THESE HORSES AND I HAVE BEEN FRIENDS A LONG TIME. STILL, I'VE NEVER SEEN THEM SO SCARED BEFORE.
WHAT IS THAT UP THERE? DOES THE ROAD TURN?

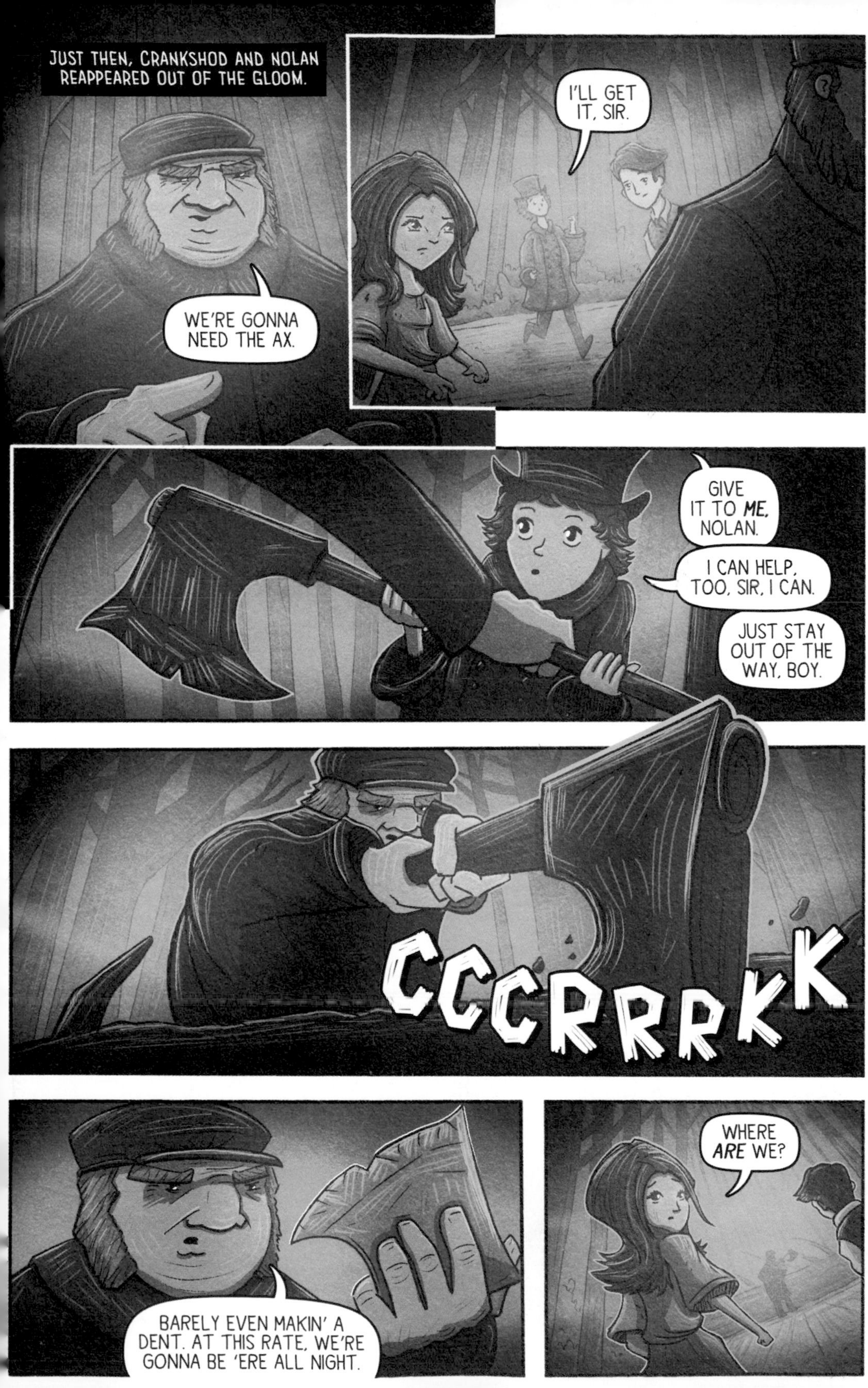
JUST THEN, CRANKSHOD AND NOLAN REAPPEARED OUT OF THE GLOOM.
WE'RE GONNA NEED THE AX.
I'LL GET IT, SIR.
GIVE IT TO *ME,* NOLAN.
I CAN HELP, TOO, SIR, I CAN.
JUST STAY OUT OF THE WAY, BOY.
CCCRRRKK
BARELY EVEN MAKIN' A DENT. AT THIS RATE, WE'RE GONNA BE 'ERE ALL NIGHT.
WHERE *ARE* WE?

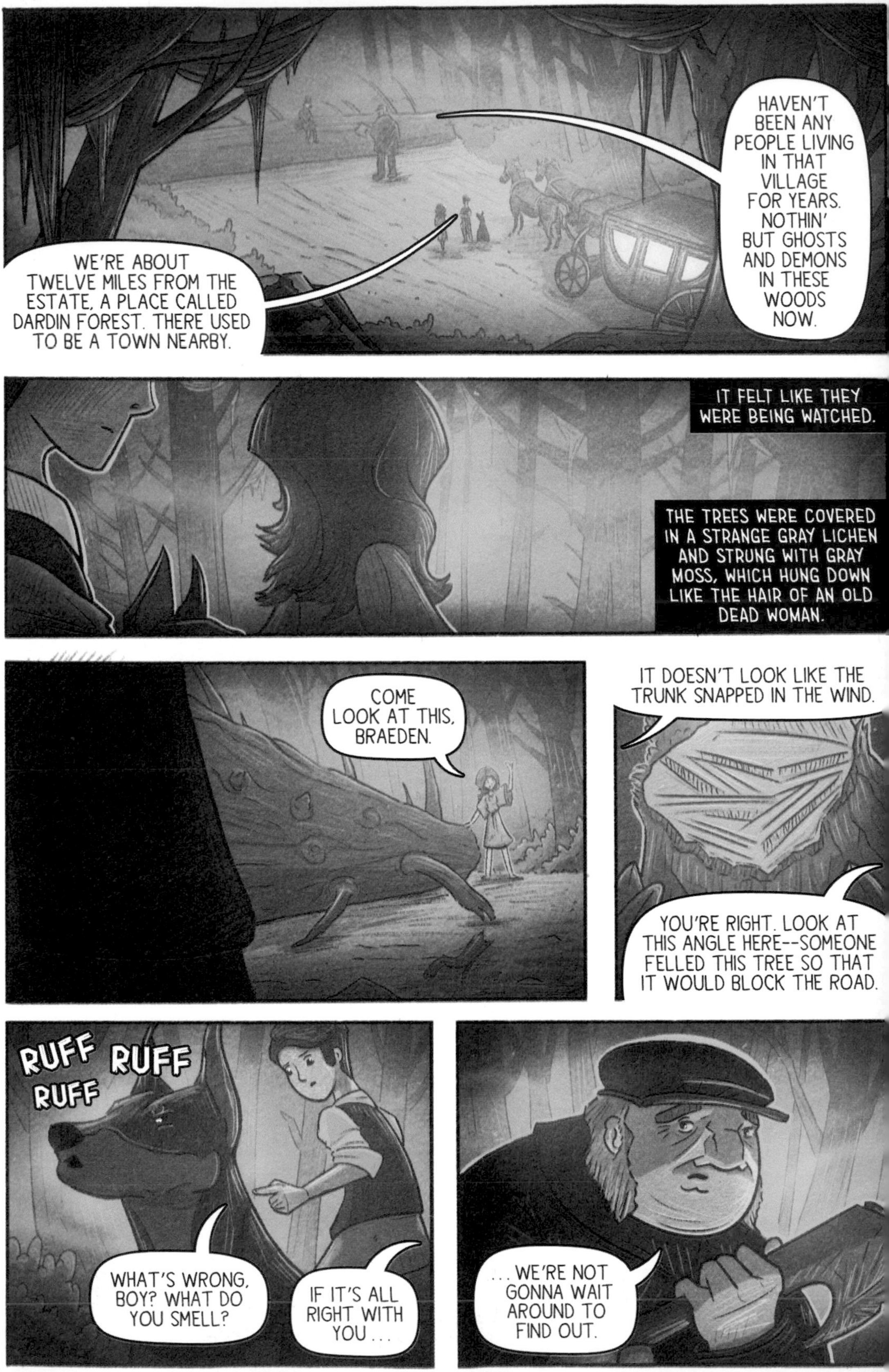
WE'RE ABOUT TWELVE MILES FROM THE ESTATE, A PLACE CALLED DARDIN FOREST. THERE USED TO BE A TOWN NEARBY.
HAVEN'T BEEN ANY PEOPLE LIVING IN THAT VILLAGE FOR YEARS. NOTHIN' BUT GHOSTS AND DEMONS IN THESE WOODS NOW.
IT FELT LIKE THEY WERE BEING WATCHED.
THE TREES WERE COVERED IN A STRANGE GRAY LICHEN AND STRUNG WITH GRAY MOSS, WHICH HUNG DOWN LIKE THE HAIR OF AN OLD DEAD WOMAN.
COME LOOK AT THIS, BRAEDEN.
IT DOESN'T LOOK LIKE THE TRUNK SNAPPED IN THE WIND.
YOU'RE RIGHT. LOOK AT THIS ANGLE HERE--SOMEONE FELLED THIS TREE SO THAT IT WOULD BLOCK THE ROAD.
RUFF RUFF
RUFF
WHAT'S WRONG, BOY? WHAT DO YOU SMELL?
IF IT'S ALL RIGHT WITH YOU . . .
. . . WE'RE NOT GONNA WAIT AROUND TO FIND OUT.

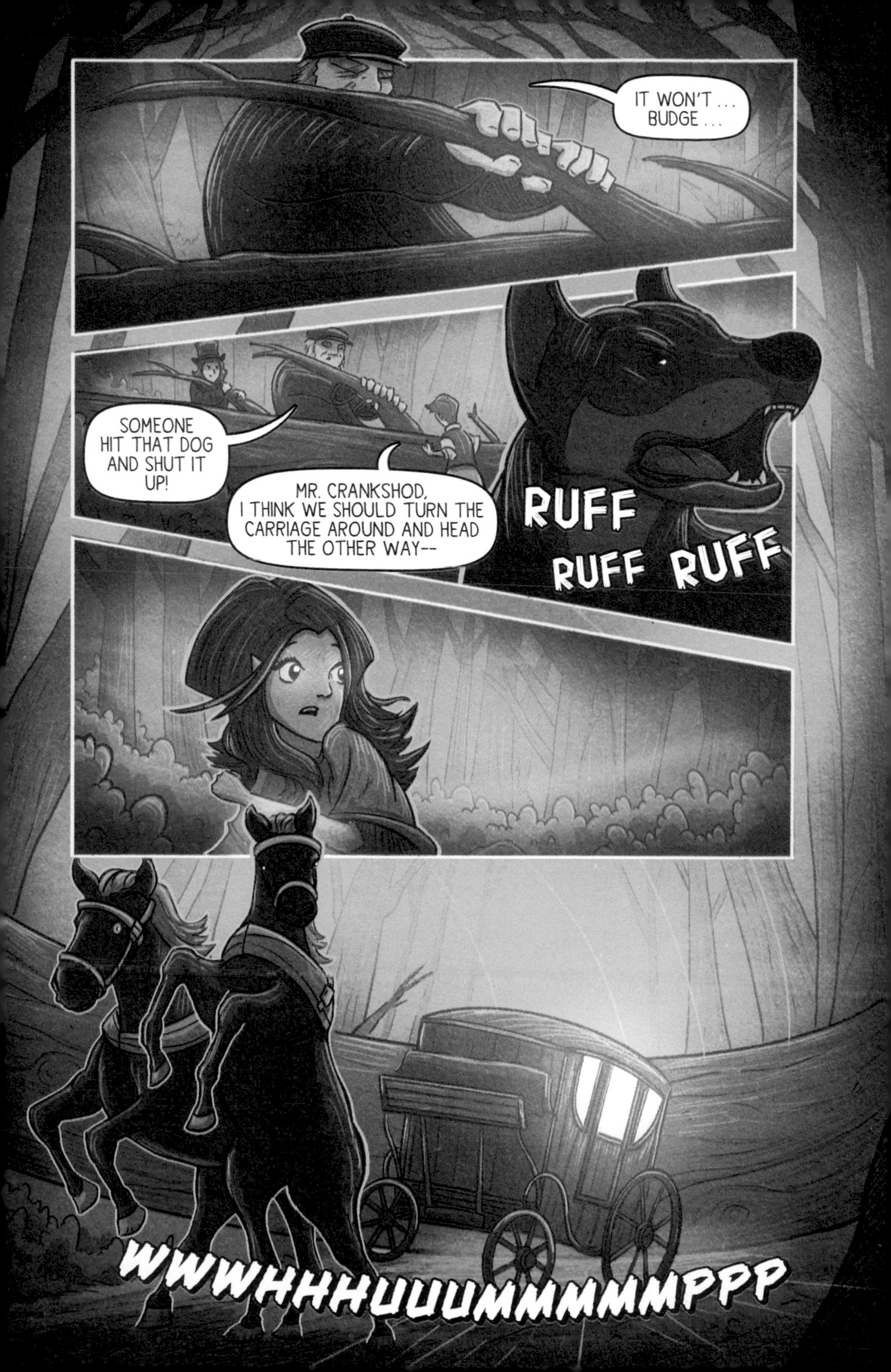
IT WON'T . . . BUDGE . . .
SOMEONE HIT THAT DOG AND SHUT IT UP!
MR. CRANKSHOD, I THINK WE SHOULD TURN THE CARRIAGE AROUND AND HEAD THE OTHER WAY--
RUFF
RUFF RUFF
WWWHHHUUUMMMMMMPPP

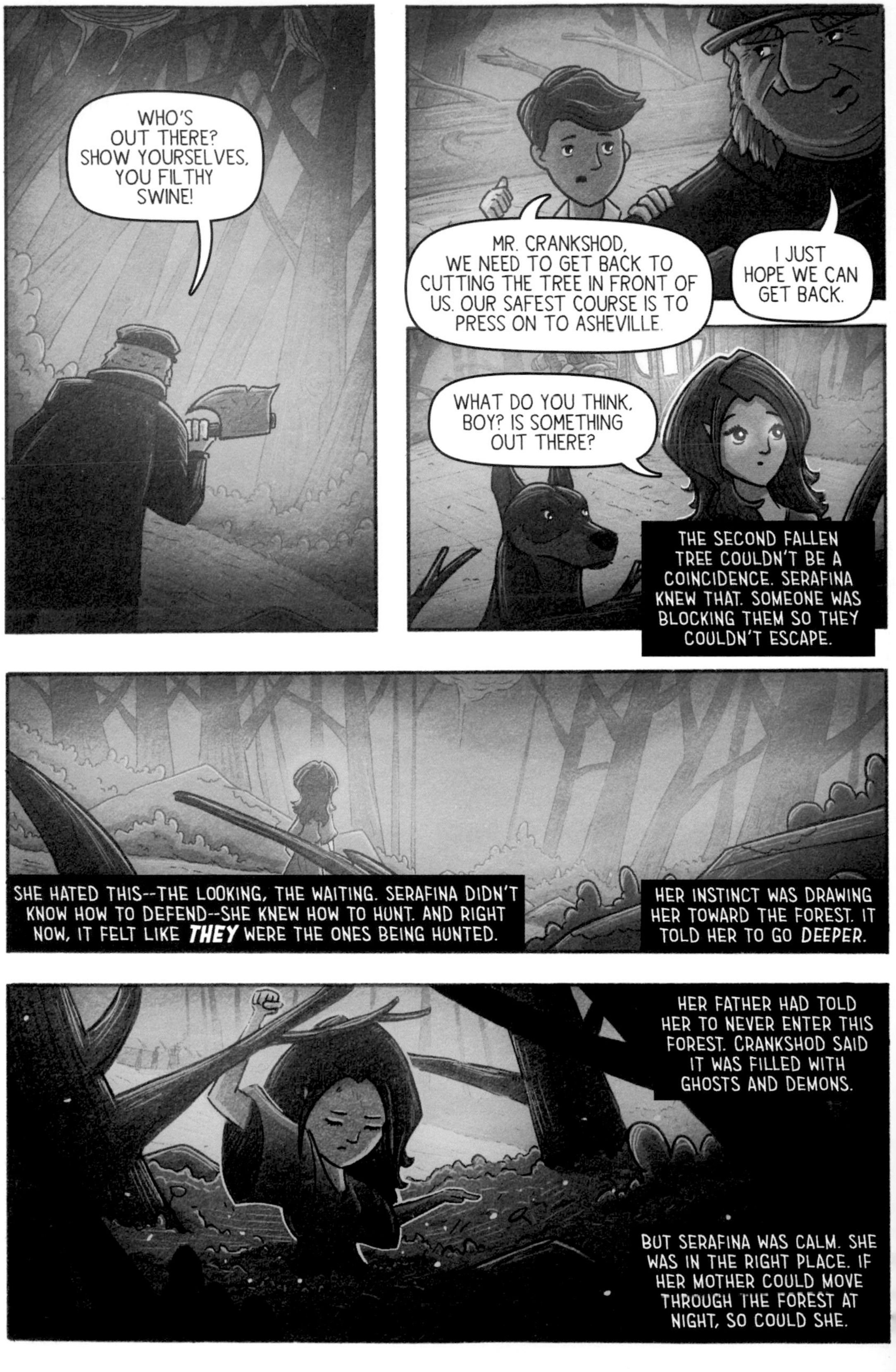

WHO'S OUT THERE? SHOW YOURSELVES, YOU FILTHY SWINE!
MR. CRANKSHOD, WE NEED TO GET BACK TO CUTTING THE TREE IN FRONT OF US. OUR SAFEST COURSE IS TO PRESS ON TO ASHEVILLE.
I JUST HOPE WE CAN GET BACK.
WHAT DO YOU THINK, BOY? IS SOMETHING OUT THERE?
THE SECOND FALLEN TREE COULDN'T BE A COINCIDENCE. SERAFINA KNEW THAT. SOMEONE WAS BLOCKING THEM SO THEY COULDN'T ESCAPE.
SHE HATED THIS--THE LOOKING, THE WAITING. SERAFINA DIDN'T KNOW HOW TO DEFEND--SHE KNEW HOW TO HUNT. AND RIGHT NOW, IT FELT LIKE THEY WERE THE ONES BEING HUNTED.
HER INSTINCT WAS DRAWING HER TOWARD THE FOREST. IT TOLD HER TO GO DEEPER.
HER FATHER HAD TOLD HER TO NEVER ENTER THIS FOREST. CRANKSHOD SAID IT WAS FILLED WITH GHOSTS AND DEMONS.
BUT SERAFINA WAS CALM. SHE WAS IN THE RIGHT PLACE. IF HER MOTHER COULD MOVE THROUGH THE FOREST AT NIGHT, SO COULD SHE.

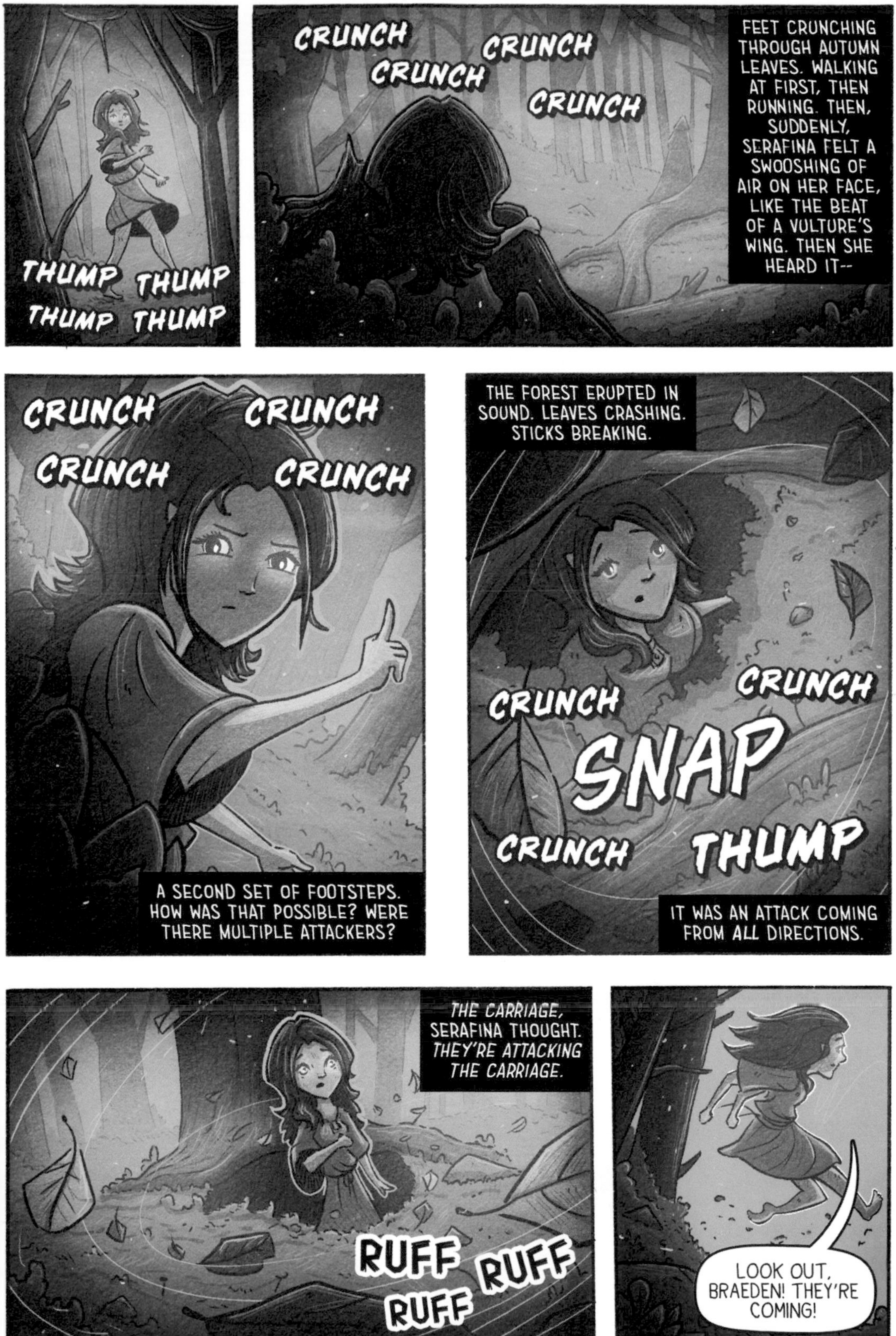
THUMP THUMP
THUMP THUMP
CRUNCH
CRUNCH
CRUNCH
CRUNCH
FEET CRUNCHING THROUGH AUTUMN LEAVES. WALKING AT FIRST, THEN RUNNING. THEN, SUDDENLY, SERAFINA FELT A SWOOSHING OF AIR ON HER FACE, LIKE THE BEAT OF A VULTURE'S WING. THEN SHE HEARD IT--
CRUNCH CRUNCH
CRUNCH CRUNCH
A SECOND SET OF FOOTSTEPS. HOW WAS THAT POSSIBLE? WERE THERE MULTIPLE ATTACKERS?
THE FOREST ERUPTED IN SOUND. LEAVES CRASHING. STICKS BREAKING.
CRUNCH
CRUNCH
SNAP
CRUNCH
THUMP
IT WAS AN ATTACK COMING FROM *ALL* DIRECTIONS.
THE CARRIAGE, SERAFINA THOUGHT. *THEY'RE ATTACKING THE CARRIAGE.*
RUFF
RUFF
RUFF
LOOK OUT, BRAEDEN! THEY'RE COMING!

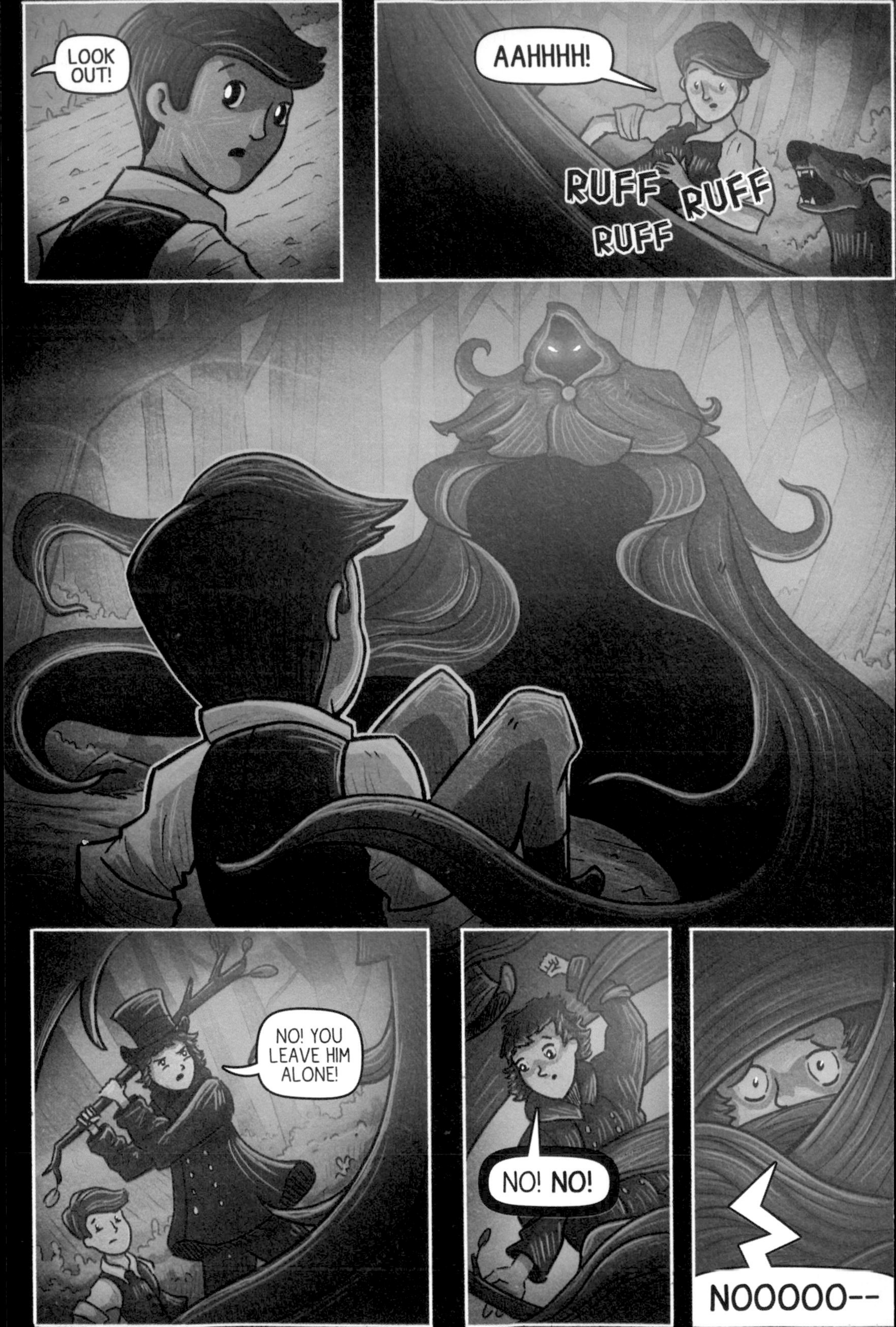
LOOK OUT!
AAHHHH!
RUFF RUFF
RUFF
NO! YOU LEAVE HIM ALONE!
NO! NO!
NOOOOO--

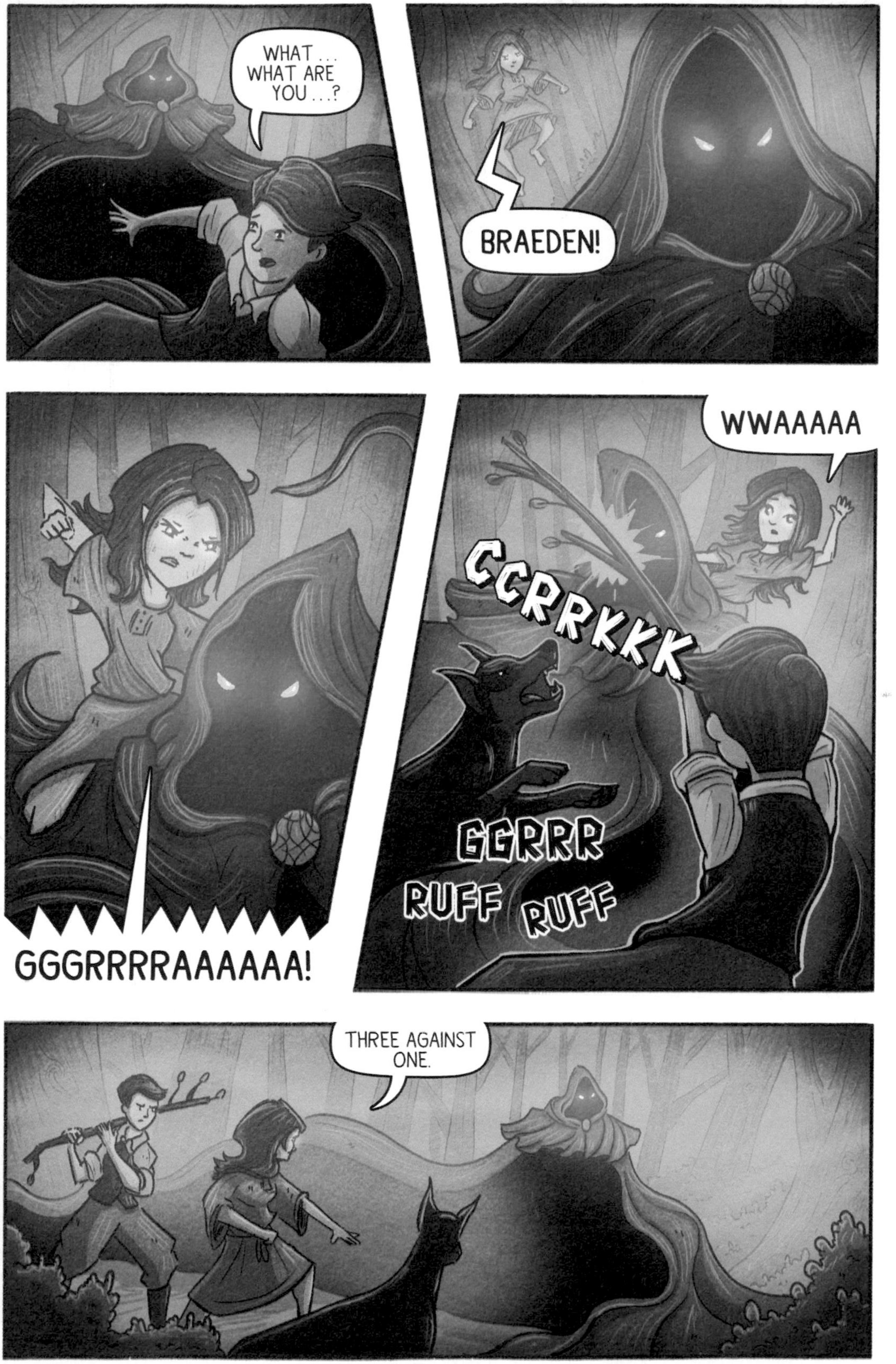
WHAT ... WHAT ARE YOU ...?
BRAEDEN!
GGGRRRRAAAAAA!
WWAAAAA
CCRRKKK
GGRRR
RUFF RUFF
THREE AGAINST ONE.

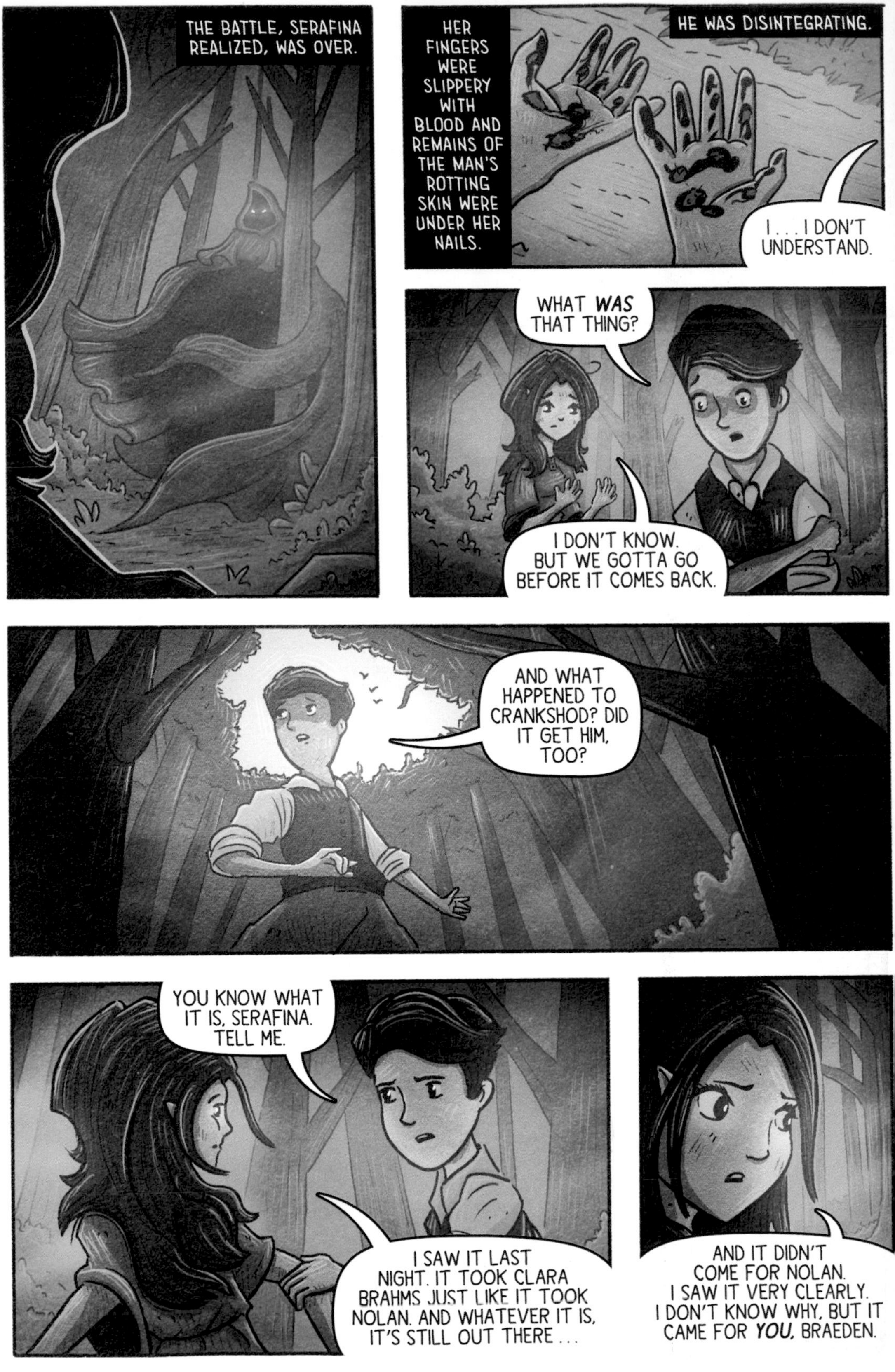
THE BATTLE, SERAFINA REALIZED, WAS OVER.
HER FINGERS WERE SLIPPERY WITH BLOOD AND REMAINS OF THE MAN'S ROTTING SKIN WERE UNDER HER NAILS.
HE WAS DISINTEGRATING.
I . . . I DON'T UNDERSTAND.
WHAT *WAS* THAT THING?
I DON'T KNOW. BUT WE GOTTA GO BEFORE IT COMES BACK.
AND WHAT HAPPENED TO CRANKSHOD? DID IT GET HIM, TOO?
YOU KNOW WHAT IT IS, SERAFINA. TELL ME.
I SAW IT LAST NIGHT. IT TOOK CLARA BRAHMS JUST LIKE IT TOOK NOLAN. AND WHATEVER IT IS, IT'S STILL OUT THERE . . .
AND IT DIDN'T COME FOR NOLAN. I SAW IT VERY CLEARLY. I DON'T KNOW WHY, BUT IT CAME FOR *YOU*, BRAEDEN.

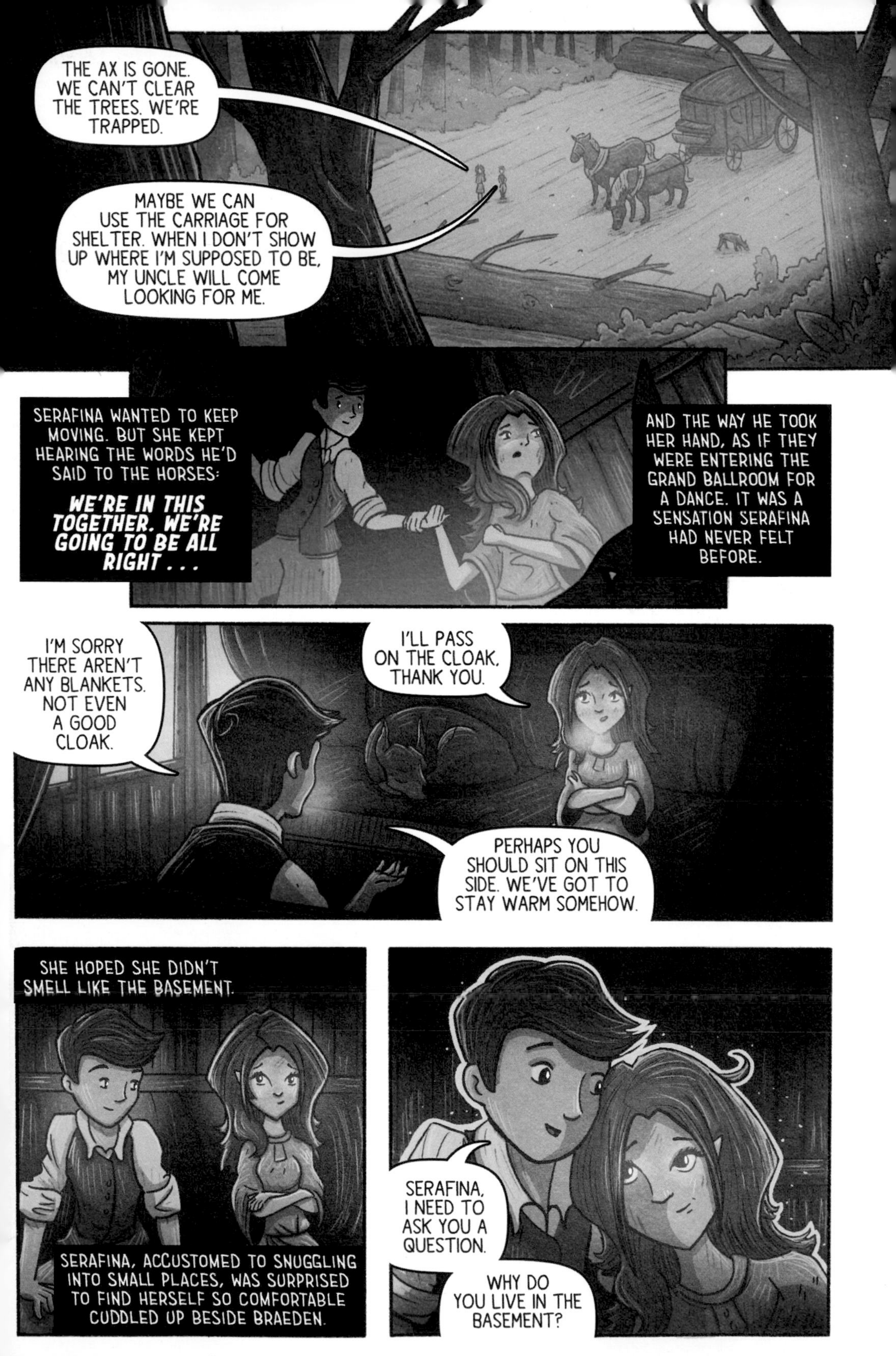

THE AX IS GONE. WE CAN'T CLEAR THE TREES. WE'RE TRAPPED.
MAYBE WE CAN USE THE CARRIAGE FOR SHELTER. WHEN I DON'T SHOW UP WHERE I'M SUPPOSED TO BE, MY UNCLE WILL COME LOOKING FOR ME.
SERAFINA WANTED TO KEEP MOVING. BUT SHE KEPT HEARING THE WORDS HE'D SAID TO THE HORSES:
WE'RE IN THIS TOGETHER. WE'RE GOING TO BE ALL RIGHT . . .
AND THE WAY HE TOOK HER HAND, AS IF THEY WERE ENTERING THE GRAND BALLROOM FOR A DANCE. IT WAS A SENSATION SERAFINA HAD NEVER FELT BEFORE.
I'M SORRY THERE AREN'T ANY BLANKETS. NOT EVEN A GOOD CLOAK.
I'LL PASS ON THE CLOAK, THANK YOU.
PERHAPS YOU SHOULD SIT ON THIS SIDE. WE'VE GOT TO STAY WARM SOMEHOW.
SHE HOPED SHE DIDN'T SMELL LIKE THE BASEMENT.
SERAFINA, ACCUSTOMED TO SNUGGLING INTO SMALL PLACES, WAS SURPRISED TO FIND HERSELF SO COMFORTABLE CUDDLED UP BESIDE BRAEDEN.
SERAFINA, I NEED TO ASK YOU A QUESTION.
WHY DO YOU LIVE IN THE BASEMENT?

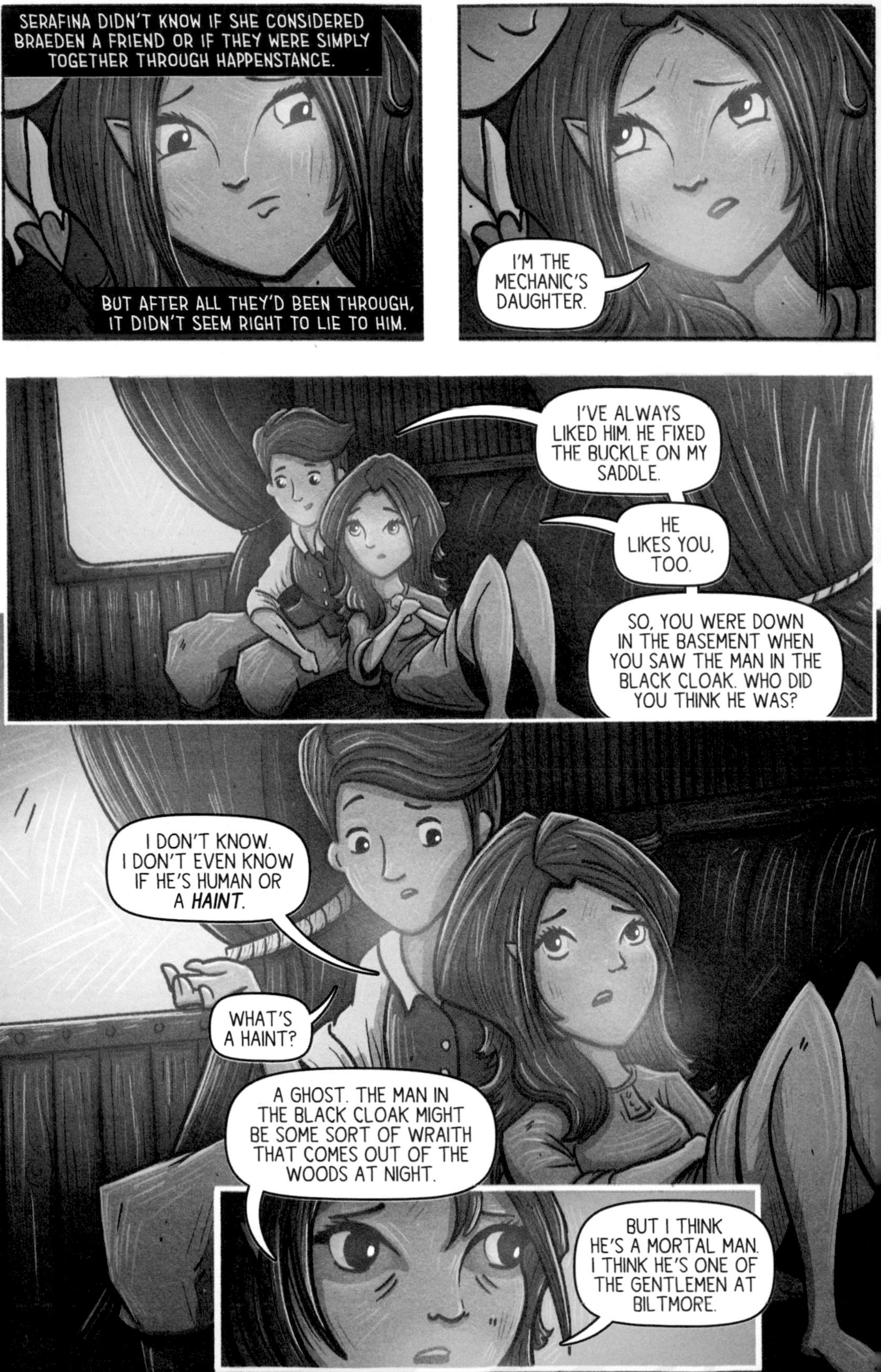
SERAFINA DIDN'T KNOW IF SHE CONSIDERED BRAEDEN A FRIEND OR IF THEY WERE SIMPLY TOGETHER THROUGH HAPPENSTANCE.
BUT AFTER ALL THEY'D BEEN THROUGH, IT DIDN'T SEEM RIGHT TO LIE TO HIM.
I'M THE MECHANIC'S DAUGHTER.
I'VE ALWAYS LIKED HIM. HE FIXED THE BUCKLE ON MY SADDLE.
HE LIKES YOU, TOO.
SO, YOU WERE DOWN IN THE BASEMENT WHEN YOU SAW THE MAN IN THE BLACK CLOAK. WHO DID YOU THINK HE WAS?
I DON'T KNOW. I DON'T EVEN KNOW IF HE'S HUMAN OR A ***HAINT***.
WHAT'S A HAINT?
A GHOST. THE MAN IN THE BLACK CLOAK MIGHT BE SOME SORT OF WRAITH THAT COMES OUT OF THE WOODS AT NIGHT.
BUT I THINK HE'S A MORTAL MAN. I THINK HE'S ONE OF THE GENTLEMEN AT BILTMORE.

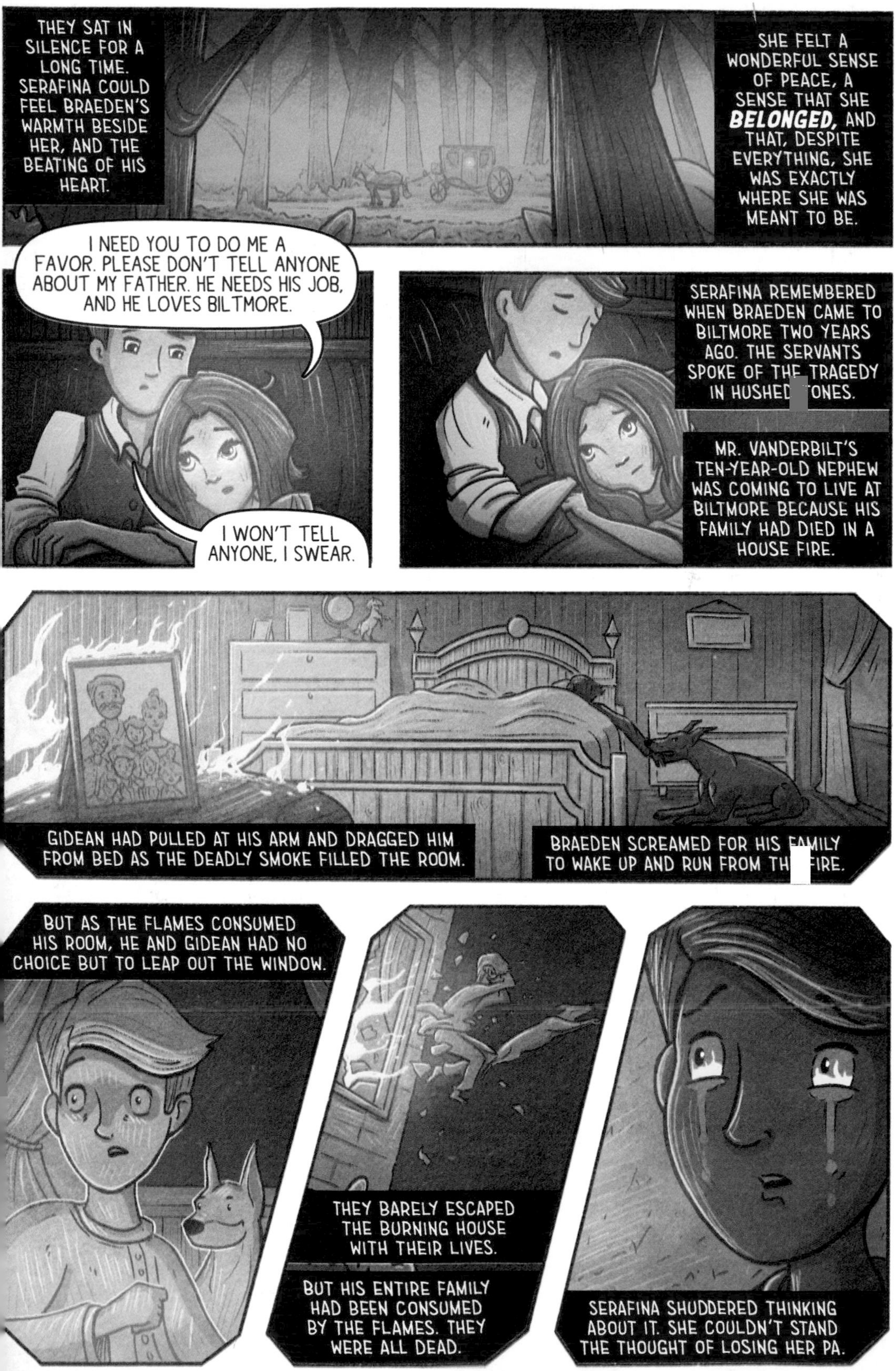
THEY SAT IN SILENCE FOR A LONG TIME. SERAFINA COULD FEEL BRAEDEN'S WARMTH BESIDE HER, AND THE BEATING OF HIS HEART.
SHE FELT A WONDERFUL SENSE OF PEACE, A SENSE THAT SHE **BELONGED,** AND THAT, DESPITE EVERYTHING, SHE WAS EXACTLY WHERE SHE WAS MEANT TO BE.
I NEED YOU TO DO ME A FAVOR. PLEASE DON'T TELL ANYONE ABOUT MY FATHER. HE NEEDS HIS JOB, AND HE LOVES BILTMORE.
I WON'T TELL ANYONE, I SWEAR.
SERAFINA REMEMBERED WHEN BRAEDEN CAME TO BILTMORE TWO YEARS AGO. THE SERVANTS SPOKE OF THE TRAGEDY IN HUSHED TONES.
MR. VANDERBILT'S TEN-YEAR-OLD NEPHEW WAS COMING TO LIVE AT BILTMORE BECAUSE HIS FAMILY HAD DIED IN A HOUSE FIRE.
GIDEAN HAD PULLED AT HIS ARM AND DRAGGED HIM FROM BED AS THE DEADLY SMOKE FILLED THE ROOM.
BRAEDEN SCREAMED FOR HIS FAMILY TO WAKE UP AND RUN FROM THE FIRE.
BUT AS THE FLAMES CONSUMED HIS ROOM, HE AND GIDEAN HAD NO CHOICE BUT TO LEAP OUT THE WINDOW.
THEY BARELY ESCAPED THE BURNING HOUSE WITH THEIR LIVES.
BUT HIS ENTIRE FAMILY HAD BEEN CONSUMED BY THE FLAMES. THEY WERE ALL DEAD.
SERAFINA SHUDDERED THINKING ABOUT IT. SHE COULDN'T STAND THE THOUGHT OF LOSING HER PA.

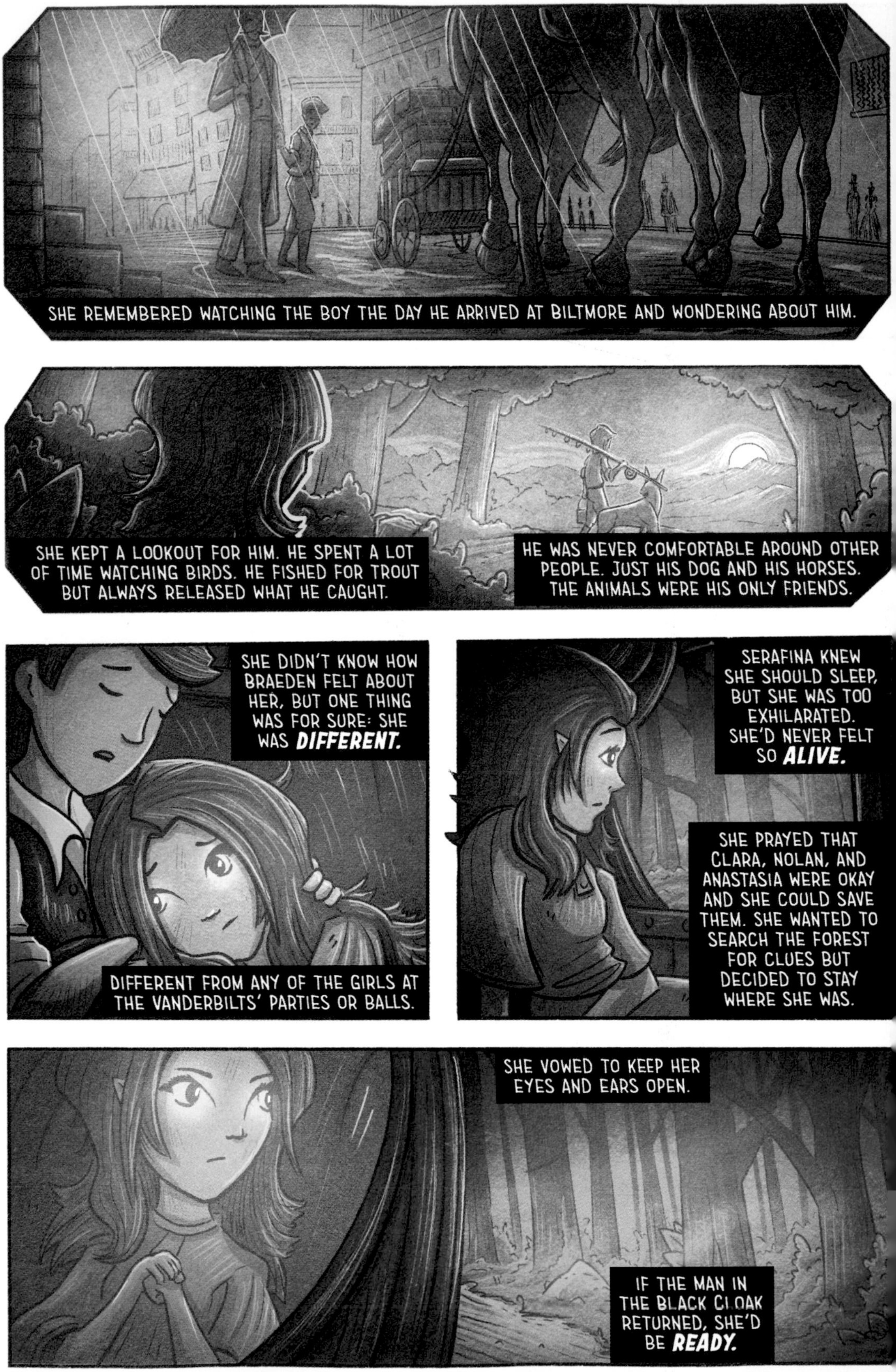
SHE REMEMBERED WATCHING THE BOY THE DAY HE ARRIVED AT BILTMORE AND WONDERING ABOUT HIM.
SHE KEPT A LOOKOUT FOR HIM. HE SPENT A LOT OF TIME WATCHING BIRDS. HE FISHED FOR TROUT BUT ALWAYS RELEASED WHAT HE CAUGHT.
HE WAS NEVER COMFORTABLE AROUND OTHER PEOPLE. JUST HIS DOG AND HIS HORSES. THE ANIMALS WERE HIS ONLY FRIENDS.
SHE DIDN'T KNOW HOW BRAEDEN FELT ABOUT HER, BUT ONE THING WAS FOR SURE: SHE WAS ***DIFFERENT.***
DIFFERENT FROM ANY OF THE GIRLS AT THE VANDERBILTS' PARTIES OR BALLS.
SERAFINA KNEW SHE SHOULD SLEEP, BUT SHE WAS TOO EXHILARATED. SHE'D NEVER FELT SO ***ALIVE.***
SHE PRAYED THAT CLARA, NOLAN, AND ANASTASIA WERE OKAY AND SHE COULD SAVE THEM. SHE WANTED TO SEARCH THE FOREST FOR CLUES BUT DECIDED TO STAY WHERE SHE WAS.
SHE VOWED TO KEEP HER EYES AND EARS OPEN.
IF THE MAN IN THE BLACK CLOAK RETURNED, SHE'D BE ***READY.***

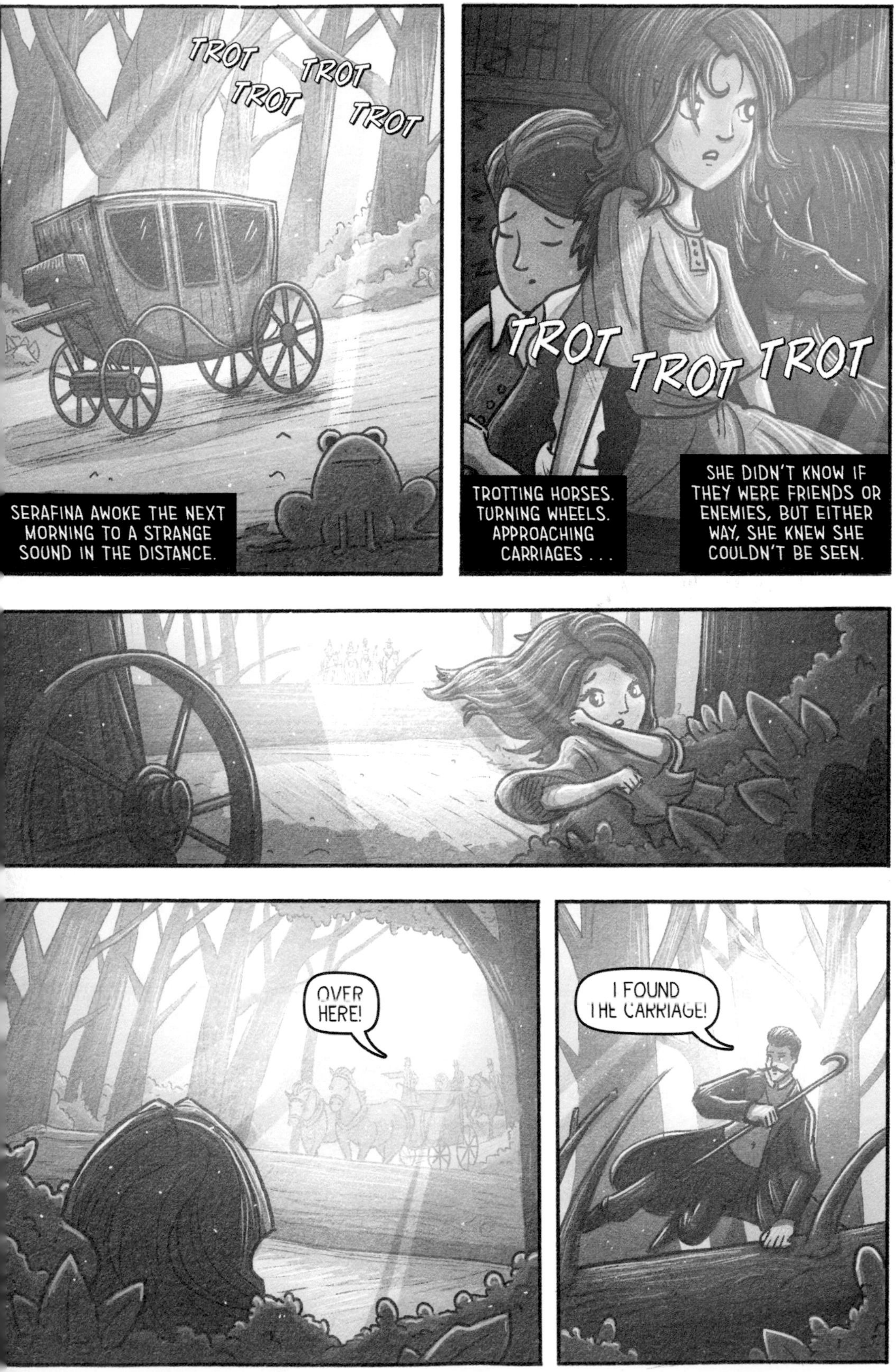
TROT
TROT
TROT
TROT
SERAFINA AWOKE THE NEXT MORNING TO A STRANGE SOUND IN THE DISTANCE.
TROT TROT TROT
TROTTING HORSES. TURNING WHEELS. APPROACHING CARRIAGES . . .
SHE DIDN'T KNOW IF THEY WERE FRIENDS OR ENEMIES, BUT EITHER WAY, SHE KNEW SHE COULDN'T BE SEEN.
OVER HERE!
I FOUND THE CARRIAGE!

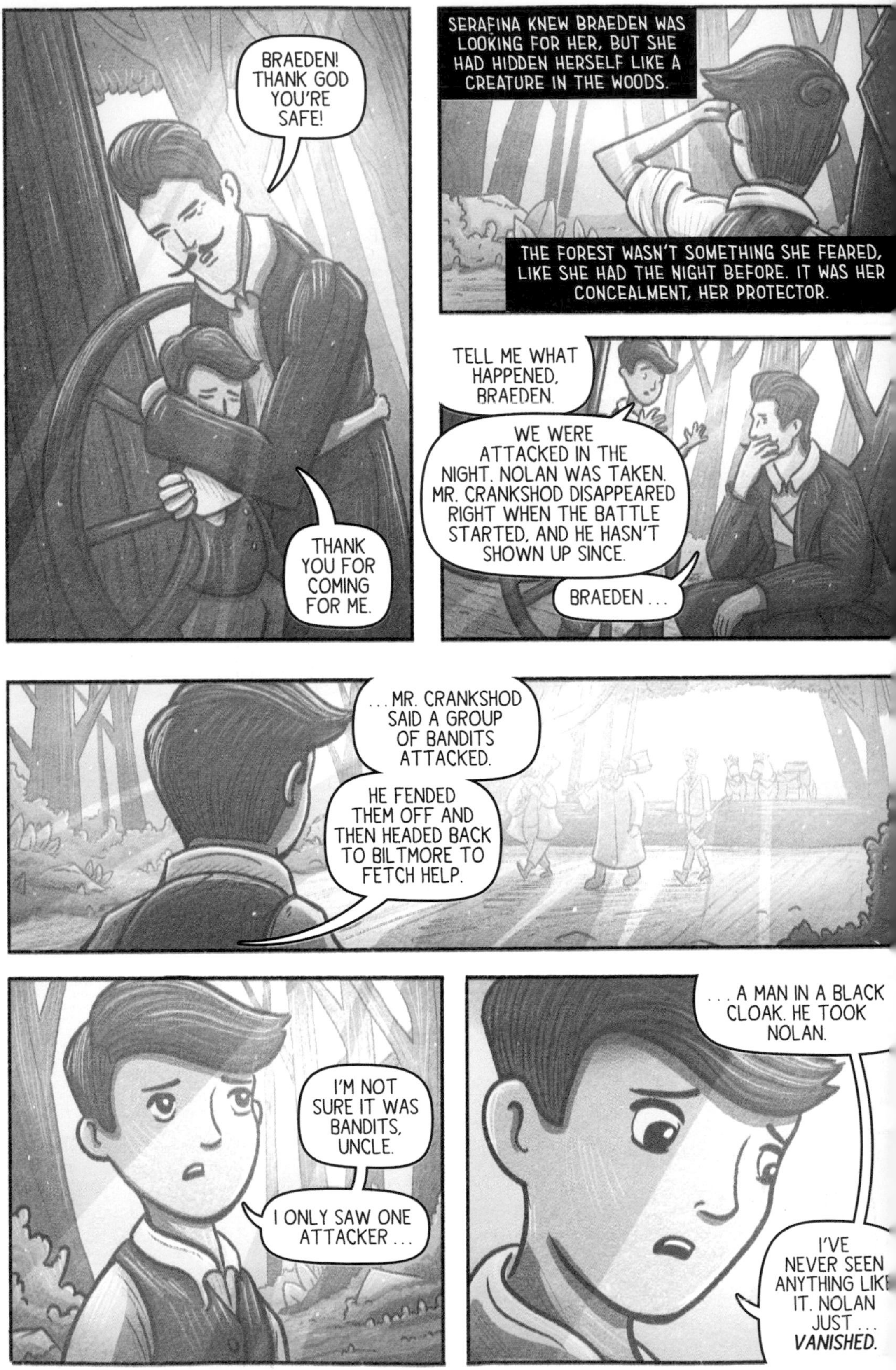
BRAEDEN! THANK GOD YOU'RE SAFE!
THANK YOU FOR COMING FOR ME.
SERAFINA KNEW BRAEDEN WAS LOOKING FOR HER, BUT SHE HAD HIDDEN HERSELF LIKE A CREATURE IN THE WOODS.
THE FOREST WASN'T SOMETHING SHE FEARED, LIKE SHE HAD THE NIGHT BEFORE. IT WAS HER CONCEALMENT, HER PROTECTOR.
TELL ME WHAT HAPPENED, BRAEDEN.
WE WERE ATTACKED IN THE NIGHT. NOLAN WAS TAKEN. MR. CRANKSHOD DISAPPEARED RIGHT WHEN THE BATTLE STARTED, AND HE HASN'T SHOWN UP SINCE.
BRAEDEN . . .
. . . MR. CRANKSHOD SAID A GROUP OF BANDITS ATTACKED.
HE FENDED THEM OFF AND THEN HEADED BACK TO BILTMORE TO FETCH HELP.
I'M NOT SURE IT WAS BANDITS, UNCLE.
I ONLY SAW ONE ATTACKER . . .
. . . A MAN IN A BLACK CLOAK. HE TOOK NOLAN.
I'VE NEVER SEEN ANYTHING LIKE IT. NOLAN JUST . . . *VANISHED*.

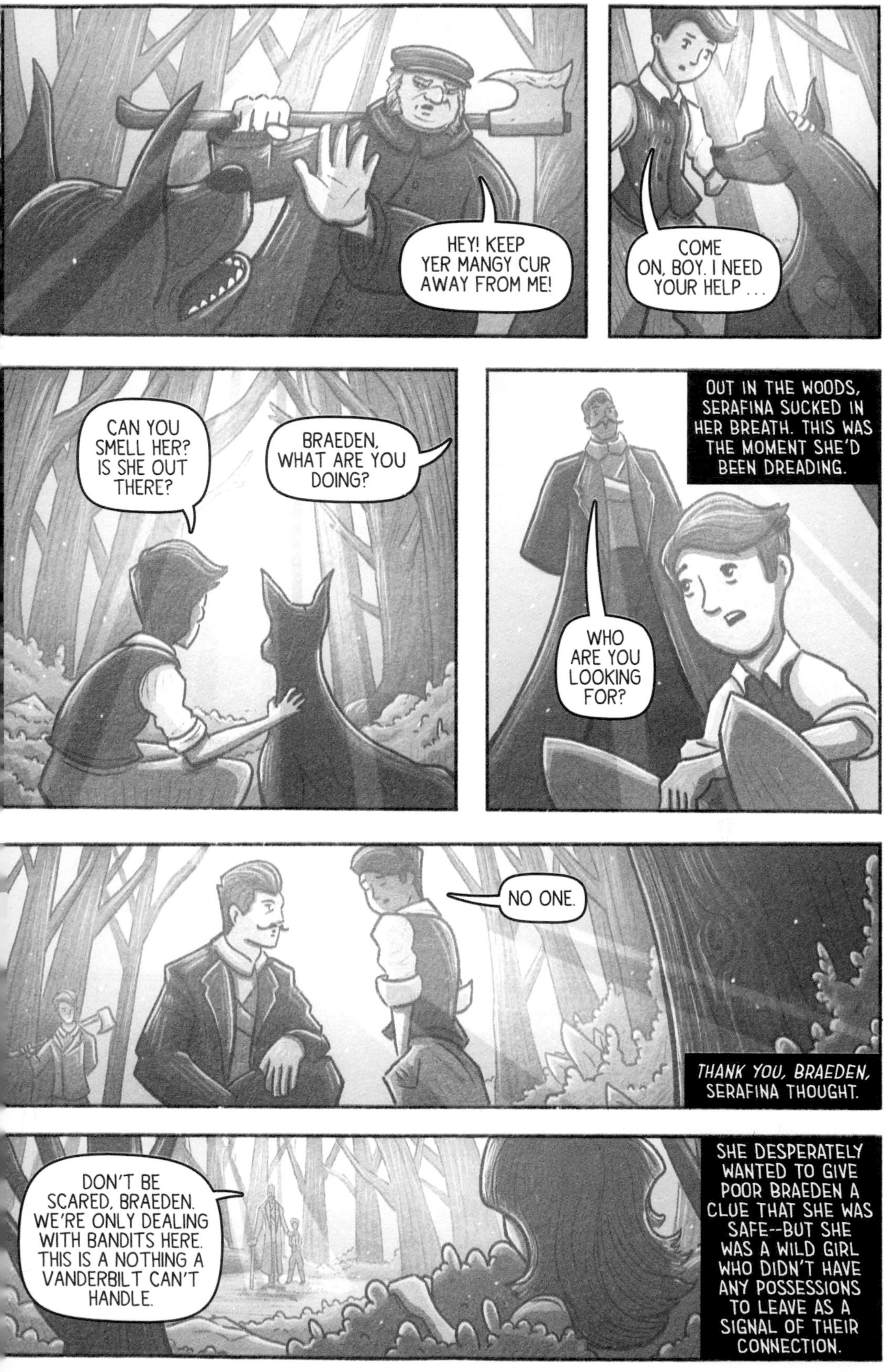
HEY! KEEP YER MANGY CUR AWAY FROM ME!
COME ON, BOY. I NEED YOUR HELP . . .
CAN YOU SMELL HER? IS SHE OUT THERE?
BRAEDEN, WHAT ARE YOU DOING?
OUT IN THE WOODS, SERAFINA SUCKED IN HER BREATH. THIS WAS THE MOMENT SHE'D BEEN DREADING.
WHO ARE YOU LOOKING FOR?
NO ONE.
THANK YOU, BRAEDEN, SERAFINA THOUGHT.
DON'T BE SCARED, BRAEDEN. WE'RE ONLY DEALING WITH BANDITS HERE. THIS IS A NOTHING A VANDERBILT CAN'T HANDLE.
SHE DESPERATELY WANTED TO GIVE POOR BRAEDEN A CLUE THAT SHE WAS SAFE--BUT SHE WAS A WILD GIRL WHO DIDN'T HAVE ANY POSSESSIONS TO LEAVE AS A SIGNAL OF THEIR CONNECTION.

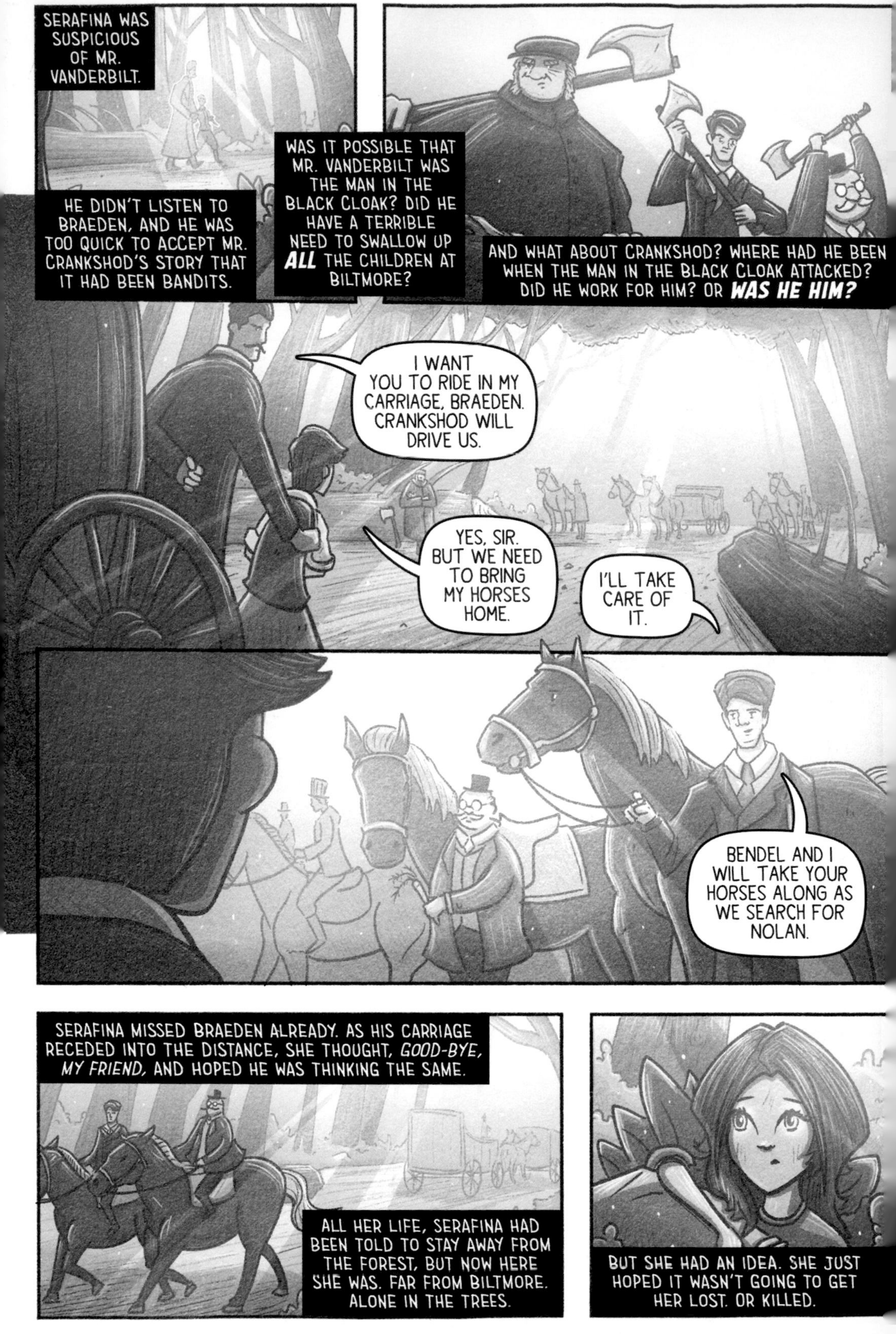

SERAFINA WAS SUSPICIOUS OF MR. VANDERBILT.
HE DIDN'T LISTEN TO BRAEDEN, AND HE WAS TOO QUICK TO ACCEPT MR. CRANKSHOD'S STORY THAT IT HAD BEEN BANDITS.
WAS IT POSSIBLE THAT MR. VANDERBILT WAS THE MAN IN THE BLACK CLOAK? DID HE HAVE A TERRIBLE NEED TO SWALLOW UP ***ALL*** THE CHILDREN AT BILTMORE?
AND WHAT ABOUT CRANKSHOD? WHERE HAD HE BEEN WHEN THE MAN IN THE BLACK CLOAK ATTACKED? DID HE WORK FOR HIM? OR ***WAS HE HIM?***
I WANT YOU TO RIDE IN MY CARRIAGE, BRAEDEN. CRANKSHOD WILL DRIVE US.
YES, SIR. BUT WE NEED TO BRING MY HORSES HOME.
I'LL TAKE CARE OF IT.
BENDEL AND I WILL TAKE YOUR HORSES ALONG AS WE SEARCH FOR NOLAN.
SERAFINA MISSED BRAEDEN ALREADY. AS HIS CARRIAGE RECEDED INTO THE DISTANCE, SHE THOUGHT, *GOOD-BYE, MY FRIEND,* AND HOPED HE WAS THINKING THE SAME.
ALL HER LIFE, SERAFINA HAD BEEN TOLD TO STAY AWAY FROM THE FOREST, BUT NOW HERE SHE WAS. FAR FROM BILTMORE. ALONE IN THE TREES.
BUT SHE HAD AN IDEA. SHE JUST HOPED IT WASN'T GOING TO GET HER LOST. OR KILLED.

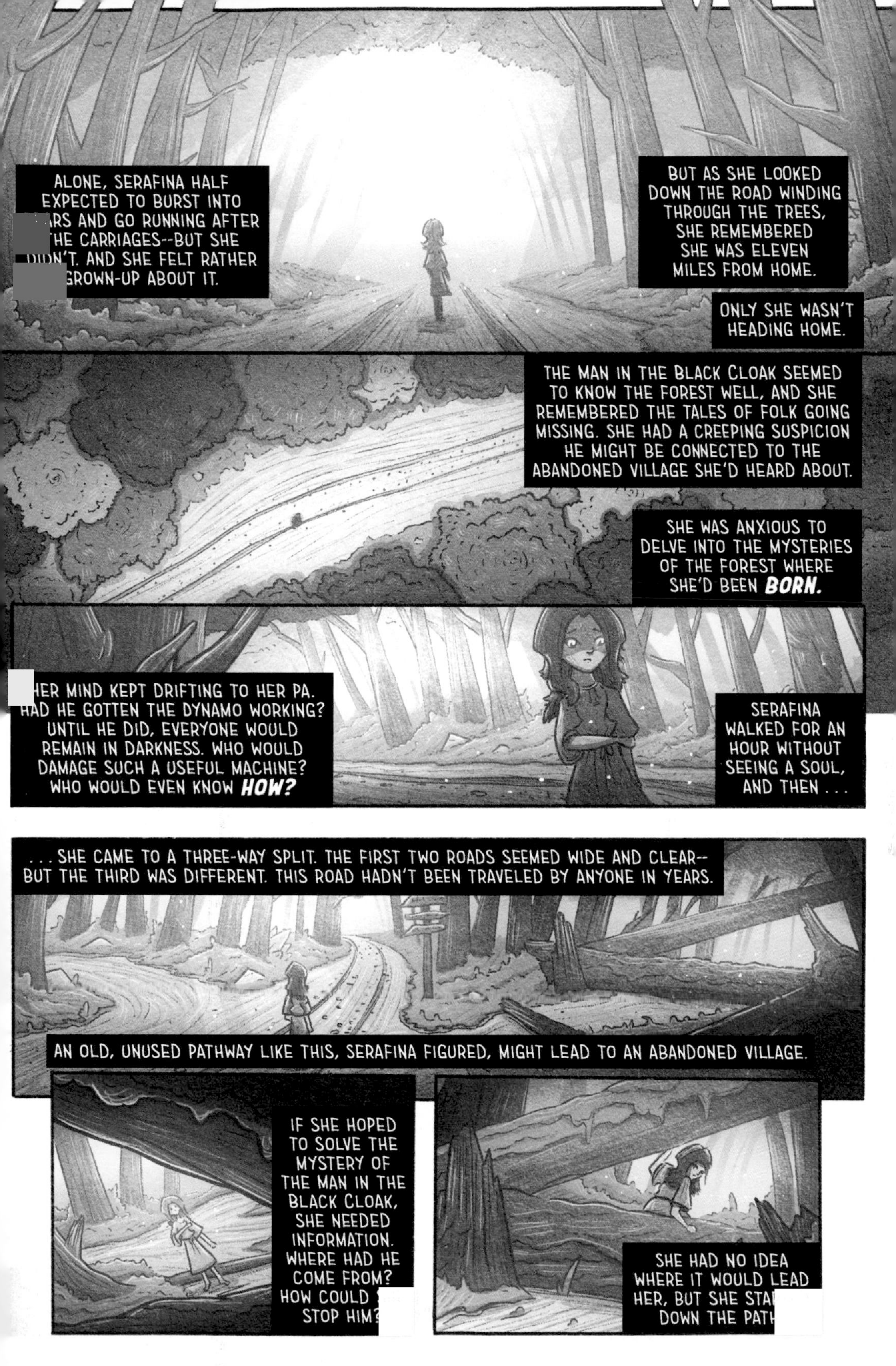
ALONE, SERAFINA HALF EXPECTED TO BURST INTO
ARS AND GO RUNNING AFTER THE CARRIAGES--BUT SHE
DN'T. AND SHE FELT RATHER GROWN-UP ABOUT IT.
BUT AS SHE LOOKED DOWN THE ROAD WINDING THROUGH THE TREES, SHE REMEMBERED SHE WAS ELEVEN MILES FROM HOME.
ONLY SHE WASN'T HEADING HOME.
THE MAN IN THE BLACK CLOAK SEEMED TO KNOW THE FOREST WELL, AND SHE REMEMBERED THE TALES OF FOLK GOING MISSING. SHE HAD A CREEPING SUSPICION HE MIGHT BE CONNECTED TO THE ABANDONED VILLAGE SHE'D HEARD ABOUT.
SHE WAS ANXIOUS TO DELVE INTO THE MYSTERIES OF THE FOREST WHERE SHE'D BEEN **BORN.**
HER MIND KEPT DRIFTING TO HER PA. HAD HE GOTTEN THE DYNAMO WORKING? UNTIL HE DID, EVERYONE WOULD REMAIN IN DARKNESS. WHO WOULD DAMAGE SUCH A USEFUL MACHINE? WHO WOULD EVEN KNOW **HOW?**
SERAFINA WALKED FOR AN HOUR WITHOUT SEEING A SOUL, AND THEN . . .
. . . SHE CAME TO A THREE-WAY SPLIT. THE FIRST TWO ROADS SEEMED WIDE AND CLEAR-- BUT THE THIRD WAS DIFFERENT. THIS ROAD HADN'T BEEN TRAVELED BY ANYONE IN YEARS.
AN OLD, UNUSED PATHWAY LIKE THIS, SERAFINA FIGURED, MIGHT LEAD TO AN ABANDONED VILLAGE.
IF SHE HOPED TO SOLVE THE MYSTERY OF THE MAN IN THE BLACK CLOAK, SHE NEEDED INFORMATION. WHERE HAD HE COME FROM? HOW COULD
STOP HIM
SHE HAD NO IDEA WHERE IT WOULD LEAD HER, BUT SHE STA
DOWN THE PATH

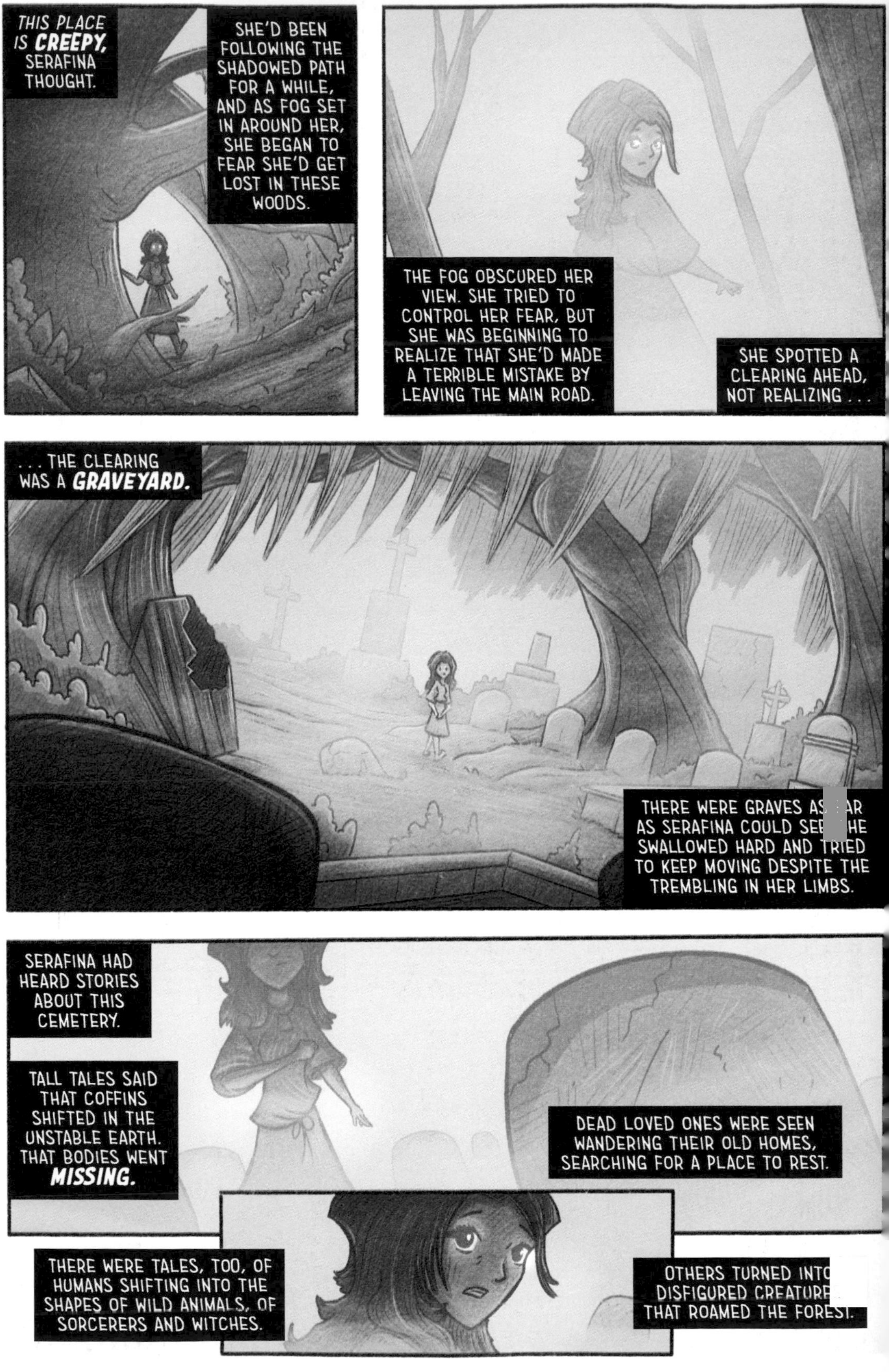
THIS PLACE IS CREEPY, SERAFINA THOUGHT.
SHE'D BEEN FOLLOWING THE SHADOWED PATH FOR A WHILE, AND AS FOG SET IN AROUND HER, SHE BEGAN TO FEAR SHE'D GET LOST IN THESE WOODS.
THE FOG OBSCURED HER VIEW. SHE TRIED TO CONTROL HER FEAR, BUT SHE WAS BEGINNING TO REALIZE THAT SHE'D MADE A TERRIBLE MISTAKE BY LEAVING THE MAIN ROAD.
SHE SPOTTED A CLEARING AHEAD, NOT REALIZING . . .
. . . THE CLEARING WAS A GRAVEYARD.
THERE WERE GRAVES AS FAR AS SERAFINA COULD SEE. SHE SWALLOWED HARD AND TRIED TO KEEP MOVING DESPITE THE TREMBLING IN HER LIMBS.
SERAFINA HAD HEARD STORIES ABOUT THIS CEMETERY.
TALL TALES SAID THAT COFFINS SHIFTED IN THE UNSTABLE EARTH. THAT BODIES WENT MISSING.
DEAD LOVED ONES WERE SEEN WANDERING THEIR OLD HOMES, SEARCHING FOR A PLACE TO REST.
THERE WERE TALES, TOO, OF HUMANS SHIFTING INTO THE SHAPES OF WILD ANIMALS, OF SORCERERS AND WITCHES.
OTHERS TURNED INTO DISFIGURED CREATURES THAT ROAMED THE FOREST.

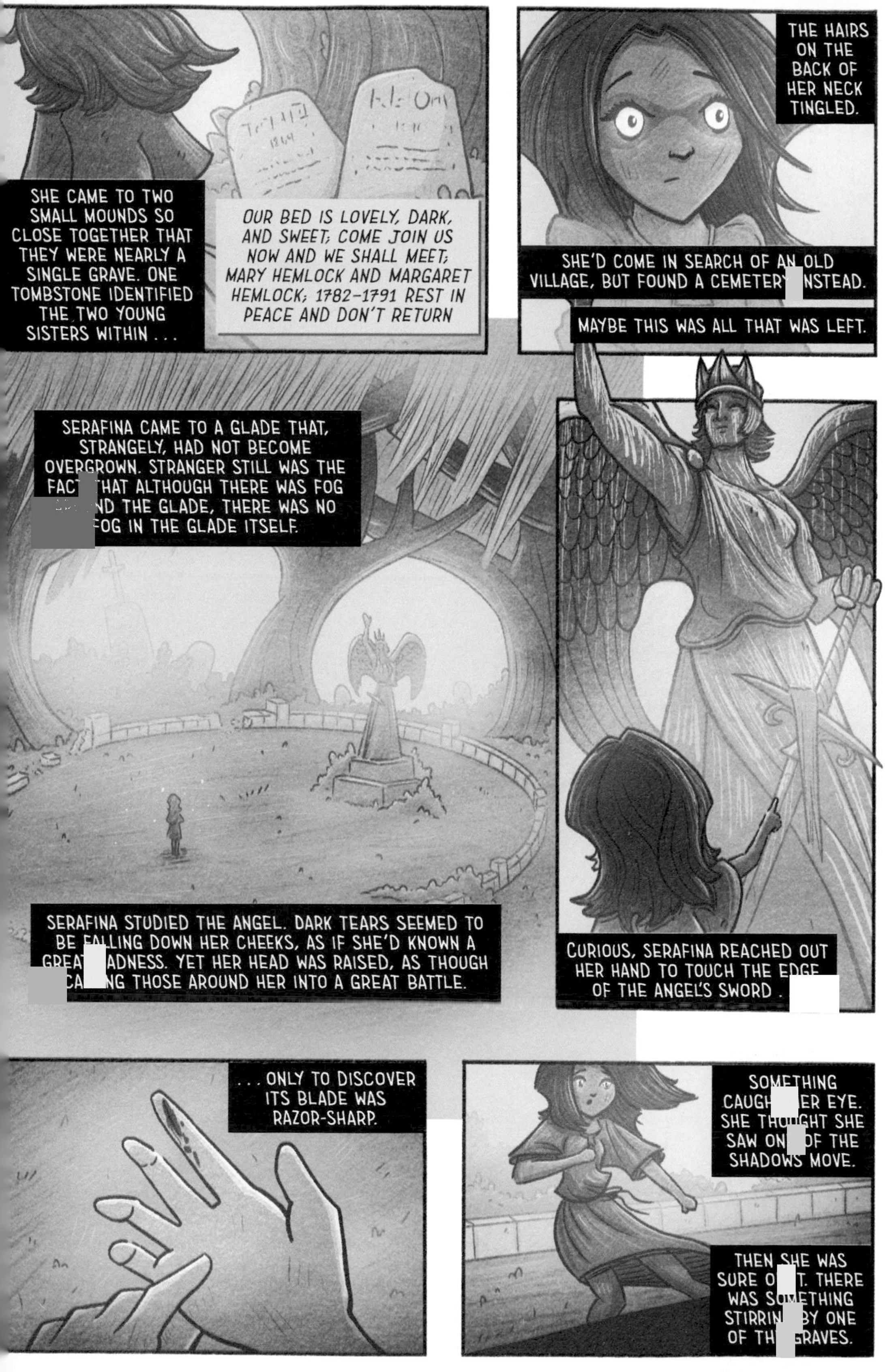
SHE CAME TO TWO SMALL MOUNDS SO CLOSE TOGETHER THAT THEY WERE NEARLY A SINGLE GRAVE. ONE TOMBSTONE IDENTIFIED THE TWO YOUNG SISTERS WITHIN . . .
OUR BED IS LOVELY, DARK, AND SWEET; COME JOIN US NOW AND WE SHALL MEET; MARY HEMLOCK AND MARGARET HEMLOCK; 1782–1791 REST IN PEACE AND DON'T RETURN
THE HAIRS ON THE BACK OF HER NECK TINGLED.
SHE'D COME IN SEARCH OF AN OLD VILLAGE, BUT FOUND A CEMETERY INSTEAD.
MAYBE THIS WAS ALL THAT WAS LEFT.
SERAFINA CAME TO A GLADE THAT, STRANGELY, HAD NOT BECOME OVERGROWN. STRANGER STILL WAS THE FACT THAT ALTHOUGH THERE WAS FOG AROUND THE GLADE, THERE WAS NO FOG IN THE GLADE ITSELF.
SERAFINA STUDIED THE ANGEL. DARK TEARS SEEMED TO BE FALLING DOWN HER CHEEKS, AS IF SHE'D KNOWN A GREAT SADNESS. YET HER HEAD WAS RAISED, AS THOUGH CALLING THOSE AROUND HER INTO A GREAT BATTLE.
CURIOUS, SERAFINA REACHED OUT HER HAND TO TOUCH THE EDGE OF THE ANGEL'S SWORD . . .
. . . ONLY TO DISCOVER ITS BLADE WAS RAZOR-SHARP.
SOMETHING CAUGHT HER EYE. SHE THOUGHT SHE SAW ONE OF THE SHADOWS MOVE.
THEN SHE WAS SURE OF IT. THERE WAS SOMETHING STIRRING BY ONE OF THE GRAVES.

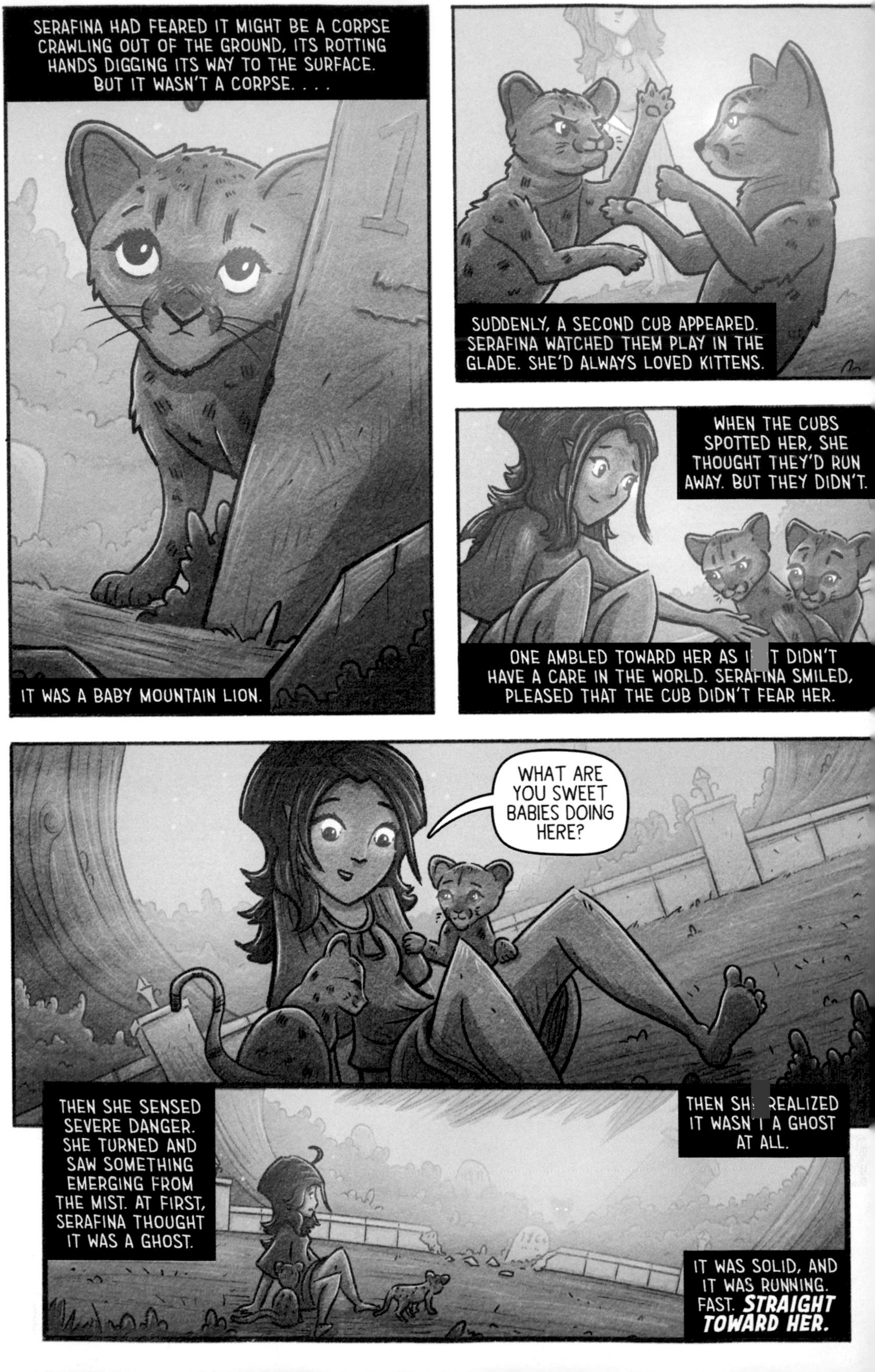
SERAFINA HAD FEARED IT MIGHT BE A CORPSE CRAWLING OUT OF THE GROUND, ITS ROTTING HANDS DIGGING ITS WAY TO THE SURFACE. BUT IT WASN'T A CORPSE. . . .
IT WAS A BABY MOUNTAIN LION.
SUDDENLY, A SECOND CUB APPEARED. SERAFINA WATCHED THEM PLAY IN THE GLADE. SHE'D ALWAYS LOVED KITTENS.
WHEN THE CUBS SPOTTED HER, SHE THOUGHT THEY'D RUN AWAY. BUT THEY DIDN'T.
ONE AMBLED TOWARD HER AS I[redacted]T DIDN'T HAVE A CARE IN THE WORLD. SERAFINA SMILED, PLEASED THAT THE CUB DIDN'T FEAR HER.
WHAT ARE YOU SWEET BABIES DOING HERE?
THEN SHE SENSED SEVERE DANGER. SHE TURNED AND SAW SOMETHING EMERGING FROM THE MIST. AT FIRST, SERAFINA THOUGHT IT WAS A GHOST.
THEN SH[redacted]REALIZED IT WASN[redacted] A GHOST AT ALL.
IT WAS SOLID, AND IT WAS RUNNING. FAST. ***STRAIGHT TOWARD HER.***

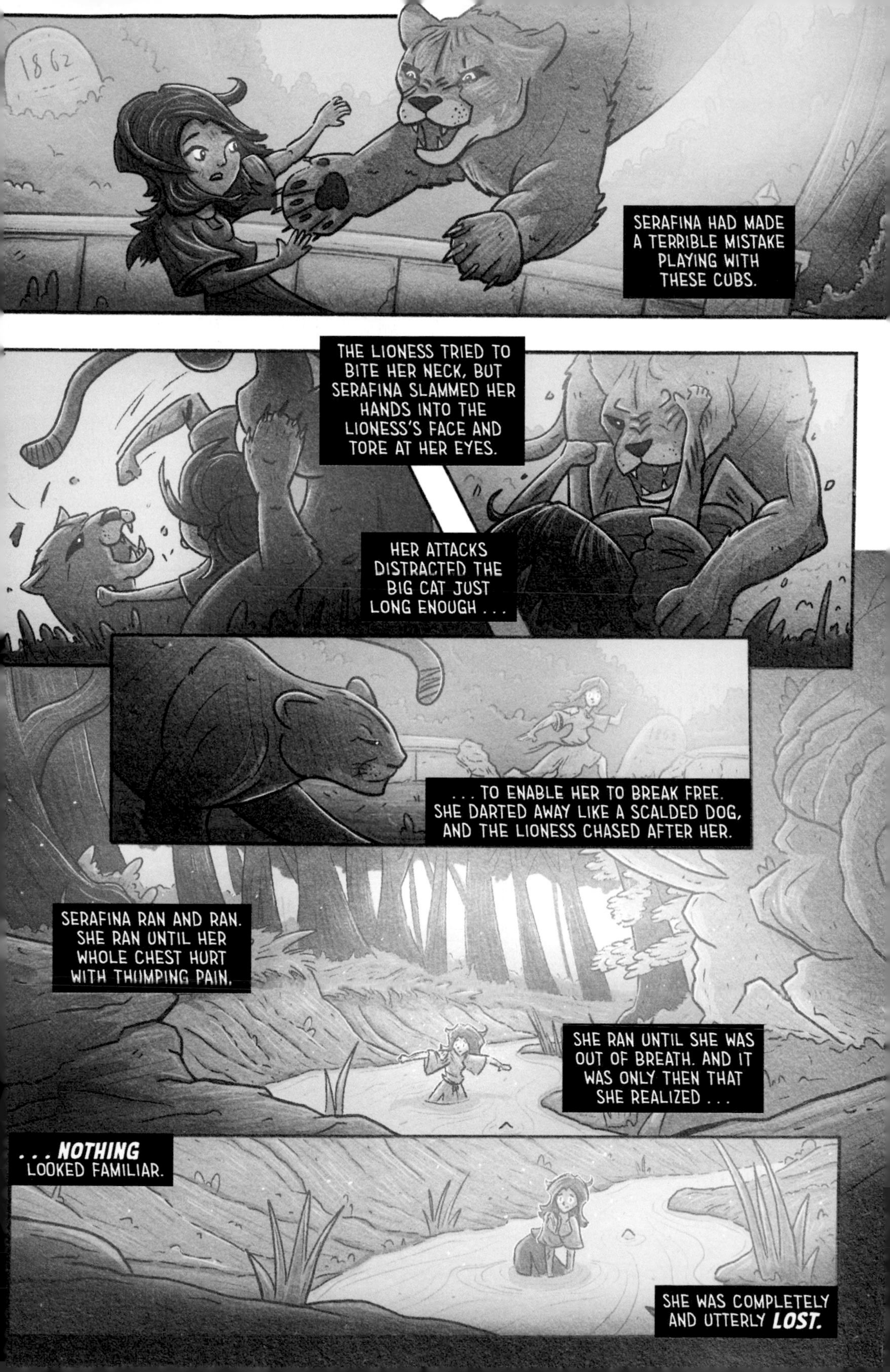
1862
SERAFINA HAD MADE A TERRIBLE MISTAKE PLAYING WITH THESE CUBS.
THE LIONESS TRIED TO BITE HER NECK, BUT SERAFINA SLAMMED HER HANDS INTO THE LIONESS'S FACE AND TORE AT HER EYES.
HER ATTACKS DISTRACTED THE BIG CAT JUST LONG ENOUGH . . .
. . . TO ENABLE HER TO BREAK FREE. SHE DARTED AWAY LIKE A SCALDED DOG, AND THE LIONESS CHASED AFTER HER.
SERAFINA RAN AND RAN. SHE RAN UNTIL HER WHOLE CHEST HURT WITH THUMPING PAIN.
SHE RAN UNTIL SHE WAS OUT OF BREATH. AND IT WAS ONLY THEN THAT SHE REALIZED . . .
. . . NOTHING LOOKED FAMILIAR.
SHE WAS COMPLETELY AND UTTERLY LOST.

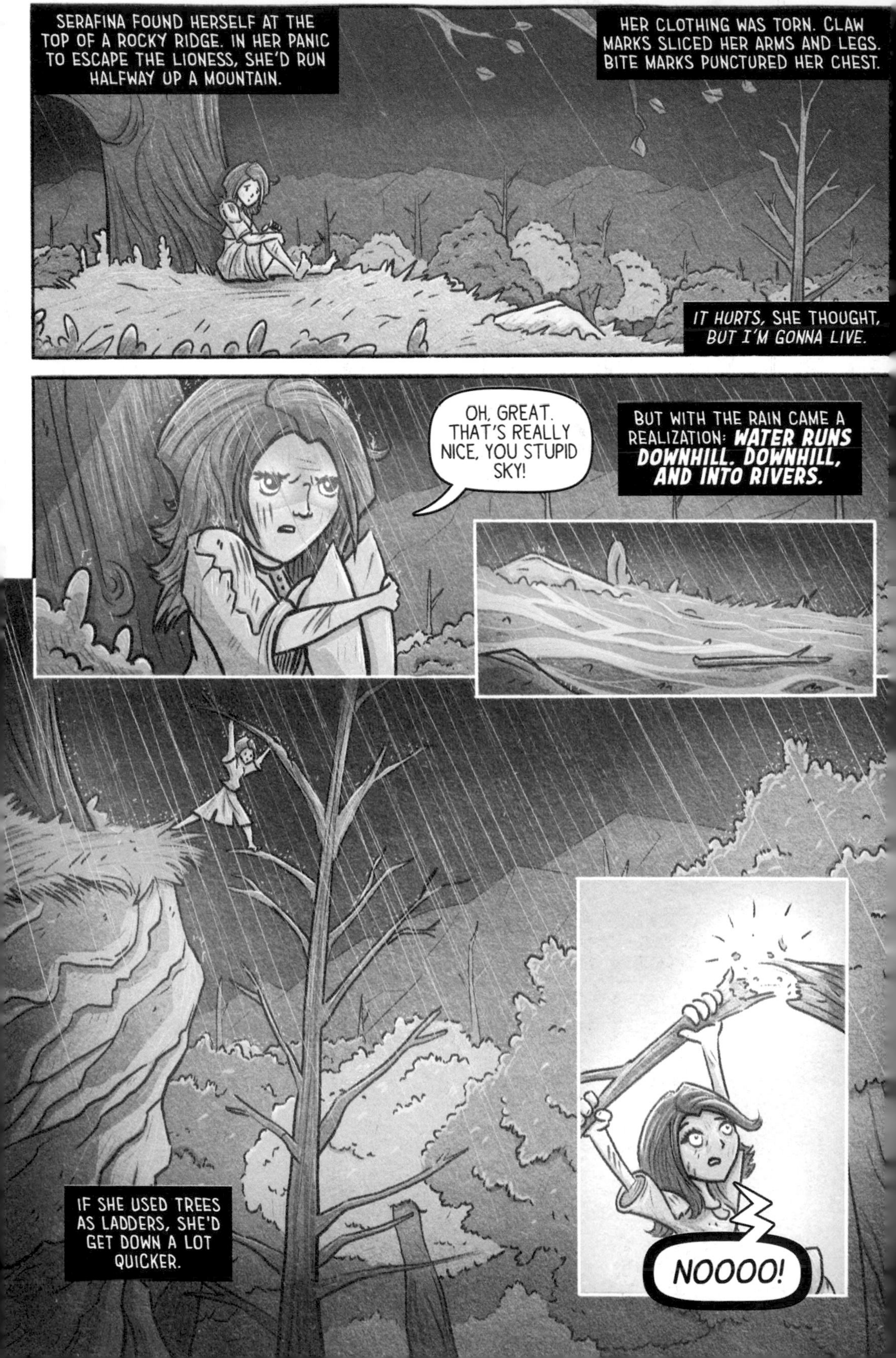
SERAFINA FOUND HERSELF AT THE TOP OF A ROCKY RIDGE. IN HER PANIC TO ESCAPE THE LIONESS, SHE'D RUN HALFWAY UP A MOUNTAIN.
HER CLOTHING WAS TORN. CLAW MARKS SLICED HER ARMS AND LEGS. BITE MARKS PUNCTURED HER CHEST.
IT HURTS, SHE THOUGHT, BUT I'M GONNA LIVE.
OH, GREAT. THAT'S REALLY NICE, YOU STUPID SKY!
BUT WITH THE RAIN CAME A REALIZATION: ***WATER RUNS DOWNHILL. DOWNHILL, AND INTO RIVERS.***
IF SHE USED TREES AS LADDERS, SHE'D GET DOWN A LOT QUICKER.
NOOOO!

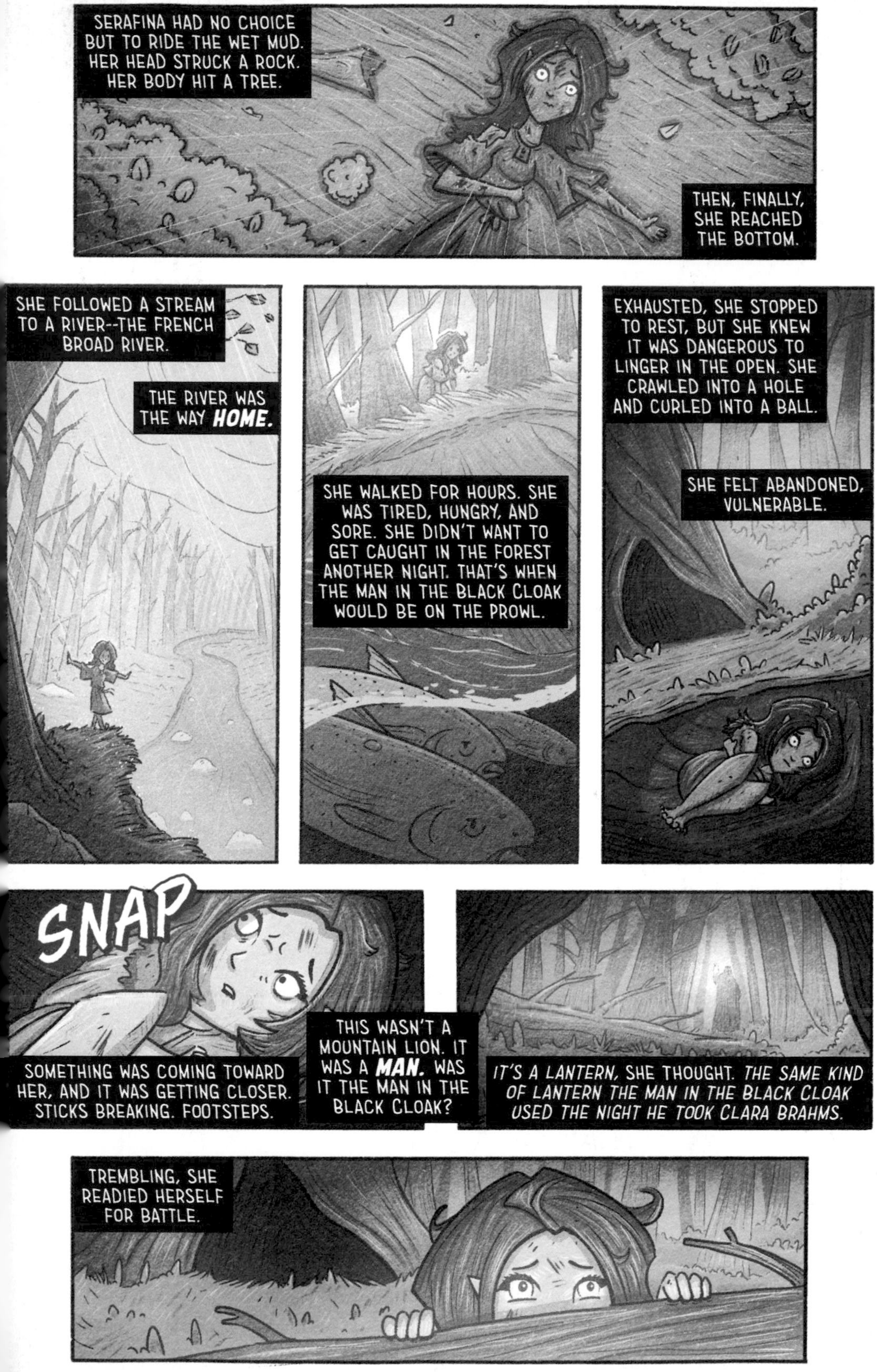
SERAFINA HAD NO CHOICE BUT TO RIDE THE WET MUD. HER HEAD STRUCK A ROCK. HER BODY HIT A TREE.
THEN, FINALLY, SHE REACHED THE BOTTOM.
SHE FOLLOWED A STREAM TO A RIVER--THE FRENCH BROAD RIVER.
THE RIVER WAS THE WAY **HOME.**
SHE WALKED FOR HOURS. SHE WAS TIRED, HUNGRY, AND SORE. SHE DIDN'T WANT TO GET CAUGHT IN THE FOREST ANOTHER NIGHT. THAT'S WHEN THE MAN IN THE BLACK CLOAK WOULD BE ON THE PROWL.
EXHAUSTED, SHE STOPPED TO REST, BUT SHE KNEW IT WAS DANGEROUS TO LINGER IN THE OPEN. SHE CRAWLED INTO A HOLE AND CURLED INTO A BALL.
SHE FELT ABANDONED, VULNERABLE.
SNAP
SOMETHING WAS COMING TOWARD HER, AND IT WAS GETTING CLOSER. STICKS BREAKING. FOOTSTEPS.
THIS WASN'T A MOUNTAIN LION. IT WAS A **MAN.** WAS IT THE MAN IN THE BLACK CLOAK?
IT'S A LANTERN, SHE THOUGHT. *THE SAME KIND OF LANTERN THE MAN IN THE BLACK CLOAK USED THE NIGHT HE TOOK CLARA BRAHMS.*
TREMBLING, SHE READIED HERSELF FOR BATTLE.

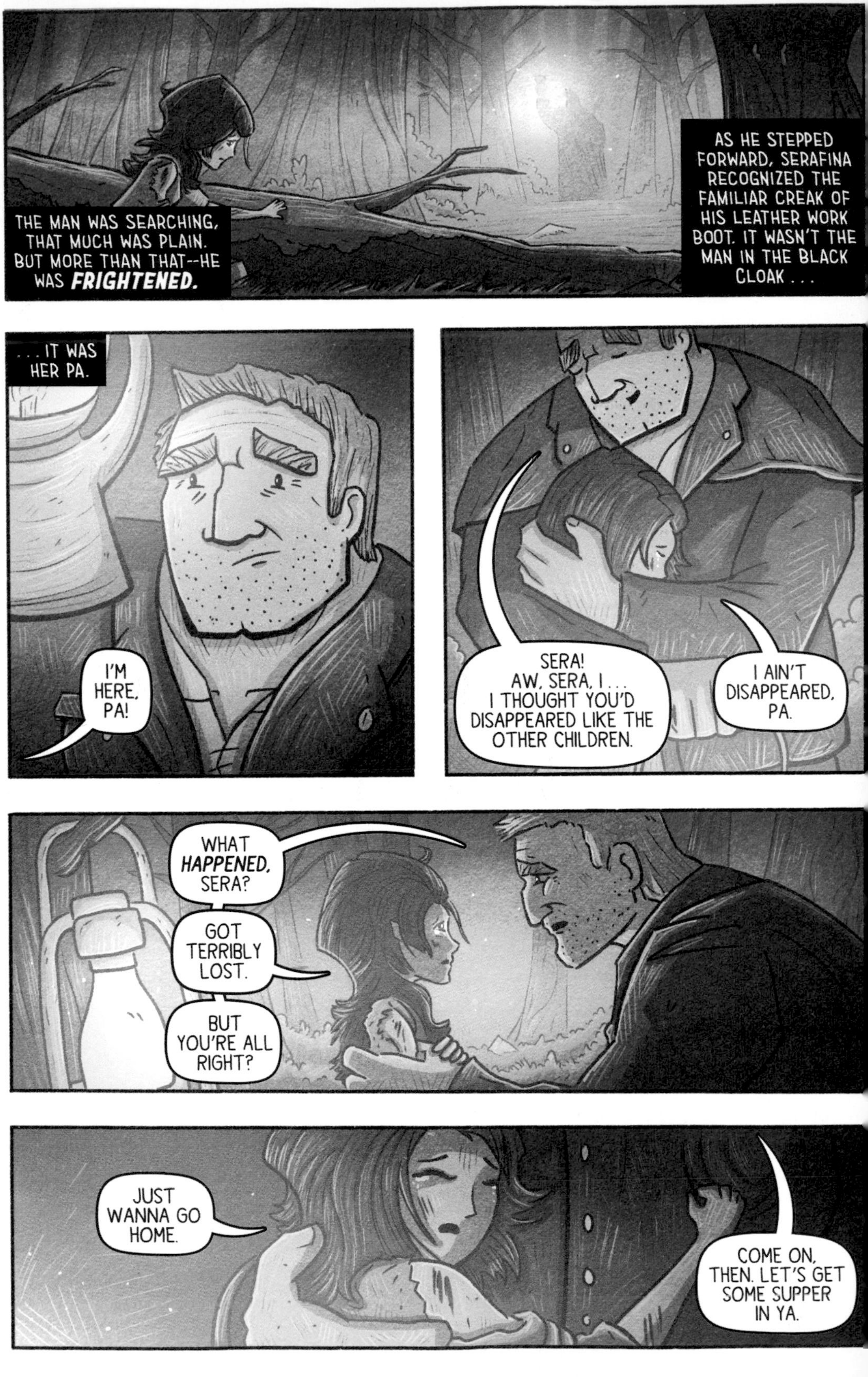
THE MAN WAS SEARCHING, THAT MUCH WAS PLAIN. BUT MORE THAN THAT--HE WAS FRIGHTENED.
AS HE STEPPED FORWARD, SERAFINA RECOGNIZED THE FAMILIAR CREAK OF HIS LEATHER WORK BOOT. IT WASN'T THE MAN IN THE BLACK CLOAK . . .
. . . IT WAS HER PA.
I'M HERE, PA!
SERA! AW, SERA, I . . . I THOUGHT YOU'D DISAPPEARED LIKE THE OTHER CHILDREN.
I AIN'T DISAPPEARED, PA.
WHAT HAPPENED, SERA?
GOT TERRIBLY LOST.
BUT YOU'RE ALL RIGHT?
JUST WANNA GO HOME.
COME ON, THEN. LET'S GET SOME SUPPER IN YA.

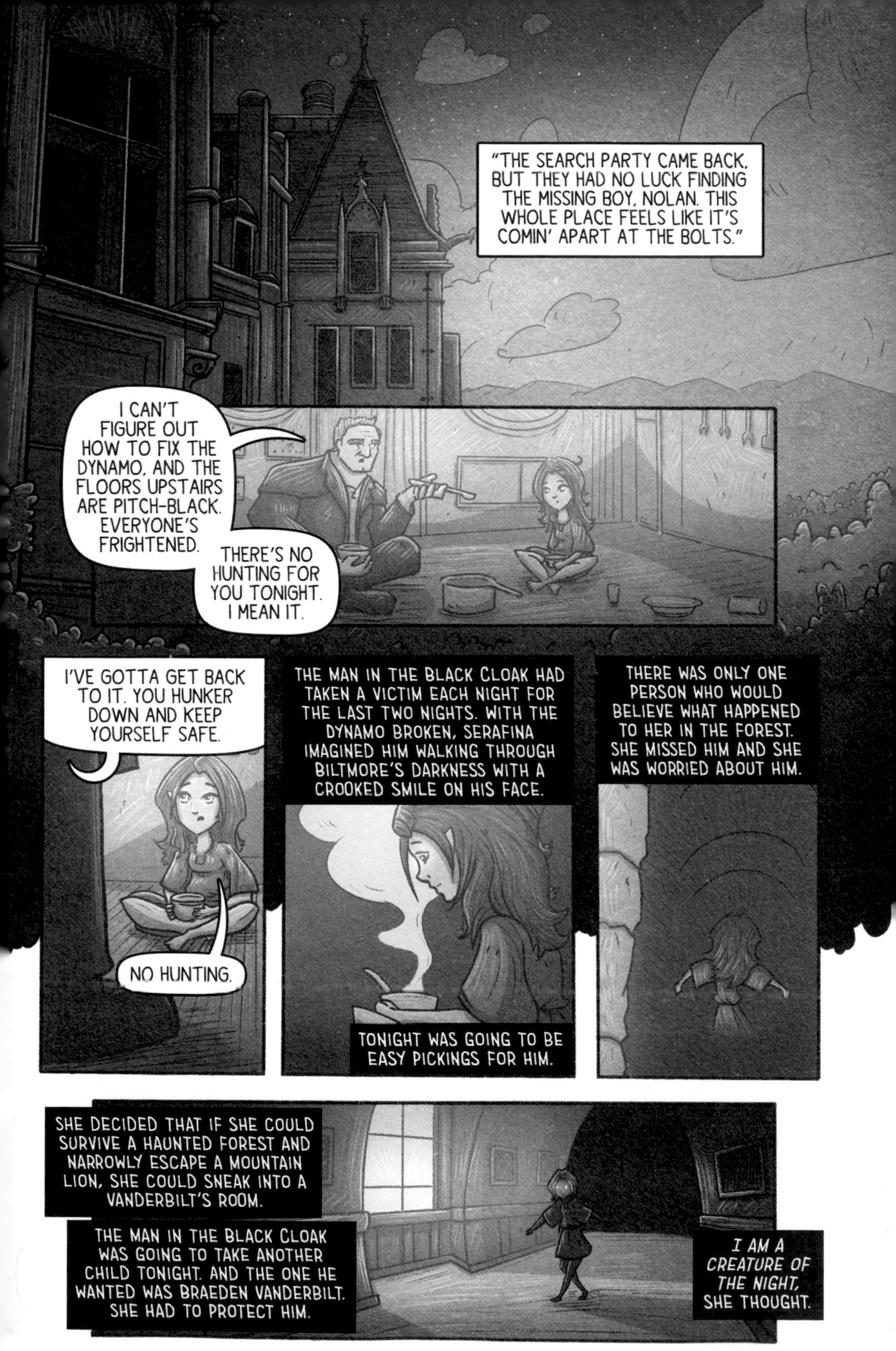
"THE SEARCH PARTY CAME BACK, BUT THEY HAD NO LUCK FINDING THE MISSING BOY, NOLAN. THIS WHOLE PLACE FEELS LIKE IT'S COMIN' APART AT THE BOLTS."
I CAN'T FIGURE OUT HOW TO FIX THE DYNAMO, AND THE FLOORS UPSTAIRS ARE PITCH-BLACK. EVERYONE'S FRIGHTENED.
THERE'S NO HUNTING FOR YOU TONIGHT. I MEAN IT.
I'VE GOTTA GET BACK TO IT. YOU HUNKER DOWN AND KEEP YOURSELF SAFE.
NO HUNTING.
THE MAN IN THE BLACK CLOAK HAD TAKEN A VICTIM EACH NIGHT FOR THE LAST TWO NIGHTS. WITH THE DYNAMO BROKEN, SERAFINA IMAGINED HIM WALKING THROUGH BILTMORE'S DARKNESS WITH A CROOKED SMILE ON HIS FACE.
TONIGHT WAS GOING TO BE EASY PICKINGS FOR HIM.
THERE WAS ONLY ONE PERSON WHO WOULD BELIEVE WHAT HAPPENED TO HER IN THE FOREST. SHE MISSED HIM AND SHE WAS WORRIED ABOUT HIM.
SHE DECIDED THAT IF SHE COULD SURVIVE A HAUNTED FOREST AND NARROWLY ESCAPE A MOUNTAIN LION, SHE COULD SNEAK INTO A VANDERBILT'S ROOM.
THE MAN IN THE BLACK CLOAK WAS GOING TO TAKE ANOTHER CHILD TONIGHT. AND THE ONE HE WANTED WAS BRAEDEN VANDERBILT. SHE HAD TO PROTECT HIM.
I AM A CREATURE OF THE NIGHT, SHE THOUGHT.

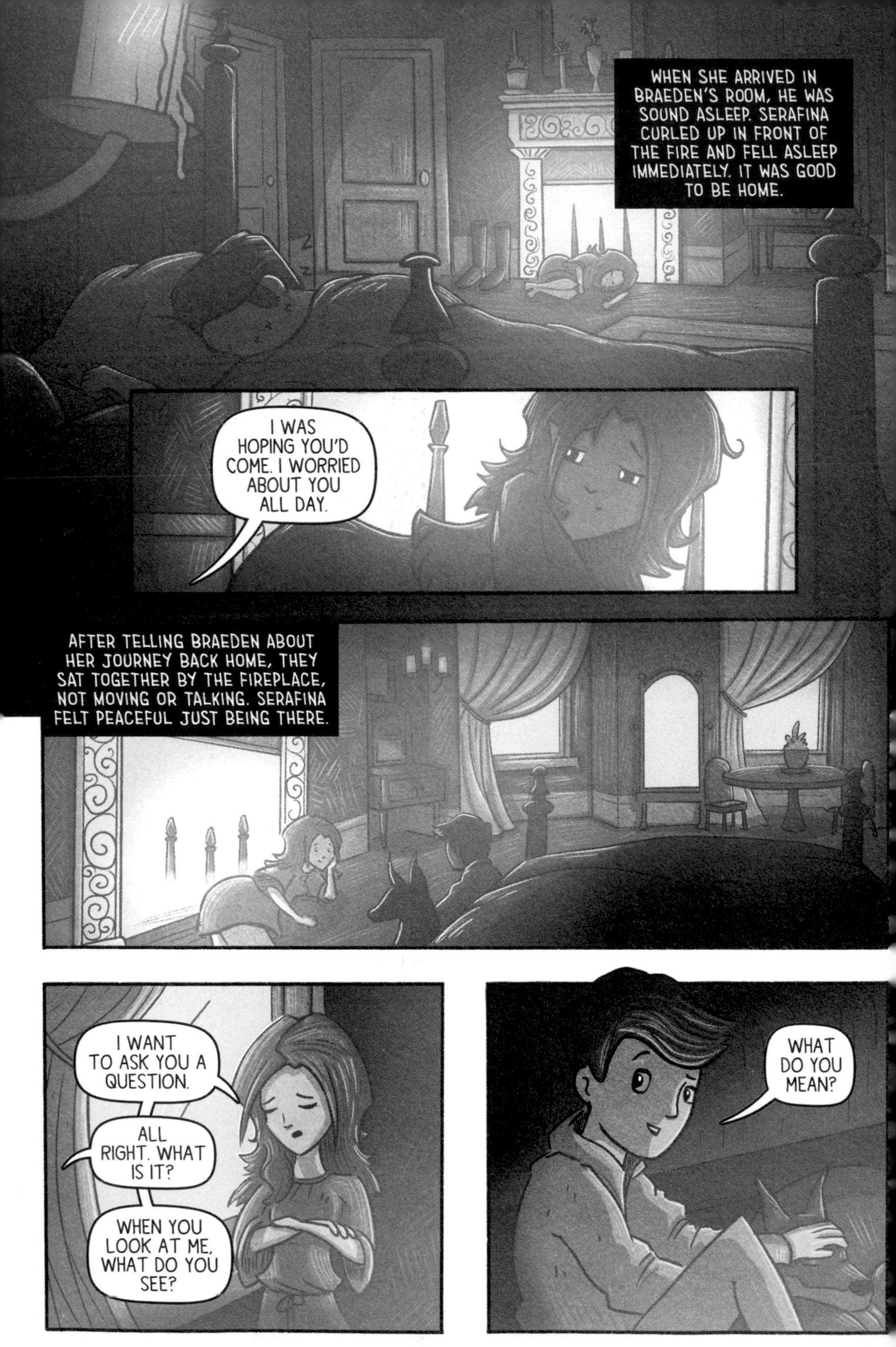
WHEN SHE ARRIVED IN BRAEDEN'S ROOM, HE WAS SOUND ASLEEP. SERAFINA CURLED UP IN FRONT OF THE FIRE AND FELL ASLEEP IMMEDIATELY. IT WAS GOOD TO BE HOME.
I WAS HOPING YOU'D COME. I WORRIED ABOUT YOU ALL DAY.
AFTER TELLING BRAEDEN ABOUT HER JOURNEY BACK HOME, THEY SAT TOGETHER BY THE FIREPLACE, NOT MOVING OR TALKING. SERAFINA FELT PEACEFUL JUST BEING THERE.
I WANT TO ASK YOU A QUESTION.
ALL RIGHT. WHAT IS IT?
WHEN YOU LOOK AT ME, WHAT DO YOU SEE?
WHAT DO YOU MEAN?

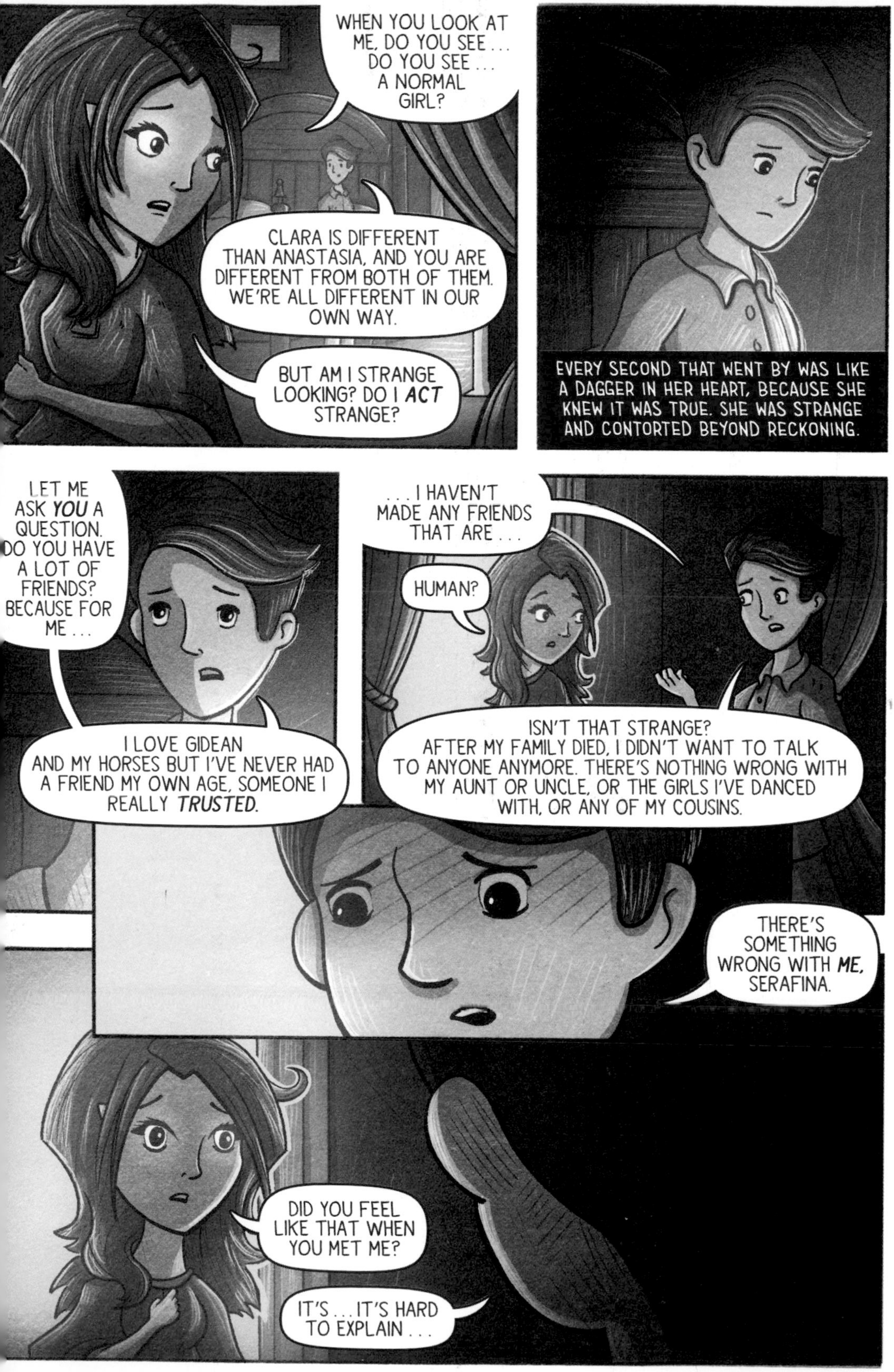
WHEN YOU LOOK AT ME, DO YOU SEE . . . DO YOU SEE . . . A NORMAL GIRL?
CLARA IS DIFFERENT THAN ANASTASIA, AND YOU ARE DIFFERENT FROM BOTH OF THEM. WE'RE ALL DIFFERENT IN OUR OWN WAY.
BUT AM I STRANGE LOOKING? DO I *ACT* STRANGE?
EVERY SECOND THAT WENT BY WAS LIKE A DAGGER IN HER HEART, BECAUSE SHE KNEW IT WAS TRUE. SHE WAS STRANGE AND CONTORTED BEYOND RECKONING.
LET ME ASK *YOU* A QUESTION. DO YOU HAVE A LOT OF FRIENDS? BECAUSE FOR ME . . .
I LOVE GIDEAN AND MY HORSES BUT I'VE NEVER HAD A FRIEND MY OWN AGE, SOMEONE I REALLY *TRUSTED*.
. . . I HAVEN'T MADE ANY FRIENDS THAT ARE . . .
HUMAN?
ISN'T THAT STRANGE? AFTER MY FAMILY DIED, I DIDN'T WANT TO TALK TO ANYONE ANYMORE. THERE'S NOTHING WRONG WITH MY AUNT OR UNCLE, OR THE GIRLS I'VE DANCED WITH, OR ANY OF MY COUSINS.
THERE'S SOMETHING WRONG WITH *ME*, SERAFINA.
DID YOU FEEL LIKE THAT WHEN YOU MET ME?
IT'S . . . IT'S HARD TO EXPLAIN . . .

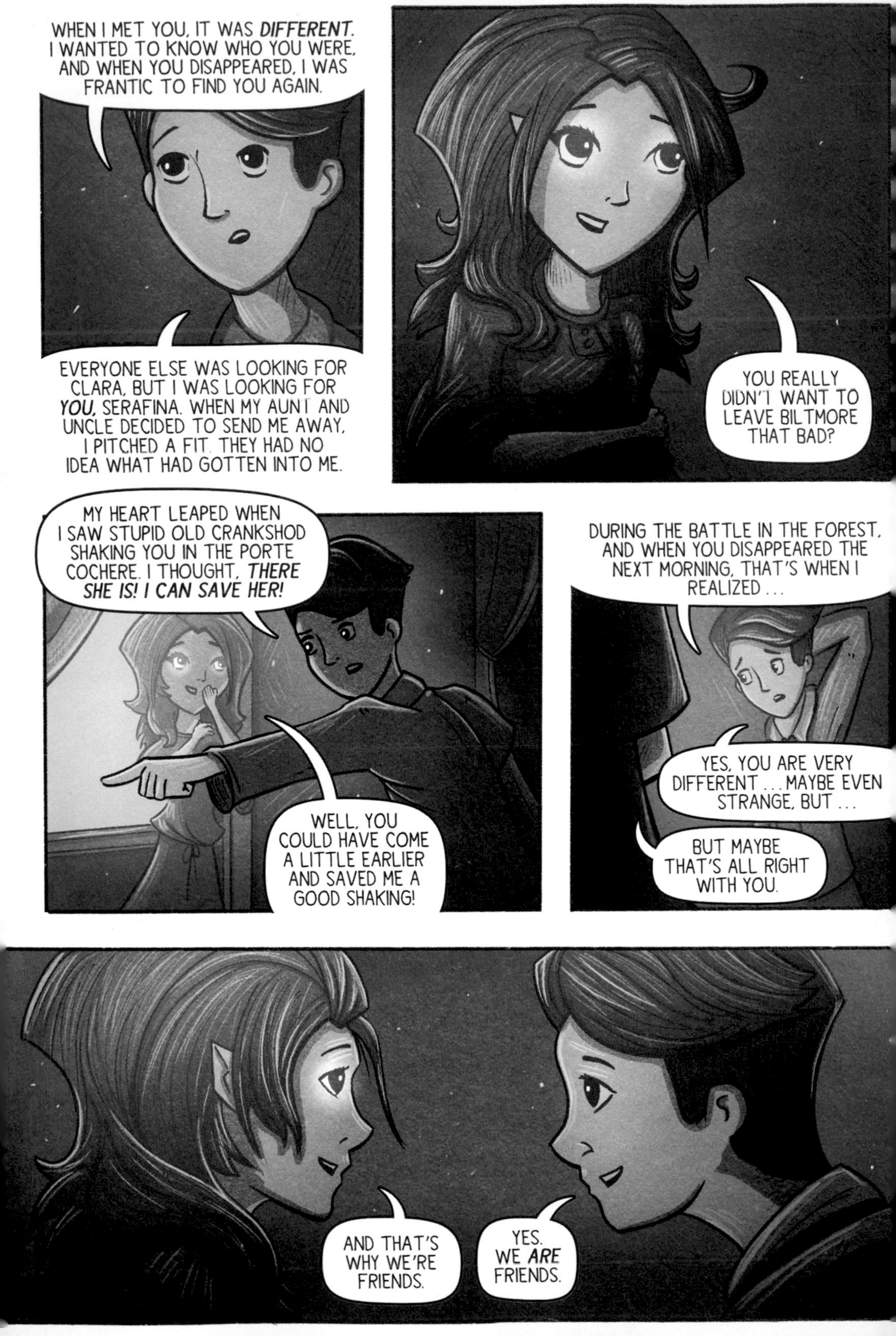

WHEN I MET YOU, IT WAS *DIFFERENT*. I WANTED TO KNOW WHO YOU WERE, AND WHEN YOU DISAPPEARED, I WAS FRANTIC TO FIND YOU AGAIN.
EVERYONE ELSE WAS LOOKING FOR CLARA, BUT I WAS LOOKING FOR *YOU,* SERAFINA. WHEN MY AUNT AND UNCLE DECIDED TO SEND ME AWAY, I PITCHED A FIT. THEY HAD NO IDEA WHAT HAD GOTTEN INTO ME.
YOU REALLY DIDN'T WANT TO LEAVE BILTMORE THAT BAD?
MY HEART LEAPED WHEN I SAW STUPID OLD CRANKSHOD SHAKING YOU IN THE PORTE COCHERE. I THOUGHT, *THERE SHE IS! I CAN SAVE HER!*
WELL, YOU COULD HAVE COME A LITTLE EARLIER AND SAVED ME A GOOD SHAKING!
DURING THE BATTLE IN THE FOREST, AND WHEN YOU DISAPPEARED THE NEXT MORNING, THAT'S WHEN I REALIZED . . .
YES, YOU ARE VERY DIFFERENT . . . MAYBE EVEN STRANGE, BUT . . .
BUT MAYBE THAT'S ALL RIGHT WITH YOU.
AND THAT'S WHY WE'RE FRIENDS.
YES. WE *ARE* FRIENDS.

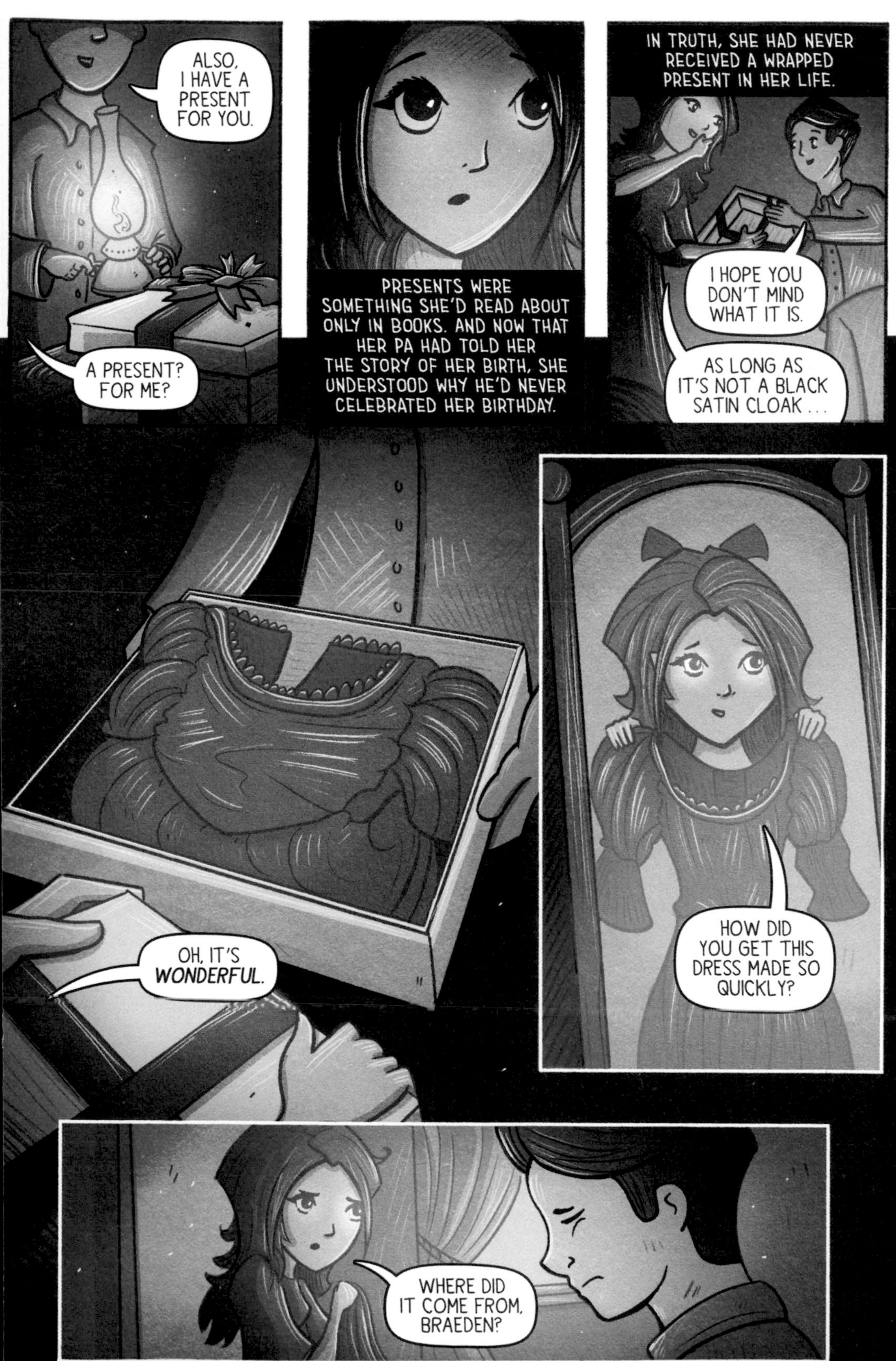
ALSO, I HAVE A PRESENT FOR YOU.
A PRESENT? FOR ME?
PRESENTS WERE SOMETHING SHE'D READ ABOUT ONLY IN BOOKS. AND NOW THAT HER PA HAD TOLD HER THE STORY OF HER BIRTH, SHE UNDERSTOOD WHY HE'D NEVER CELEBRATED HER BIRTHDAY.
IN TRUTH, SHE HAD NEVER RECEIVED A WRAPPED PRESENT IN HER LIFE.
I HOPE YOU DON'T MIND WHAT IT IS.
AS LONG AS IT'S NOT A BLACK SATIN CLOAK . . .
OH, IT'S *WONDERFUL.*
HOW DID YOU GET THIS DRESS MADE SO QUICKLY?
WHERE DID IT COME FROM, BRAEDEN?

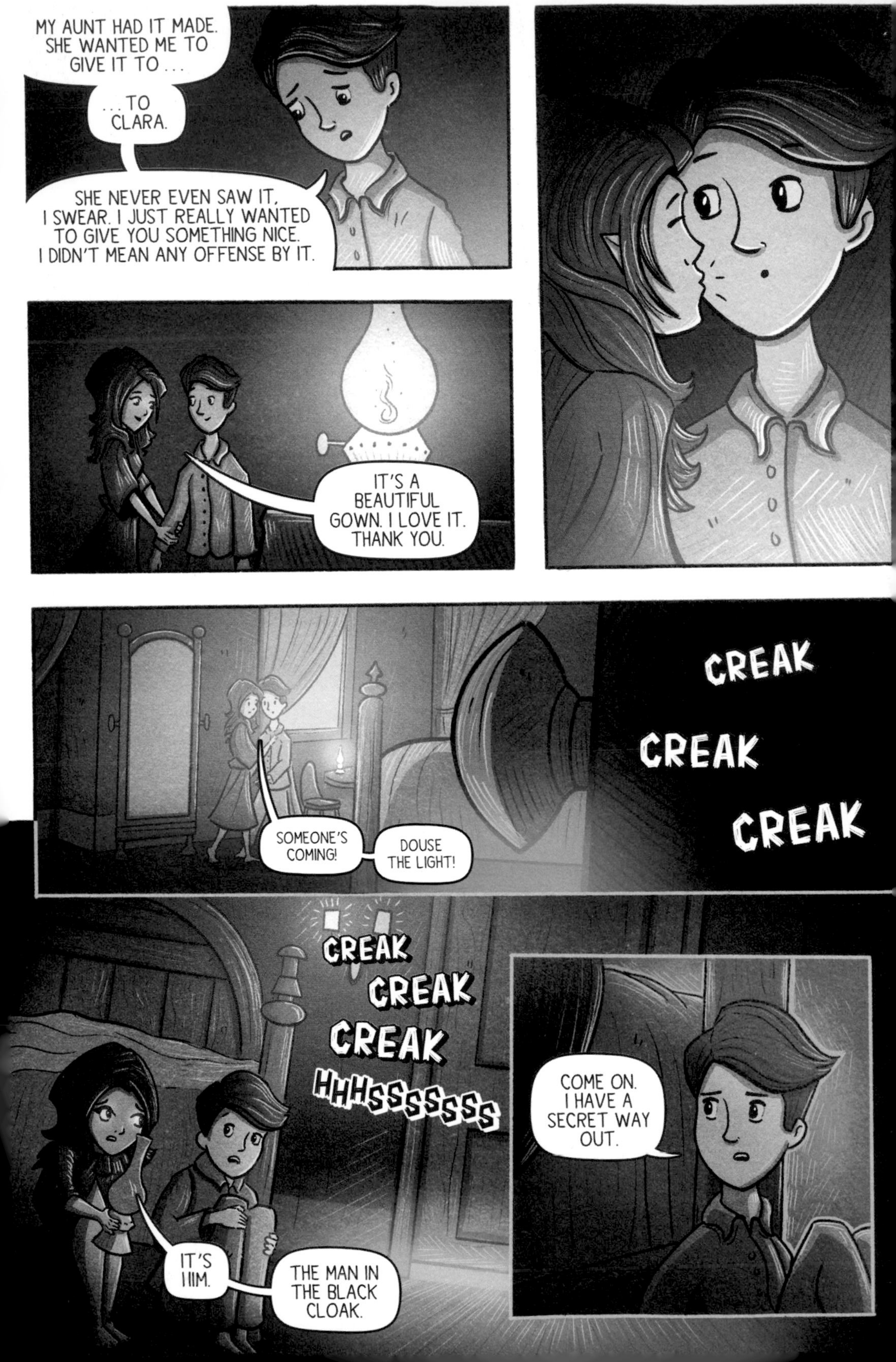
MY AUNT HAD IT MADE. SHE WANTED ME TO GIVE IT TO . . .
. . . TO CLARA.
SHE NEVER EVEN SAW IT, I SWEAR. I JUST REALLY WANTED TO GIVE YOU SOMETHING NICE. I DIDN'T MEAN ANY OFFENSE BY IT.
IT'S A BEAUTIFUL GOWN. I LOVE IT. THANK YOU.
SOMEONE'S COMING!
DOUSE THE LIGHT!
CREAK
CREAK
CREAK
CREAK
CREAK
CREAK
HHHSSSSSSS
IT'S HIM.
THE MAN IN THE BLACK CLOAK.
COME ON. I HAVE A SECRET WAY OUT.

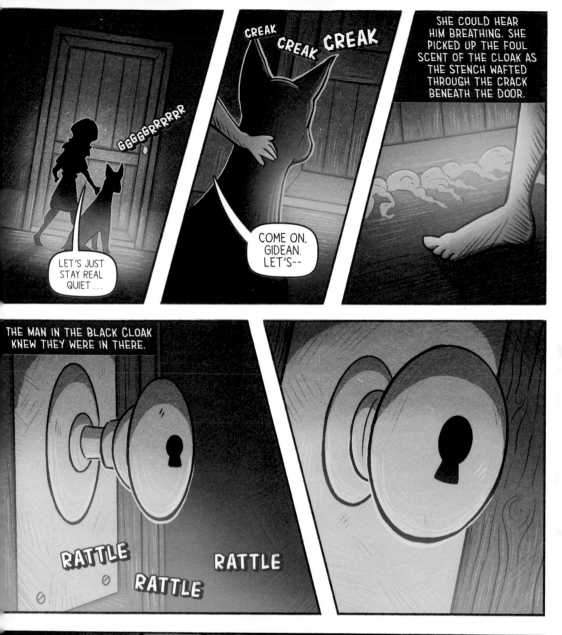

GGGGGRRRRR

LET'S JUST STAY REAL QUIET...

CREAK CREAK CREAK

COME ON, GIDEAN. LET'S--

SHE COULD HEAR HIM BREATHING. SHE PICKED UP THE FOUL SCENT OF THE CLOAK AS THE STENCH WAFTED THROUGH THE CRACK BENEATH THE DOOR.

THE MAN IN THE BLACK CLOAK KNEW THEY WERE IN THERE.

RATTLE

RATTLE

RATTLE

SERAFINA HAD LOCKED THE DOOR WHEN SHE CAME IN. AFTER SEVERAL SECONDS THEY HEARD THE FOOTSTEPS RESUME, RECEDING DOWN THE HALLWAY.

THAT... WAS A *CLOSE* ONE.

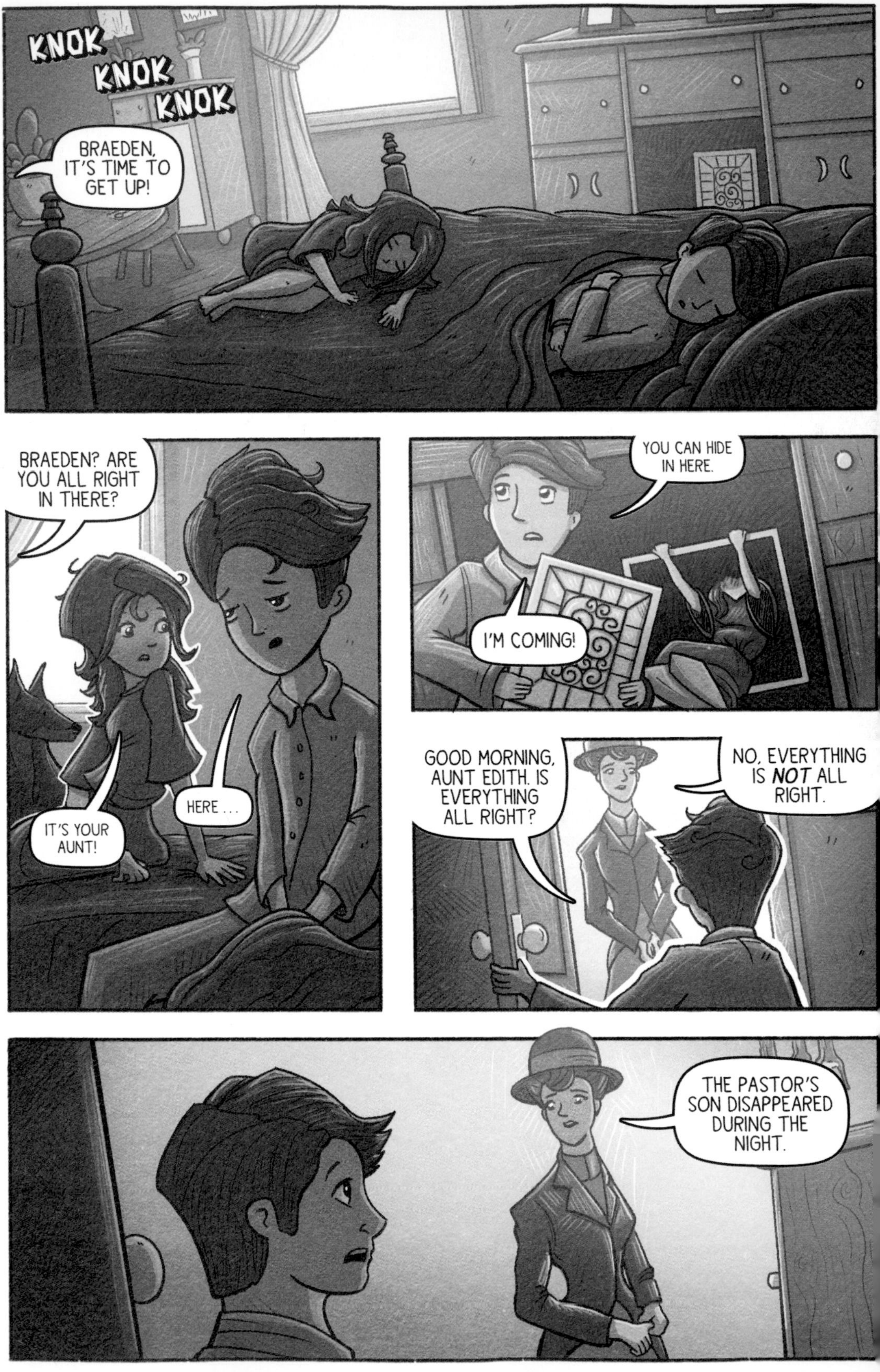
KNOK KNOK KNOK
BRAEDEN, IT'S TIME TO GET UP!
BRAEDEN? ARE YOU ALL RIGHT IN THERE?
IT'S YOUR AUNT!
HERE . . .
YOU CAN HIDE IN HERE.
I'M COMING!
GOOD MORNING, AUNT EDITH. IS EVERYTHING ALL RIGHT?
NO, EVERYTHING IS **NOT** ALL RIGHT.
THE PASTOR'S SON DISAPPEARED DURING THE NIGHT.

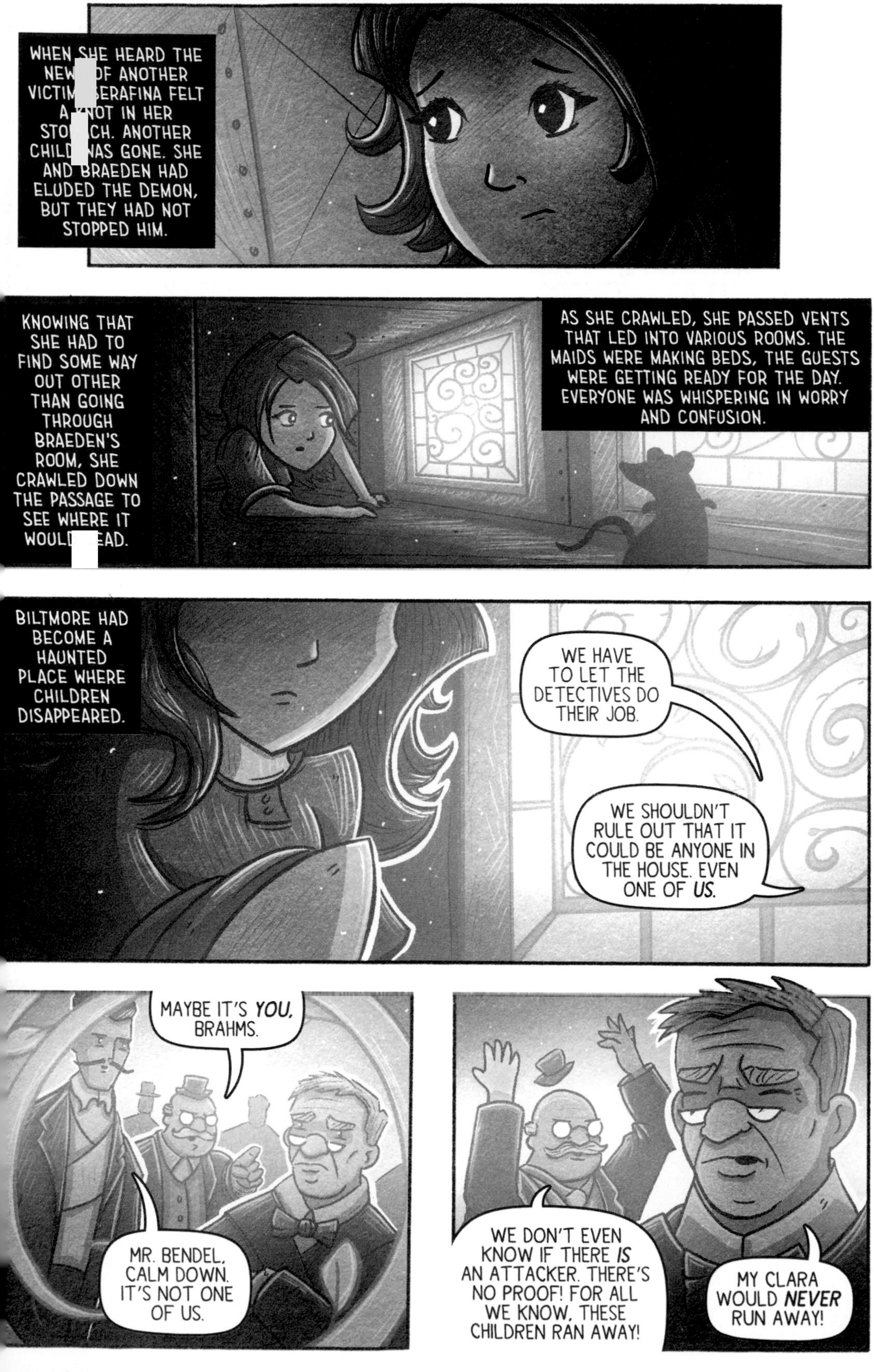
WHEN SHE HEARD THE NEWS OF ANOTHER VICTIM, SERAFINA FELT A KNOT IN HER STOMACH. ANOTHER CHILD WAS GONE. SHE AND BRAEDEN HAD ELUDED THE DEMON, BUT THEY HAD NOT STOPPED HIM.
KNOWING THAT SHE HAD TO FIND SOME WAY OUT OTHER THAN GOING THROUGH BRAEDEN'S ROOM, SHE CRAWLED DOWN THE PASSAGE TO SEE WHERE IT WOULD LEAD.
AS SHE CRAWLED, SHE PASSED VENTS THAT LED INTO VARIOUS ROOMS. THE MAIDS WERE MAKING BEDS, THE GUESTS WERE GETTING READY FOR THE DAY. EVERYONE WAS WHISPERING IN WORRY AND CONFUSION.
BILTMORE HAD BECOME A HAUNTED PLACE WHERE CHILDREN DISAPPEARED.
WE HAVE TO LET THE DETECTIVES DO THEIR JOB.
WE SHOULDN'T RULE OUT THAT IT COULD BE ANYONE IN THE HOUSE. EVEN ONE OF *US*.
MAYBE IT'S *YOU*, BRAHMS.
MR. BENDEL, CALM DOWN. IT'S NOT ONE OF US.
WE DON'T EVEN KNOW IF THERE *IS* AN ATTACKER. THERE'S NO PROOF! FOR ALL WE KNOW, THESE CHILDREN RAN AWAY!
MY CLARA WOULD *NEVER* RUN AWAY!

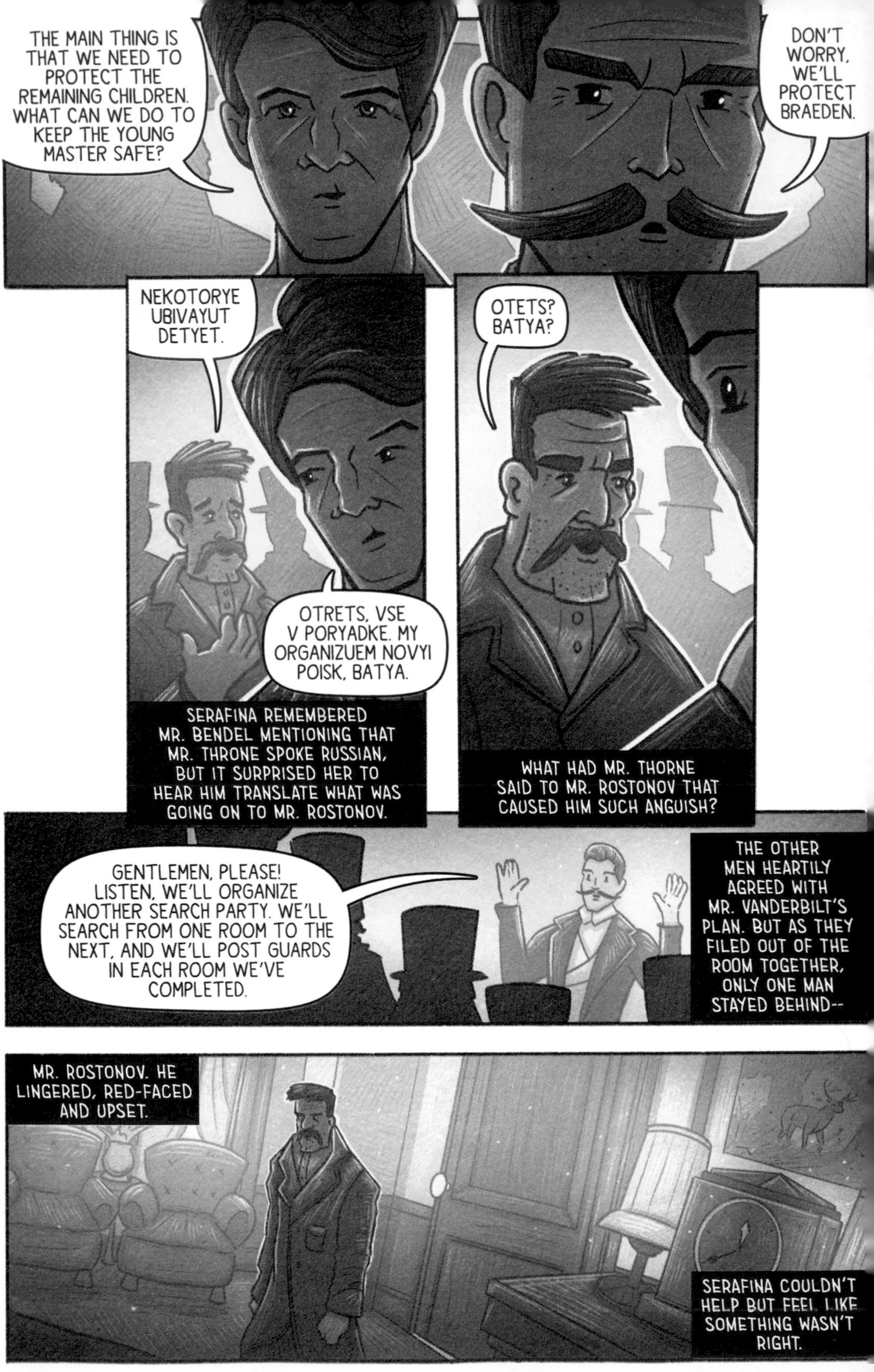
THE MAIN THING IS THAT WE NEED TO PROTECT THE REMAINING CHILDREN. WHAT CAN WE DO TO KEEP THE YOUNG MASTER SAFE?
DON'T WORRY, WE'LL PROTECT BRAEDEN.
NEKOTORYE UBIVAYUT DETYET.
OTRETS, VSE V PORYADKE. MY ORGANIZUEM NOVYI POISK, BATYA.
SERAFINA REMEMBERED MR. BENDEL MENTIONING THAT MR. THRONE SPOKE RUSSIAN, BUT IT SURPRISED HER TO HEAR HIM TRANSLATE WHAT WAS GOING ON TO MR. ROSTONOV.
OTETS? BATYA?
WHAT HAD MR. THORNE SAID TO MR. ROSTONOV THAT CAUSED HIM SUCH ANGUISH?
GENTLEMEN, PLEASE! LISTEN, WE'LL ORGANIZE ANOTHER SEARCH PARTY. WE'LL SEARCH FROM ONE ROOM TO THE NEXT, AND WE'LL POST GUARDS IN EACH ROOM WE'VE COMPLETED.
THE OTHER MEN HEARTILY AGREED WITH MR. VANDERBILT'S PLAN. BUT AS THEY FILED OUT OF THE ROOM TOGETHER, ONLY ONE MAN STAYED BEHIND--
MR. ROSTONOV. HE LINGERED, RED-FACED AND UPSET.
SERAFINA COULDN'T HELP BUT FEEL LIKE SOMETHING WASN'T RIGHT.

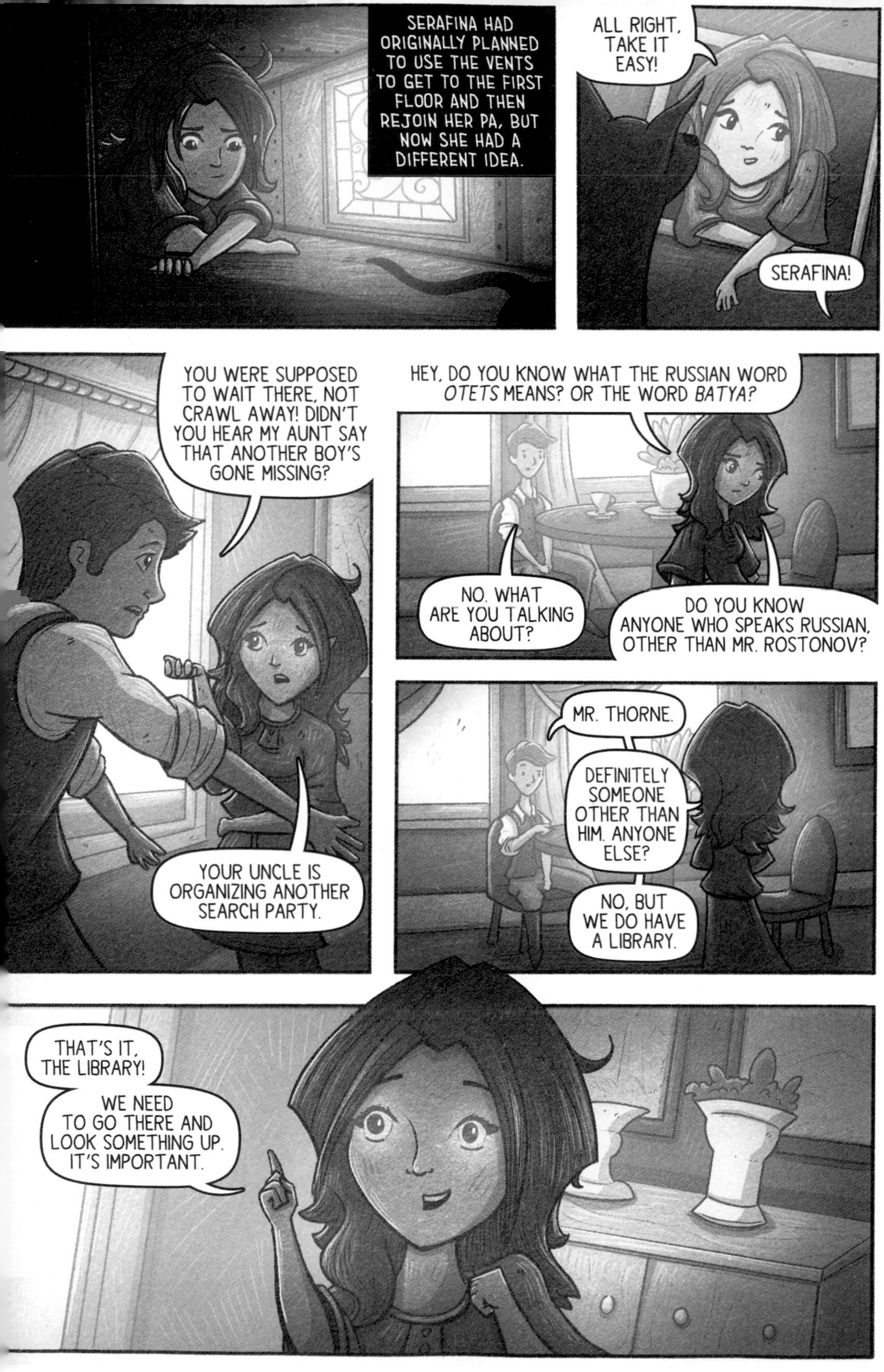
SERAFINA HAD ORIGINALLY PLANNED TO USE THE VENTS TO GET TO THE FIRST FLOOR AND THEN REJOIN HER PA, BUT NOW SHE HAD A DIFFERENT IDEA.
ALL RIGHT, TAKE IT EASY!
SERAFINA!
YOU WERE SUPPOSED TO WAIT THERE, NOT CRAWL AWAY! DIDN'T YOU HEAR MY AUNT SAY THAT ANOTHER BOY'S GONE MISSING?
YOUR UNCLE IS ORGANIZING ANOTHER SEARCH PARTY.
HEY, DO YOU KNOW WHAT THE RUSSIAN WORD *OTETS* MEANS? OR THE WORD *BATYA?*
NO. WHAT ARE YOU TALKING ABOUT?
DO YOU KNOW ANYONE WHO SPEAKS RUSSIAN, OTHER THAN MR. ROSTONOV?
MR. THORNE.
DEFINITELY SOMEONE OTHER THAN HIM. ANYONE ELSE?
NO, BUT WE DO HAVE A LIBRARY.
THAT'S IT, THE LIBRARY!
WE NEED TO GO THERE AND LOOK SOMETHING UP. IT'S IMPORTANT.

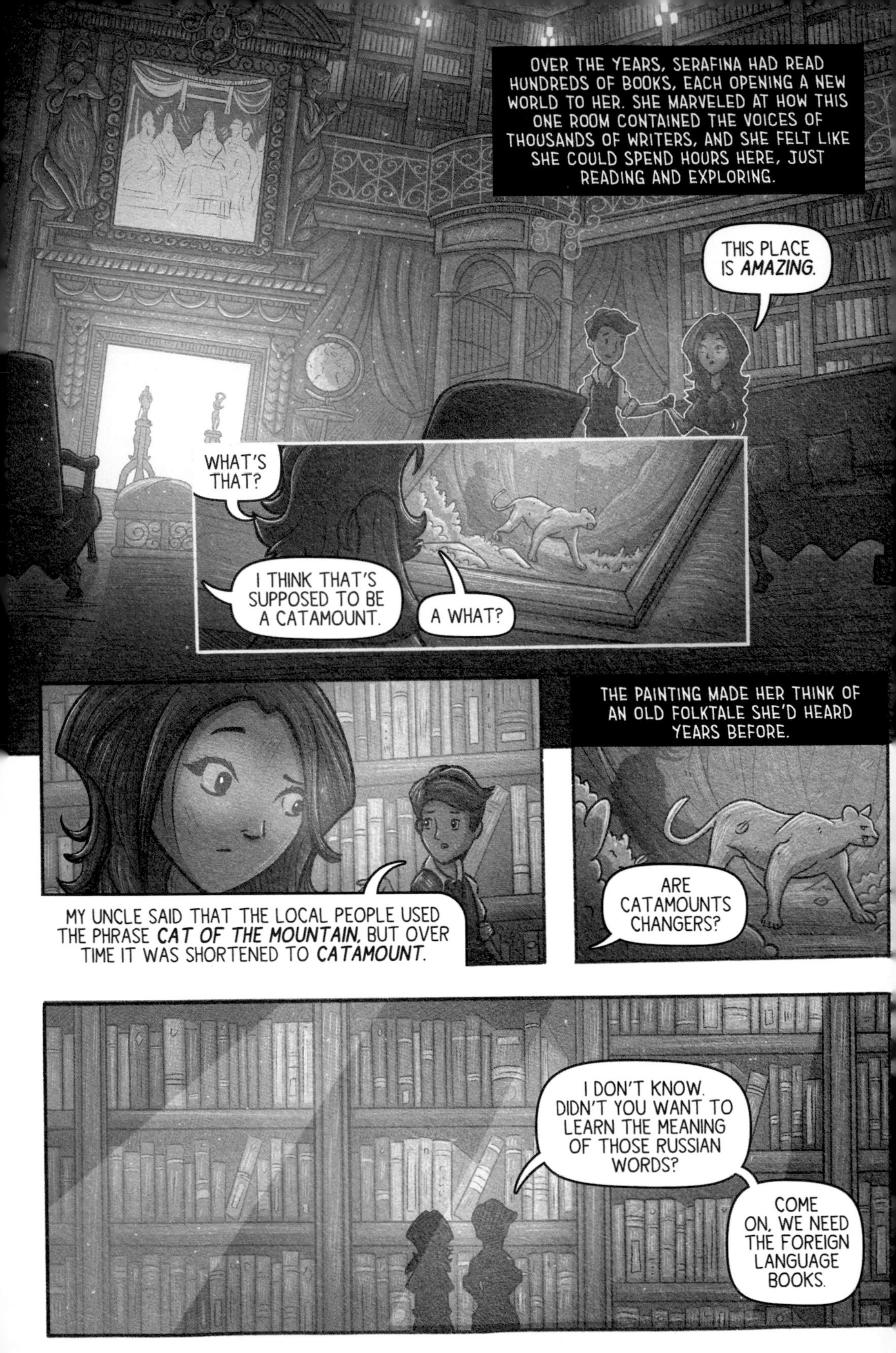

OVER THE YEARS, SERAFINA HAD READ HUNDREDS OF BOOKS, EACH OPENING A NEW WORLD TO HER. SHE MARVELED AT HOW THIS ONE ROOM CONTAINED THE VOICES OF THOUSANDS OF WRITERS, AND SHE FELT LIKE SHE COULD SPEND HOURS HERE, JUST READING AND EXPLORING.
THIS PLACE IS *AMAZING*.
WHAT'S THAT?
I THINK THAT'S SUPPOSED TO BE A CATAMOUNT.
A WHAT?
MY UNCLE SAID THAT THE LOCAL PEOPLE USED THE PHRASE ***CAT OF THE MOUNTAIN,*** BUT OVER TIME IT WAS SHORTENED TO ***CATAMOUNT***.
THE PAINTING MADE HER THINK OF AN OLD FOLKTALE SHE'D HEARD YEARS BEFORE.
ARE CATAMOUNTS CHANGERS?
I DON'T KNOW. DIDN'T YOU WANT TO LEARN THE MEANING OF THOSE RUSSIAN WORDS?
COME ON, WE NEED THE FOREIGN LANGUAGE BOOKS.

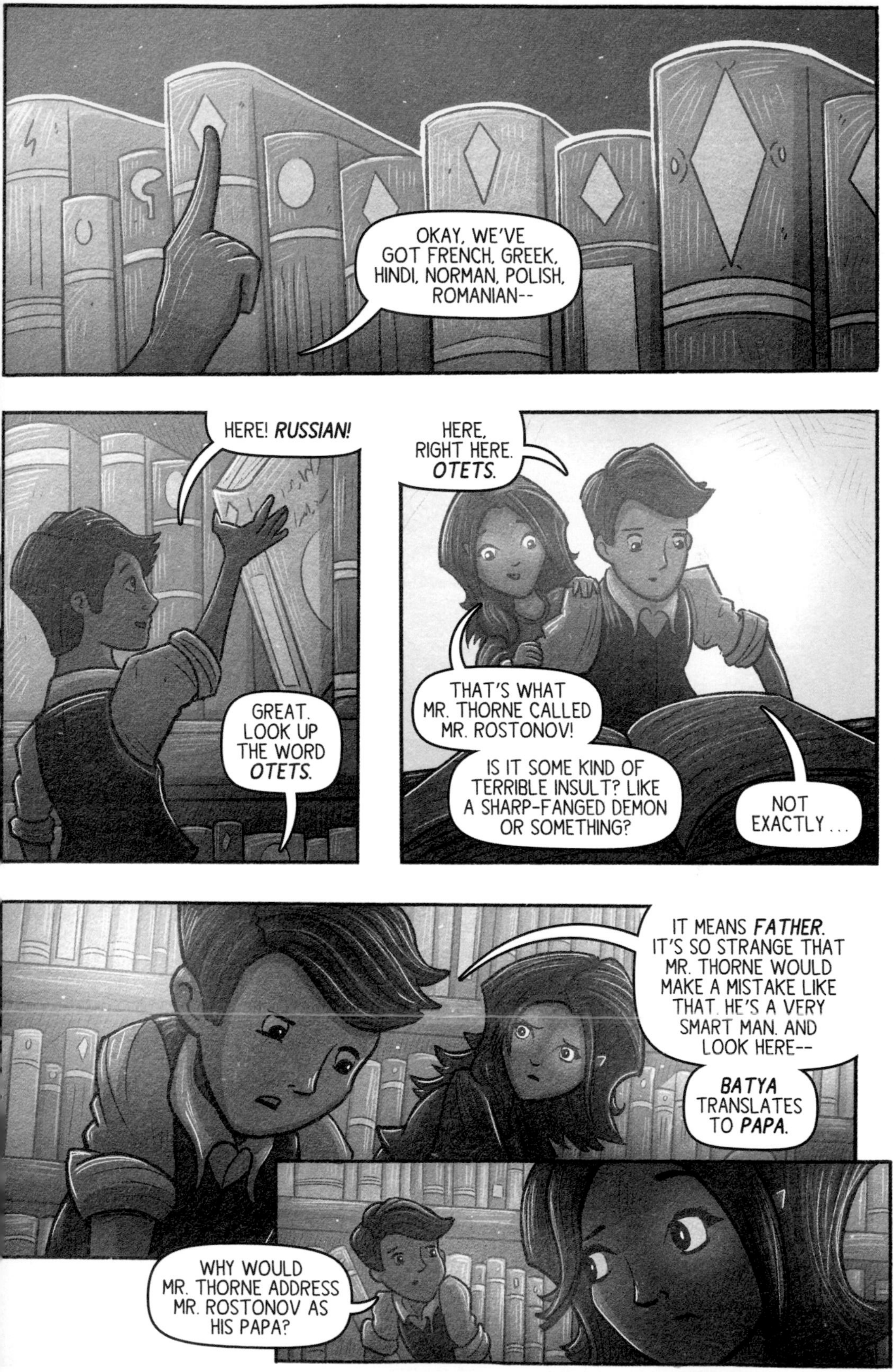
OKAY, WE'VE GOT FRENCH, GREEK, HINDI, NORMAN, POLISH, ROMANIAN--
HERE! ***RUSSIAN!***
GREAT. LOOK UP THE WORD ***OTETS.***
HERE, RIGHT HERE. ***OTETS.***
THAT'S WHAT MR. THORNE CALLED MR. ROSTONOV!
IS IT SOME KIND OF TERRIBLE INSULT? LIKE A SHARP-FANGED DEMON OR SOMETHING?
NOT EXACTLY . . .
IT MEANS ***FATHER.*** IT'S SO STRANGE THAT MR. THORNE WOULD MAKE A MISTAKE LIKE THAT. HE'S A VERY SMART MAN. AND LOOK HERE--
BATYA TRANSLATES TO ***PAPA.***
WHY WOULD MR. THORNE ADDRESS MR. ROSTONOV AS HIS PAPA?

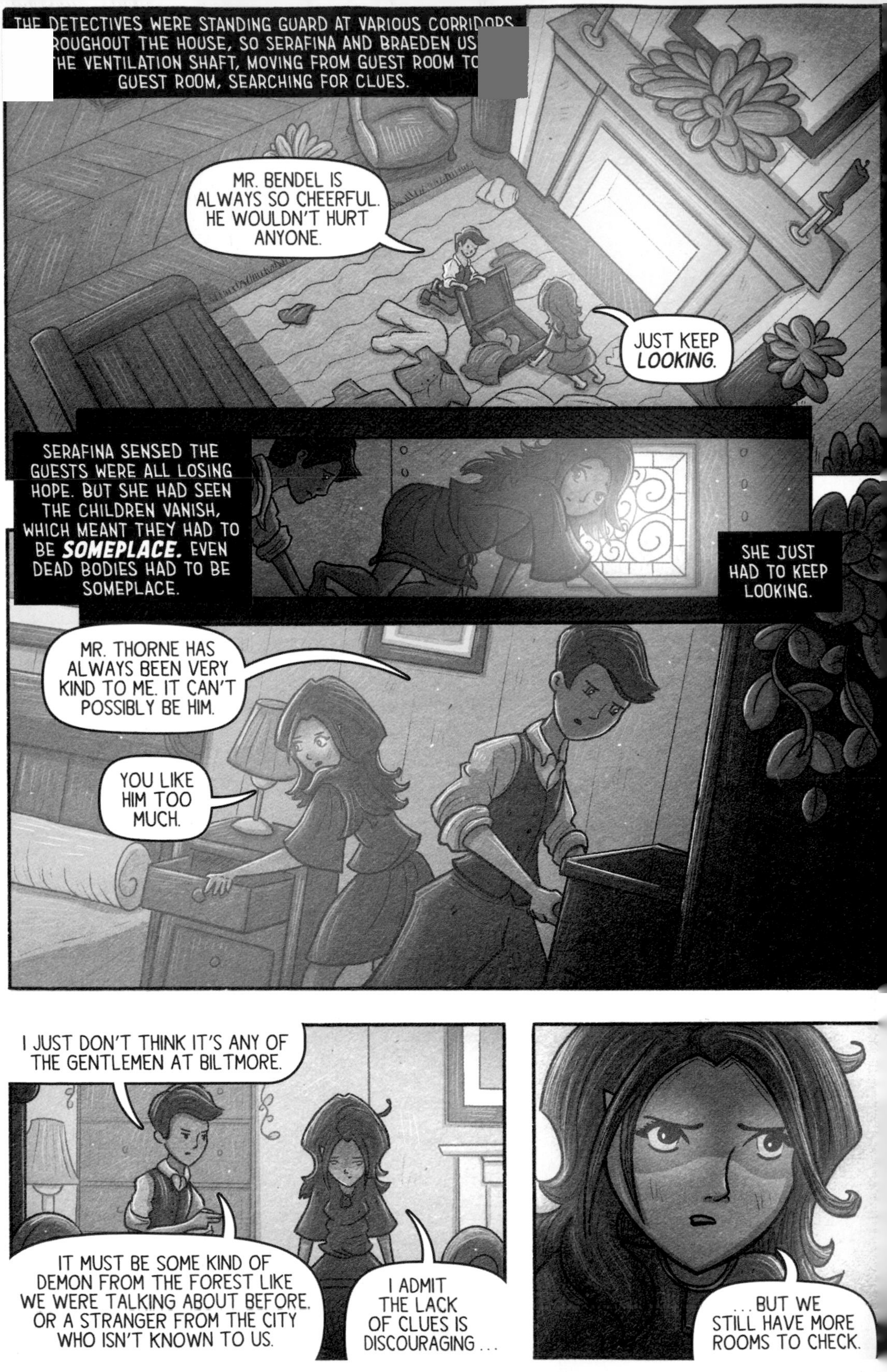
THE DETECTIVES WERE STANDING GUARD AT VARIOUS CORRIDORS
ROUGHOUT THE HOUSE, SO SERAFINA AND BRAEDEN US
THE VENTILATION SHAFT, MOVING FROM GUEST ROOM TO
GUEST ROOM, SEARCHING FOR CLUES.
MR. BENDEL IS ALWAYS SO CHEERFUL. HE WOULDN'T HURT ANYONE.
JUST KEEP *LOOKING.*
SERAFINA SENSED THE GUESTS WERE ALL LOSING HOPE. BUT SHE HAD SEEN THE CHILDREN VANISH, WHICH MEANT THEY HAD TO BE ***SOMEPLACE.*** EVEN DEAD BODIES HAD TO BE SOMEPLACE.
SHE JUST HAD TO KEEP LOOKING.
MR. THORNE HAS ALWAYS BEEN VERY KIND TO ME. IT CAN'T POSSIBLY BE HIM.
YOU LIKE HIM TOO MUCH.
I JUST DON'T THINK IT'S ANY OF THE GENTLEMEN AT BILTMORE.
IT MUST BE SOME KIND OF DEMON FROM THE FOREST LIKE WE WERE TALKING ABOUT BEFORE, OR A STRANGER FROM THE CITY WHO ISN'T KNOWN TO US.
I ADMIT THE LACK OF CLUES IS DISCOURAGING . . .
. . . BUT WE STILL HAVE MORE ROOMS TO CHECK.

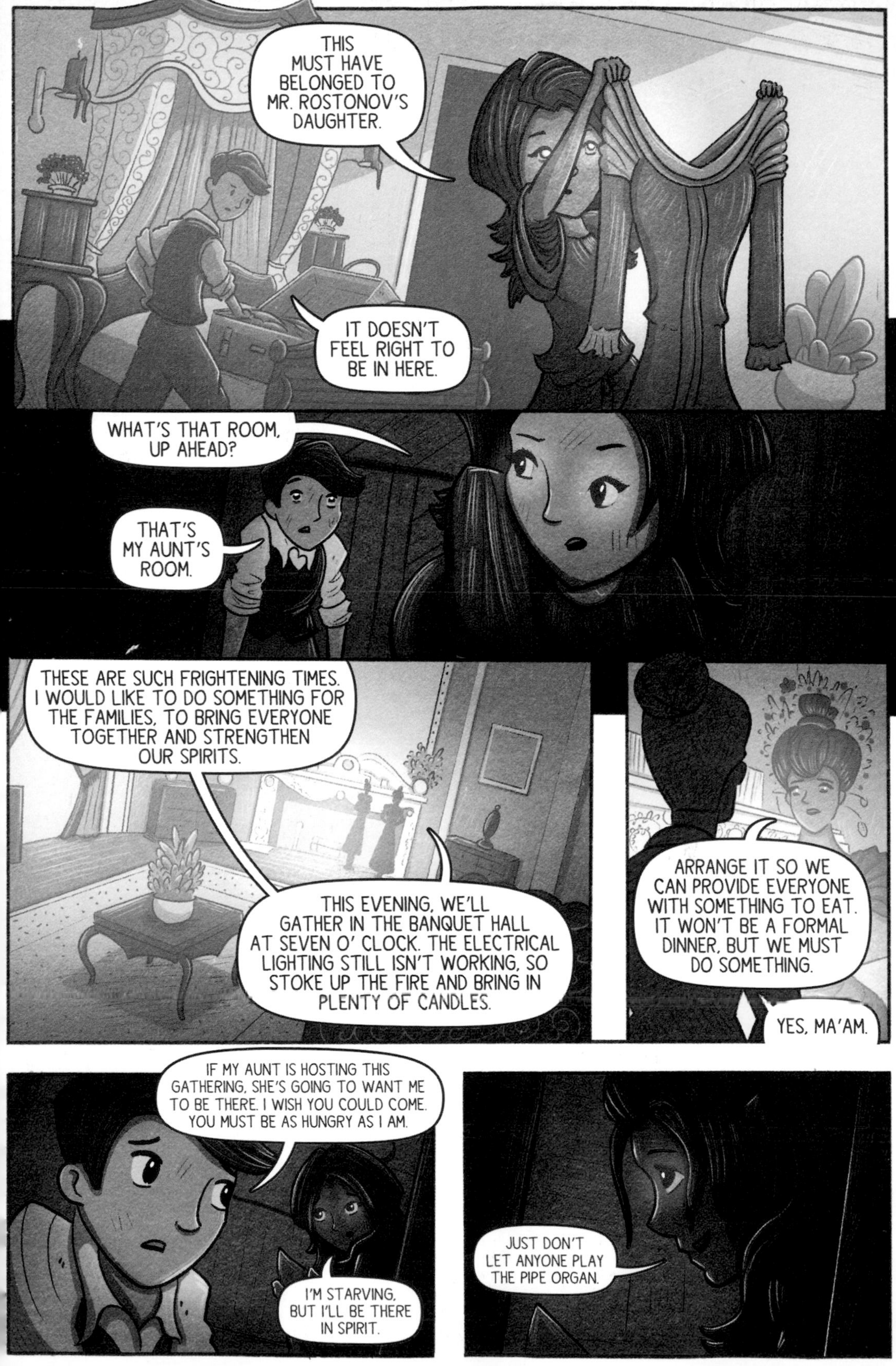
THIS MUST HAVE BELONGED TO MR. ROSTONOV'S DAUGHTER.
IT DOESN'T FEEL RIGHT TO BE IN HERE.
WHAT'S THAT ROOM, UP AHEAD?
THAT'S MY AUNT'S ROOM.
THESE ARE SUCH FRIGHTENING TIMES. I WOULD LIKE TO DO SOMETHING FOR THE FAMILIES, TO BRING EVERYONE TOGETHER AND STRENGTHEN OUR SPIRITS.
THIS EVENING, WE'LL GATHER IN THE BANQUET HALL AT SEVEN O' CLOCK. THE ELECTRICAL LIGHTING STILL ISN'T WORKING, SO STOKE UP THE FIRE AND BRING IN PLENTY OF CANDLES.
ARRANGE IT SO WE CAN PROVIDE EVERYONE WITH SOMETHING TO EAT. IT WON'T BE A FORMAL DINNER, BUT WE MUST DO SOMETHING.
YES, MA'AM.
IF MY AUNT IS HOSTING THIS GATHERING, SHE'S GOING TO WANT ME TO BE THERE. I WISH YOU COULD COME. YOU MUST BE AS HUNGRY AS I AM.
I'M STARVING, BUT I'LL BE THERE IN SPIRIT.
JUST DON'T LET ANYONE PLAY THE PIPE ORGAN.

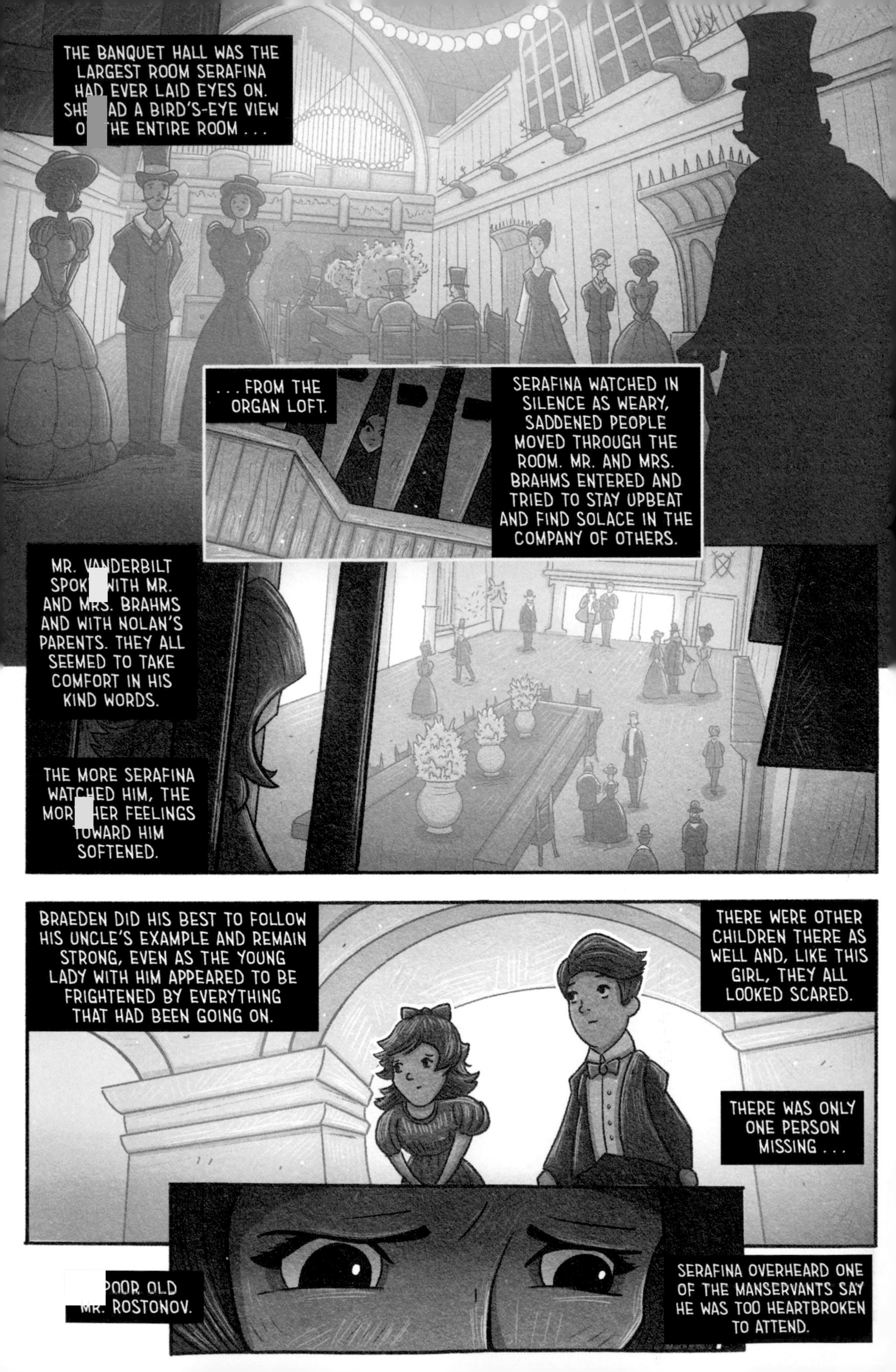
THE BANQUET HALL WAS THE LARGEST ROOM SERAFINA HAD EVER LAID EYES ON. SHE HAD A BIRD'S-EYE VIEW OF THE ENTIRE ROOM . . .
. . . FROM THE ORGAN LOFT.
SERAFINA WATCHED IN SILENCE AS WEARY, SADDENED PEOPLE MOVED THROUGH THE ROOM. MR. AND MRS. BRAHMS ENTERED AND TRIED TO STAY UPBEAT AND FIND SOLACE IN THE COMPANY OF OTHERS.
MR. VANDERBILT SPOKE WITH MR. AND MRS. BRAHMS AND WITH NOLAN'S PARENTS. THEY ALL SEEMED TO TAKE COMFORT IN HIS KIND WORDS.
THE MORE SERAFINA WATCHED HIM, THE MORE HER FEELINGS TOWARD HIM SOFTENED.
BRAEDEN DID HIS BEST TO FOLLOW HIS UNCLE'S EXAMPLE AND REMAIN STRONG, EVEN AS THE YOUNG LADY WITH HIM APPEARED TO BE FRIGHTENED BY EVERYTHING THAT HAD BEEN GOING ON.
THERE WERE OTHER CHILDREN THERE AS WELL AND, LIKE THIS GIRL, THEY ALL LOOKED SCARED.
THERE WAS ONLY ONE PERSON MISSING . . .
POOR OLD MR. ROSTONOV.
SERAFINA OVERHEARD ONE OF THE MANSERVANTS SAY HE WAS TOO HEARTBROKEN TO ATTEND.

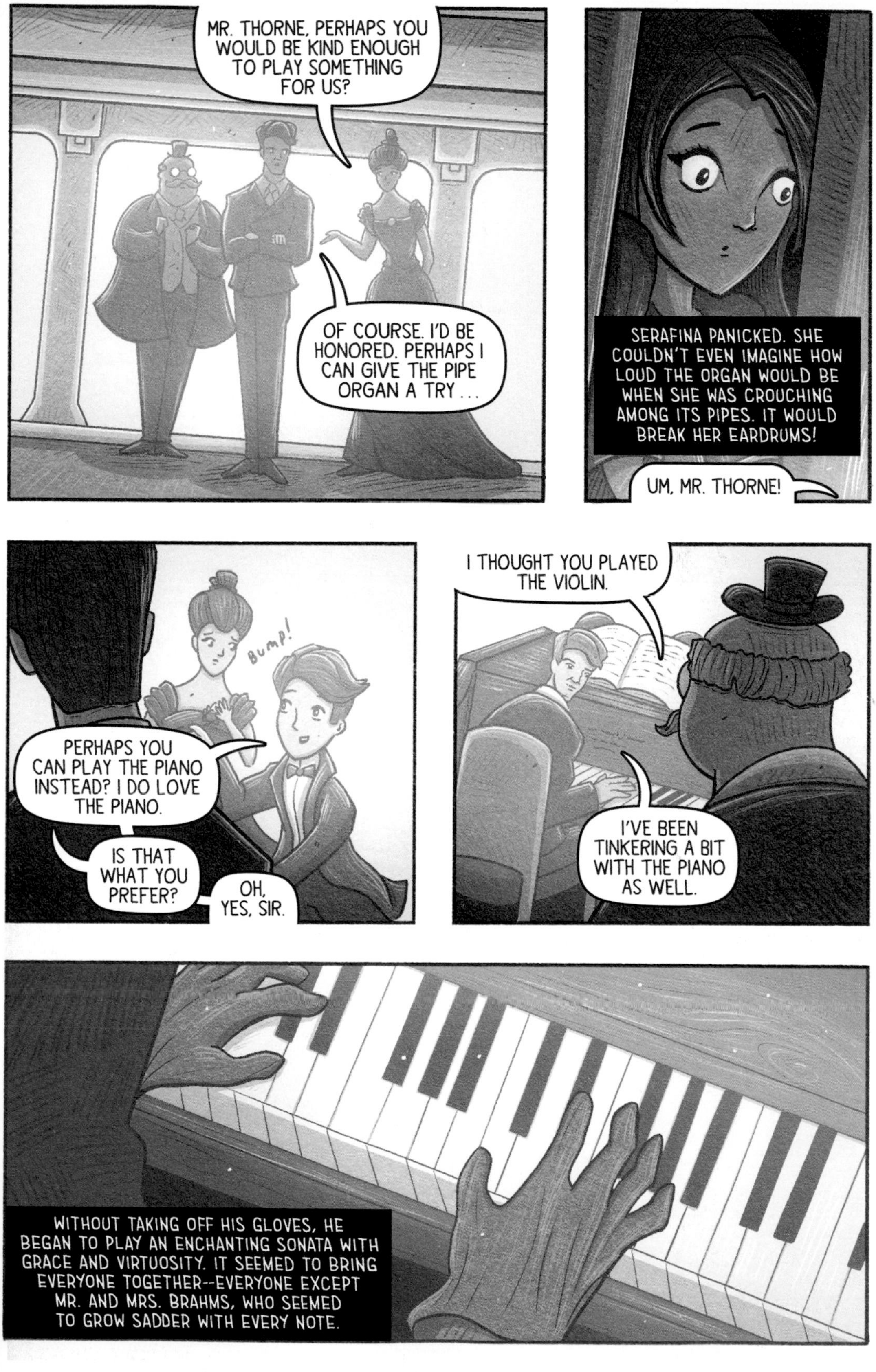
MR. THORNE, PERHAPS YOU WOULD BE KIND ENOUGH TO PLAY SOMETHING FOR US?
OF COURSE. I'D BE HONORED. PERHAPS I CAN GIVE THE PIPE ORGAN A TRY . . .
SERAFINA PANICKED. SHE COULDN'T EVEN IMAGINE HOW LOUD THE ORGAN WOULD BE WHEN SHE WAS CROUCHING AMONG ITS PIPES. IT WOULD BREAK HER EARDRUMS!
UM, MR. THORNE!
BUMP!
PERHAPS YOU CAN PLAY THE PIANO INSTEAD? I DO LOVE THE PIANO.
IS THAT WHAT YOU PREFER?
OH, YES, SIR.
I THOUGHT YOU PLAYED THE VIOLIN.
I'VE BEEN TINKERING A BIT WITH THE PIANO AS WELL.
WITHOUT TAKING OFF HIS GLOVES, HE BEGAN TO PLAY AN ENCHANTING SONATA WITH GRACE AND VIRTUOSITY. IT SEEMED TO BRING EVERYONE TOGETHER--EVERYONE EXCEPT MR. AND MRS. BRAHMS, WHO SEEMED TO GROW SADDER WITH EVERY NOTE.

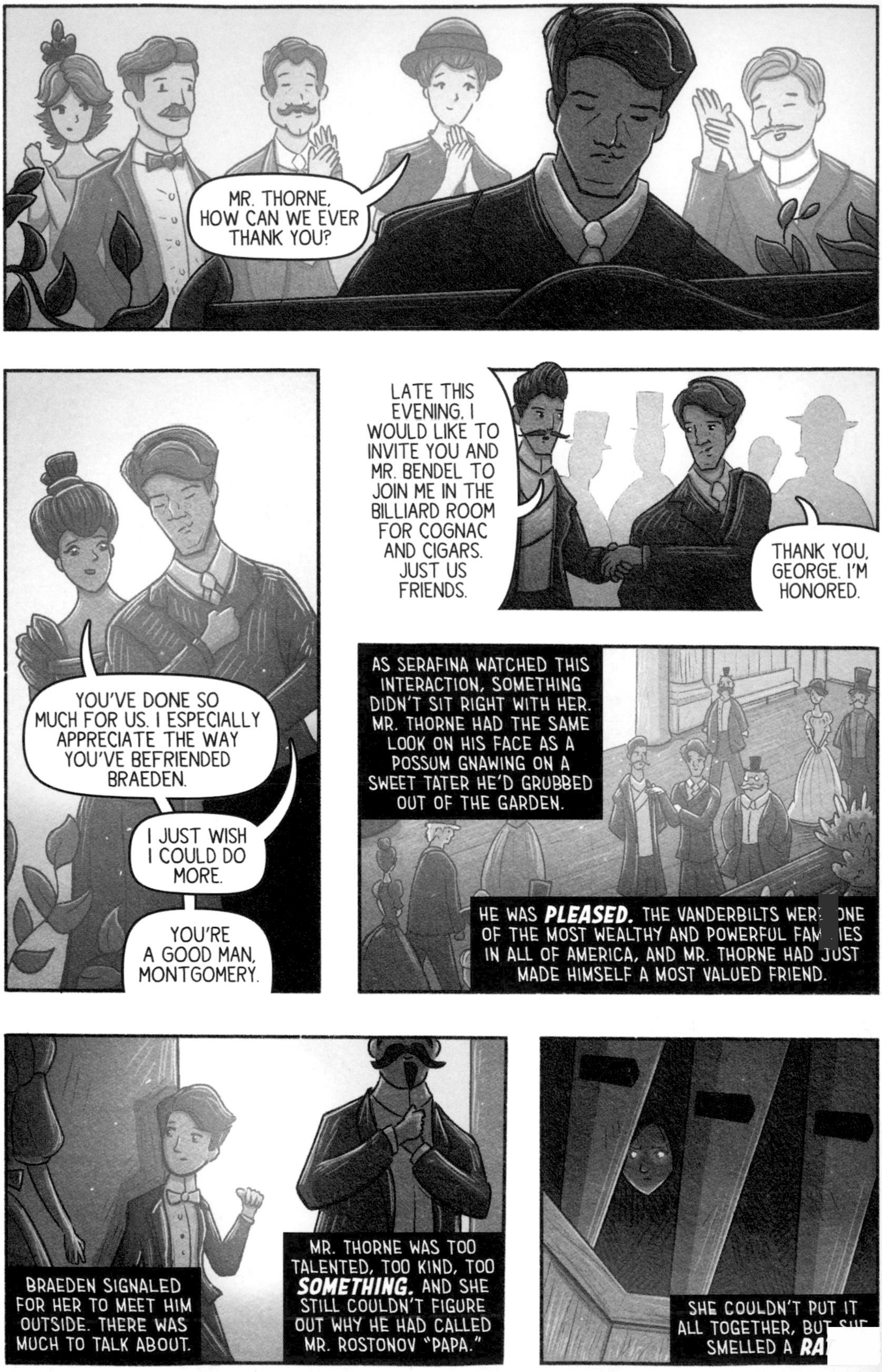
MR. THORNE, HOW CAN WE EVER THANK YOU?
YOU'VE DONE SO MUCH FOR US. I ESPECIALLY APPRECIATE THE WAY YOU'VE BEFRIENDED BRAEDEN.
I JUST WISH I COULD DO MORE.
YOU'RE A GOOD MAN, MONTGOMERY.
LATE THIS EVENING, I WOULD LIKE TO INVITE YOU AND MR. BENDEL TO JOIN ME IN THE BILLIARD ROOM FOR COGNAC AND CIGARS. JUST US FRIENDS.
THANK YOU, GEORGE. I'M HONORED.
AS SERAFINA WATCHED THIS INTERACTION, SOMETHING DIDN'T SIT RIGHT WITH HER. MR. THORNE HAD THE SAME LOOK ON HIS FACE AS A POSSUM GNAWING ON A SWEET TATER HE'D GRUBBED OUT OF THE GARDEN.
HE WAS ***PLEASED.*** THE VANDERBILTS WER[redacted]ONE OF THE MOST WEALTHY AND POWERFUL FAM[redacted]IES IN ALL OF AMERICA, AND MR. THORNE HAD JUST MADE HIMSELF A MOST VALUED FRIEND.
BRAEDEN SIGNALED FOR HER TO MEET HIM OUTSIDE. THERE WAS MUCH TO TALK ABOUT.
MR. THORNE WAS TOO TALENTED, TOO KIND, TOO ***SOMETHING.*** AND SHE STILL COULDN'T FIGURE OUT WHY HE HAD CALLED MR. ROSTONOV "PAPA."
SHE COULDN'T PUT IT ALL TOGETHER, BUT
SMELLED A ***RA***

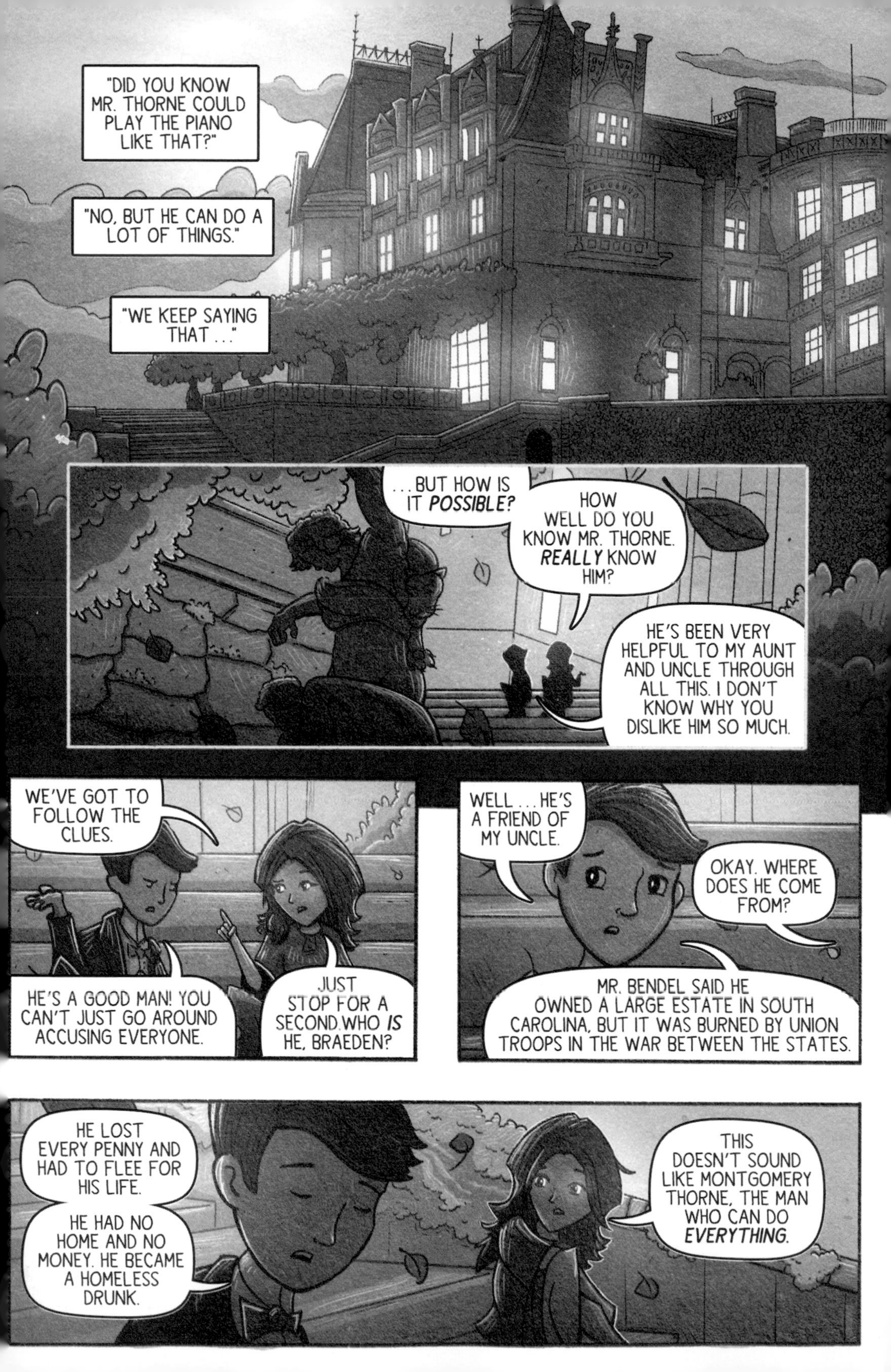
"DID YOU KNOW MR. THORNE COULD PLAY THE PIANO LIKE THAT?"
"NO, BUT HE CAN DO A LOT OF THINGS."
"WE KEEP SAYING THAT . . ."
. . . BUT HOW IS IT *POSSIBLE?*
HOW WELL DO YOU KNOW MR. THORNE. *REALLY* KNOW HIM?
HE'S BEEN VERY HELPFUL TO MY AUNT AND UNCLE THROUGH ALL THIS. I DON'T KNOW WHY YOU DISLIKE HIM SO MUCH.
WE'VE GOT TO FOLLOW THE CLUES.
HE'S A GOOD MAN! YOU CAN'T JUST GO AROUND ACCUSING EVERYONE.
JUST STOP FOR A SECOND. WHO *IS* HE, BRAEDEN?
WELL . . . HE'S A FRIEND OF MY UNCLE.
OKAY. WHERE DOES HE COME FROM?
MR. BENDEL SAID HE OWNED A LARGE ESTATE IN SOUTH CAROLINA, BUT IT WAS BURNED BY UNION TROOPS IN THE WAR BETWEEN THE STATES.
HE LOST EVERY PENNY AND HAD TO FLEE FOR HIS LIFE.
HE HAD NO HOME AND NO MONEY. HE BECAME A HOMELESS DRUNK.
THIS DOESN'T SOUND LIKE MONTGOMERY THORNE, THE MAN WHO CAN DO *EVERYTHING*.

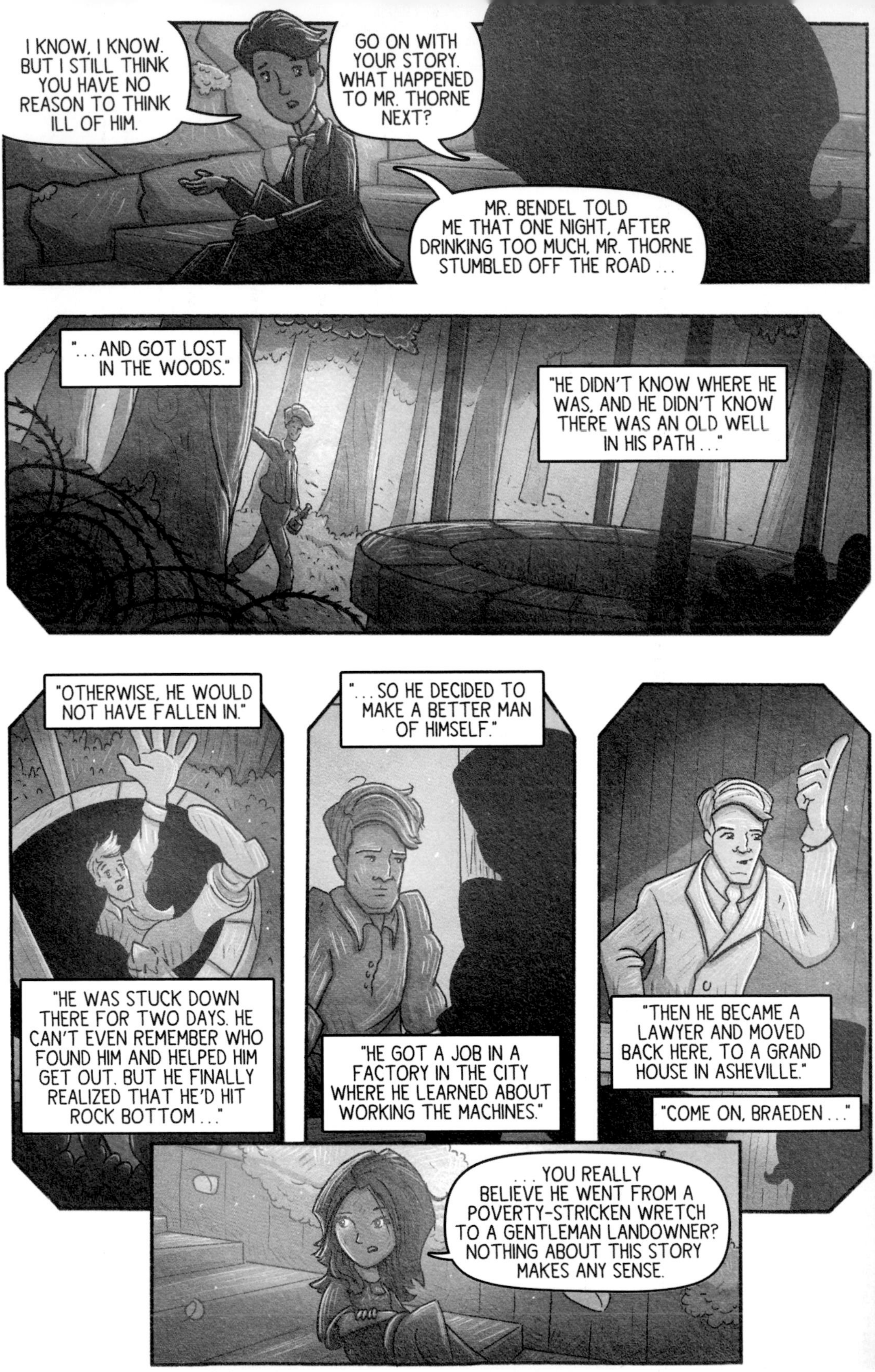

I KNOW, I KNOW. BUT I STILL THINK YOU HAVE NO REASON TO THINK ILL OF HIM.
GO ON WITH YOUR STORY. WHAT HAPPENED TO MR. THORNE NEXT?
MR. BENDEL TOLD ME THAT ONE NIGHT, AFTER DRINKING TOO MUCH, MR. THORNE STUMBLED OFF THE ROAD . . .
". . . AND GOT LOST IN THE WOODS."
"HE DIDN'T KNOW WHERE HE WAS, AND HE DIDN'T KNOW THERE WAS AN OLD WELL IN HIS PATH . . ."
"OTHERWISE, HE WOULD NOT HAVE FALLEN IN."
"HE WAS STUCK DOWN THERE FOR TWO DAYS. HE CAN'T EVEN REMEMBER WHO FOUND HIM AND HELPED HIM GET OUT. BUT HE FINALLY REALIZED THAT HE'D HIT ROCK BOTTOM . . ."
". . . SO HE DECIDED TO MAKE A BETTER MAN OF HIMSELF."
"HE GOT A JOB IN A FACTORY IN THE CITY WHERE HE LEARNED ABOUT WORKING THE MACHINES."
"THEN HE BECAME A LAWYER AND MOVED BACK HERE, TO A GRAND HOUSE IN ASHEVILLE."
"COME ON, BRAEDEN . . ."
. . . YOU REALLY BELIEVE HE WENT FROM A POVERTY-STRICKEN WRETCH TO A GENTLEMAN LANDOWNER? NOTHING ABOUT THIS STORY MAKES ANY SENSE.

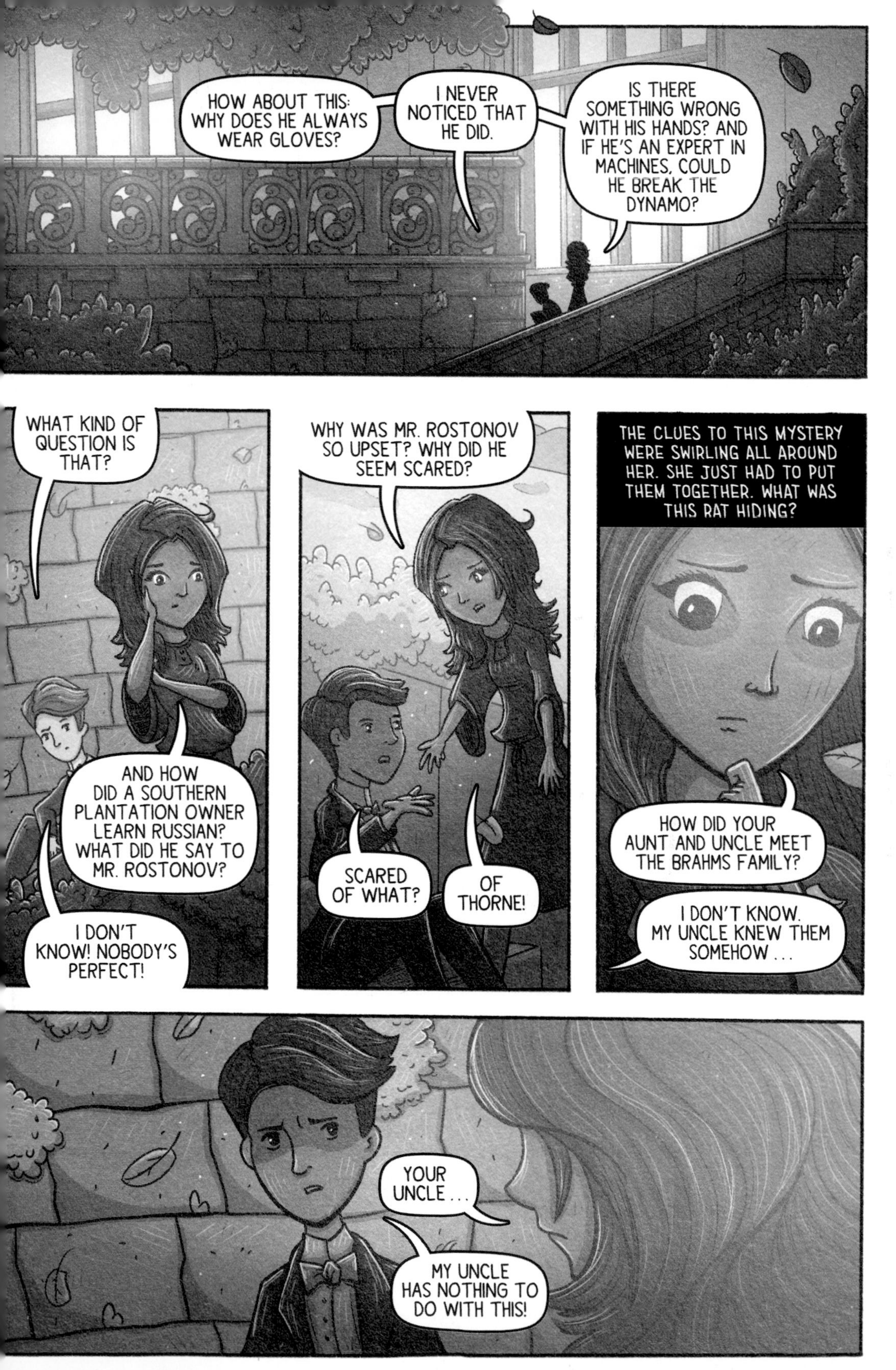
HOW ABOUT THIS: WHY DOES HE ALWAYS WEAR GLOVES?
I NEVER NOTICED THAT HE DID.
IS THERE SOMETHING WRONG WITH HIS HANDS? AND IF HE'S AN EXPERT IN MACHINES, COULD HE BREAK THE DYNAMO?
WHAT KIND OF QUESTION IS THAT?
AND HOW DID A SOUTHERN PLANTATION OWNER LEARN RUSSIAN? WHAT DID HE SAY TO MR. ROSTONOV?
I DON'T KNOW! NOBODY'S PERFECT!
WHY WAS MR. ROSTONOV SO UPSET? WHY DID HE SEEM SCARED?
SCARED OF WHAT?
OF THORNE!
THE CLUES TO THIS MYSTERY WERE SWIRLING ALL AROUND HER. SHE JUST HAD TO PUT THEM TOGETHER. WHAT WAS THIS RAT HIDING?
HOW DID YOUR AUNT AND UNCLE MEET THE BRAHMS FAMILY?
I DON'T KNOW. MY UNCLE KNEW THEM SOMEHOW . . .
YOUR UNCLE . . .
MY UNCLE HAS NOTHING TO DO WITH THIS!

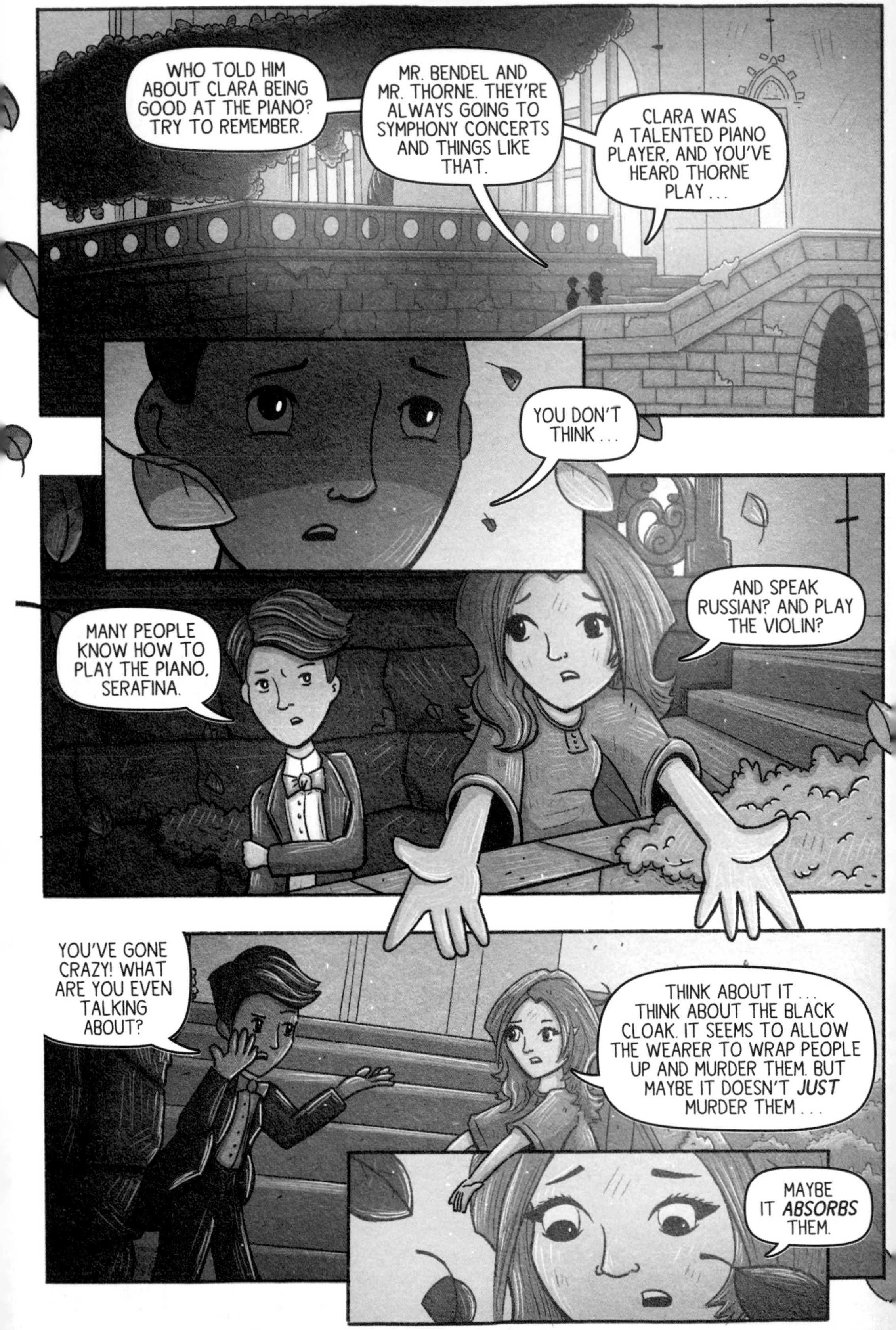
WHO TOLD HIM ABOUT CLARA BEING GOOD AT THE PIANO? TRY TO REMEMBER.
MR. BENDEL AND MR. THORNE. THEY'RE ALWAYS GOING TO SYMPHONY CONCERTS AND THINGS LIKE THAT.
CLARA WAS A TALENTED PIANO PLAYER, AND YOU'VE HEARD THORNE PLAY . . .
YOU DON'T THINK . . .
MANY PEOPLE KNOW HOW TO PLAY THE PIANO, SERAFINA.
AND SPEAK RUSSIAN? AND PLAY THE VIOLIN?
YOU'VE GONE CRAZY! WHAT ARE YOU EVEN TALKING ABOUT?
THINK ABOUT IT . . . THINK ABOUT THE BLACK CLOAK. IT SEEMS TO ALLOW THE WEARER TO WRAP PEOPLE UP AND MURDER THEM. BUT MAYBE IT DOESN'T *JUST* MURDER THEM . . .
MAYBE IT ***ABSORBS*** THEM.

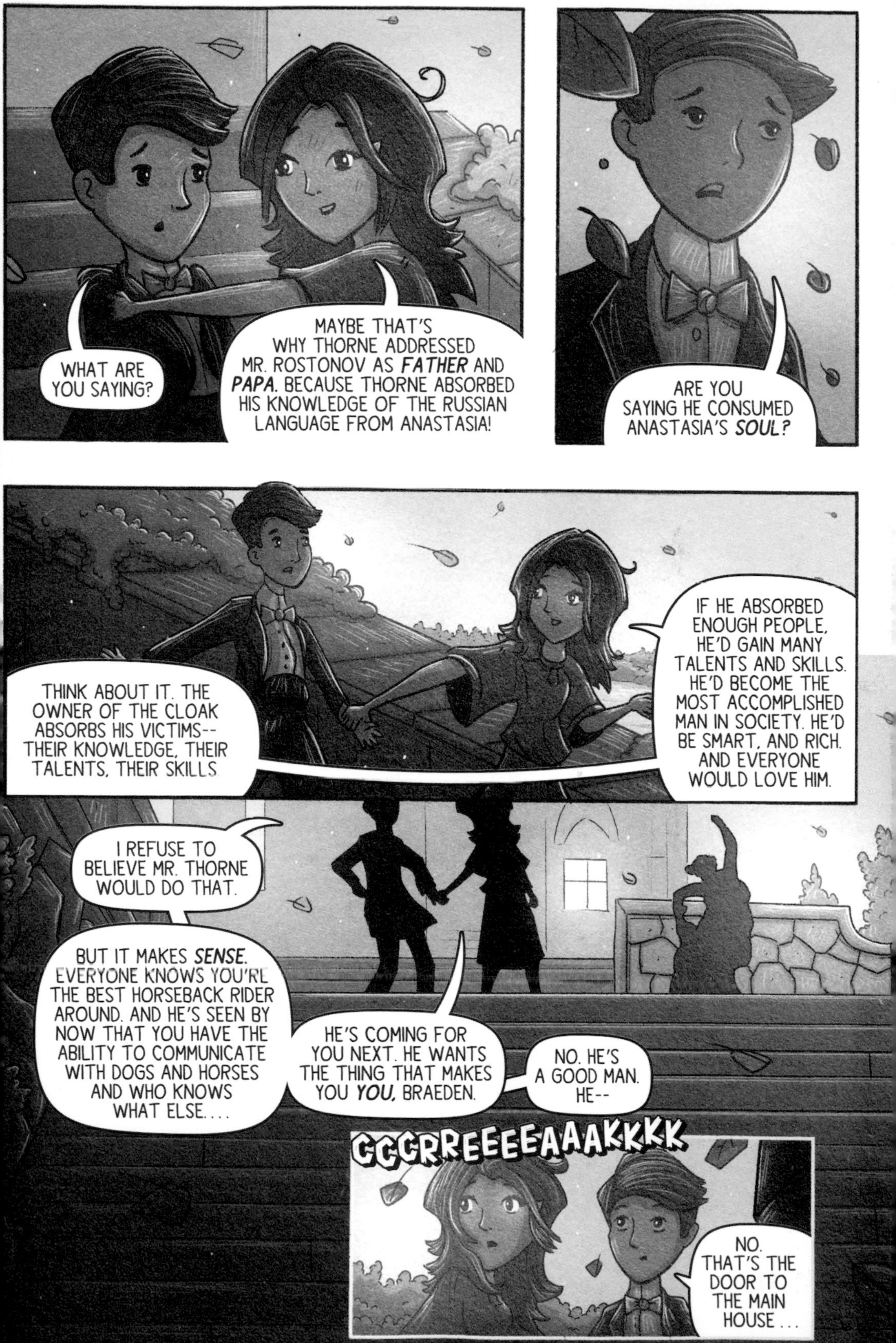
WHAT ARE YOU SAYING?
MAYBE THAT'S WHY THORNE ADDRESSED MR. ROSTONOV AS FATHER AND PAPA. BECAUSE THORNE ABSORBED HIS KNOWLEDGE OF THE RUSSIAN LANGUAGE FROM ANASTASIA!
ARE YOU SAYING HE CONSUMED ANASTASIA'S SOUL?
THINK ABOUT IT. THE OWNER OF THE CLOAK ABSORBS HIS VICTIMS-- THEIR KNOWLEDGE, THEIR TALENTS, THEIR SKILLS.
IF HE ABSORBED ENOUGH PEOPLE, HE'D GAIN MANY TALENTS AND SKILLS. HE'D BECOME THE MOST ACCOMPLISHED MAN IN SOCIETY. HE'D BE SMART, AND RICH. AND EVERYONE WOULD LOVE HIM.
I REFUSE TO BELIEVE MR. THORNE WOULD DO THAT.
BUT IT MAKES SENSE. EVERYONE KNOWS YOU'RE THE BEST HORSEBACK RIDER AROUND. AND HE'S SEEN BY NOW THAT YOU HAVE THE ABILITY TO COMMUNICATE WITH DOGS AND HORSES AND WHO KNOWS WHAT ELSE. . . .
HE'S COMING FOR YOU NEXT. HE WANTS THE THING THAT MAKES YOU YOU, BRAEDEN.
NO. HE'S A GOOD MAN. HE--
CCCRREEEEEAAAKKKK
NO. THAT'S THE DOOR TO THE MAIN HOUSE . . .

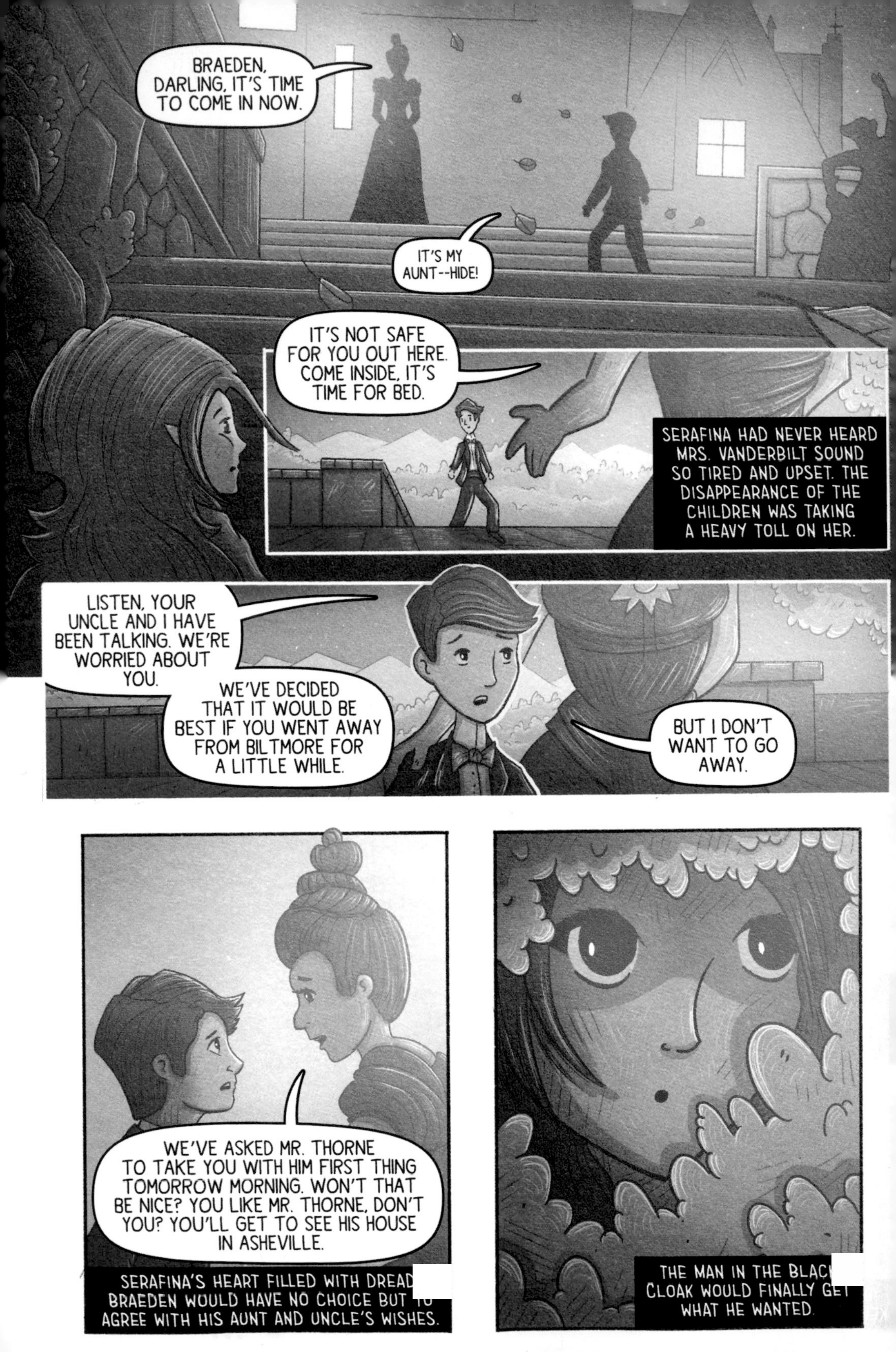
BRAEDEN, DARLING, IT'S TIME TO COME IN NOW.
IT'S MY AUNT--HIDE!
IT'S NOT SAFE FOR YOU OUT HERE. COME INSIDE, IT'S TIME FOR BED.
SERAFINA HAD NEVER HEARD MRS. VANDERBILT SOUND SO TIRED AND UPSET. THE DISAPPEARANCE OF THE CHILDREN WAS TAKING A HEAVY TOLL ON HER.
LISTEN, YOUR UNCLE AND I HAVE BEEN TALKING. WE'RE WORRIED ABOUT YOU.
WE'VE DECIDED THAT IT WOULD BE BEST IF YOU WENT AWAY FROM BILTMORE FOR A LITTLE WHILE.
BUT I DON'T WANT TO GO AWAY.
WE'VE ASKED MR. THORNE TO TAKE YOU WITH HIM FIRST THING TOMORROW MORNING. WON'T THAT BE NICE? YOU LIKE MR. THORNE, DON'T YOU? YOU'LL GET TO SEE HIS HOUSE IN ASHEVILLE.
SERAFINA'S HEART FILLED WITH DREAD
BRAEDEN WOULD HAVE NO CHOICE BUT
AGREE WITH HIS AUNT AND UNCLE'S WISHES.
THE MAN IN THE BLAC
CLOAK WOULD FINALLY GET
WHAT HE WANTED.

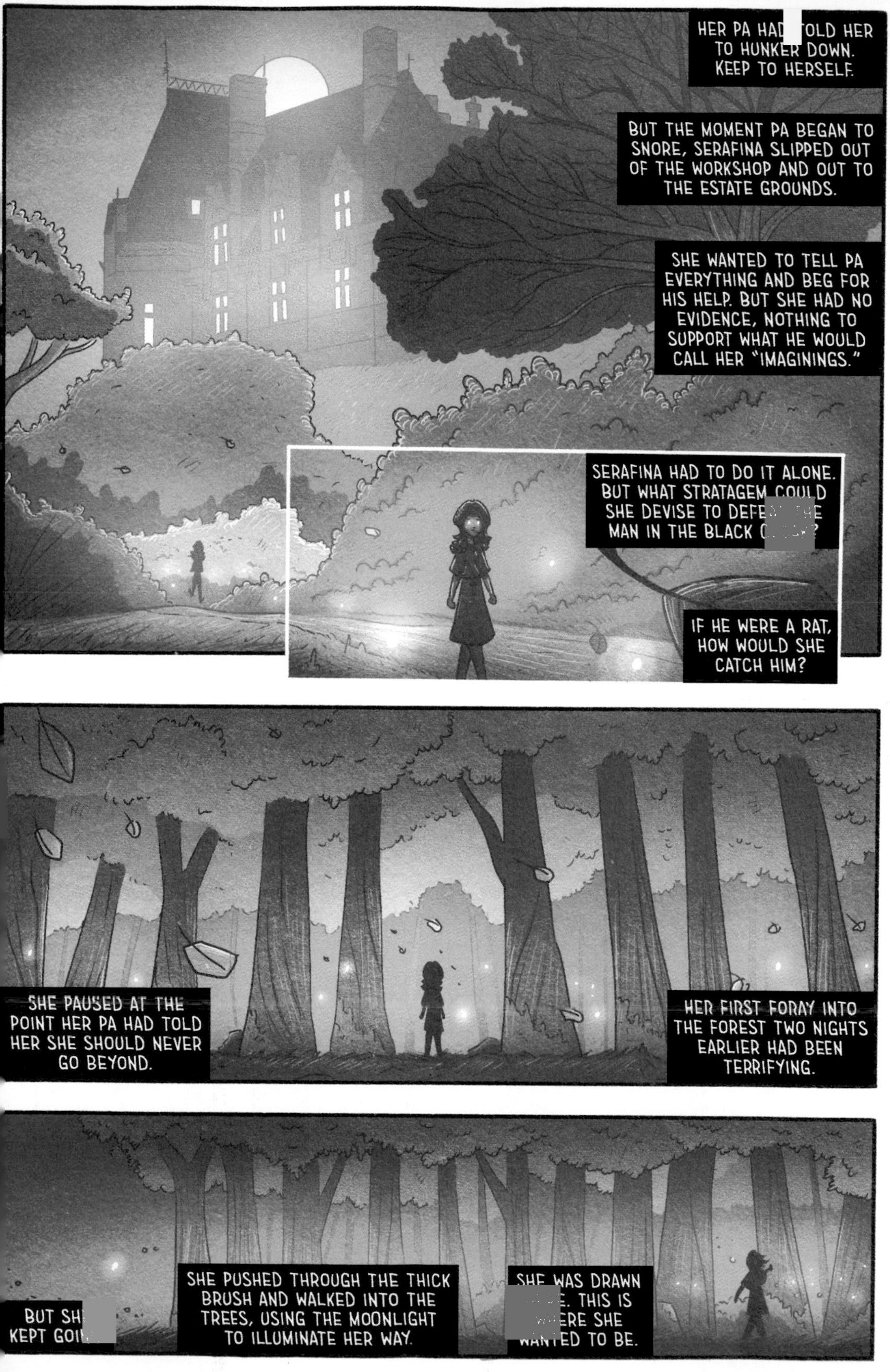

HER PA HAD OLD HER TO HUNKER DOWN. KEEP TO HERSELF.
BUT THE MOMENT PA BEGAN TO SNORE, SERAFINA SLIPPED OUT OF THE WORKSHOP AND OUT TO THE ESTATE GROUNDS.
SHE WANTED TO TELL PA EVERYTHING AND BEG FOR HIS HELP. BUT SHE HAD NO EVIDENCE, NOTHING TO SUPPORT WHAT HE WOULD CALL HER "IMAGININGS."
SERAFINA HAD TO DO IT ALONE. BUT WHAT STRATAGEM COULD SHE DEVISE TO DEFE MAN IN THE BLACK ?
IF HE WERE A RAT, HOW WOULD SHE CATCH HIM?
SHE PAUSED AT THE POINT HER PA HAD TOLD HER SHE SHOULD NEVER GO BEYOND.
HER FIRST FORAY INTO THE FOREST TWO NIGHTS EARLIER HAD BEEN TERRIFYING.
BUT SH KEPT GOI
SHE PUSHED THROUGH THE THICK BRUSH AND WALKED INTO THE TREES, USING THE MOONLIGHT TO ILLUMINATE HER WAY.
SHE WAS DRAWN E. THIS IS ERE SHE WANTED TO BE.

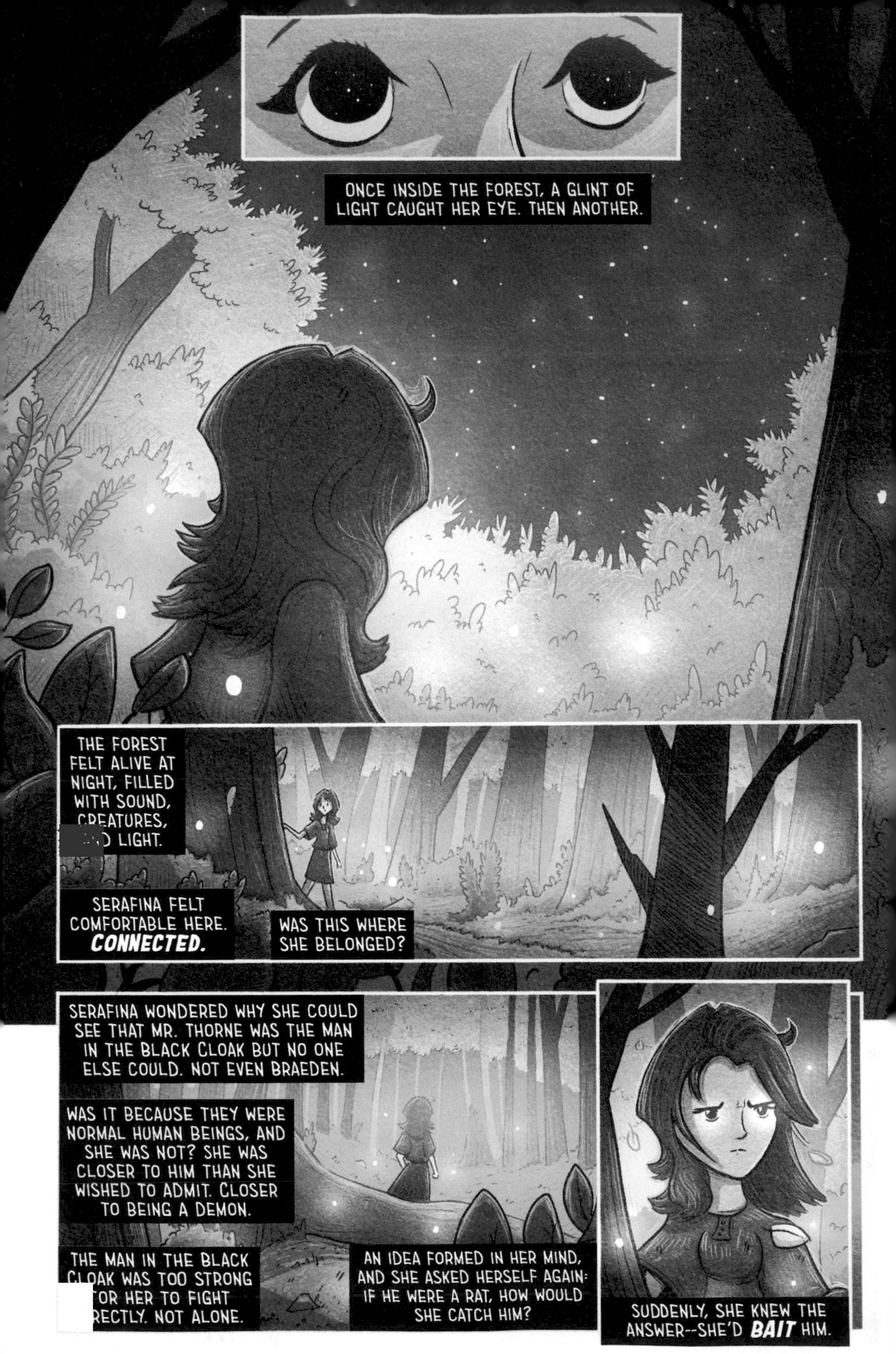

ONCE INSIDE THE FOREST, A GLINT OF LIGHT CAUGHT HER EYE. THEN ANOTHER.
THE FOREST FELT ALIVE AT NIGHT, FILLED WITH SOUND, CREATURES, D LIGHT.
SERAFINA FELT COMFORTABLE HERE. ***CONNECTED.***
WAS THIS WHERE SHE BELONGED?
SERAFINA WONDERED WHY SHE COULD SEE THAT MR. THORNE WAS THE MAN IN THE BLACK CLOAK BUT NO ONE ELSE COULD. NOT EVEN BRAEDEN.
WAS IT BECAUSE THEY WERE NORMAL HUMAN BEINGS, AND SHE WAS NOT? SHE WAS CLOSER TO HIM THAN SHE WISHED TO ADMIT. CLOSER TO BEING A DEMON.
THE MAN IN THE BLACK CLOAK WAS TOO STRONG OR HER TO FIGHT RECTLY. NOT ALONE.
AN IDEA FORMED IN HER MIND, AND SHE ASKED HERSELF AGAIN: IF HE WERE A RAT, HOW WOULD SHE CATCH HIM?
SUDDENLY, SHE KNEW THE ANSWER--SHE'D ***BAIT*** HIM.

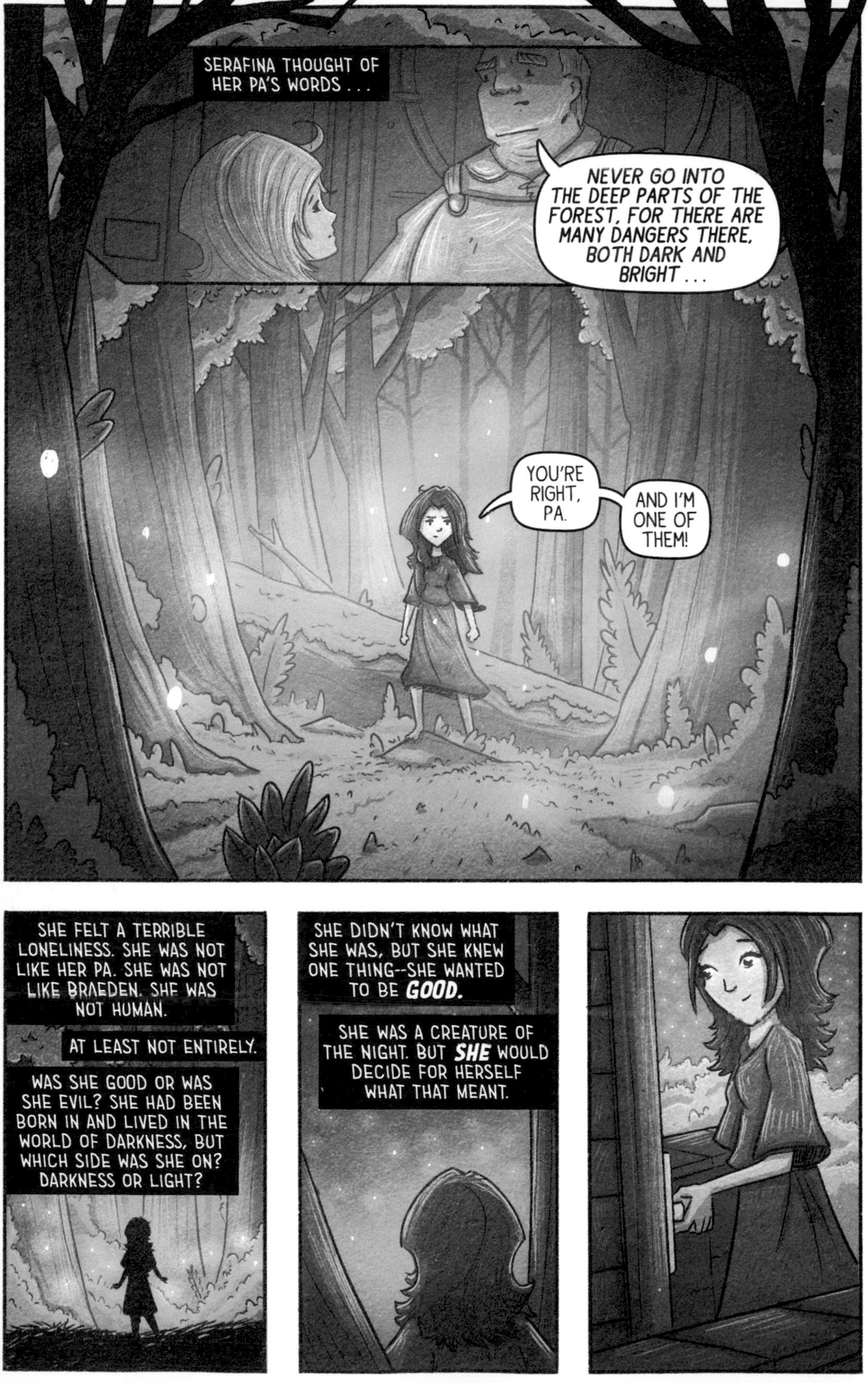
SERAFINA THOUGHT OF HER PA'S WORDS . . .
NEVER GO INTO THE DEEP PARTS OF THE FOREST, FOR THERE ARE MANY DANGERS THERE, BOTH DARK AND BRIGHT . . .
YOU'RE RIGHT, PA.
AND I'M ONE OF THEM!
SHE FELT A TERRIBLE LONELINESS. SHE WAS NOT LIKE HER PA. SHE WAS NOT LIKE BRAEDEN. SHE WAS NOT HUMAN.
AT LEAST NOT ENTIRELY.
WAS SHE GOOD OR WAS SHE EVIL? SHE HAD BEEN BORN IN AND LIVED IN THE WORLD OF DARKNESS, BUT WHICH SIDE WAS SHE ON? DARKNESS OR LIGHT?
SHE DIDN'T KNOW WHAT SHE WAS, BUT SHE KNEW ONE THING--SHE WANTED TO BE GOOD.
SHE WAS A CREATURE OF THE NIGHT. BUT SHE WOULD DECIDE FOR HERSELF WHAT THAT MEANT.

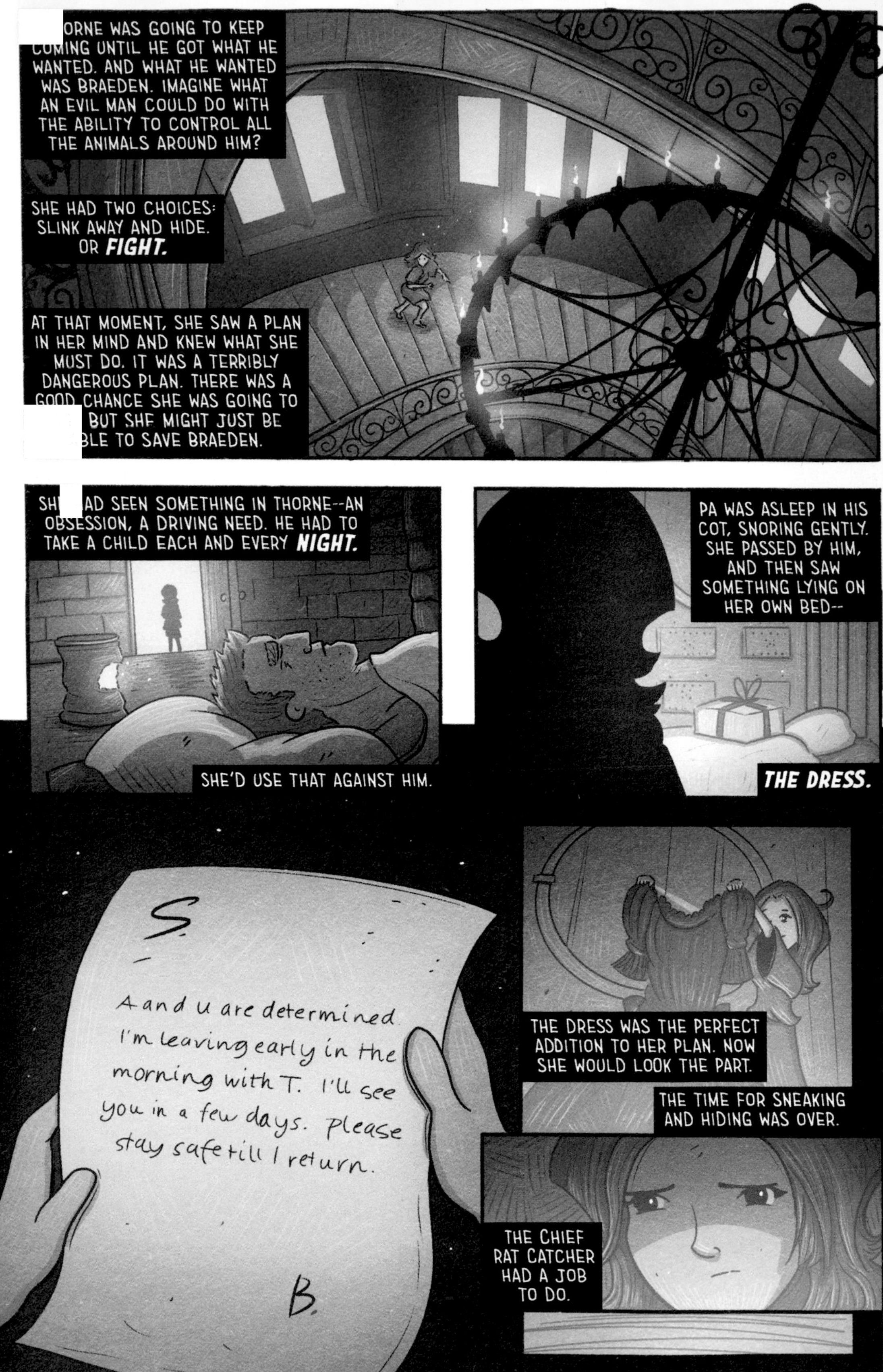

ORNE WAS GOING TO KEEP COMING UNTIL HE GOT WHAT HE WANTED. AND WHAT HE WANTED WAS BRAEDEN. IMAGINE WHAT AN EVIL MAN COULD DO WITH THE ABILITY TO CONTROL ALL THE ANIMALS AROUND HIM?
SHE HAD TWO CHOICES: SLINK AWAY AND HIDE. OR FIGHT.
AT THAT MOMENT, SHE SAW A PLAN IN HER MIND AND KNEW WHAT SHE MUST DO. IT WAS A TERRIBLY DANGEROUS PLAN. THERE WAS A GOOD CHANCE SHE WAS GOING TO BUT SHE MIGHT JUST BE BLE TO SAVE BRAEDEN.
SH AD SEEN SOMETHING IN THORNE--AN OBSESSION, A DRIVING NEED. HE HAD TO TAKE A CHILD EACH AND EVERY NIGHT.
SHE'D USE THAT AGAINST HIM.
PA WAS ASLEEP IN HIS COT, SNORING GENTLY. SHE PASSED BY HIM, AND THEN SAW SOMETHING LYING ON HER OWN BED--
THE DRESS.
S.
A and u are determined. I'm leaving early in the morning with T. I'll see you in a few days. Please stay safe till I return.
B.
THE DRESS WAS THE PERFECT ADDITION TO HER PLAN. NOW SHE WOULD LOOK THE PART.
THE TIME FOR SNEAKING AND HIDING WAS OVER.
THE CHIEF RAT CATCHER HAD A JOB TO DO.

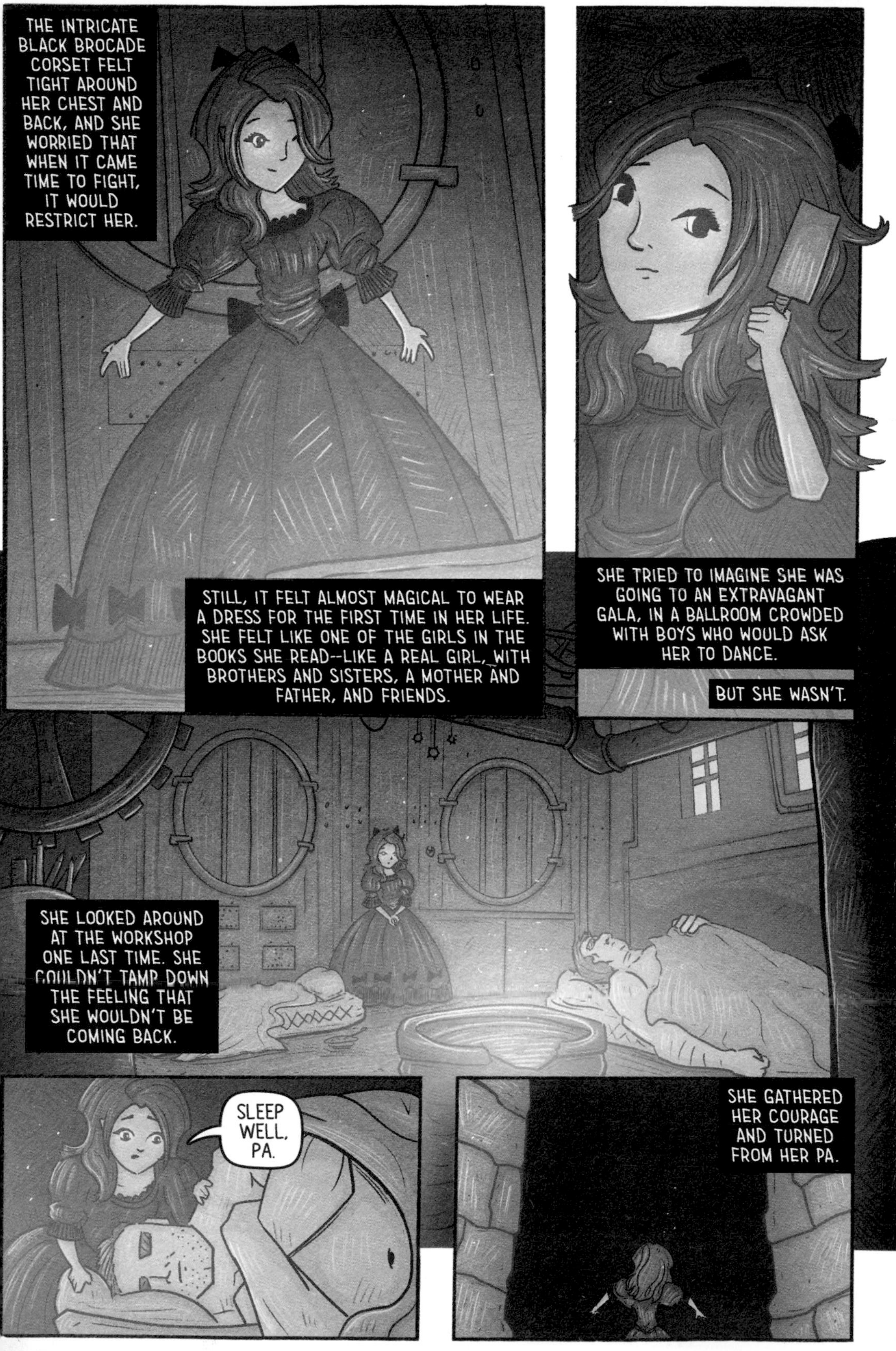
THE INTRICATE BLACK BROCADE CORSET FELT TIGHT AROUND HER CHEST AND BACK, AND SHE WORRIED THAT WHEN IT CAME TIME TO FIGHT, IT WOULD RESTRICT HER.
STILL, IT FELT ALMOST MAGICAL TO WEAR A DRESS FOR THE FIRST TIME IN HER LIFE. SHE FELT LIKE ONE OF THE GIRLS IN THE BOOKS SHE READ--LIKE A REAL GIRL, WITH BROTHERS AND SISTERS, A MOTHER AND FATHER, AND FRIENDS.
SHE TRIED TO IMAGINE SHE WAS GOING TO AN EXTRAVAGANT GALA, IN A BALLROOM CROWDED WITH BOYS WHO WOULD ASK HER TO DANCE.
BUT SHE WASN'T.
SHE LOOKED AROUND AT THE WORKSHOP ONE LAST TIME. SHE COULDN'T TAMP DOWN THE FEELING THAT SHE WOULDN'T BE COMING BACK.
SLEEP WELL, PA.
SHE GATHERED HER COURAGE AND TURNED FROM HER PA.

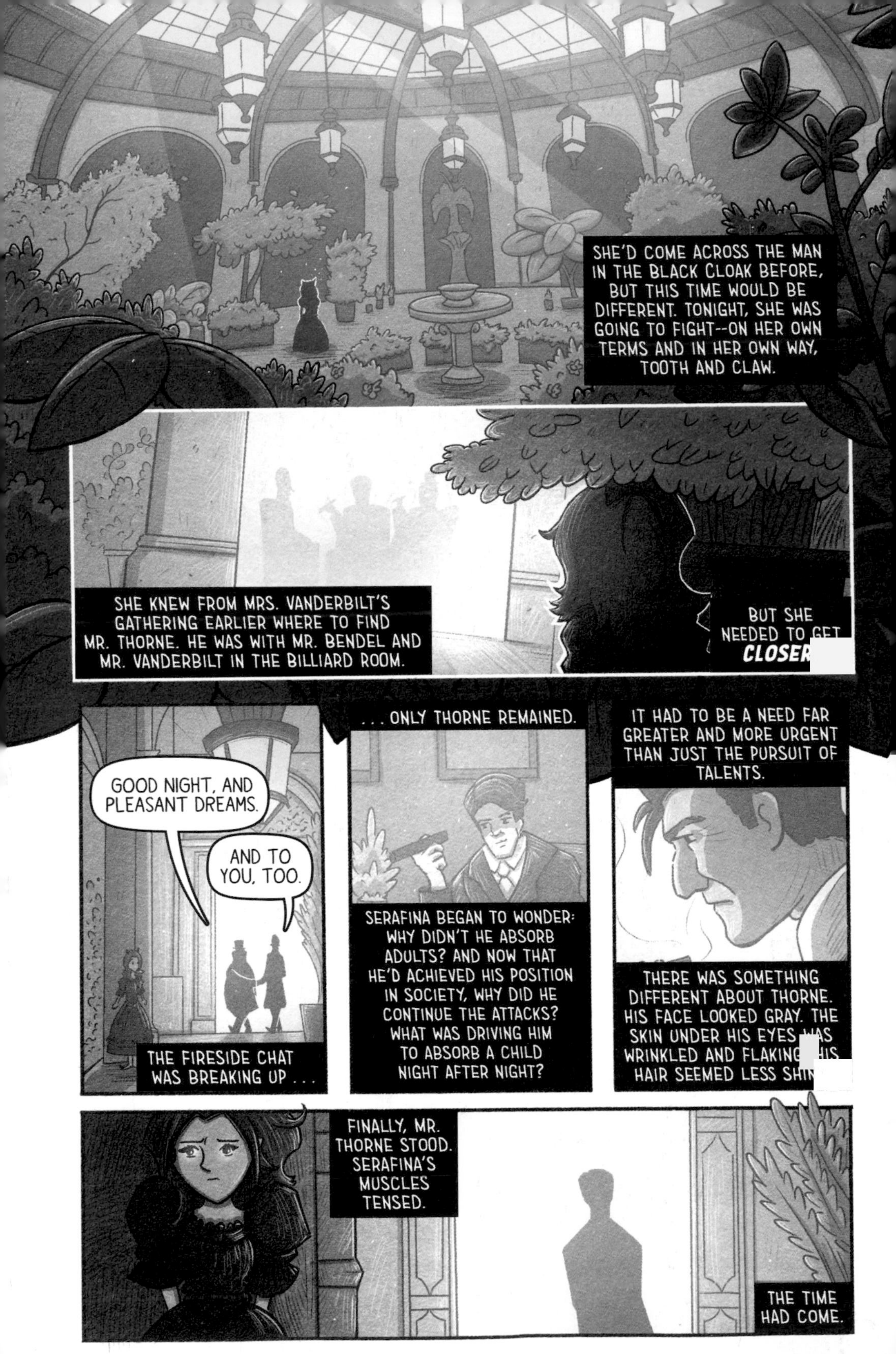
SHE'D COME ACROSS THE MAN IN THE BLACK CLOAK BEFORE, BUT THIS TIME WOULD BE DIFFERENT. TONIGHT, SHE WAS GOING TO FIGHT--ON HER OWN TERMS AND IN HER OWN WAY, TOOTH AND CLAW.
SHE KNEW FROM MRS. VANDERBILT'S GATHERING EARLIER WHERE TO FIND MR. THORNE. HE WAS WITH MR. BENDEL AND MR. VANDERBILT IN THE BILLIARD ROOM.
BUT SHE NEEDED TO GET CLOSER
GOOD NIGHT, AND PLEASANT DREAMS.
AND TO YOU, TOO.
THE FIRESIDE CHAT WAS BREAKING UP . . .
. . . ONLY THORNE REMAINED.
SERAFINA BEGAN TO WONDER: WHY DIDN'T HE ABSORB ADULTS? AND NOW THAT HE'D ACHIEVED HIS POSITION IN SOCIETY, WHY DID HE CONTINUE THE ATTACKS? WHAT WAS DRIVING HIM TO ABSORB A CHILD NIGHT AFTER NIGHT?
IT HAD TO BE A NEED FAR GREATER AND MORE URGENT THAN JUST THE PURSUIT OF TALENTS.
THERE WAS SOMETHING DIFFERENT ABOUT THORNE. HIS FACE LOOKED GRAY. THE SKIN UNDER HIS EYES WAS WRINKLED AND FLAKING HIS HAIR SEEMED LESS SHIN
FINALLY, MR. THORNE STOOD. SERAFINA'S MUSCLES TENSED.
THE TIME HAD COME.

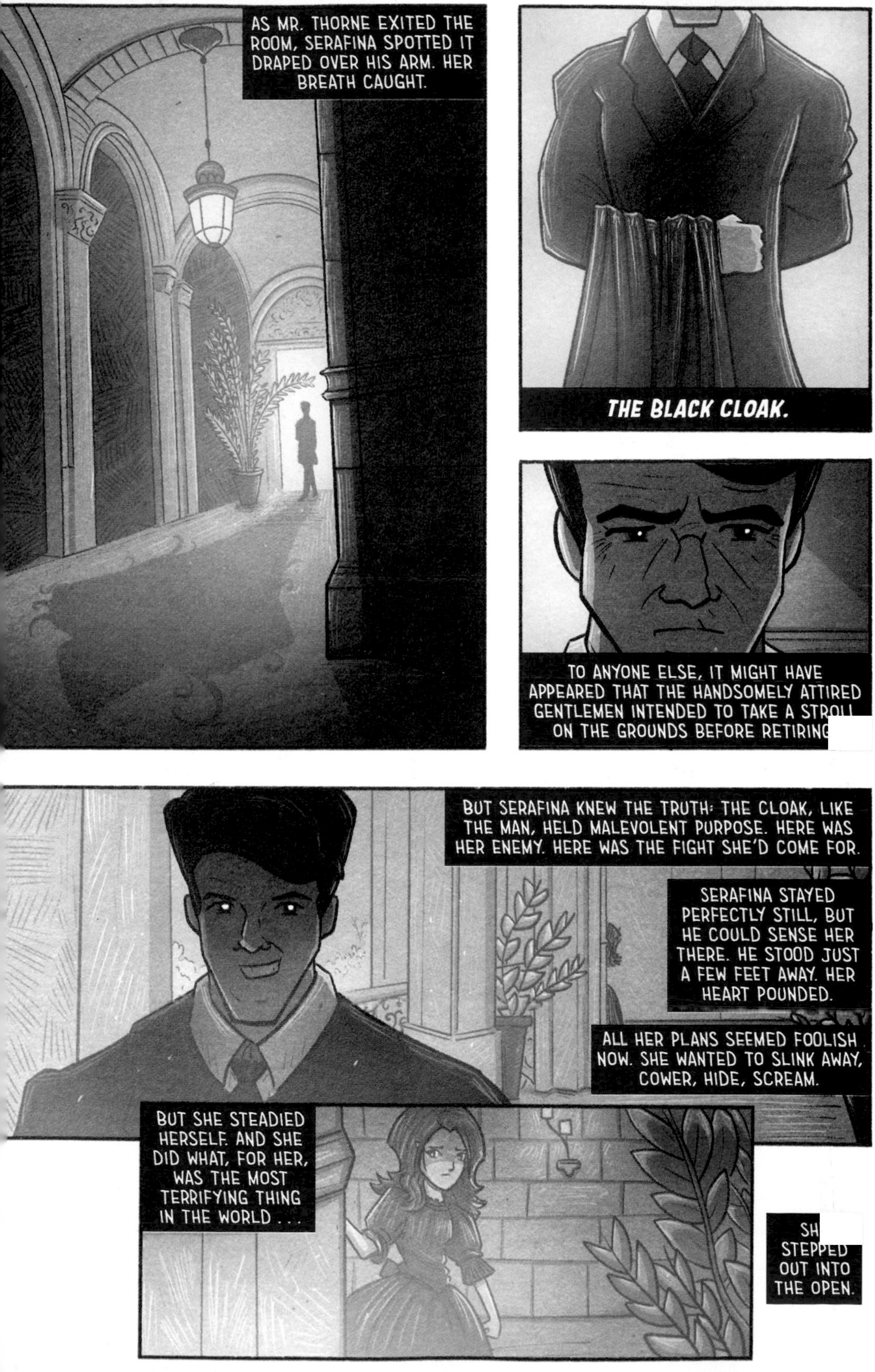

AS MR. THORNE EXITED THE ROOM, SERAFINA SPOTTED IT DRAPED OVER HIS ARM. HER BREATH CAUGHT.
THE BLACK CLOAK.
TO ANYONE ELSE, IT MIGHT HAVE APPEARED THAT THE HANDSOMELY ATTIRED GENTLEMEN INTENDED TO TAKE A STROLL ON THE GROUNDS BEFORE RETIRING
BUT SERAFINA KNEW THE TRUTH: THE CLOAK, LIKE THE MAN, HELD MALEVOLENT PURPOSE. HERE WAS HER ENEMY. HERE WAS THE FIGHT SHE'D COME FOR.
SERAFINA STAYED PERFECTLY STILL, BUT HE COULD SENSE HER THERE. HE STOOD JUST A FEW FEET AWAY. HER HEART POUNDED.
ALL HER PLANS SEEMED FOOLISH NOW. SHE WANTED TO SLINK AWAY, COWER, HIDE, SCREAM.
BUT SHE STEADIED HERSELF. AND SHE DID WHAT, FOR HER, WAS THE MOST TERRIFYING THING IN THE WORLD . . .
SH STEPPED OUT INTO THE OPEN.

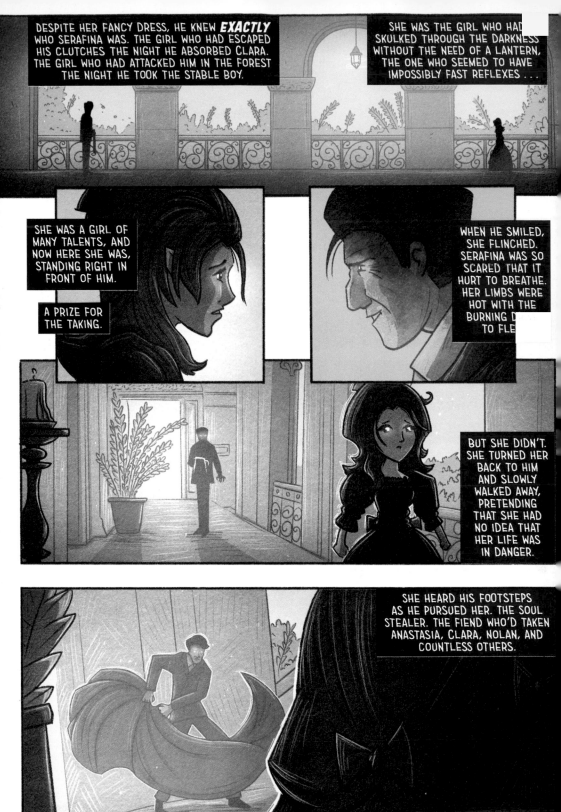

DESPITE HER FANCY DRESS, HE KNEW *EXACTLY* WHO SERAFINA WAS. THE GIRL WHO HAD ESCAPED HIS CLUTCHES THE NIGHT HE ABSORBED CLARA. THE GIRL WHO HAD ATTACKED HIM IN THE FOREST THE NIGHT HE TOOK THE STABLE BOY.

SHE WAS THE GIRL WHO HAD SKULKED THROUGH THE DARKNESS WITHOUT THE NEED OF A LANTERN, THE ONE WHO SEEMED TO HAVE IMPOSSIBLY FAST REFLEXES . . .

SHE WAS A GIRL OF MANY TALENTS, AND NOW HERE SHE WAS, STANDING RIGHT IN FRONT OF HIM.

A PRIZE FOR THE TAKING.

WHEN HE SMILED, SHE FLINCHED. SERAFINA WAS SO SCARED THAT IT HURT TO BREATHE. HER LIMBS WERE HOT WITH THE BURNING D TO FLE

BUT SHE DIDN'T. SHE TURNED HER BACK TO HIM AND SLOWLY WALKED AWAY, PRETENDING THAT SHE HAD NO IDEA THAT HER LIFE WAS IN DANGER.

SHE HEARD HIS FOOTSTEPS AS HE PURSUED HER. THE SOUL STEALER. THE FIEND WHO'D TAKEN ANASTASIA, CLARA, NOLAN, AND COUNTLESS OTHERS.

AND HE WAS RIGHT BEHIND HER.

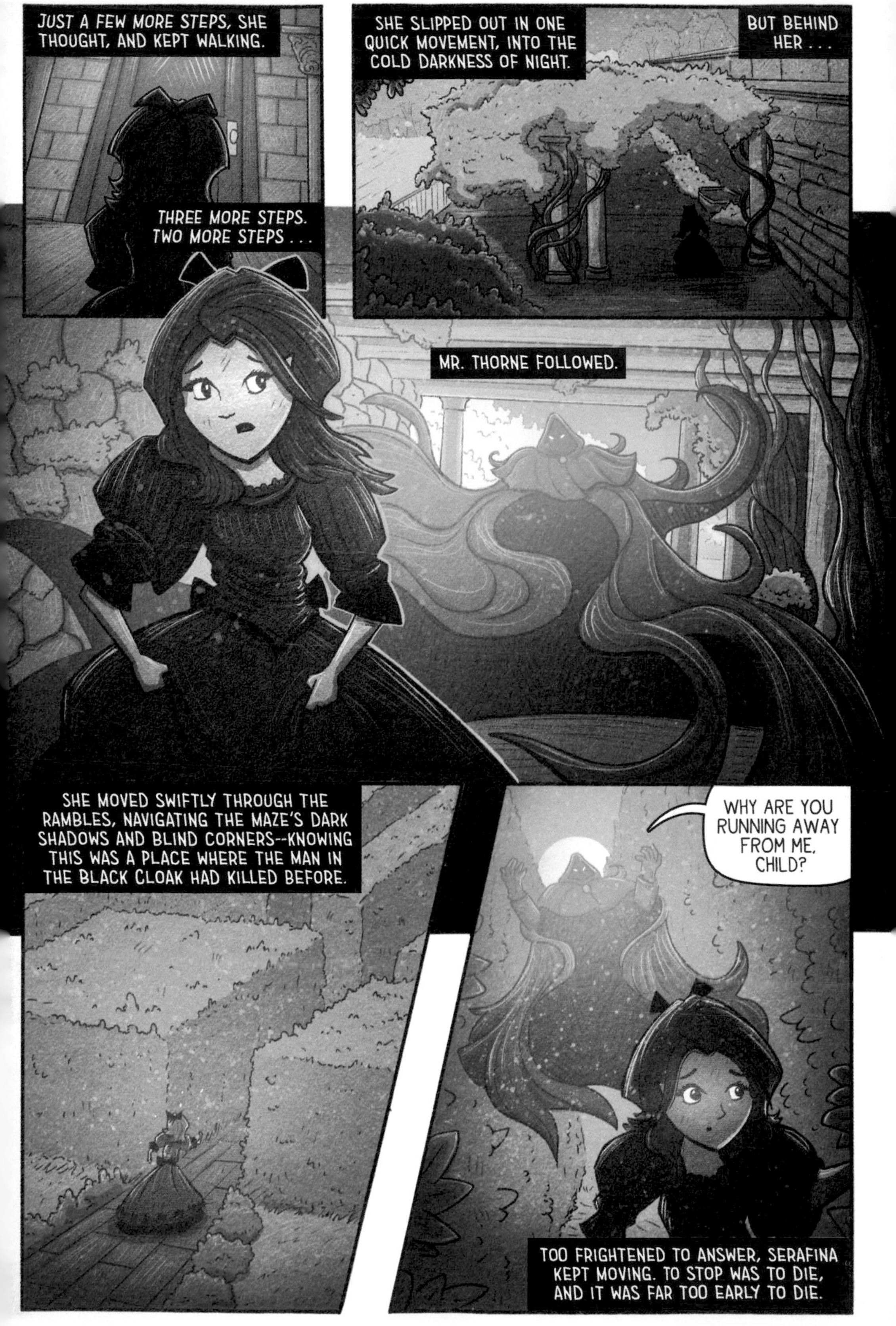
JUST A FEW MORE STEPS, SHE THOUGHT, AND KEPT WALKING.
THREE MORE STEPS. TWO MORE STEPS . . .
SHE SLIPPED OUT IN ONE QUICK MOVEMENT, INTO THE COLD DARKNESS OF NIGHT.
BUT BEHIND HER . . .
MR. THORNE FOLLOWED.
SHE MOVED SWIFTLY THROUGH THE RAMBLES, NAVIGATING THE MAZE'S DARK SHADOWS AND BLIND CORNERS--KNOWING THIS WAS A PLACE WHERE THE MAN IN THE BLACK CLOAK HAD KILLED BEFORE.
WHY ARE YOU RUNNING AWAY FROM ME, CHILD?
TOO FRIGHTENED TO ANSWER, SERAFINA KEPT MOVING. TO STOP WAS TO DIE, AND IT WAS FAR TOO EARLY TO DIE.

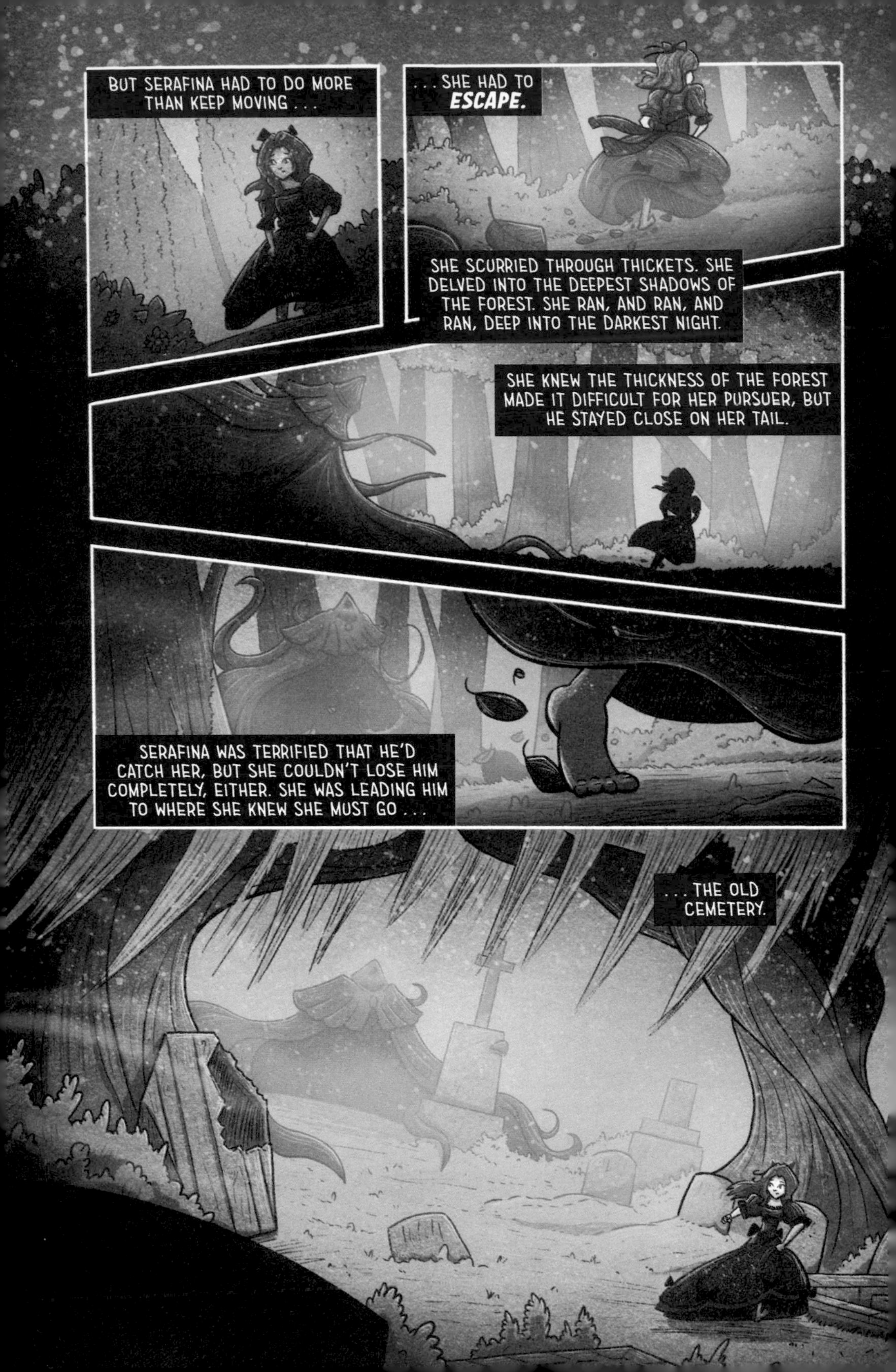
BUT SERAFINA HAD TO DO MORE THAN KEEP MOVING . . .
. . . SHE HAD TO *ESCAPE.*
SHE SCURRIED THROUGH THICKETS. SHE DELVED INTO THE DEEPEST SHADOWS OF THE FOREST. SHE RAN, AND RAN, AND RAN, DEEP INTO THE DARKEST NIGHT.
SHE KNEW THE THICKNESS OF THE FOREST MADE IT DIFFICULT FOR HER PURSUER, BUT HE STAYED CLOSE ON HER TAIL.
SERAFINA WAS TERRIFIED THAT HE'D CATCH HER, BUT SHE COULDN'T LOSE HIM COMPLETELY, EITHER. SHE WAS LEADING HIM TO WHERE SHE KNEW SHE MUST GO . . .
. . . THE OLD CEMETERY.

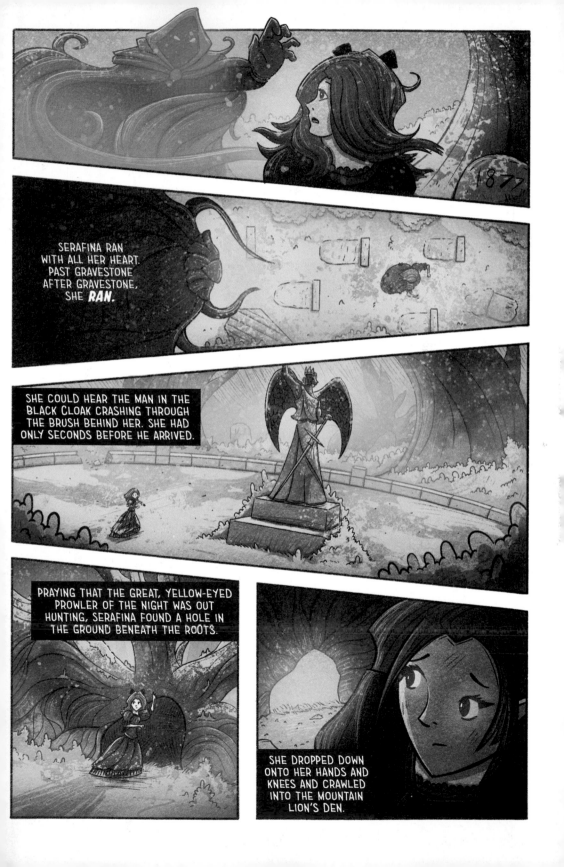

SERAFINA RAN WITH ALL HER HEART. PAST GRAVESTONE AFTER GRAVESTONE, SHE *RAN.*

SHE COULD HEAR THE MAN IN THE BLACK CLOAK CRASHING THROUGH THE BRUSH BEHIND HER. SHE HAD ONLY SECONDS BEFORE HE ARRIVED.

PRAYING THAT THE GREAT, YELLOW-EYED PROWLER OF THE NIGHT WAS OUT HUNTING, SERAFINA FOUND A HOLE IN THE GROUND BENEATH THE ROOTS.

SHE DROPPED DOWN ONTO HER HANDS AND KNEES AND CRAWLED INTO THE MOUNTAIN LION'S DEN.

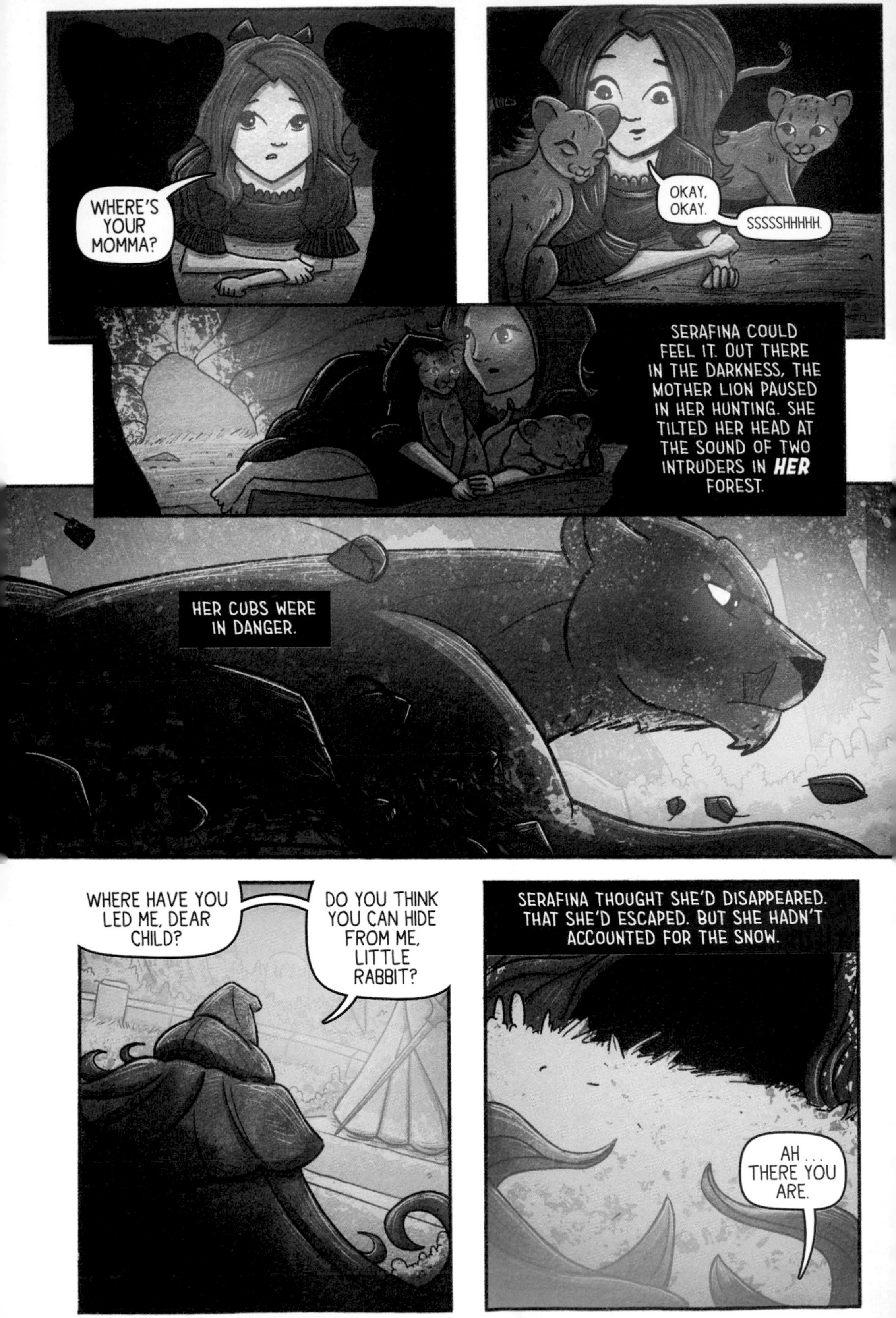
WHERE'S YOUR MOMMA?
OKAY, OKAY.
SSSSSHHHHH.
SERAFINA COULD FEEL IT. OUT THERE IN THE DARKNESS, THE MOTHER LION PAUSED IN HER HUNTING. SHE TILTED HER HEAD AT THE SOUND OF TWO INTRUDERS IN ***HER*** FOREST.
HER CUBS WERE IN DANGER.
WHERE HAVE YOU LED ME, DEAR CHILD?
DO YOU THINK YOU CAN HIDE FROM ME, LITTLE RABBIT?
SERAFINA THOUGHT SHE'D DISAPPEARED. THAT SHE'D ESCAPED. BUT SHE HADN'T ACCOUNTED FOR THE SNOW.
AH . . . THERE YOU ARE.

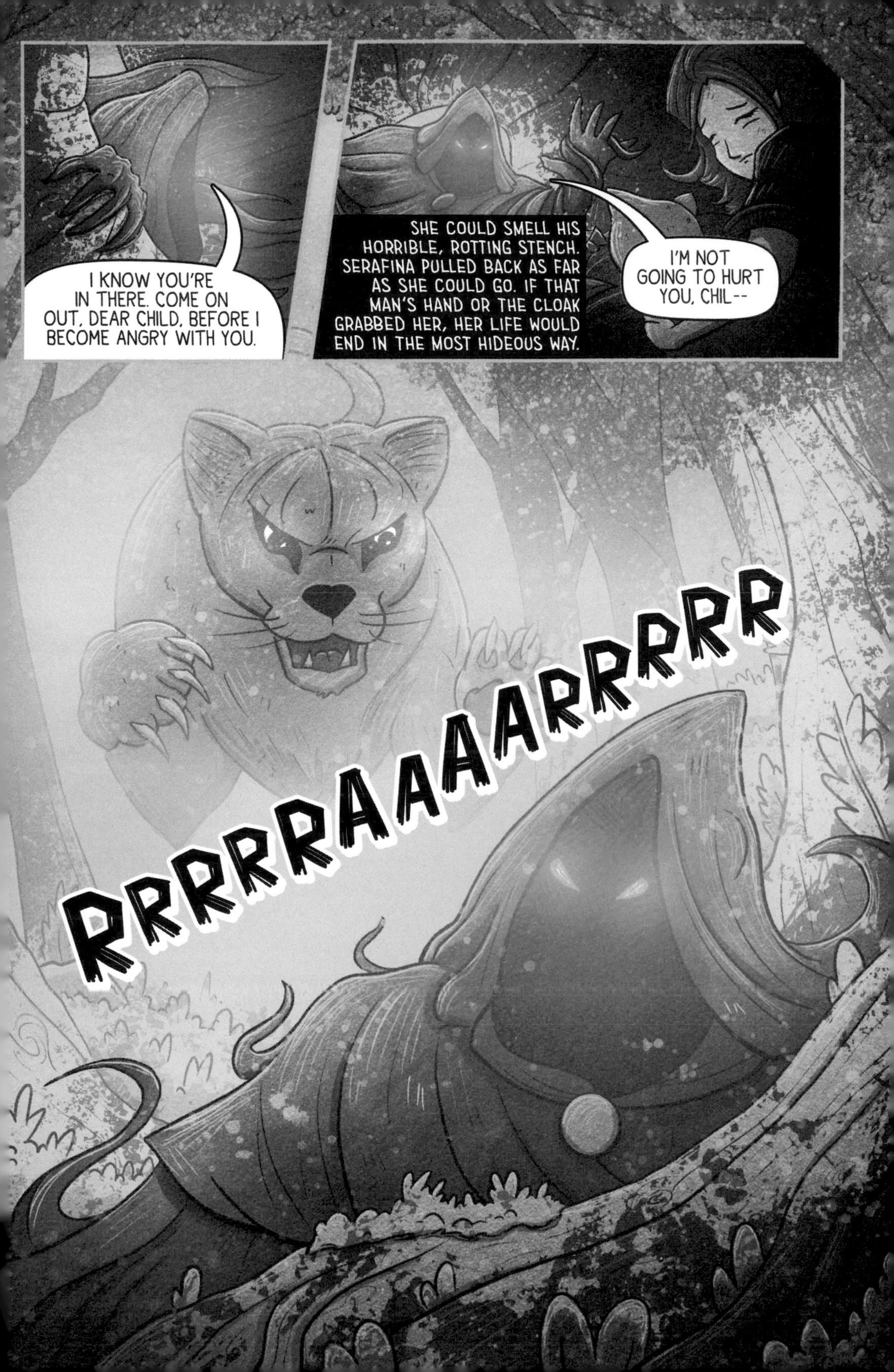
I KNOW YOU'RE IN THERE. COME ON OUT, DEAR CHILD, BEFORE I BECOME ANGRY WITH YOU.
SHE COULD SMELL HIS HORRIBLE, ROTTING STENCH. SERAFINA PULLED BACK AS FAR AS SHE COULD GO. IF THAT MAN'S HAND OR THE CLOAK GRABBED HER, HER LIFE WOULD END IN THE MOST HIDEOUS WAY.
I'M NOT GOING TO HURT YOU, CHIL--
RRRRRAAAAARRRRRR

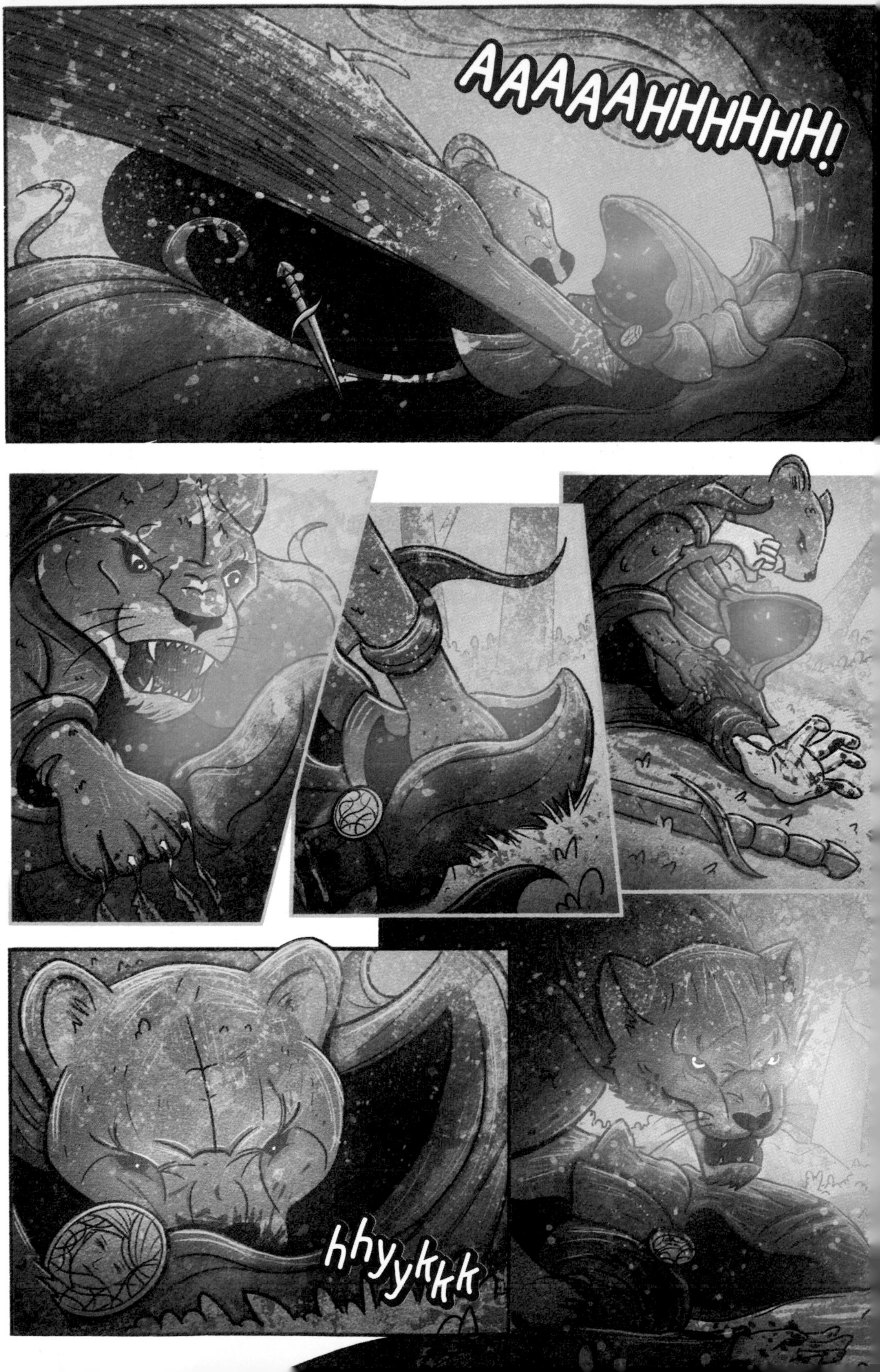
AAAAAHHHHHH!
hhyykkk

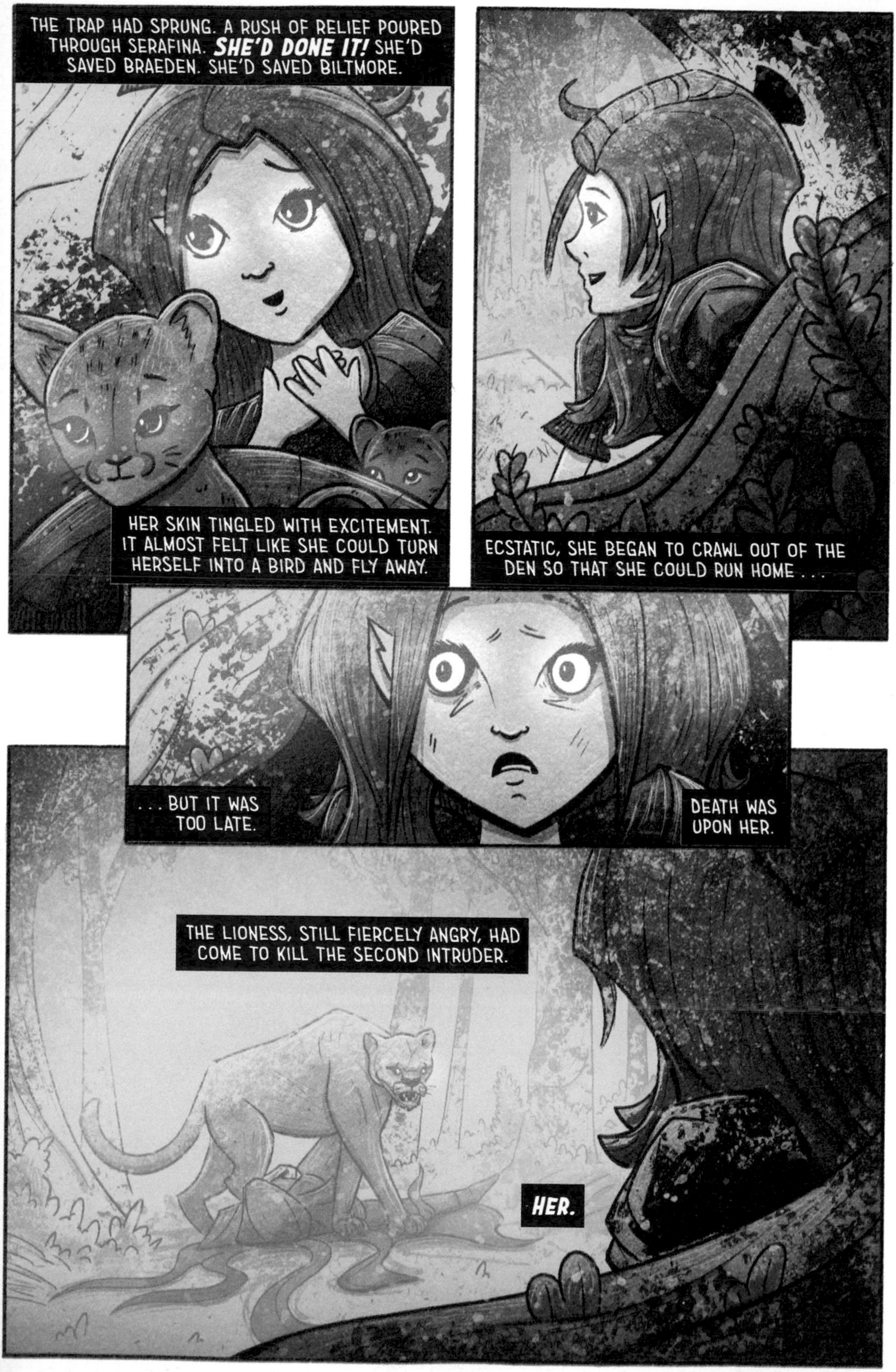

THE TRAP HAD SPRUNG. A RUSH OF RELIEF POURED THROUGH SERAFINA. SHE'D DONE IT! SHE'D SAVED BRAEDEN. SHE'D SAVED BILTMORE.
HER SKIN TINGLED WITH EXCITEMENT. IT ALMOST FELT LIKE SHE COULD TURN HERSELF INTO A BIRD AND FLY AWAY.
ECSTATIC, SHE BEGAN TO CRAWL OUT OF THE DEN SO THAT SHE COULD RUN HOME . . .
. . . BUT IT WAS TOO LATE.
DEATH WAS UPON HER.
THE LIONESS, STILL FIERCELY ANGRY, HAD COME TO KILL THE SECOND INTRUDER.
HER.

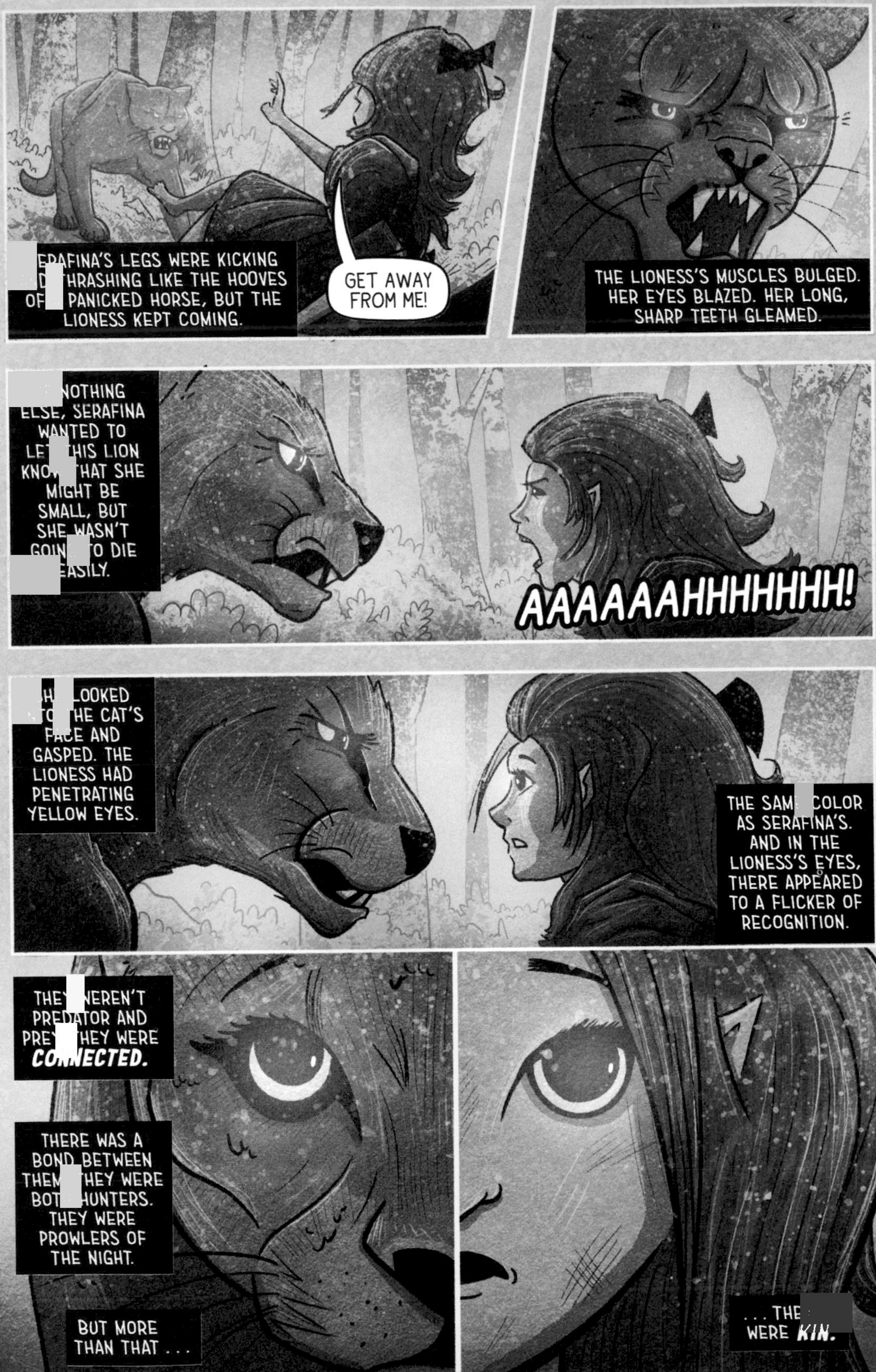
ERAFINA'S LEGS WERE KICKING
D THRASHING LIKE THE HOOVES
OF PANICKED HORSE, BUT THE
LIONESS KEPT COMING.
GET AWAY FROM ME!
THE LIONESS'S MUSCLES BULGED. HER EYES BLAZED. HER LONG, SHARP TEETH GLEAMED.
NOTHING ELSE, SERAFINA WANTED TO LET THIS LION KNO HAT SHE MIGHT BE SMALL, BUT SHE WASN'T GOIN TO DIE ASILY.
AAAAAAHHHHHHH!
H LOOKED TO HE CAT'S FACE AND GASPED. THE LIONESS HAD PENETRATING YELLOW EYES.
THE SAM COLOR AS SERAFINA'S. AND IN THE LIONESS'S EYES, THERE APPEARED TO A FLICKER OF RECOGNITION.
THEY EREN'T PREDATOR AND PREY HEY WERE CONNECTED.
THERE WAS A BOND BETWEEN THEM HEY WERE BOT HUNTERS. THEY WERE PROWLERS OF THE NIGHT.
BUT MORE THAN THAT . . .
. . . THE WERE KIN.

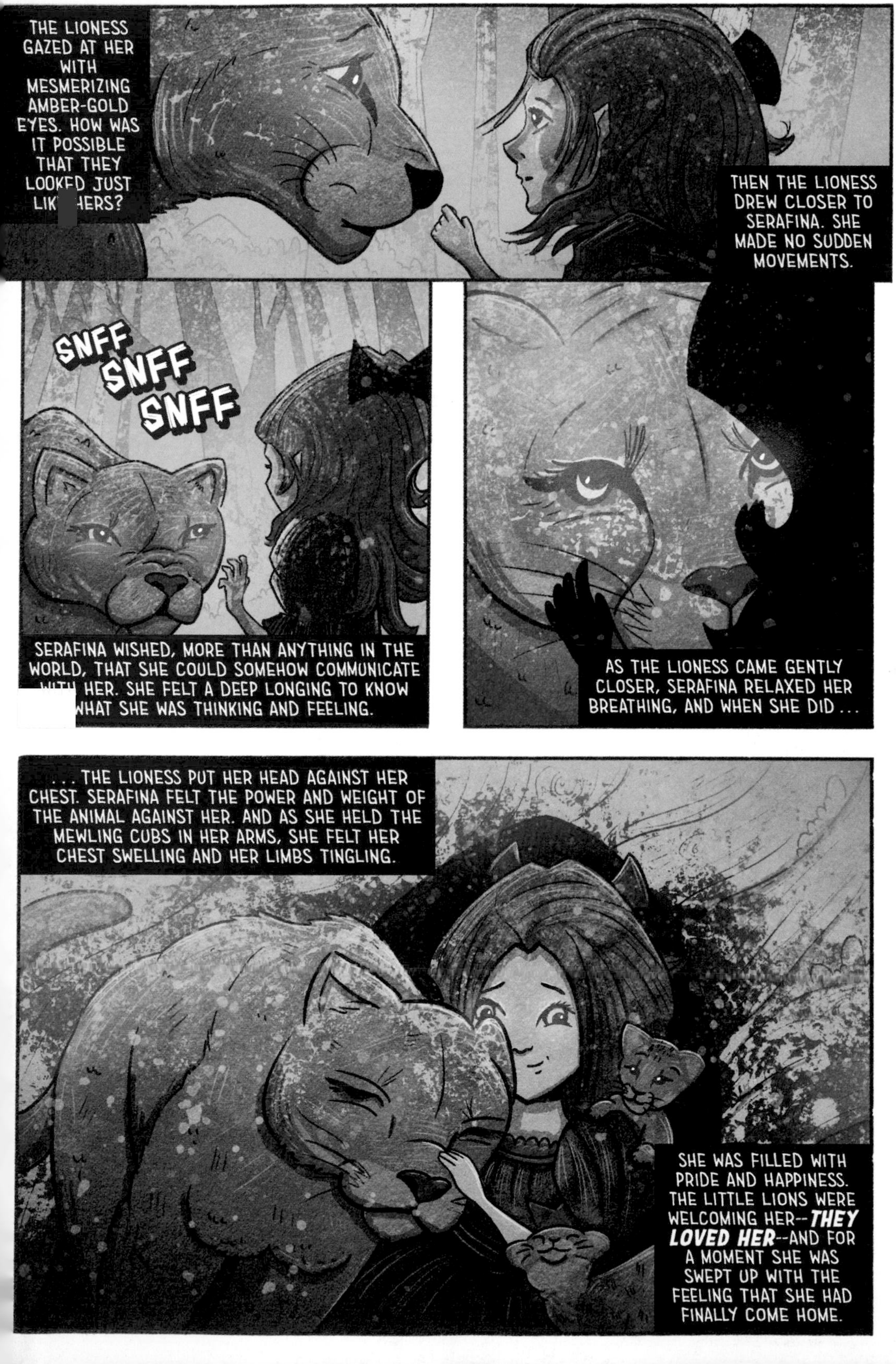
THE LIONESS GAZED AT HER WITH MESMERIZING AMBER-GOLD EYES. HOW WAS IT POSSIBLE THAT THEY LOOKED JUST LIK HERS?
THEN THE LIONESS DREW CLOSER TO SERAFINA. SHE MADE NO SUDDEN MOVEMENTS.
SNFF SNFF SNFF
SERAFINA WISHED, MORE THAN ANYTHING IN THE WORLD, THAT SHE COULD SOMEHOW COMMUNICATE WITH HER. SHE FELT A DEEP LONGING TO KNOW WHAT SHE WAS THINKING AND FEELING.
AS THE LIONESS CAME GENTLY CLOSER, SERAFINA RELAXED HER BREATHING, AND WHEN SHE DID . . .
. . . THE LIONESS PUT HER HEAD AGAINST HER CHEST. SERAFINA FELT THE POWER AND WEIGHT OF THE ANIMAL AGAINST HER. AND AS SHE HELD THE MEWLING CUBS IN HER ARMS, SHE FELT HER CHEST SWELLING AND HER LIMBS TINGLING.
SHE WAS FILLED WITH PRIDE AND HAPPINESS. THE LITTLE LIONS WERE WELCOMING HER--***THEY LOVED HER***--AND FOR A MOMENT SHE WAS SWEPT UP WITH THE FEELING THAT SHE HAD FINALLY COME HOME.

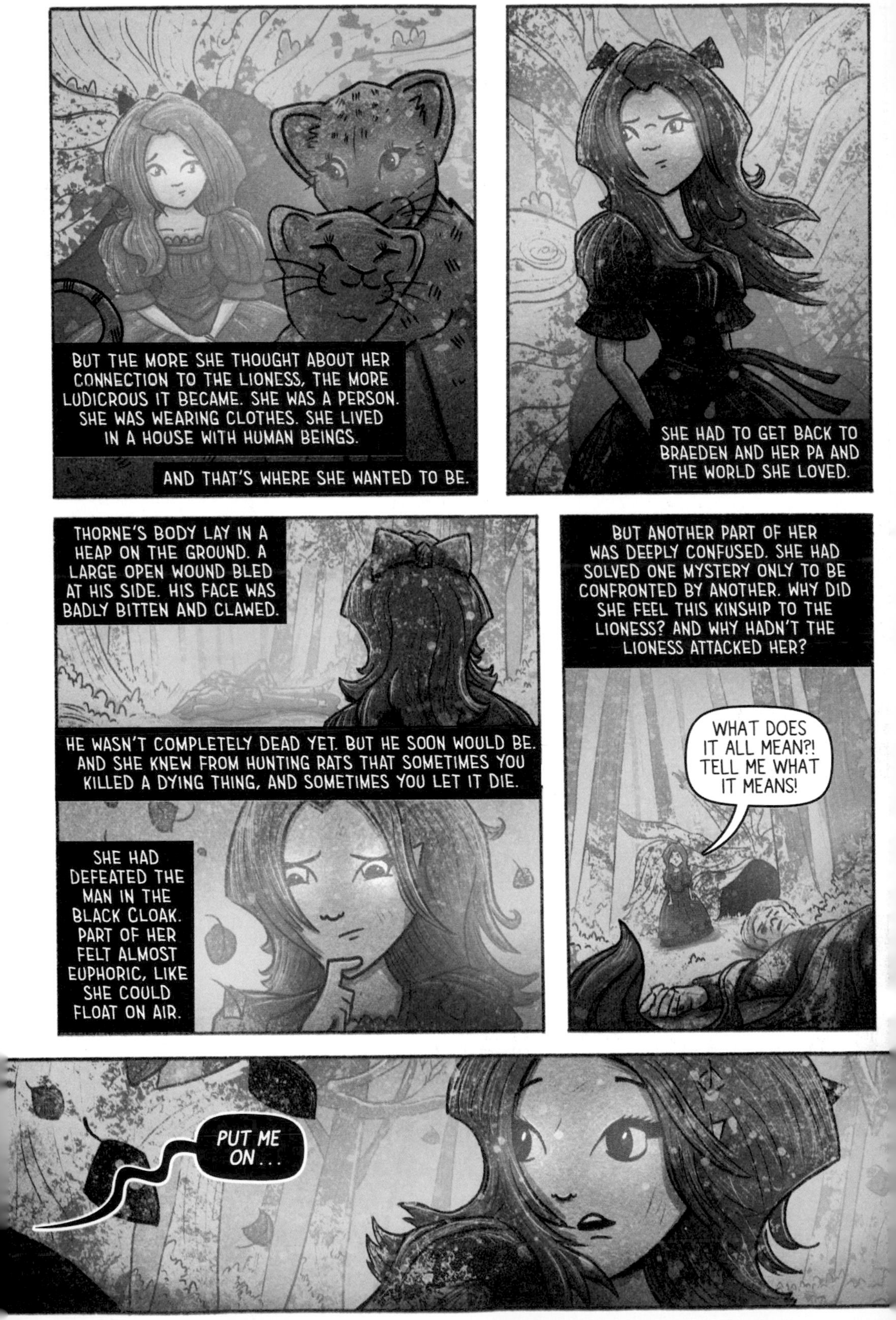
BUT THE MORE SHE THOUGHT ABOUT HER CONNECTION TO THE LIONESS, THE MORE LUDICROUS IT BECAME. SHE WAS A PERSON. SHE WAS WEARING CLOTHES. SHE LIVED IN A HOUSE WITH HUMAN BEINGS.
AND THAT'S WHERE SHE WANTED TO BE.
SHE HAD TO GET BACK TO BRAEDEN AND HER PA AND THE WORLD SHE LOVED.
THORNE'S BODY LAY IN A HEAP ON THE GROUND. A LARGE OPEN WOUND BLED AT HIS SIDE. HIS FACE WAS BADLY BITTEN AND CLAWED.
HE WASN'T COMPLETELY DEAD YET. BUT HE SOON WOULD BE. AND SHE KNEW FROM HUNTING RATS THAT SOMETIMES YOU KILLED A DYING THING, AND SOMETIMES YOU LET IT DIE.
SHE HAD DEFEATED THE MAN IN THE BLACK CLOAK. PART OF HER FELT ALMOST EUPHORIC, LIKE SHE COULD FLOAT ON AIR.
BUT ANOTHER PART OF HER WAS DEEPLY CONFUSED. SHE HAD SOLVED ONE MYSTERY ONLY TO BE CONFRONTED BY ANOTHER. WHY DID SHE FEEL THIS KINSHIP TO THE LIONESS? AND WHY HADN'T THE LIONESS ATTACKED HER?
WHAT DOES IT ALL MEAN?! TELL ME WHAT IT MEANS!
PUT ME ON . . .

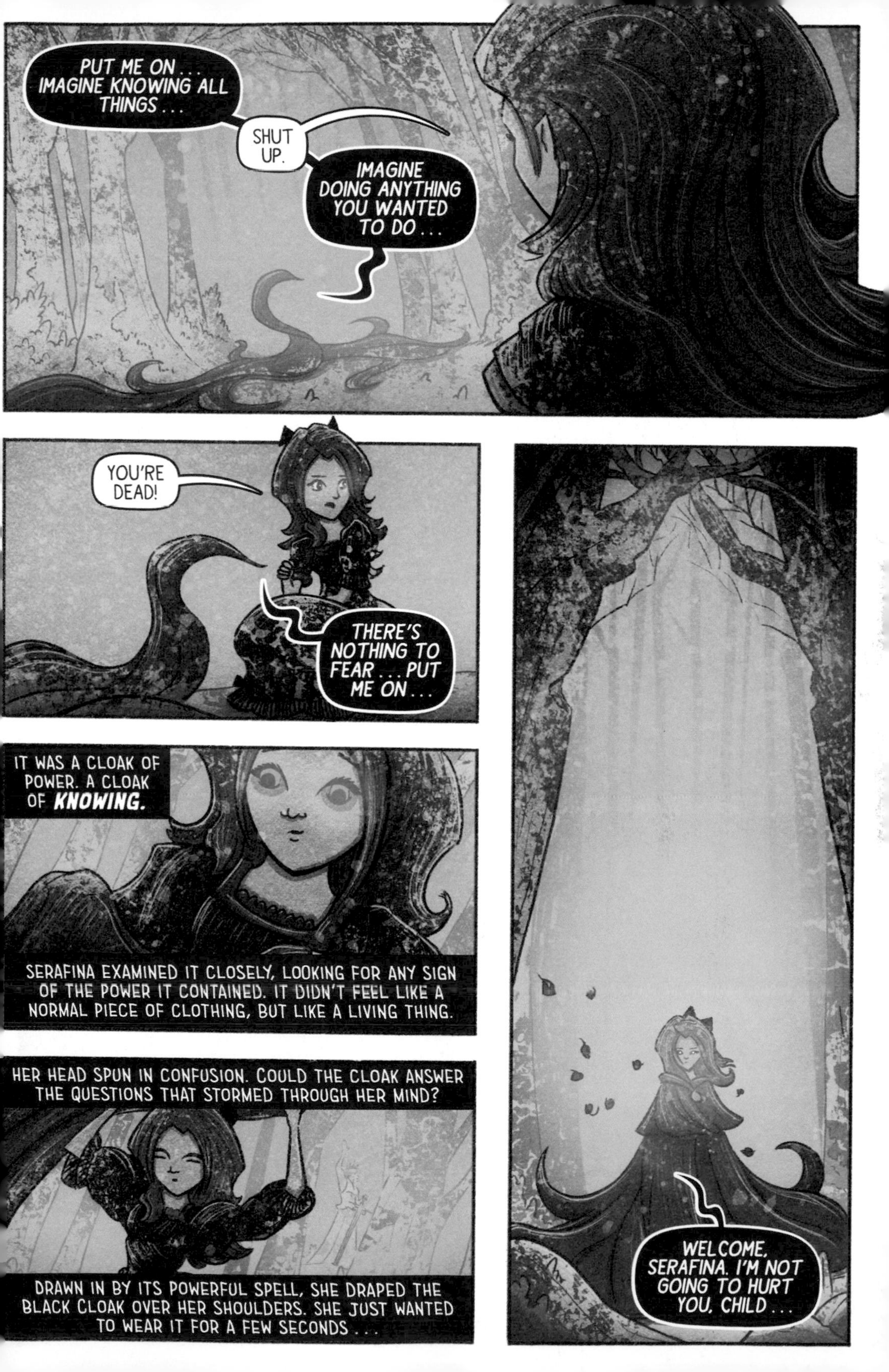
PUT ME ON . . . IMAGINE KNOWING ALL THINGS . . .
SHUT UP.
IMAGINE DOING ANYTHING YOU WANTED TO DO . . .
YOU'RE DEAD!
THERE'S NOTHING TO FEAR . . . PUT ME ON . . .
IT WAS A CLOAK OF POWER. A CLOAK OF ***KNOWING.***
SERAFINA EXAMINED IT CLOSELY, LOOKING FOR ANY SIGN OF THE POWER IT CONTAINED. IT DIDN'T FEEL LIKE A NORMAL PIECE OF CLOTHING, BUT LIKE A LIVING THING.
HER HEAD SPUN IN CONFUSION. COULD THE CLOAK ANSWER THE QUESTIONS THAT STORMED THROUGH HER MIND?
DRAWN IN BY ITS POWERFUL SPELL, SHE DRAPED THE BLACK CLOAK OVER HER SHOULDERS. SHE JUST WANTED TO WEAR IT FOR A FEW SECONDS . . .
WELCOME, SERAFINA. I'M NOT GOING TO HURT YOU, CHILD . . .

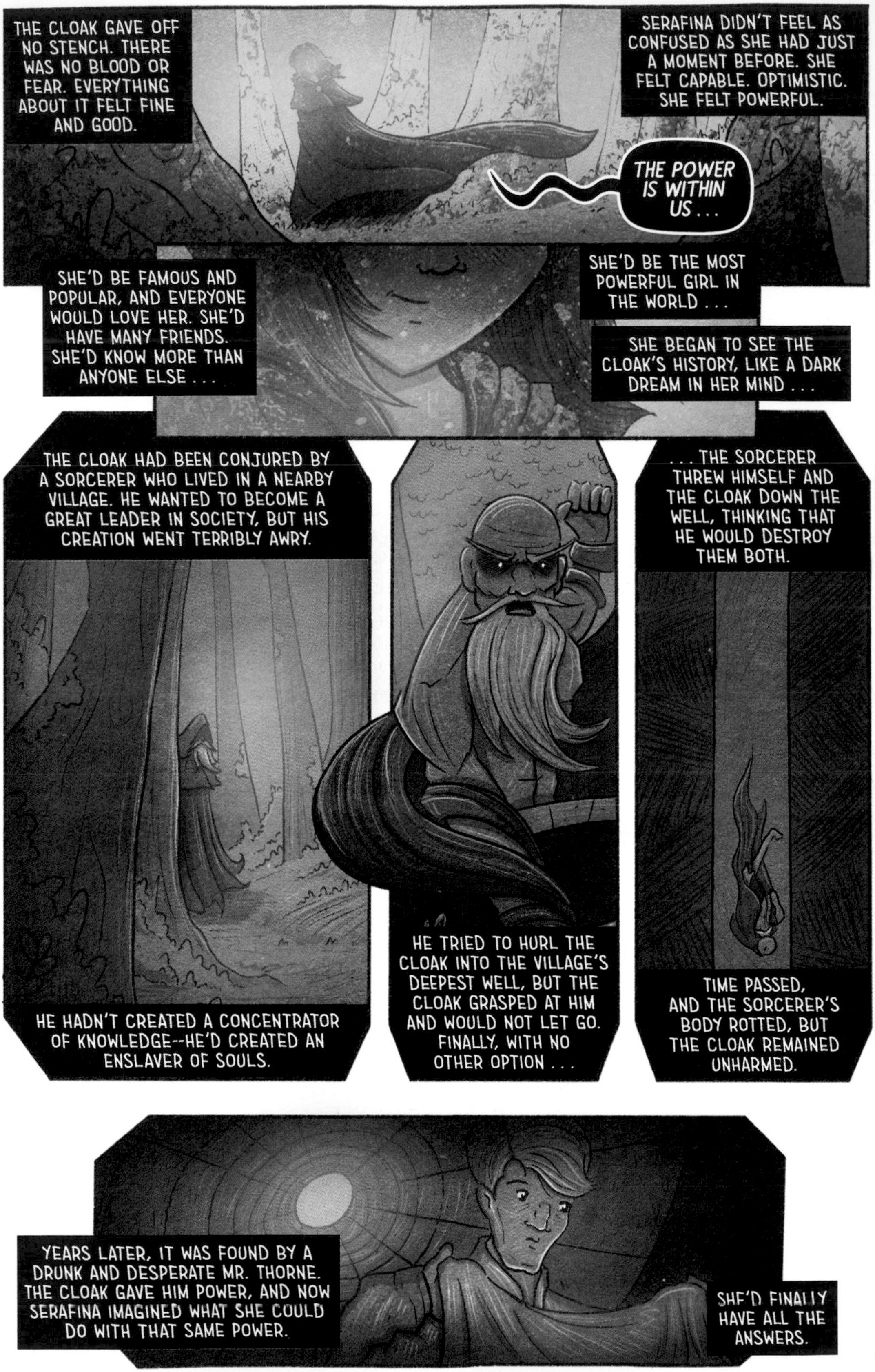
THE CLOAK GAVE OFF NO STENCH. THERE WAS NO BLOOD OR FEAR. EVERYTHING ABOUT IT FELT FINE AND GOOD.
SERAFINA DIDN'T FEEL AS CONFUSED AS SHE HAD JUST A MOMENT BEFORE. SHE FELT CAPABLE. OPTIMISTIC. SHE FELT POWERFUL.
THE POWER IS WITHIN US . . .
SHE'D BE FAMOUS AND POPULAR, AND EVERYONE WOULD LOVE HER. SHE'D HAVE MANY FRIENDS. SHE'D KNOW MORE THAN ANYONE ELSE . . .
SHE'D BE THE MOST POWERFUL GIRL IN THE WORLD . . .
SHE BEGAN TO SEE THE CLOAK'S HISTORY, LIKE A DARK DREAM IN HER MIND . . .
THE CLOAK HAD BEEN CONJURED BY A SORCERER WHO LIVED IN A NEARBY VILLAGE. HE WANTED TO BECOME A GREAT LEADER IN SOCIETY, BUT HIS CREATION WENT TERRIBLY AWRY.
HE HADN'T CREATED A CONCENTRATOR OF KNOWLEDGE--HE'D CREATED AN ENSLAVER OF SOULS.
HE TRIED TO HURL THE CLOAK INTO THE VILLAGE'S DEEPEST WELL, BUT THE CLOAK GRASPED AT HIM AND WOULD NOT LET GO. FINALLY, WITH NO OTHER OPTION . . .
. . . THE SORCERER THREW HIMSELF AND THE CLOAK DOWN THE WELL, THINKING THAT HE WOULD DESTROY THEM BOTH.
TIME PASSED, AND THE SORCERER'S BODY ROTTED, BUT THE CLOAK REMAINED UNHARMED.
YEARS LATER, IT WAS FOUND BY A DRUNK AND DESPERATE MR. THORNE. THE CLOAK GAVE HIM POWER, AND NOW SERAFINA IMAGINED WHAT SHE COULD DO WITH THAT SAME POWER.
SHE'D FINALLY HAVE ALL THE ANSWERS.

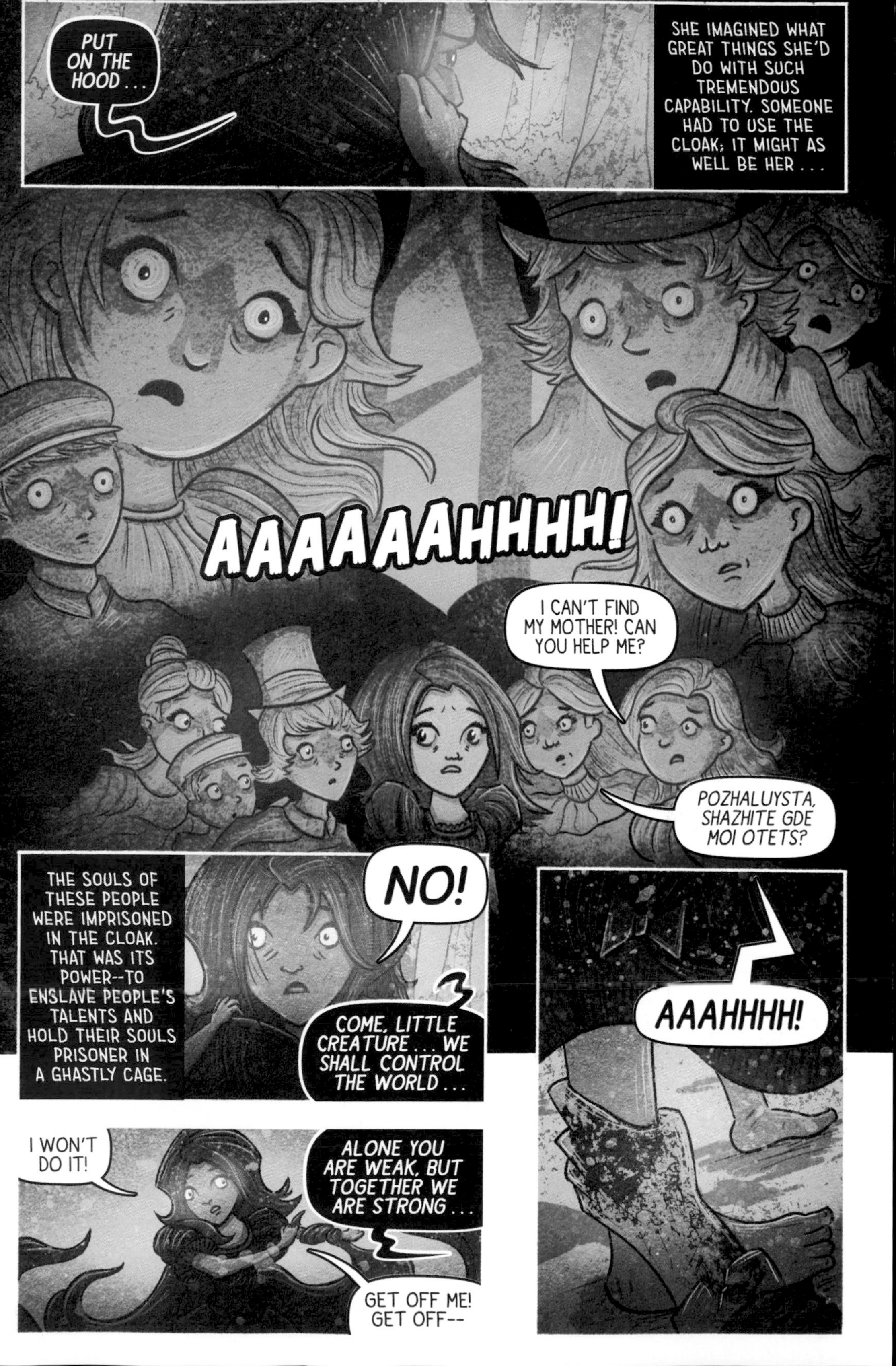
PUT ON THE HOOD . . .
SHE IMAGINED WHAT GREAT THINGS SHE'D DO WITH SUCH TREMENDOUS CAPABILITY. SOMEONE HAD TO USE THE CLOAK; IT MIGHT AS WELL BE HER . . .
AAAAAAHHHH!
I CAN'T FIND MY MOTHER! CAN YOU HELP ME?
POZHALUYSTA, SHAZHITE GDE MOI OTETS?
THE SOULS OF THESE PEOPLE WERE IMPRISONED IN THE CLOAK. THAT WAS ITS POWER--TO ENSLAVE PEOPLE'S TALENTS AND HOLD THEIR SOULS PRISONER IN A GHASTLY CAGE.
NO!
COME, LITTLE CREATURE . . . WE SHALL CONTROL THE WORLD . . .
I WON'T DO IT!
ALONE YOU ARE WEAK, BUT TOGETHER WE ARE STRONG . . .
GET OFF ME! GET OFF--
AAAHHHH!

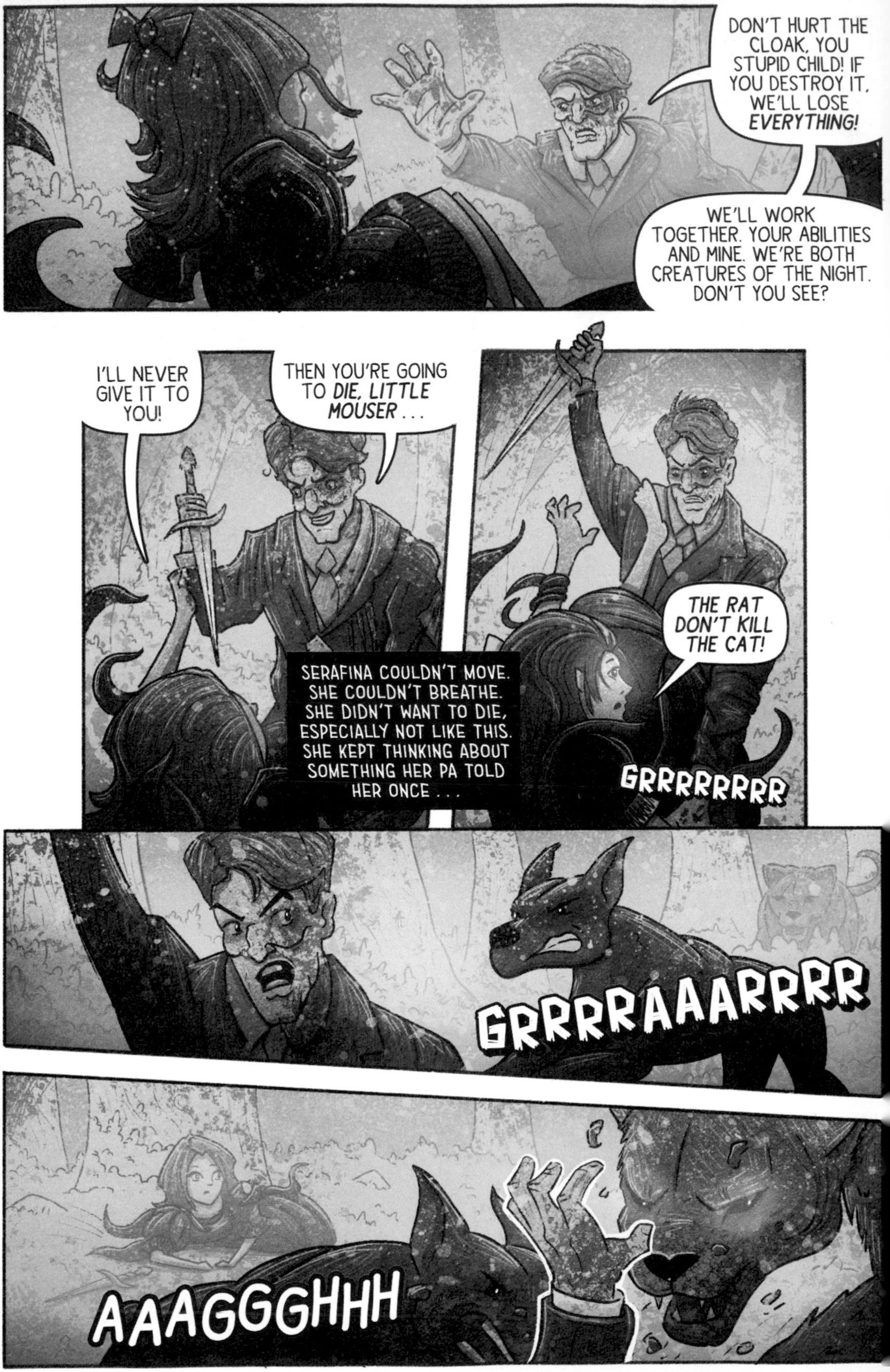
DON'T HURT THE CLOAK, YOU STUPID CHILD! IF YOU DESTROY IT, WE'LL LOSE *EVERYTHING!*
WE'LL WORK TOGETHER. YOUR ABILITIES AND MINE. WE'RE BOTH CREATURES OF THE NIGHT. DON'T YOU SEE?
I'LL NEVER GIVE IT TO YOU!
THEN YOU'RE GOING TO *DIE, LITTLE MOUSER* . . .
SERAFINA COULDN'T MOVE. SHE COULDN'T BREATHE. SHE DIDN'T WANT TO DIE, ESPECIALLY NOT LIKE THIS. SHE KEPT THINKING ABOUT SOMETHING HER PA TOLD HER ONCE . . .
THE RAT DON'T KILL THE CAT!
GRRRRRRRR
GRRRRAAARRRR
AAAGGGHHH

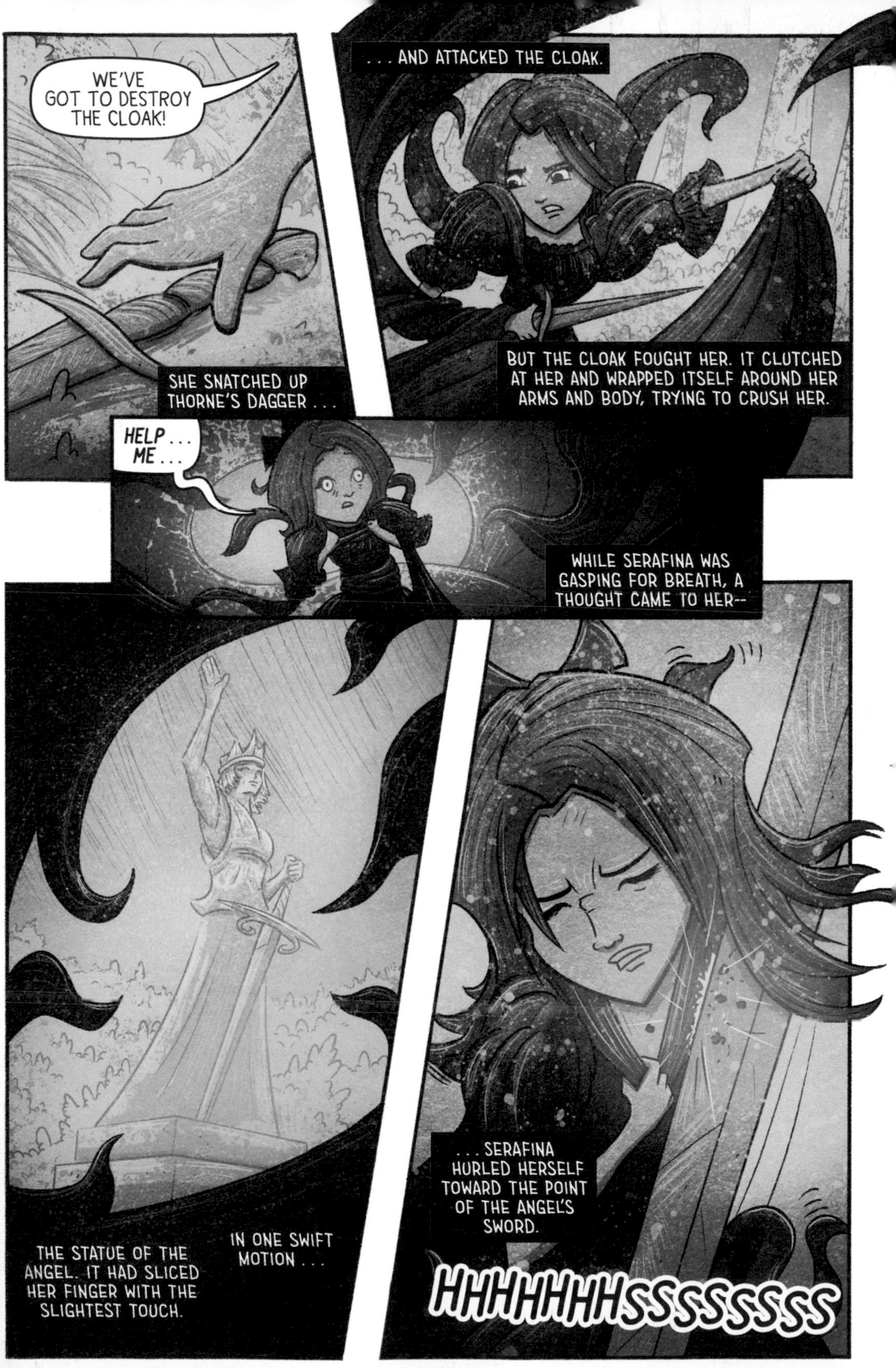
WE'VE GOT TO DESTROY THE CLOAK!
SHE SNATCHED UP THORNE'S DAGGER . . .
. . . AND ATTACKED THE CLOAK.
BUT THE CLOAK FOUGHT HER. IT CLUTCHED AT HER AND WRAPPED ITSELF AROUND HER ARMS AND BODY, TRYING TO CRUSH HER.
HELP . . . ME . . .
WHILE SERAFINA WAS GASPING FOR BREATH, A THOUGHT CAME TO HER--
THE STATUE OF THE ANGEL. IT HAD SLICED HER FINGER WITH THE SLIGHTEST TOUCH.
IN ONE SWIFT MOTION . . .
. . . SERAFINA HURLED HERSELF TOWARD THE POINT OF THE ANGEL'S SWORD.
HHHHHHHSSSSSSSS

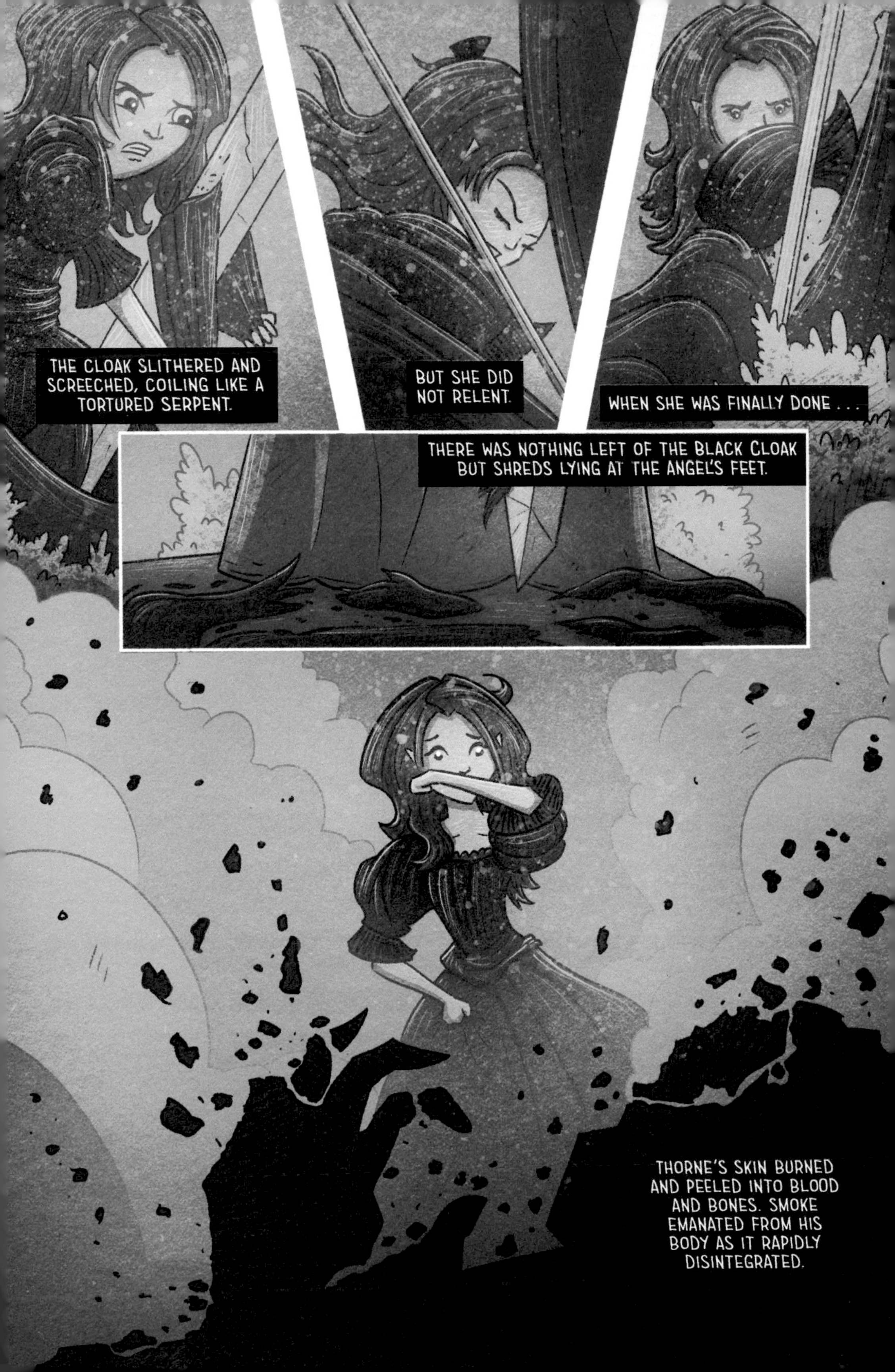

THE CLOAK SLITHERED AND SCREECHED, COILING LIKE A TORTURED SERPENT.
BUT SHE DID NOT RELENT.
WHEN SHE WAS FINALLY DONE . . .
THERE WAS NOTHING LEFT OF THE BLACK CLOAK BUT SHREDS LYING AT THE ANGEL'S FEET.
THORNE'S SKIN BURNED AND PEELED INTO BLOOD AND BONES. SMOKE EMANATED FROM HIS BODY AS IT RAPIDLY DISINTEGRATED.

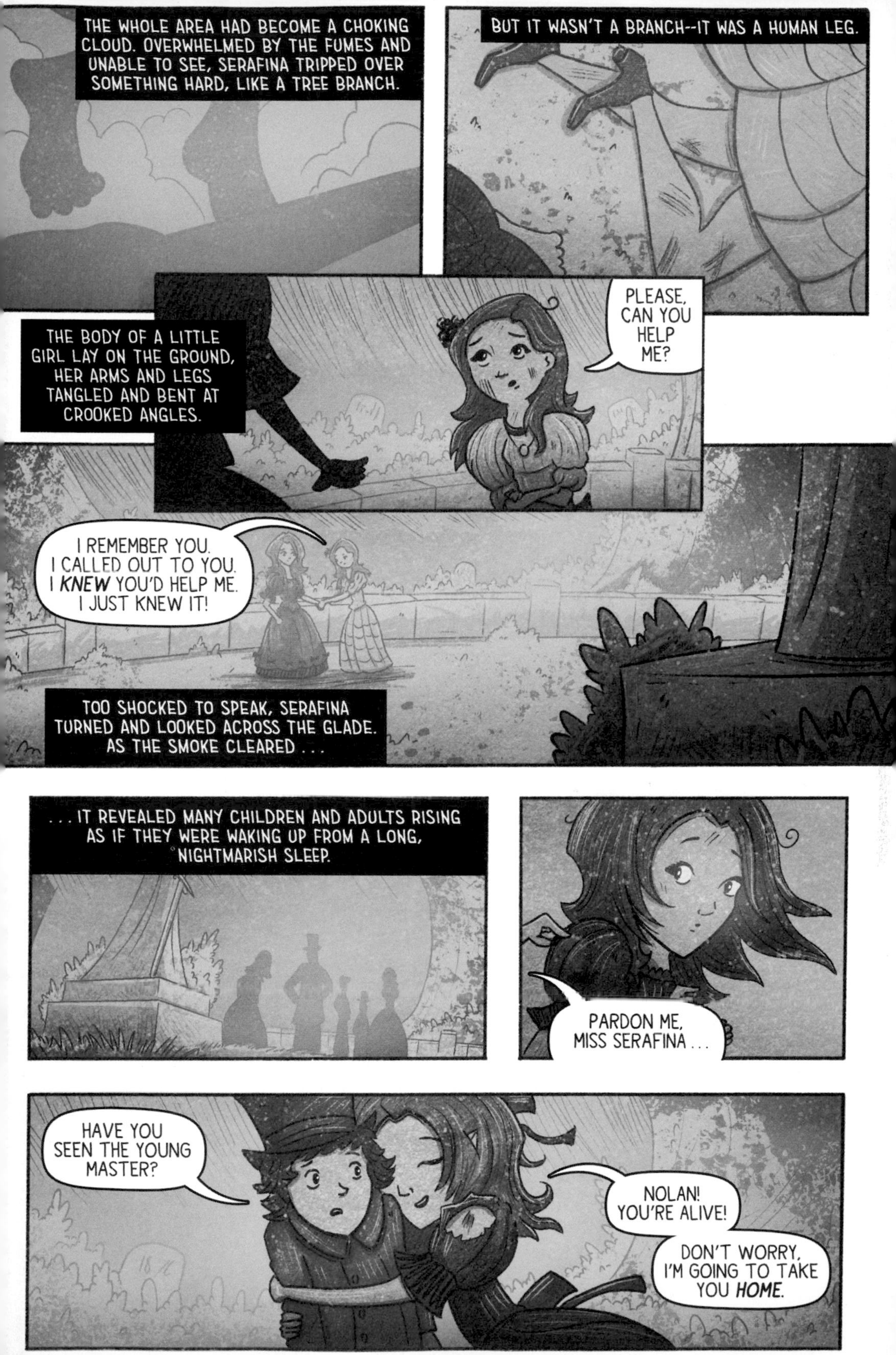

THE WHOLE AREA HAD BECOME A CHOKING CLOUD. OVERWHELMED BY THE FUMES AND UNABLE TO SEE, SERAFINA TRIPPED OVER SOMETHING HARD, LIKE A TREE BRANCH.
BUT IT WASN'T A BRANCH--IT WAS A HUMAN LEG.
THE BODY OF A LITTLE GIRL LAY ON THE GROUND, HER ARMS AND LEGS TANGLED AND BENT AT CROOKED ANGLES.
PLEASE, CAN YOU HELP ME?
I REMEMBER YOU. I CALLED OUT TO YOU. I KNEW YOU'D HELP ME. I JUST KNEW IT!
TOO SHOCKED TO SPEAK, SERAFINA TURNED AND LOOKED ACROSS THE GLADE. AS THE SMOKE CLEARED . . .
. . . IT REVEALED MANY CHILDREN AND ADULTS RISING AS IF THEY WERE WAKING UP FROM A LONG, NIGHTMARISH SLEEP.
PARDON ME, MISS SERAFINA . . .
HAVE YOU SEEN THE YOUNG MASTER?
NOLAN! YOU'RE ALIVE!
DON'T WORRY, I'M GOING TO TAKE YOU HOME.

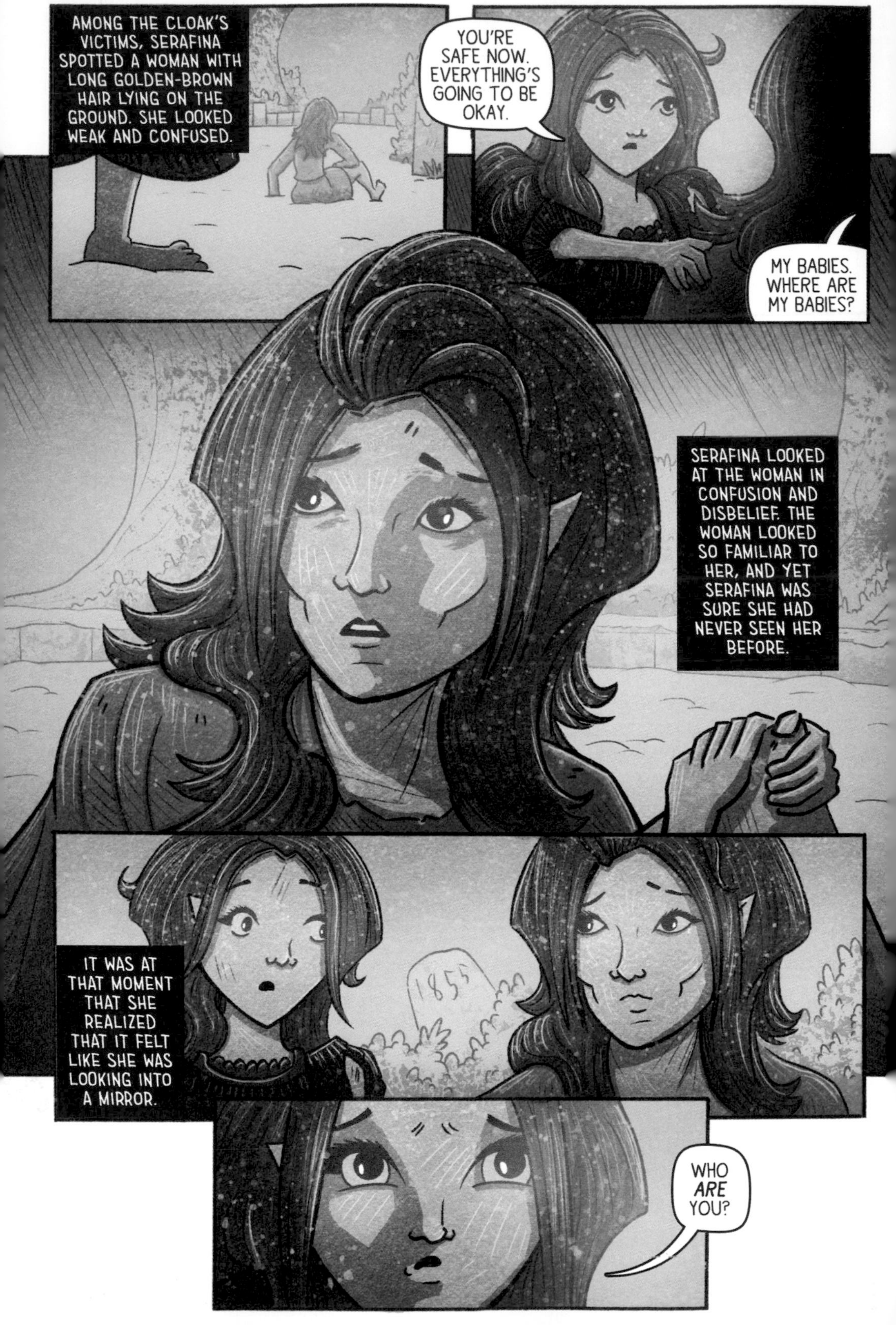
AMONG THE CLOAK'S VICTIMS, SERAFINA SPOTTED A WOMAN WITH LONG GOLDEN-BROWN HAIR LYING ON THE GROUND. SHE LOOKED WEAK AND CONFUSED.
YOU'RE SAFE NOW. EVERYTHING'S GOING TO BE OKAY.
MY BABIES. WHERE ARE MY BABIES?
SERAFINA LOOKED AT THE WOMAN IN CONFUSION AND DISBELIEF. THE WOMAN LOOKED SO FAMILIAR TO HER, AND YET SERAFINA WAS SURE SHE HAD NEVER SEEN HER BEFORE.
IT WAS AT THAT MOMENT THAT SHE REALIZED THAT IT FELT LIKE SHE WAS LOOKING INTO A MIRROR.
1855
WHO *ARE* YOU?

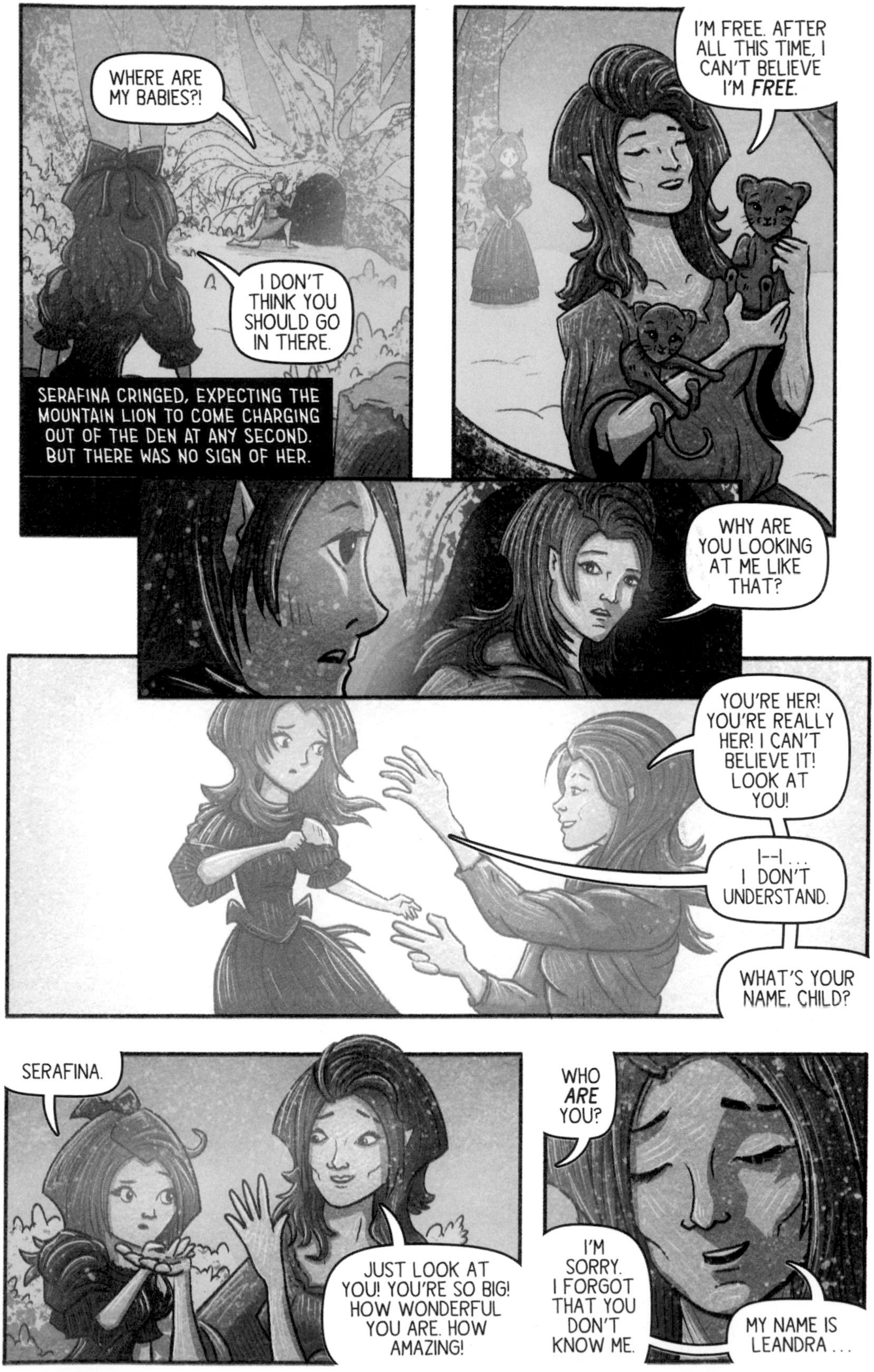
WHERE ARE MY BABIES?!
I DON'T THINK YOU SHOULD GO IN THERE.
SERAFINA CRINGED, EXPECTING THE MOUNTAIN LION TO COME CHARGING OUT OF THE DEN AT ANY SECOND. BUT THERE WAS NO SIGN OF HER.
I'M FREE. AFTER ALL THIS TIME, I CAN'T BELIEVE I'M *FREE*.
WHY ARE YOU LOOKING AT ME LIKE THAT?
YOU'RE HER! YOU'RE REALLY HER! I CAN'T BELIEVE IT! LOOK AT YOU!
I—I . . . I DON'T UNDERSTAND.
WHAT'S YOUR NAME, CHILD?
SERAFINA.
JUST LOOK AT YOU! YOU'RE SO BIG! HOW WONDERFUL YOU ARE. HOW AMAZING!
WHO *ARE* YOU?
I'M SORRY. I FORGOT THAT YOU DON'T KNOW ME.
MY NAME IS LEANDRA . . .

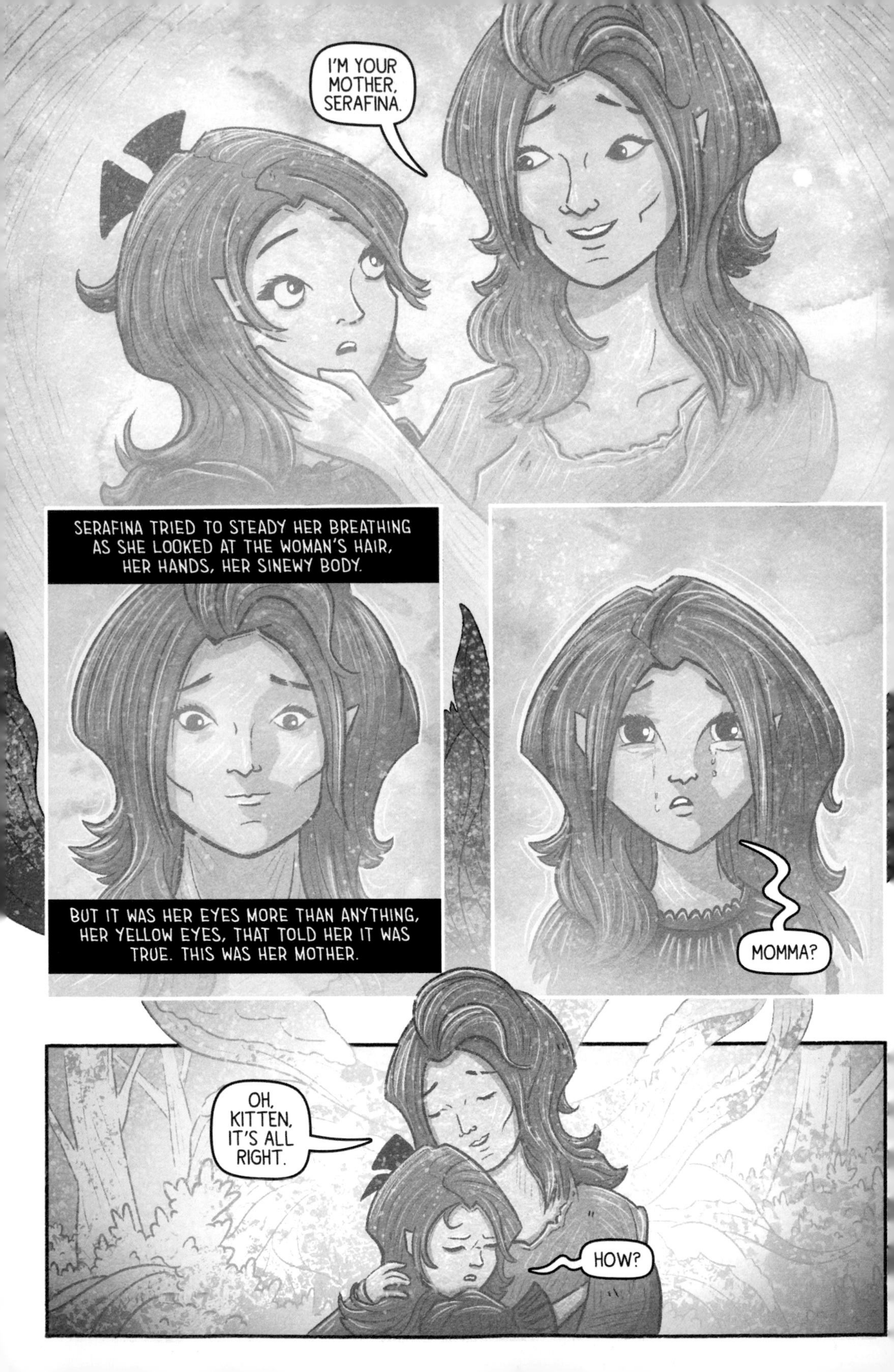
I'M YOUR MOTHER, SERAFINA.
SERAFINA TRIED TO STEADY HER BREATHING AS SHE LOOKED AT THE WOMAN'S HAIR, HER HANDS, HER SINEWY BODY.
BUT IT WAS HER EYES MORE THAN ANYTHING, HER YELLOW EYES, THAT TOLD HER IT WAS TRUE. THIS WAS HER MOTHER.
MOMMA?
OH, KITTEN, IT'S ALL RIGHT.
HOW?

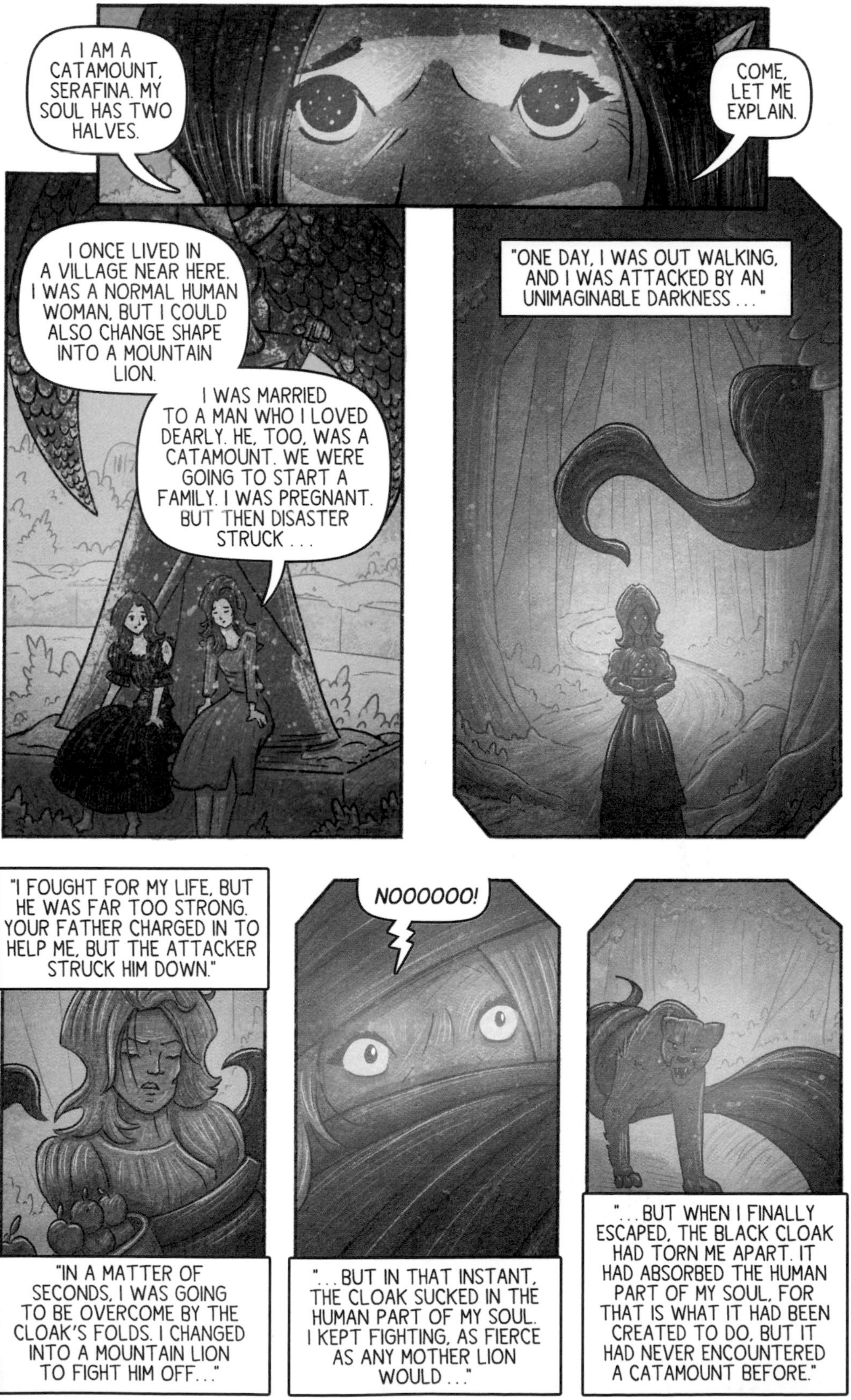
I AM A CATAMOUNT, SERAFINA. MY SOUL HAS TWO HALVES.
COME, LET ME EXPLAIN.
I ONCE LIVED IN A VILLAGE NEAR HERE. I WAS A NORMAL HUMAN WOMAN, BUT I COULD ALSO CHANGE SHAPE INTO A MOUNTAIN LION.
I WAS MARRIED TO A MAN WHO I LOVED DEARLY. HE, TOO, WAS A CATAMOUNT. WE WERE GOING TO START A FAMILY. I WAS PREGNANT. BUT THEN DISASTER STRUCK . . .
"ONE DAY, I WAS OUT WALKING, AND I WAS ATTACKED BY AN UNIMAGINABLE DARKNESS . . ."
"I FOUGHT FOR MY LIFE, BUT HE WAS FAR TOO STRONG. YOUR FATHER CHARGED IN TO HELP ME, BUT THE ATTACKER STRUCK HIM DOWN."
"IN A MATTER OF SECONDS, I WAS GOING TO BE OVERCOME BY THE CLOAK'S FOLDS. I CHANGED INTO A MOUNTAIN LION TO FIGHT HIM OFF . . ."
NOOOOOO!
". . . BUT IN THAT INSTANT, THE CLOAK SUCKED IN THE HUMAN PART OF MY SOUL. I KEPT FIGHTING, AS FIERCE AS ANY MOTHER LION WOULD . . ."
". . . BUT WHEN I FINALLY ESCAPED, THE BLACK CLOAK HAD TORN ME APART. IT HAD ABSORBED THE HUMAN PART OF MY SOUL, FOR THAT IS WHAT IT HAD BEEN CREATED TO DO, BUT IT HAD NEVER ENCOUNTERED A CATAMOUNT BEFORE."

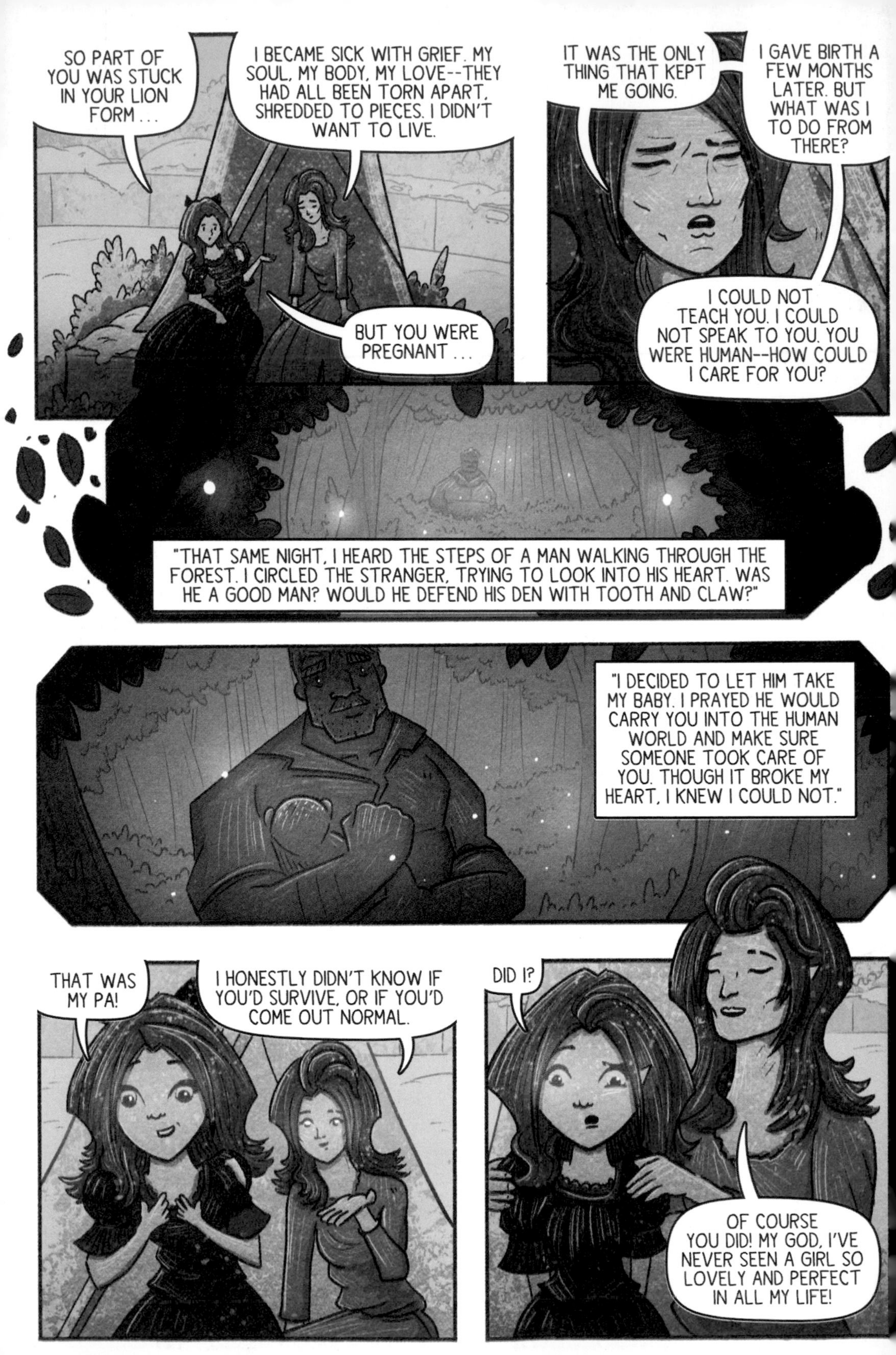
SO PART OF YOU WAS STUCK IN YOUR LION FORM . . .
I BECAME SICK WITH GRIEF. MY SOUL, MY BODY, MY LOVE--THEY HAD ALL BEEN TORN APART, SHREDDED TO PIECES. I DIDN'T WANT TO LIVE.
BUT YOU WERE PREGNANT . . .
IT WAS THE ONLY THING THAT KEPT ME GOING.
I GAVE BIRTH A FEW MONTHS LATER. BUT WHAT WAS I TO DO FROM THERE?
I COULD NOT TEACH YOU. I COULD NOT SPEAK TO YOU. YOU WERE HUMAN--HOW COULD I CARE FOR YOU?
"THAT SAME NIGHT, I HEARD THE STEPS OF A MAN WALKING THROUGH THE FOREST. I CIRCLED THE STRANGER, TRYING TO LOOK INTO HIS HEART. WAS HE A GOOD MAN? WOULD HE DEFEND HIS DEN WITH TOOTH AND CLAW?"
"I DECIDED TO LET HIM TAKE MY BABY. I PRAYED HE WOULD CARRY YOU INTO THE HUMAN WORLD AND MAKE SURE SOMEONE TOOK CARE OF YOU. THOUGH IT BROKE MY HEART, I KNEW I COULD NOT."
THAT WAS MY PA!
I HONESTLY DIDN'T KNOW IF YOU'D SURVIVE, OR IF YOU'D COME OUT NORMAL.
DID I?
OF COURSE YOU DID! MY GOD, I'VE NEVER SEEN A GIRL SO LOVELY AND PERFECT IN ALL MY LIFE!

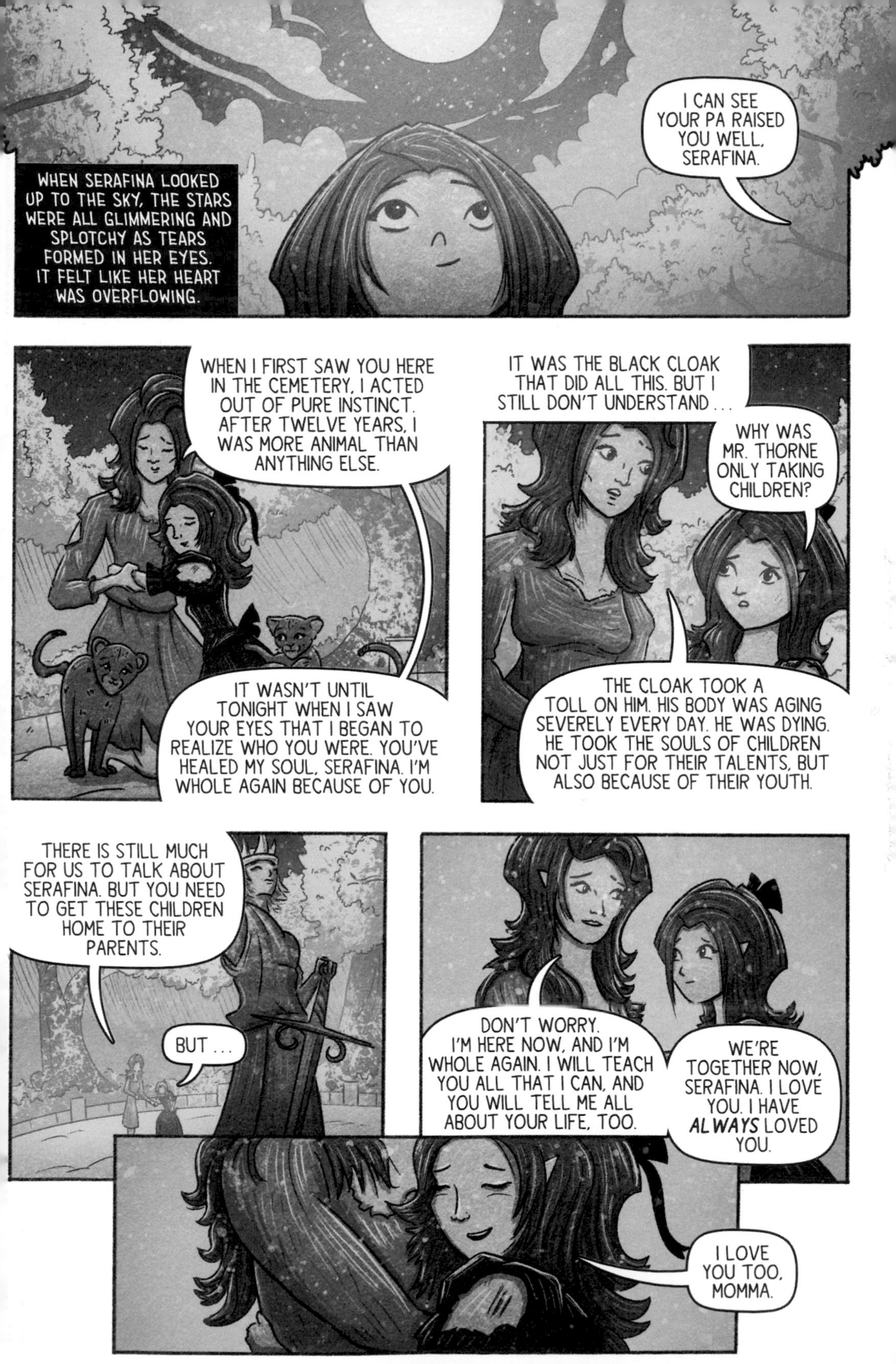
WHEN SERAFINA LOOKED UP TO THE SKY, THE STARS WERE ALL GLIMMERING AND SPLOTCHY AS TEARS FORMED IN HER EYES. IT FELT LIKE HER HEART WAS OVERFLOWING.
I CAN SEE YOUR PA RAISED YOU WELL, SERAFINA.
WHEN I FIRST SAW YOU HERE IN THE CEMETERY, I ACTED OUT OF PURE INSTINCT. AFTER TWELVE YEARS, I WAS MORE ANIMAL THAN ANYTHING ELSE.
IT WASN'T UNTIL TONIGHT WHEN I SAW YOUR EYES THAT I BEGAN TO REALIZE WHO YOU WERE. YOU'VE HEALED MY SOUL, SERAFINA. I'M WHOLE AGAIN BECAUSE OF YOU.
IT WAS THE BLACK CLOAK THAT DID ALL THIS. BUT I STILL DON'T UNDERSTAND . . .
WHY WAS MR. THORNE ONLY TAKING CHILDREN?
THE CLOAK TOOK A TOLL ON HIM. HIS BODY WAS AGING SEVERELY EVERY DAY. HE WAS DYING. HE TOOK THE SOULS OF CHILDREN NOT JUST FOR THEIR TALENTS, BUT ALSO BECAUSE OF THEIR YOUTH.
THERE IS STILL MUCH FOR US TO TALK ABOUT SERAFINA. BUT YOU NEED TO GET THESE CHILDREN HOME TO THEIR PARENTS.
BUT . . .
DON'T WORRY. I'M HERE NOW, AND I'M WHOLE AGAIN. I WILL TEACH YOU ALL THAT I CAN, AND YOU WILL TELL ME ALL ABOUT YOUR LIFE, TOO.
WE'RE TOGETHER NOW, SERAFINA. I LOVE YOU. I HAVE *ALWAYS* LOVED YOU.
I LOVE YOU TOO, MOMMA.

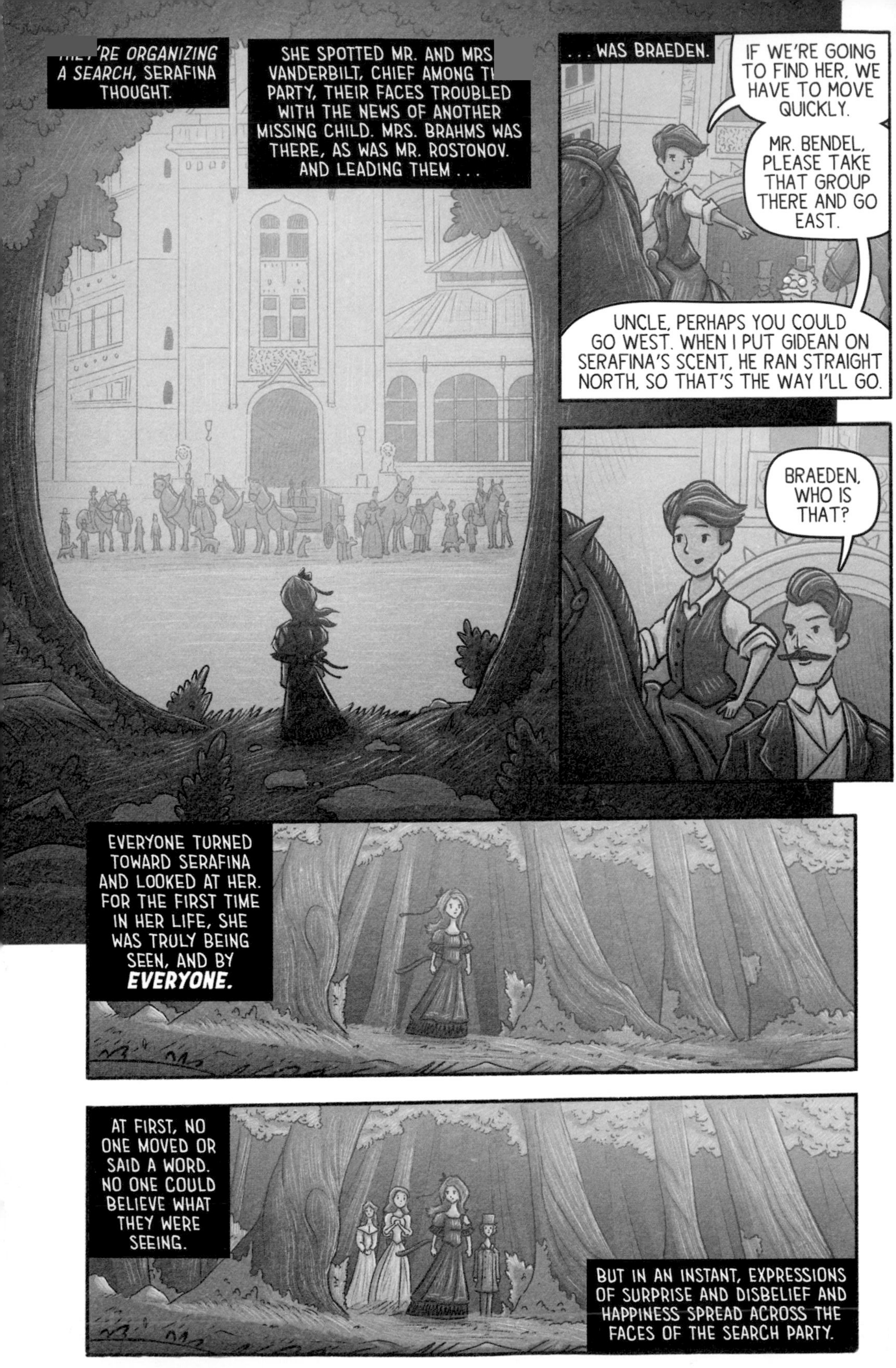

[redacted]'RE ORGANIZING A SEARCH, SERAFINA THOUGHT.
SHE SPOTTED MR. AND MRS[redacted] VANDERBILT, CHIEF AMONG [redacted] PARTY, THEIR FACES TROUBLED WITH THE NEWS OF ANOTHER MISSING CHILD. MRS. BRAHMS WAS THERE, AS WAS MR. ROSTONOV. AND LEADING THEM . . .
. . . WAS BRAEDEN.
IF WE'RE GOING TO FIND HER, WE HAVE TO MOVE QUICKLY.
MR. BENDEL, PLEASE TAKE THAT GROUP THERE AND GO EAST.
UNCLE, PERHAPS YOU COULD GO WEST. WHEN I PUT GIDEAN ON SERAFINA'S SCENT, HE RAN STRAIGHT NORTH, SO THAT'S THE WAY I'LL GO.
BRAEDEN, WHO IS THAT?
EVERYONE TURNED TOWARD SERAFINA AND LOOKED AT HER. FOR THE FIRST TIME IN HER LIFE, SHE WAS TRULY BEING SEEN, AND BY ***EVERYONE.***
AT FIRST, NO ONE MOVED OR SAID A WORD. NO ONE COULD BELIEVE WHAT THEY WERE SEEING.
BUT IN AN INSTANT, EXPRESSIONS OF SURPRISE AND DISBELIEF AND HAPPINESS SPREAD ACROSS THE FACES OF THE SEARCH PARTY.

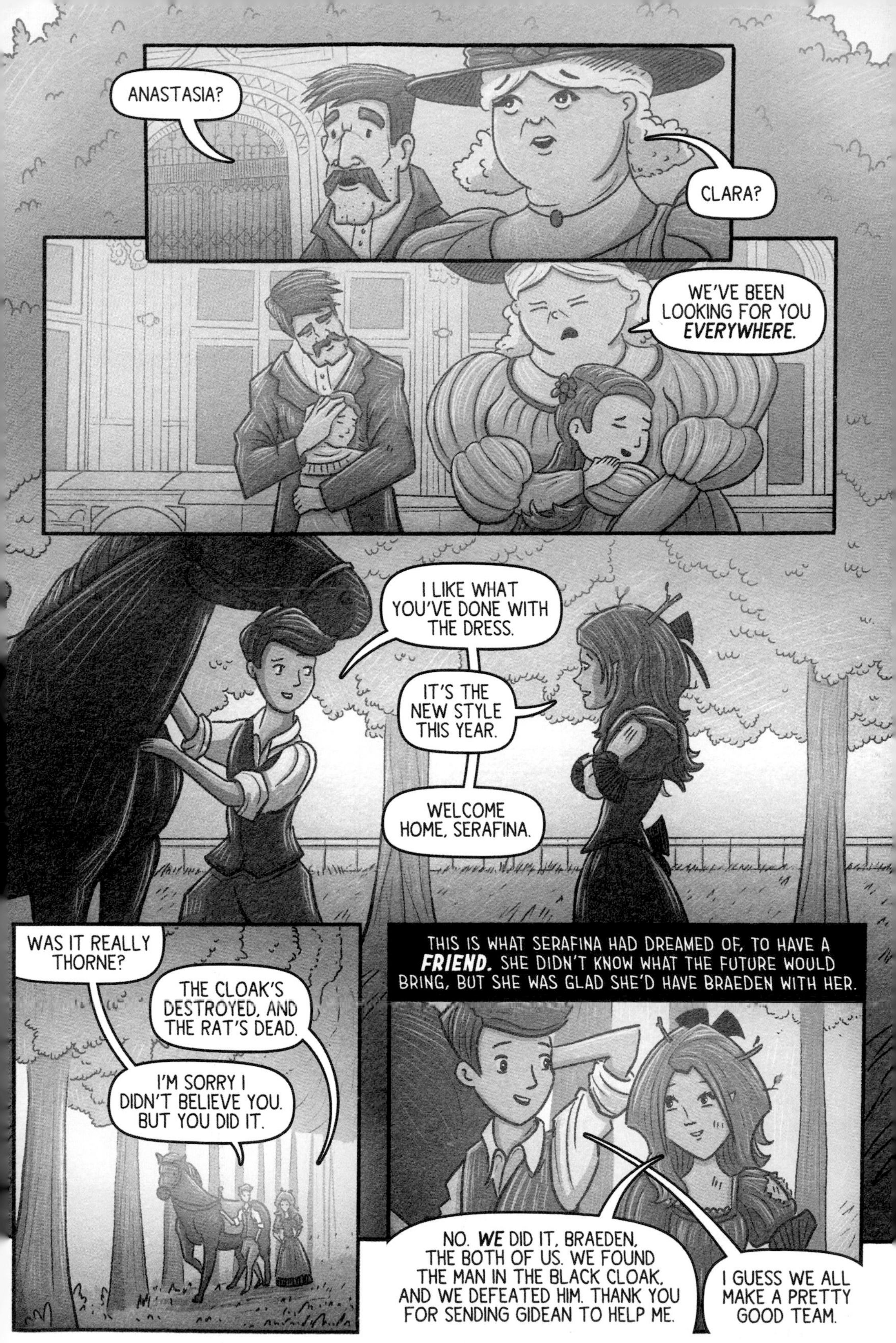

ANASTASIA?
CLARA?
WE'VE BEEN LOOKING FOR YOU *EVERYWHERE*.
I LIKE WHAT YOU'VE DONE WITH THE DRESS.
IT'S THE NEW STYLE THIS YEAR.
WELCOME HOME, SERAFINA.
WAS IT REALLY THORNE?
THE CLOAK'S DESTROYED, AND THE RAT'S DEAD.
I'M SORRY I DIDN'T BELIEVE YOU. BUT YOU DID IT.
THIS IS WHAT SERAFINA HAD DREAMED OF, TO HAVE A ***FRIEND.*** SHE DIDN'T KNOW WHAT THE FUTURE WOULD BRING, BUT SHE WAS GLAD SHE'D HAVE BRAEDEN WITH HER.
NO. ***WE*** DID IT, BRAEDEN, THE BOTH OF US. WE FOUND THE MAN IN THE BLACK CLOAK, AND WE DEFEATED HIM. THANK YOU FOR SENDING GIDEAN TO HELP ME.
I GUESS WE ALL MAKE A PRETTY GOOD TEAM.

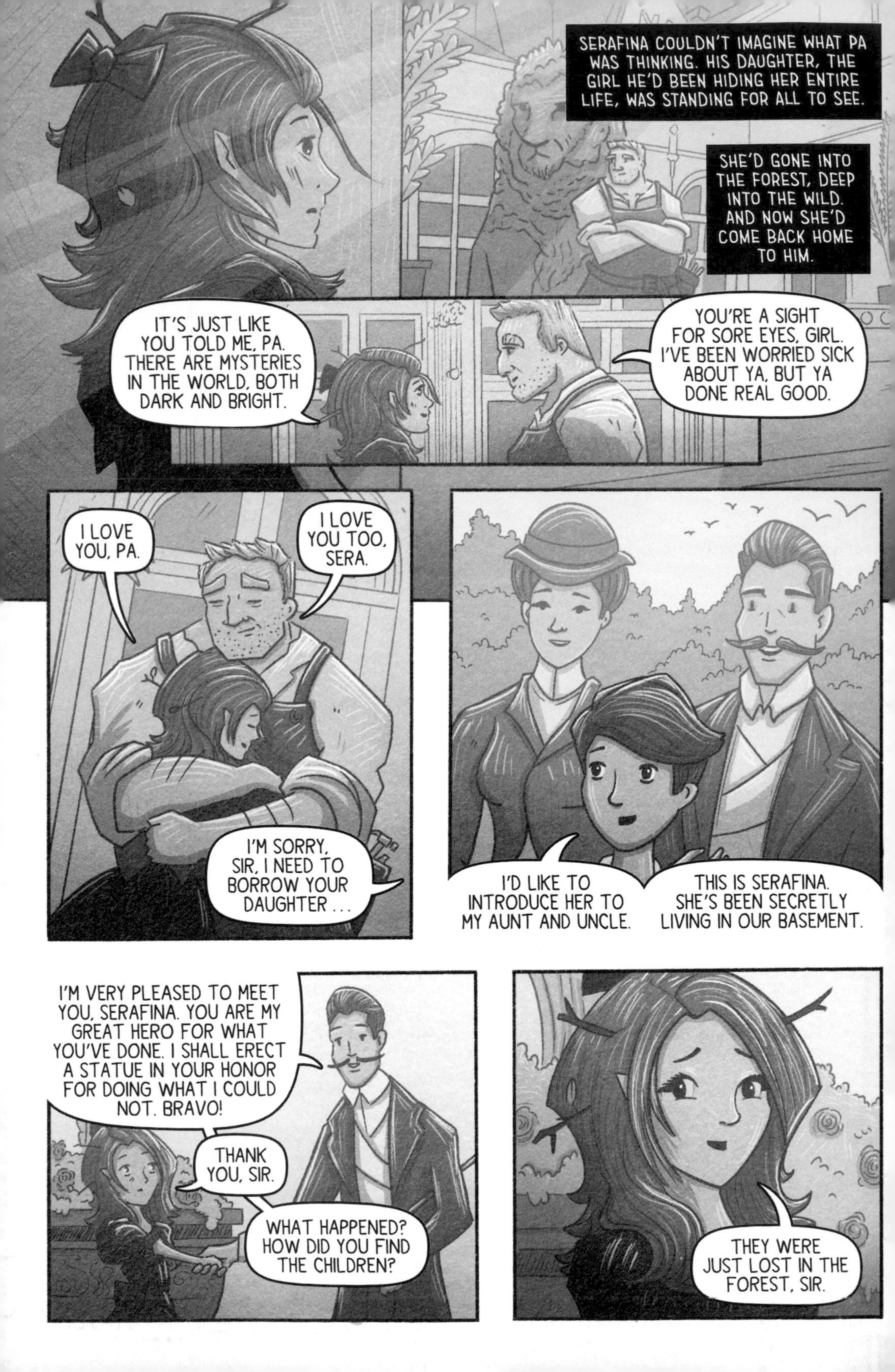
SERAFINA COULDN'T IMAGINE WHAT PA WAS THINKING. HIS DAUGHTER, THE GIRL HE'D BEEN HIDING HER ENTIRE LIFE, WAS STANDING FOR ALL TO SEE.
SHE'D GONE INTO THE FOREST, DEEP INTO THE WILD. AND NOW SHE'D COME BACK HOME TO HIM.
IT'S JUST LIKE YOU TOLD ME, PA. THERE ARE MYSTERIES IN THE WORLD, BOTH DARK AND BRIGHT.
YOU'RE A SIGHT FOR SORE EYES, GIRL. I'VE BEEN WORRIED SICK ABOUT YA, BUT YA DONE REAL GOOD.
I LOVE YOU, PA.
I LOVE YOU TOO, SERA.
I'M SORRY, SIR, I NEED TO BORROW YOUR DAUGHTER . . .
THIS IS SERAFINA. SHE'S BEEN SECRETLY LIVING IN OUR BASEMENT.
I'D LIKE TO INTRODUCE HER TO MY AUNT AND UNCLE.
I'M VERY PLEASED TO MEET YOU, SERAFINA. YOU ARE MY GREAT HERO FOR WHAT YOU'VE DONE. I SHALL ERECT A STATUE IN YOUR HONOR FOR DOING WHAT I COULD NOT. BRAVO!
THANK YOU, SIR.
WHAT HAPPENED? HOW DID YOU FIND THE CHILDREN?
THEY WERE JUST LOST IN THE FOREST, SIR.

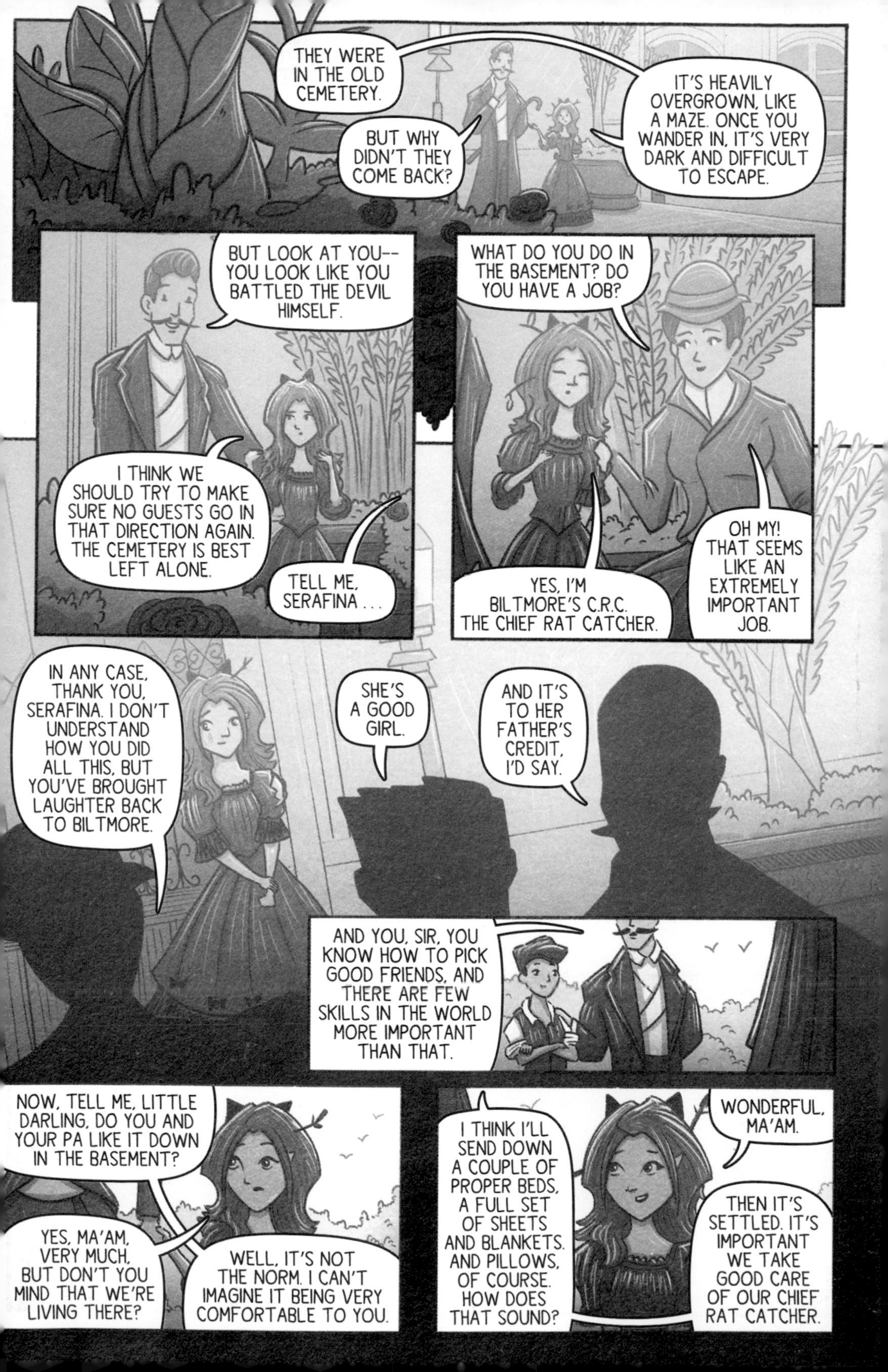
THEY WERE IN THE OLD CEMETERY.
BUT WHY DIDN'T THEY COME BACK?
IT'S HEAVILY OVERGROWN, LIKE A MAZE. ONCE YOU WANDER IN, IT'S VERY DARK AND DIFFICULT TO ESCAPE.
BUT LOOK AT YOU-- YOU LOOK LIKE YOU BATTLED THE DEVIL HIMSELF.
I THINK WE SHOULD TRY TO MAKE SURE NO GUESTS GO IN THAT DIRECTION AGAIN. THE CEMETERY IS BEST LEFT ALONE.
TELL ME, SERAFINA . . .
WHAT DO YOU DO IN THE BASEMENT? DO YOU HAVE A JOB?
YES, I'M BILTMORE'S C.R.C. THE CHIEF RAT CATCHER.
OH MY! THAT SEEMS LIKE AN EXTREMELY IMPORTANT JOB.
IN ANY CASE, THANK YOU, SERAFINA. I DON'T UNDERSTAND HOW YOU DID ALL THIS, BUT YOU'VE BROUGHT LAUGHTER BACK TO BILTMORE.
SHE'S A GOOD GIRL.
AND IT'S TO HER FATHER'S CREDIT, I'D SAY.
AND YOU, SIR, YOU KNOW HOW TO PICK GOOD FRIENDS, AND THERE ARE FEW SKILLS IN THE WORLD MORE IMPORTANT THAN THAT.
NOW, TELL ME, LITTLE DARLING, DO YOU AND YOUR PA LIKE IT DOWN IN THE BASEMENT?
YES, MA'AM, VERY MUCH, BUT DON'T YOU MIND THAT WE'RE LIVING THERE?
WELL, IT'S NOT THE NORM. I CAN'T IMAGINE IT BEING VERY COMFORTABLE TO YOU.
I THINK I'LL SEND DOWN A COUPLE OF PROPER BEDS, A FULL SET OF SHEETS AND BLANKETS. AND PILLOWS, OF COURSE. HOW DOES THAT SOUND?
WONDERFUL, MA'AM.
THEN IT'S SETTLED. IT'S IMPORTANT WE TAKE GOOD CARE OF OUR CHIEF RAT CATCHER.

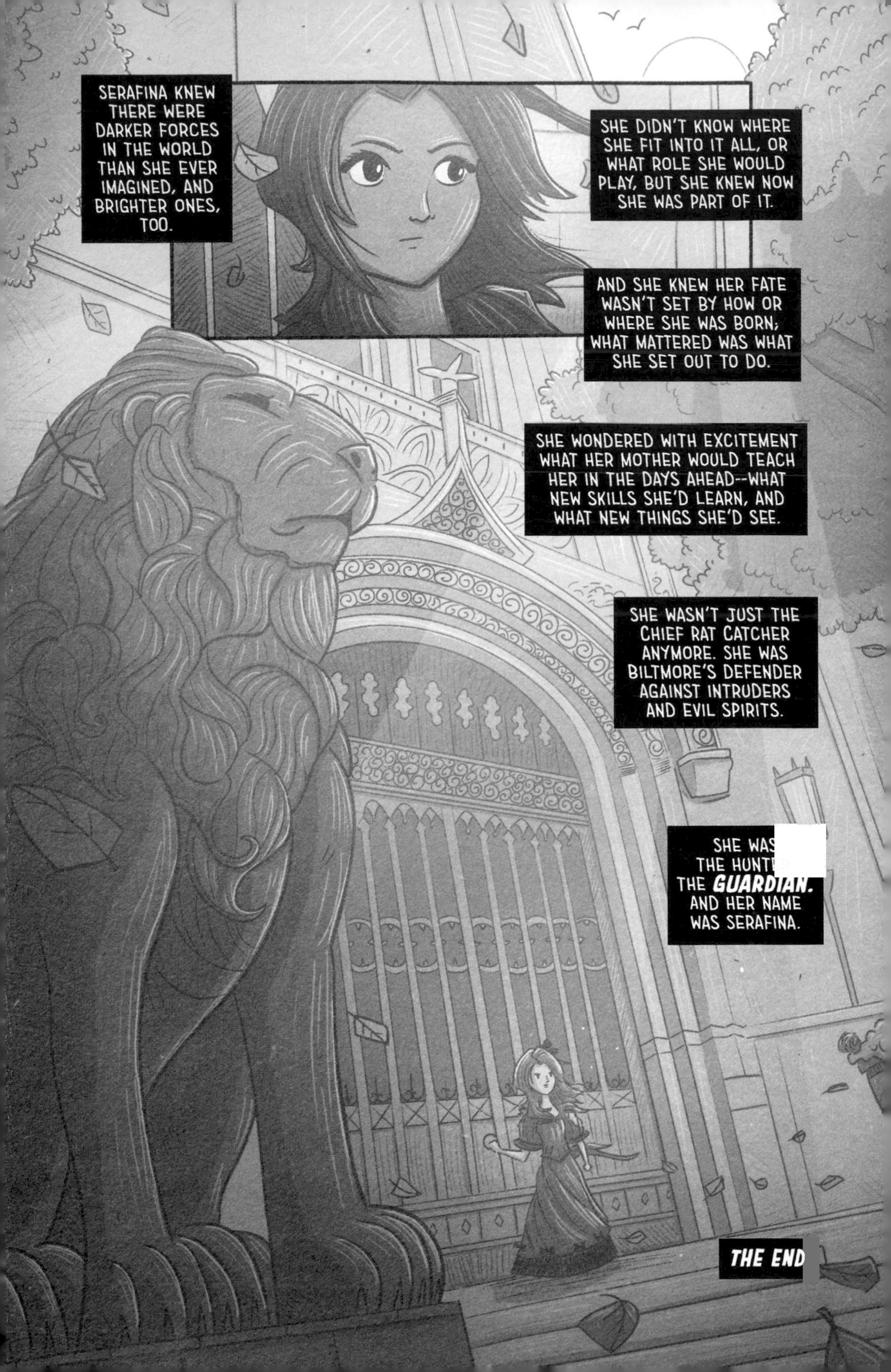
SERAFINA KNEW THERE WERE DARKER FORCES IN THE WORLD THAN SHE EVER IMAGINED, AND BRIGHTER ONES, TOO.
SHE DIDN'T KNOW WHERE SHE FIT INTO IT ALL, OR WHAT ROLE SHE WOULD PLAY, BUT SHE KNEW NOW SHE WAS PART OF IT.
AND SHE KNEW HER FATE WASN'T SET BY HOW OR WHERE SHE WAS BORN; WHAT MATTERED WAS WHAT SHE SET OUT TO DO.
SHE WONDERED WITH EXCITEMENT WHAT HER MOTHER WOULD TEACH HER IN THE DAYS AHEAD--WHAT NEW SKILLS SHE'D LEARN, AND WHAT NEW THINGS SHE'D SEE.
SHE WASN'T JUST THE CHIEF RAT CATCHER ANYMORE. SHE WAS BILTMORE'S DEFENDER AGAINST INTRUDERS AND EVIL SPIRITS.
SHE WAS
THE HUNTE
THE **GUARDIAN.**
AND HER NAME WAS SERAFINA.
THE END

BOOKS BY

ROBERT BEATTY

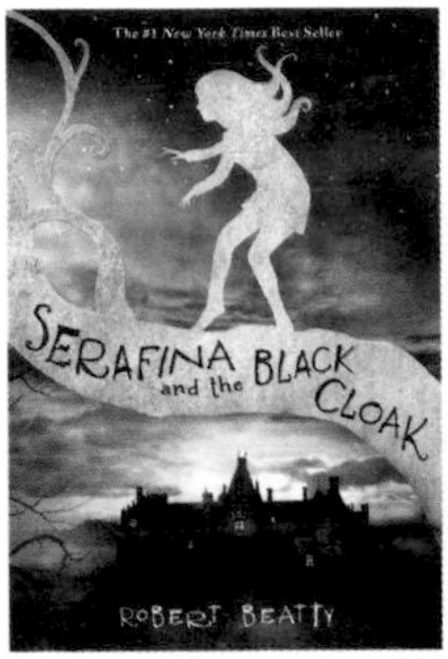
The #1 New York Times Best Seller
SERAFINA and the BLACK CLOAK
ROBERT BEATTY

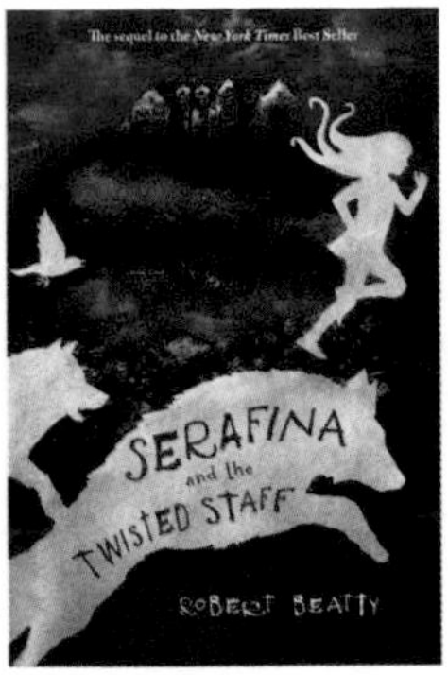
The sequel to the New York Times Best Seller
SERAFINA and the TWISTED STAFF
ROBERT BEATTY

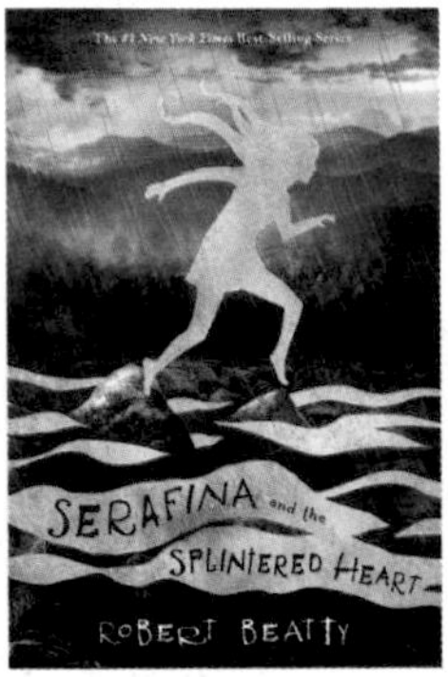
The #1 New York Times Best-Selling Series
SERAFINA and the SPLINTERED HEART
ROBERT BEATTY

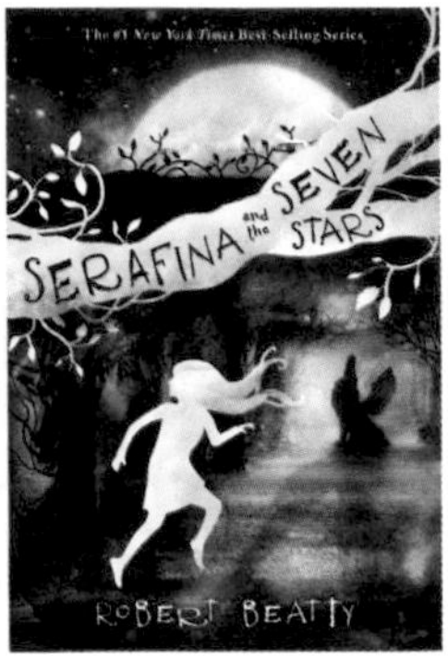
The #1 New York Times Best-Selling Series
SERAFINA and the SEVEN STARS
ROBERT BEATTY

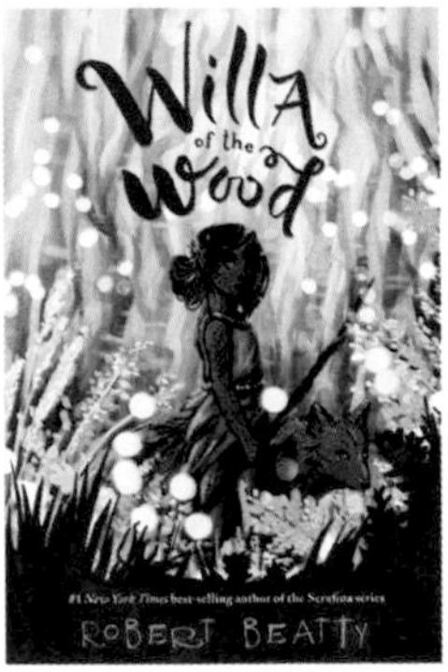
Willa of the Wood
#1 New York Times best-selling author of the Serafina series
ROBERT BEATTY

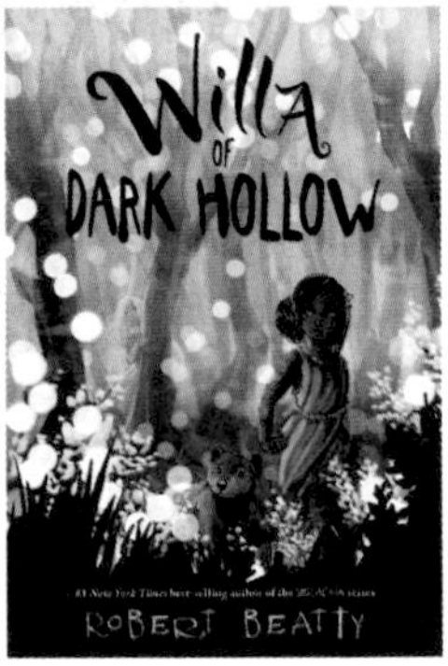
Willa of DARK HOLLOW
ROBERT BEATTY